GATEWAY

TO THE

MOON

✳

GATEWAY

TO THE

MOON

A NOVEL

MARY MORRIS

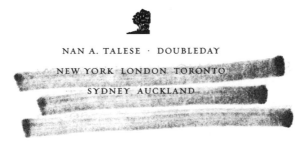

NAN A. TALESE · DOUBLEDAY

NEW YORK LONDON TORONTO

SYDNEY AUCKLAND

Copyright © 2018 by Mary Morris

All rights reserved. Published in the United States by Nan A. Talese/Doubleday, a division of Penguin Random House LLC, New York, and distributed in Canada by Random House of Canada, a division of Penguin Random House Canada Limited, Toronto.

www.nanatalese.com

Doubleday is a registered trademark of Penguin Random House LLC. Nan A. Talese and the colophon are trademarks of Penguin Random House LLC.

Jacket design by Emily Mahon
Jacket photograph by Matt Anderson/Moment/Getty Images

LIBRARY OF CONGRESS CATALOGING-IN-PUBLICATION DATA
Names: Morris, Mary, 1947– author.
Title: Gateway to the moon : a novel / Mary Morris.
Description: First edition. | New York : NAN A. TALESE/Doubleday, [2018]
Identifiers: LCCN 2017016953 | ISBN 9780385542906 (hardcover) | ISBN 9780385542913 (ebook)
Classification: LCC PS3563.O87445 G38 2018 | DDC 813/.54—dc23
LC record available at https://lccn.loc.gov/2017016953

MANUFACTURED IN THE UNITED STATES OF AMERICA

First Edition

This book is for Ellen Levine and Nan A. Talese—

Fierce readers, believers, friends.

In memory of Jane Supino whose wisdom remains,

And to Larry for everything.

The great mystery is not that we have been flung at random among the profusion of the earth and the galaxy of the stars, but that in this prison we can fashion images of ourselves sufficiently powerful to deny our nothingness.

—ANDRÉ MALRAUX

CONTENTS

✳

CONTENTS

HISTORICAL NOTE

✳

In 1492 with the Alhambra Decree, King Ferdinand and Queen Isabella ordered all Jews and Muslims to convert to Christianity or be expelled from Spain. It was their decision, along with the Vatican, to make Spain an entirely Catholic nation. It is estimated that among the Jewish population a hundred thousand converted; the Inquisition killed another thirty thousand, and hundreds of thousands fled. Of the Jews who converted, many were Christian only in name. They practiced what the Inquisition referred to as "the dead Law of Moses" and became what are known as secret or crypto-Jews.

As the New World was being settled, crypto-Jews followed, making their homes in Mexico City and Nuevo León. But as the hand of the Inquisition reached farther into Mexico, some of these crypto-Jews moved north into what would become New Mexico. They lived as Catholics in the remote hills while still maintaining their Jewish traditions. Eventually they forgot that they were Jews. Though they continued to practice Jewish rituals, such as the lighting of candles on Friday night and the refusal to eat pork, for generations they did not know why.

CHRONOLOGY

✳

This is the historic timeline regarding the Jews and the Inquisition.

1478 + Pope authorizes the establishment of the Inquisition in Spain

1492 + Edict calls for the conversion or expulsion of Jews and Muslims from Spain

1492 + Columbus's first voyage of discovery

1493 + Columbus's second voyage of discovery

1497 + Forced conversion of all Jews of Portugal

1506 + Massacre of the conversos in Lisbon

1510 + Birth of Beatrice de Luna in Portugal

1536 + Authorization of an Inquisition in Portugal

1540 + Escape route begins for conversos from Portugal, orchestrated by Beatrice de Luna

1569 + Inquisition arrives in Mexico

1579 + Establishment of first crypto-Jewish settlements in northern New Mexico

PRINCIPAL CHARACTERS

✳

FIFTEENTH AND SIXTEENTH CENTURIES

Luis de Torres—crypto-Jew and interpreter for Christopher
    Columbus *
Catalina de Torres—his wife *
Juan de Torres—his eldest son
Eduardo de Torres—his youngest son
Christopher Columbus—explorer *
Pedro de Terrenos—cabin boy on the *Santa María* *
Rodrigo de Triano—sailor and secret Jew *
Benjamin Cordero—possible son of Luis de Torres
Inez Cordero—Benjamin's adoptive mother
Diego Cordero—Inez's father
Olivia Cordero—Inez's mother
Leonora Cordero—Benjamin's wife
Alejandro Cordero—Benjamin's son

Francisco Mendes—head of the House of Mendes in
    Lisbon *
Dona Gracia Nasi (Beatrice de Luna)—his wife *
Ana—their daughter *

N.B. * indicates historical figures

Federico Pera de Torres—son of Eduardo de Torres
Sofia Pera—his wife and the cousin of Alejandro Cordero
Bernadine—Sofia's maid

LATE TWENTIETH CENTURY

Rafael Torres
Rosa Torres—his wife
Elena Torres—their daughter
Roberto Torres—their son
Morning Glory "MG" Torres—Roberto's ex-wife
Miguel Torres—their son

Vincent Roybal—owner of general store
Esmeralda Roybal—his wife
Pascual Roybal—their dead son

Rachel Rothstein—Miguel's boss
Nathan Rothstein—her husband
Davie Rothstein—their youngest son
Jeremy Rothstein—their eldest son

THE DE TORRES FAMILY

✳

15TH–16TH CENTURY
++++++++++++++++++++++++

Diego Cordero = Olivia

Catalina = Luis de Torres = ?   Inez Cordero (Benjamin's adoptive mother)

(Parents not named)

Juan   Eduardo = ?   Benjamin = Leonora   Gabriella = Renaldo Pera

Alejandro Magdalena Simon Balthazar

Federico   =   Sofia Pera

20TH CENTURY
++++++++++++++++++

Rafael Torres = Rosa

Elena   Roberto = MG

Miguel

GATEWAY

TO THE

MOON

✳

PERFECT DARKNESS—1992

M iguel Torres stands in the old cemetery and aims his telescope at the sky. It's a clear, cloudless evening. And there's no moon. It is easier to see the stars when there's no moon. Miguel stumbles as he adjusts his scope. He has difficulty navigating the uneven terrain of tree roots and crumbling stone. Still he likes the old cemetery. It gives him the best view of the night sky. Near the trailer where he lives with his mother, there is too much light. He comes here for the darkness.

A brisk wind blows through the branches of the old oak tree. It blows through piñon trees, and the air is redolent with the scent of pine. But it is also a dry, dusty wind and Miguel has to keep wiping his lens with a soft cloth. He buttons his thin jacket and peers into the eyepiece. Squinting, he pans the sky. It is late spring and a good night to be out. The days are already hot on the high desert plain, but the nights remain cool.

He focuses on Cassiopeia. He likes to begin with this constellation because her major stars form an M. The Celestial M some call it. Or the Lazy M. Whatever the case, Miguel feels as if it's his signature in the sky. From Cassiopeia he moves up to Ursa Major and then over to the North Star. This orients him. Once he gets his bearings, he locates Jupiter and sharpens his focus on its moons. Named after Zeus's lovers, the largest moons of Jupiter and their orbits were what Galileo used to determine that the Earth is not the center of the universe. But, of course, Galileo went to prison, recanted, and spent the rest of his life under house arrest.

Miguel has never been to prison, though he has spent a month in juvenile detention. But juvie was a little more like what he imagined summer camp to be—bunk beds, sports, three meals a day—except for the razor wire. It was a year ago when he'd gotten caught with a gang of his pals playing chicken on the highway, and next thing he knew, the cops were rounding them up. His father, who lives down the road, thought it might be good for him to spend some time straightening out, and his mother didn't argue. He'd shared a room with three other boys and they all had lice. The room had a small window, and the only pleasure he'd gotten that entire month was staring at the night sky. Since getting out, it seems as if that's all he wants to do. As his father likes to say, there are worse things to be hooked on.

Miguel stumbles again, almost toppling over as he makes a fine adjustment to his scope. But then he often stumbles. His feet don't seem to know where the rest of him is going. His mother calls him a long tall drink of water. Over six feet tall, lanky. His muscles haven't caught up with his bones. And those bones have just grown and grown. He is almost odd-looking. He has green eyes like his father. Some of his friends call him the Praying Mantis because he is so skinny and because he falls for girls usually a few years older who are known to devour boys.

As he stands with his feet apart in the cemetery, he can see the skies. He is hoping to find a moon. Not a moon that anyone else has ever found but one of his own. A moon that no one else knows is there. What will he name it? Maybe after a character in *Star Wars*? Han Solo? Luke Skywalker? Princess Leia? He's always surprised at the names given to the moons. Ganymede, Callisto, Locaste. So why not *Star Wars*? Miguel can never dream of discovering a galaxy or a comet. Or even a new planet somewhere deep in the Milky Way. That's for people who spend their lives with high-powered scopes fixed to the stars. But it is not out of the question for a boy to find a moon.

Moons have long been a preoccupation of Miguel's. He is drawn to them more than he is drawn to other celestial bodies. Moons are manageable. You can stare at one and it won't hurt your eyes. And they have low expectations. He prefers the cooler, reflected light to the burning stars. In this high desert where Miguel lives, the sun cracks his lips and makes his throat dry. Whenever possible he seeks the shade. If he could, he'd be nocturnal.

Miguel doesn't like his position so he moves the telescope to the right until he is on firmer ground. Carefully he sweeps the skies as he looks for Arcturus in the constellation of Boötes. It is one of the brightest stars. He feels certain that Arcturus has planets in its orbit, and he's sure that those planets must have moons. The universe interests him. He doesn't know why. Perhaps it's because each night when he steps out of his mother's trailer and stares at the sky, he wonders if there isn't a better life for him somewhere out there. When he was younger, he'd go outside to get away from his parents' fighting. He spent months trying to invent a device that would contact a spacecraft to come and get him. In his early teens he went out to sneak a smoke. But since juvie he just does it to watch.

Miguel never cared that much about the earth sciences, but he cares about space. The first time he gazed through a lens, he saw a crater on the moon the size of Texas. He learned that the Earth could slip through the gap between the rings of Saturn. That is how big they are. His science teacher, Mr. Garcia, taught him to ask questions. Why is it that a supernova is in the same shape as a snail? Why does nature repeat its patterns? He ponders the three-body problem, trying to understand what keeps the Earth in its orbit. How is it that we keep spinning at all?

For years he wanted his own telescope but knew he'd never be able to afford it. Then last year his science teacher, Mr. Garcia, gave him a gift: a membership to the Amateur Astronomers of America. In one of its newsletters he read about a man named John Dobson who taught people how to build their own telescopes from scratch and at almost no cost. In the Santa Fe Public Library, Miguel found a book by Dobson, in which he learned the intricacies of magnification.

He began with the mirror. He spent weeks grinding it down, polishing it, getting the shape just right. In flea markets and pawnshops he scavenged lenses from an old pair of 7/35 binoculars and these he used for his eyepiece. Then he built his own sixteen-inch scope with an eight-inch focal length that is strong enough to see galaxies and star clusters that are light-years away. The telescope cost him seven dollars to make and he can see Cassiopeia and Andromeda, her daughter. He can see Perseus. He can even see Algol, the evil winking eye in the center of Medusa's head in the constellation Perseus. When he presented the telescope to his teacher, Mr. Garcia was amazed at its strength.

Miguel pans along the outer ridges of his own galaxy. The ground is too rocky and he can't get the scope stable so he moves over a few graves. At least he assumes they are graves. Mostly there are grassy mounds and broken headstones with their strange writing that nobody can decipher. No one has been buried in this cemetery for at least a hundred years. That's what his mother tells him. In fact no one in the town remembers the last time anyone was buried here. No one comes to tend the graves. When he was younger, he came here on dares to see who could mingle longer with the ghosts. Then he came with his girlfriend because it was a good place to slip his hand under her shirt and run it along her smooth, warm skin. But since he joined the Amateur Astronomers of America, he's been trying to get better purchase on the sky.

He folds up his telescope. Though he is reluctant to leave this crystal night behind, it's Friday and his mother expects him home. He makes his way down the hill toward the lights. When he gets to Roybal's General Store, he'll give her a call. As he was heading out that evening, she asked him to pick up milk. It is one of the things that makes Miguel crazy. She's always asking him to do something. They can't have a conversation without her saying "Would you mind fixing this?" or "Will you pick this up after school?" Someday this will drive him away.

He'll leave the way his aunt Elena did. He barely knows his father's sister. He can only recall seeing her a few times. She left Entrada to go to New York City and become a ballerina. Even after she had her accident and couldn't dance anymore, she still didn't come back to Entrada. Instead she travels the world. She sends him postcards from places he's never even heard of. Kuala Lumpur and Cádiz. Bombay and Melbourne. He uses an old globe to locate them. He keeps the postcards in a shoebox in his room. Cards with rust-colored animals sleeping in trees, carved figures that rise out of the ground, pyramids of spices and fruits he's never seen. Someday he'll travel too—though it is intergalactic travel that interests him. The speed of light. He'll be the first tourist on Mars.

As he reaches the steps of Roybal's, he begins digging in his pockets for change. He is hoping he can get a candy bar as well. The best thing, as far as Miguel is concerned, about living in Entrada is that Roybal's is pretty much always open. He can pick up a candy bar, a can of soda, or some loose cigarettes at just about any time of day or night.

The Roybals live in a house attached to their store and it seems to Miguel as if they must be a family of insomniacs because there are always lights on and there is always someone to ring up a purchase even if it is just for a package of bubble gum and some beef jerky. Miguel is an insomniac as well. Or at least a night owl, for which he has recently learned there is an actual genetic disposition. At times Miguel feels more closely related to bats and raccoons than to humans.

Old man Roybal is at the cash register when Miguel walks in and gives him a wave. "Hola, m'hijo," Vincent Roybal calls out to him as he always does. But then the old man calls everyone "my daughter" or "my son," and in some ways he is correct. If you go back far enough, everyone in Entrada is related in one way or another to everyone else. Almost everyone is a Roybal or a Torres. Miguel's great-grandmother was a Roybal. They are so inbred it is a wonder that they don't have tails and pointed ears. "Qué tal?"

"Hola, papi," Miguel calls back. "It's all good."

Miguel leans his telescope against the counter as Vincent Roybal takes a long drag on his cigarette. "See any ghosts?" Miguel laughs. The old man likes to tease him about going to the cemetery at night. "How about spaceships? Any landing up there?"

Once more Miguel laughs. It's always the same joke with the old man, but Miguel doesn't mind. Besides everyone in Entrada knows that Miguel is crazy about spaceships. The ones that might come here and the ones that NASA has sent off into space. He's read everything he could get his hands on about Roswell and the rumors that the army has an alien in captivity. And he's obsessed with *Voyager*. Once he spent so much time staring at the sky, looking for *Voyager*, that he got a frozen neck and his mother had to massage it with hot oils and compresses. He knows every piece of music, every image and greeting on the Golden Record that ET was supposed to find and use to make sense out of human life.

"No spaceships. No aliens." He grabs a quart of milk from the fridge and also a Hershey bar for himself. He thinks about slipping the candy bar into his pocket the way most kids do, but decides to pay for it instead.

There's a short line. Old man Roybal can't just ring up an order. He has to ask how this father is or that sick cousin or how someone's favorite team is doing and at times it seems as if he'll go on talking forever. As he waits for Mr. Roybal to finish with "Señora Mendes of the large breasts," as Miguel has heard him refer to her, his eyes scan the store. He likes to look at the wall with all of the "For sale" and "To rent" flyers. There is always a missing dog with a name like Nachos or a kid's bike that has been taken from a yard and a "Please return: No Question Asks." That pretty much says everything, "No Question Asks" when it comes to Entrada. Miguel crosses out the *k*, add an *s* and a comma. "No questions, Ass."

On the wall, buried among the sad eyes of missing dogs and an offer to sell an old Honda 360 for a hundred dollars, he sees a notice, "Couple Seeks Afternoon Babysitter for Two Little Boys. Must have wheels." It's got smiley faces all over it and little tabs with the number to call. No one's taken a number yet. Miguel could use some cash. His mom is barely getting by and he has almost nothing to spend on books, gas, or girls. The job is out on Colibri Canyon Road just north of Santa Fe, about forty minutes from his place. He gets out of school at two and can easily be there before three. Besides summer vacation will be starting soon.

Miguel knows Colibri Canyon. He worked there once when his father was laying pipes. That was a long time ago but he remembers it as a dirt road that winds its way through the canyons. It's a pretty isolated spot. But Miguel isn't picky. In the summers he does construction, mostly installing drywall and painting houses, so this summer maybe he'll try babysitting. It seems like easier work. He tears a strip from the sheet and tucks it into his pocket. Though he isn't quite fifteen, he looks older, and he's been driving since he was twelve. He can get his learner's permit soon. And his father's old Chevy sits in front of their trailer.

At last Señora Mendes heads out the door, and the bell tinkles as she goes. "Papi, can I make a call?" the boy asks.

Mr. Roybal points to the old black phone. "Help yourself." Instead of calling his mother, Miguel phones the number in the notice. In two rings he hears a woman's singsongy recorded voice. She sounds as if she's doing a commercial for dish soap. "You've reached the Rothstein residence—Rachel, Nathan, Jeremy, and Davie. You know what to do!" And then there is the beep.

Miguel hesitates. "I'm interested in the position of babysitter," he says. "I saw your ad," and he leaves his name and number. When he hangs up, he goes to pay for the milk and Hershey bar. But old man Roybal has spread out on the counter the tattered copy of his family tree and he's hunched over it. Miguel leans across the counter, gazing at the maze of branches that make up the Roybal lineage, which consists, more or less, of everyone in Entrada. It makes Miguel uneasy to see his own name dangling from a stem with the year of his birth and a blank space for his death. He doesn't like to think about life having a beginning and an end. He prefers to think of it as a continuous loop that goes around and around the way the Navajo do.

Miguel takes out his wallet and is about to pay when the old man waves him away. "You'll pay me next time."

He assumes he won't pay the next time either. "Thanks, papi."

Vincent Roybal gives the boy another wave, dismissing him. "De nada, m'hijo."

Miguel walks home under the starry night, telescope under one arm, munching on his Hershey bar. He loves chocolate. Even though it's bad for his skin, he has a candy bar at least once a day. He's so skinny he'd eat them all the time if he could, but his mother always says he'll ruin his dinner. So he sneaks them on his way home. Besides he's almost starving when he walks in and is greeted by the familiar smell of the chicken stew his mother has cooked.

"You're late," she says without looking up. She's right. She's already swept the house, moving all the dirt into the center of their trailer where she scoops it up with a dustpan. He's never understood why she doesn't just sweep it out the door. But when he asks her, she just replies, "Because we don't." She's turned the portrait of the Virgin Mary to the wall and lit the candles. She's said the blessing with her eyes closed, moving her hands in a circle. His mother doesn't like to perform the Friday-night rituals without him, yet she won't complain. She'll just ignore him for a little while.

He walks over, putting his hand on her shoulder. Looking down as if she were a bonsai, he kisses the top of her head. With a ladle in her hand she pretends to bat him away. She looks tired and the lines around her eyes and mouth have deepened. But Miguel can tell from her lush black hair, the fine features hidden in the folds of her now plump face, that she had once been pretty. She'd also been a spelling whiz. Once she made it to the state competition. Miguel certainly didn't take after her in that regard. She's still spunky, but working as a hotel maid and drinking too much beer and eating tacos have taken their toll.

"Wash your hands," she tells him.

The trailer is small and narrow. Just two rooms. Miguel sleeps in the bedroom since his father moved out. His mother sleeps on the couch. Mostly they eat standing up at the counter, but on Friday nights they eat at the fold-up table. Now she serves him a large bowl of chicken stew with a crust of bread and brings a small bowl for herself.

His mother tends to graze rather than eat but she makes a point of sitting with him. He can tell that she isn't in the mood for talking. Sometimes when she's tired from her job at the hotel in Taos, she doesn't want to talk. Instead she works on one of her crossword or sudoku puzzles. Her real name is Gloria but her father called her Morning Glory because she is perkier in the morning, fading by the end of the day. Now most people just call her MG.

"It's good, mami," he says, patting her on the arm. His mother looks up at him and smiles. It makes him so happy to see her smile. Her whole face alters. It is as if he can see her as a girl—the one his father fell for when they were just kids themselves. As Miguel gets up for a second helping—one he doesn't really want, but he wants to see that smile break across her features again—the phone rings. His mother makes no attempt to answer it. "I got it," Miguel says.

When he picks up, he hears a woman's voice. "Is this Miguel?" She sounds light and breathless as if she is talking while on a treadmill. He pictures blond hair, blue eyes. Not from around here.

He hesitates. "Yes," he says.

There is a pause. "You called," she says, "about the babysitting job."

Then he remembers. "Oh, yes, I did."

"Good. So you're interested. That's great. Can you come by tomorrow?" He expected that she'd ask him something about his age or his experience, of which he has none, but she doesn't. It is as if she is hiring him sight unseen. "I'd like you to meet the boys," she says. "You can start work on Monday. Is that good?"

Miguel nods, and then realizes she can't see him. "Yes, that's good."

"And you have a car right?"

Miguel thinks about his father's old Chevy. "Yes, I do."

She gives him the address out in Colibri Canyon. And then she hangs up.

When he gets off, his mother asks what it was about.

"A job."

She nods, looking at him with her cold, dark eyes. "You need a job. But you also need to study." He looks back at her the way he always does. Nothing about his mother has ever seemed familiar. He has never seen a flick of her wrists, a grimace on her face, and thinks, "I do that."

Perhaps he is an alien. It would explain his link to the stars. Perhaps some starship deposited him in this place and wiped out his memory.

At times Miguel scans his mother's face, looking for a trace of himself in her eyes, her mouth.

"I can do both."

She makes a face. "We'll see." They finish their stew in silence. Miguel watches the hands of his grandfather's old clock as they move mysteriously backward.

CHAPTER TWO

※

THE ARCHIVIST—1992

Entrada rests in a valley north of Santa Fe and south of Taos, nestled in the Sangre de Cristo Mountains. Before it became the "Blood of Christ" range, these mountains were known as the Sierra Nevada or the Sierra Madre or just the Sierra. No one remembers when or why they became the Sangre de Cristo. Some say it is because of the color of blood that the mountains take on at sunset after a snow. Others think it is because it's hard to live here and every day is a sacrifice.

To the east there is a dip in the mountains, like a cup. Every school-child learns, as Miguel did before the sixth grade, that when Coronado slept in this valley the moon rose through the dip in the mountains, and he named it Entrada de la Luna. Gateway to the Moon. Most of the locals just call it Entrada. Locals joke that the early explorers must have mistaken this land for the moon—it is so dry and rocky.

The earth is unyielding—except in the spring when the rains come and then it can be treacherous. Flash floods rush down these hills into the villages and pueblos below. But then the desert springs to life. The cacti bloom crimson and gold and the piñons smell sweet with their sap. You will never confuse this place with a desert then. Still it is not an easy place to make things grow. Piñon nuts, chilies, and garbanzo beans are about the only things that can be sown. Garbanzo beans are as hard and dry as the land they come from. Very few can make a living from this land, though most people remain because they have nowhere to go. And some are destined to leave.

Vincent Roybal hopes that Miguel will be one of them. In the doorway of his store he lights a cigarette as he watches the shadow of the boy making his way home. Vincent is a tall man, not as tall as Miguel but tall for Entrada, and as he leans against a wooden pillar, his head almost touches the roof. As he observes Miguel disappearing down the road, he thinks about how he's always coming into his store from the old cemetery after dark, carrying that telescope of his. He has grown used to his visits and gives the boy whatever he needs. Vincent feels protective of Miguel as if he were his own grandson.

And at times Vincent wonders if he isn't. But that's a place where he will not allow himself to go. It isn't something he cares to think about. Still he likes it when Miguel stops in, always asking to use the phone and call his mother. He is a good kid. Vincent wonders when he'll leave Entrada. Maybe for college.

It is more than he can say about his own son, Pascual. Pascual only left in a hearse after a motorcycle accident on the road to Española. Of course he'd been drinking. They were always drinking. He ran himself into an old cottonwood tree just a few miles up the road. But Vincent doesn't want to go there either. If he does, he'll never get to sleep. In fact if he can help it, Vincent Roybal thinks of very little except for the family tree he is researching and his excursions into the distant past. The present doesn't interest him that much anymore.

He pauses, taking another drag. "Your mother is going to kill me," he says to his dead son. "I shouldn't smoke. And I shouldn't keep letting that kid take whatever he wants and never pay for it. But that's my business, isn't it, m'hijo?" Vincent finds himself speaking more to Pascual since he's been dead than he did when he was alive. When Esmeralda catches him mumbling, she doesn't know he's talking to their long-gone son. She thinks that he's gone mad.

Vincent steps out on the porch. As he smokes, he gazes at a broken-down truck and some old tractor wheels in his front yard, at the dry, barren land, and ponders the same thing he always ponders. Why would anyone ever settle here? And why would they stay? As he thinks, he smokes. He can't quit. He's tried, but he's surrounded by cigarettes. He sells them all day long. Everyone wants a pack, a carton, loosies too.

Years ago he quit for a month during which time he became an alcoholic. He gave Esmeralda a choice. She preferred the cigarettes.

He supposes they each blame the other for what happened. Since Pascual's death they rarely sleep in the same bed, in part because neither of them really sleeps. They both wander the house and the store at all hours and sometimes even out into the arroyo. Once Esmeralda found him snoring under the branches of the oak in the old cemetery. On the rare occasion that they find themselves in the same bed, he inches his body away from hers. Once every month or so he makes love to her, like an old car motor you turn over now and then to make sure it's still running. Of course if he thought about it, Vincent would realize that everything changed when Pascual died. But Vincent's head is filled with the things he doesn't want to think about.

Vincent Roybal is an old man now, long past the time when he should have retired from his store. He is almost seventy years old and had anticipated long ago that his surviving son, Tomas, or his daughter, Katrina, and her husband would take over. But Tomas moved to Dallas to work with a tech company and Katrina is in Albuquerque and no one wants to run the store so that he and Esmeralda can retire and move to Galveston or Orlando. Anyway Esmeralda will never move away from Entrada nor, he suspects deep down, will he. It is hard to move away from a place where your family has dwelled for four hundred years. And Vincent has lived in this house with its store his entire life, as had his father before him.

In fact Roybal's has been a general store since anyone in Entrada can remember. In the old days it sold sorghum and pintos and garbanzos in large bins. It traded with farmers for milk and eggs. He still has the bins for the beans that are the mainstay of the diet of the poor people of Entrada. Most people raise their own chickens for eggs, but still Roybal's sells eggs and cheese and milk. They also sell sodas and candy bars and cigarettes and small bottles of whiskey in brown paper bags and cans of beer. Over the years Vincent has watched the Pueblo people who come into his store getting fatter and fatter. The Hispanics too, but not like the natives.

His own people are more compact, leaner. He attributes this to their good diet and European ways. Vincent Roybal knows that his ancestors came from Spain. He likes to believe that once they were rich aristocrats (and he has found some evidence to prove this) and that for a reason he cannot conceive they settled in this valley long ago. He knows that they are among the first explorers of the New World. He just doesn't know why they came here to a place that is so remote from anything they'd known before.

He imagines his great-great-great-grandfathers—how many greats will that require?—departing from cities like Toledo, Ávila, and Seville. Men with a sense of mission and discovery. Curious men who longed to see the world, who weren't afraid to set out on perilous journeys across unknown seas where monsters might await them, rogue waves might crush them, swirling waters sink them, where they might meet cannibals who would eat them or desert islands where they would die of thirst. What made them come to rest in a dry, impoverished land of frigid winds and relentless sun that has no gold and whose soil will yield nothing much more than the hard beans that can break your wisdom tooth in half if you bite on it before it has cooked for three hours?

It is what he ponders at night when he is restless and insomnia takes over. The insomnia that makes him open his store to Jack from Santa Domingo Pueblo whenever he runs out of booze and comes in the middle of the night with the delirium tremors or half the town when they run out of cigarettes or the teenage boys who come tapping on his window at any hour of the night for a package of ribbed and lubricated Trojans. It is his insomnia that makes him open up early in the morning to the women who run out of eggs or juice and insomnia that keeps him from his siesta when children come by after school to steal Cokes and Milky Ways.

As far as Vincent Roybal is concerned, he hasn't slept in years. If he sleeps at all, it is dozing at the cash register, his head resting on his hand, or in front of the TV late at night. He rarely makes it into his bed. He sleeps wherever he seems to land, like a dog. Vincent has to sneak up on sleep. Or let it sneak up on him like a thief in an alley. If he plans to go to bed, he'll be awake all night.

He blames it on the mystery. It is what he turns over and over at night in the dark recesses of his brain. And what Vincent Roybal ponders the most is that he has no idea who he really is. Part of that answer he believes lies on the counter in his store. It is the family tree he's been working on for years the way some people work on jigsaw puzzles. He knows his own generation and all of his siblings and cousins and nieces and nephews and their children and he knows back to his father and mother and to his grandparents before them.

For the rest he has gone to Santa Fe where he scours the County Clerk's Office for the births and death of anyone with the last name of Roybal or for whoever first laid claim to his land. A few weeks ago he found it on a yellowed sheet of paper. A simple land claim filed with the county centuries ago. On it is a seal and the signature of Federico Cordero de Torres, whom Vincent believes to be his first ancestor in the New World and the man who built his house where Vincent Roybal's house and store now stand.

Vincent has also written to the Office of Records in Andalusia and here he has learned that Federico de Torres, the son of a wealthy doctor from Gerona, traveled with the famed Coronado in 1540 and had been among the first white men to lay eyes on the Grand Canyon. Vincent tries to imagine what his ancestor saw—that enormous fiery trench in the ground. And then he returned to New Mexico and founded this town.

This searching old records is an activity that his wife thinks of as a curious hobby, like collecting stamps or old bottles. Harmless, but also more or less pointless. Whenever they go down to Santa Fe to shop, Vincent leaves Esmeralda at one of the malls where she seems able to spend days on end while he slips into the County Clerk's Office. The people who work there know him so well that no one even bothers to ask where he is going or why.

Jokingly they refer to him as the archivist. They nod to him and say to one another that the archivist is back. Indeed Vincent Roybal moves in the archives as freely as any librarian would. He's learned to read the ancient scripts, the wide, rolling strokes of the pen, and decipher names and dates, land claims and marriage certificates, causes of death and minor litigations as well as any trained archivist in all of Spain and the New World. And every time he finds a new document that indicates a Roybal or a Torres has been born or died, Vincent has the pleasure of filling in a blank spot on his family tree.

Vincent puts out his cigarette. "You probably think I should get some sleep," he says to Pascual. "But you know I can't. It's all because of you." He goes back inside. Leans on the counter and stares at his family tree. He looks at the places where he is still unable to fill in the names. The spaces where entire lives can be lived. He does not know who these people might be and he does not even know why it matters so much to him.

While he spends his time in dusty archives and writes letters to the records offices in Spain and studies documents whose yellowed pages crumble in his hands, none of it has explained why four hundred years ago his ancestors decided to settle on this dried-up and distant parcel of land. And yet he knows he will never move to Orlando or San Diego or anywhere else because for as far back as anyone can remember Entrada de la Luna is the only place that his people have ever called home, and that up on the hillside in the old cemetery under the oak tree all of their bones and all of their stories are buried.

꙳

CHAPTER THREE

FRIXLANDIA—1492

L uis de Torres rises before dawn. If he is to make it to the coast by August, he must leave now. He has a long journey ahead. Though he prayed this hour would never come, at last it has. It takes all of his strength to ease himself out of the bed he has slept in for the past ten years. He is careful not to disturb Catalina. She sleeps curled up like a child, weary from weeping. Her face curves upward, her hands press beneath her chin as if in prayer.

He tries to memorize her body. The rise of her breasts, the round of her hips. The way her lush dark hair falls across the pillow. When she sleeps, she grimaces as if she has tasted lemon, furrowing her brow, her lip. Years from now these furrows will become the wrinkles of her face, but he fears he will never see her grow old. He breathes in her sweaty, pungent smell and wonders if they made love for the last time the night before. How can he leave her, sleeping like that? How can he not wake her? But it could be his death, and perhaps hers and the children's, if he stays. It is better for him to slip away. He has heard that the ports are filled with men looking to ship out. If he is lucky, he will be among them. And if he is even more fortunate, he will return when this madness is over.

In his dressing room he pulls on his linen shirt and hose, fastens his doublet, puts on his shoes and his chaperon. In the knapsack he will carry only his woolen cape and a change of shirt along with water, bread, figs, and a hunk of hard cheese. He will buy whatever else he needs along the way. When he is ready, he tiptoes into the room where his boys sleep. The youngest, Eduardo, is only a few months old, yet already he resembles his father the most with his reddish hair, his sharp blue eyes. Catalina says they will turn brown, but more and more they have taken on the color of the sky. When Luis peers into the eyes of his tiny son, he sees his own. He is the hardest to leave.

When Catalina gave birth to Eduardo in the spring, Luis thought she would die. Her cries were so fierce and desperate, not unlike those she cried for him last night. The midwife had to tear the baby from her womb. But now he is a healthy and robust boy and Catalina has healed. He will grow up, Luis imagines, to be a fine, sturdy young man. He will not remember his father when he returns, though Luis hopes that Juan, his older son, will. Juan already takes after his mother. He has dark skin with black eyes and hair to match. His laughter is deep and his tears inconsolable. If you take the smallest of toys away from Juan, he will cry from the depths of his soul. But Eduardo is not like that. It is easy to make this little boy laugh.

Luis de Torres has left his mark on his sons, circumcising them himself with the swift slice of a barber's blade. He cauterized the boys' wounds with his own mouth, sucking their blood until the bleeding stopped. He never hesitated to do this anymore than a mother would hesitate to give her child her breast. Now he is sorry that he has marked them for life, but there is nothing to be done. He prays that they will not suffer because of his sins.

He runs his fingers across Eduardo's head. He touches his face, his finger grazing the baby's lips. Luis gazes at his two sons, breathing them in. The smell of their baby sweat, the scent of talc and milk. Catalina must have nursed Eduardo just before Luis rose. She did not want the child to awaken to his father's departure. She did not want him to leave as she was nursing their infant son. The boys are deep into their slumber. Only the fluttering of their eyelids, the gentle rise and fall of their chests let him know that they are alive. He prays silently to keep them that way.

He stoops down one last time, kissing Juan on his sweaty brow. The boy does not stir. But as he bends to kiss Eduardo, a single tear slips from Luis de Torres's eye, down his cheek, and on to that of his son.

Years later Eduardo de Torres will claim that he still feels the burn of his father's tear. The baby's eyes shoot open and their blue eyes meet. Luis fears that the boy will cry out, but he doesn't. Instead he stares at his father as if he is trying to memorize him. Then the baby smiles in that joyful way he has, closes his eyes, and settles back into sleep. That smile is one of the few things Luis will carry with him as he straightens up, breathes a sigh, and walks toward the door.

Passing the mantel, he glances at the clock whose hands go backward. It is almost five. He must go soon. Seeing the old clock sitting there gives him a pang. It is just one of the many pangs he will feel as he makes his way to the sea. No one knows why its hands go backward and the numbers too, but Luis is not sure if he can tell time any other way. His grandfather, who apprenticed with the famous clockmakers of Prague, made it. It is said to be one of the first portable clocks—one that is not attached to the wall of a church or great house. But still it is too heavy for Luis to carry on his journey. He must leave this, and so much else, behind. But he can't think of that now.

He peers at his wife one more time. He wants to gather her into his arms, but he fears he will never have the strength to go. This is how he wants to remember her. Her face serene, tranquil with sleep. He will not think about the whiteness of her flesh, the body that has lain beside his for more than a decade, the girl he first glimpsed in the marketplace when she was only fifteen. He blows her a kiss and whispers her name. One more tear slides down his face. He licks its salt. Catalina hears the door close. She feels the swish of the wind and knows that the only man she will ever love is gone. She cries into her pillow the sobs one cries for the dead. As he walks away, he cups his hands over his ears.

Luis de Torres is not his real name. It is Yosef ben Ha Levi Halvri— Joseph, Son of Levi, the Hebrew. But he became Luis de Torres earlier that year when the Alhambra Decree called for the expulsion or conversion of all the Muslims and Jews. He converted, as did Catalina. She has become a devout Catholic, but in secret he remains a Jew. He says his prayers, keeps the Sabbath. He will never eat pork. He cannot stay in Murcia long. He is certain that he will be discovered as have others like him. Luis speaks five languages. He has heard rumors of a young explorer, staying at the monastery of La Rábida, who is looking for an interpreter. He could be useful, Luis was told, on a voyage planned to the Far East. The explorer was searching for a western route to China and a speaker of Hebrew and Arabic would be able to negotiate with the traders they'd encounter along the way.

The deadline for the Jews who refuse to convert to leave Spain is August 3rd. His rabbi, who was among those leaving, noted the irony. On the lunar calendar that the Jews followed the date of expulsion fell on the 9th of Av. It was on the 9th of Av that the first temple was destroyed in 423 BCE. And it was on that same day in 69 CE that the second temple was destroyed. On that date in 1290 the Jews were expelled from England. And now, two hundred years later, they are to be expelled from Spain. This year the 9th of Av will fall on August 3rd. The Jews refer to it as the day God set aside for their suffering.

As he walks down the road and out of the only city where he's ever lived, Luis de Torres doesn't look back. His wife and children will be safer without him. Yet, even half a mile down the road, it seems as if he can still hear Catalina wail. Or perhaps it is just another wife, sobbing as she is left behind. He purses his lips and walks on.

The wind blows through the olive trees. The green olives will soon ripen. He will miss the harvest. He loves to go to the fields those few nights a year when the olives must be harvested. He loves the sound of them falling into the nets, and the hauling to the presses from which he will carry home large jugs. He wonders if he will ever again taste the savory oil that comes from these pressed fruits.

As the heat of the day rises, he begins to perspire. The sores that plague him fester. He never knows what will set them off, but now they blister on his neck and arms. Is it the sadness at his leaving or just the sweat of his brow? He does not know, but he hopes that the waters of the sea might cure him. He has heard that they can heal.

As he comes down from the hills, the paths are filled with donkeys and carts and men carrying their rucksacks. Women and children are piled into carts. Young and old, rich and poor, they trudge out of the hills, heading to the seaports and frontier towns, for they have been given only days to leave Spain. Some travel with their gold and jewels sewn into their vests and petticoats. Others swallow them. They will do whatever they can to not have them confiscated when they reach the frontier.

They have left behind fine houses and estates, horses and sheep, dresses made of damask and jewels that could shimmer on the crowns of kings. They have sold everything to Christians for a trifle. One man sold all his holdings for a donkey and a cart with which to transport his family to the border of Portugal. Luis de Torres brings only enough ducats to get him to Huelva where he believes he will find work. Along the slopes he passes those who are falling, others struggling to rise. They are thirsty and hungry and tired and old. A pregnant woman in a cart screams in labor, her insides splitting, with no one to help her. Exhausted children cling to their mothers' hands or to the backs of wagons. An old man slumps by the side of the road, trying to sell the silver cover of the ketubah he and his wife signed when they made their marital vows.

On the hillsides sounders of hogs graze. As he walks past, the dark and ominous beasts grunt and forage. A year ago herds of goats and sheep roamed these hills. But they have been slaughtered, and black hoofed pigs brought in instead. This is how much the Spanish hate the Muslims and the Jews. They have filled the pasturelands with pigs. They eat pork to spite them. If they invite Luis into their homes, they serve ham hocks and pig knuckles, ribs and pork butt and bacon just to see if he will choke at the sight of them. This will prove that he is still a Jew. Then he will be relaxed, as the Inquisition calls it, to the torture chambers and the flames.

Luis de Torres knows the punishment for being a Jew who doesn't actually convert but merely pretends. The Great Inquisitor has a price list and any man tortured or executed must pay for services rendered. There is a price for having your mouth burned and your face branded, another for having appendages such as hands, fingers, ears, or toes removed. Luis knows the price for the rack where bones are separated from sinew, the *garrucha* in which your arms are tied behind your back and you are lifted until you dangle like a despondent angel. If you are burned at the stake, your family is required to cover the cost. And of course you must pay for the room and board during your imprisonment.

As he climbs through the hills, he passes others. Moors departing in haste with their goats and children piled into a cart. An old rabbi staggers under the weight of the Torah he is carrying. The holy scrolls can never touch the ground or they will have to be buried, and Luis wonders if the old man can make it to wherever he is going. A child stands alone in a ditch, crying, and it pains Luis to walk on, but how can he take a child with him when he has left his own behind? An old Moorish woman crumples by the side of the road and he pauses to give her water. "Please," she begs, pointing toward the sea. "Please . . ."

Luis gives her another sip. "Your son will come back for you," he promises, not knowing if it is a son or daughter or even her own husband who has left her to die by the side of the road. The Moors and the Jews pour out of the hills. Hundreds, thousands of them. Along with their exodus go the spices. The hills were redolent with the cardamom and ginger, the cinnamon and turmeric that they carry away—spices that will never find their way back to Spain. He gives the old woman one more sip, wondering if it will be her last, and then he walks on.

Luis de Torres is a delicate man with fine white hands, pale skin, and reddish hair. His skin, which opens into painful sores, is his curse. Every day he bathes with olive oil and almond soap, but still his flesh curses him. Many nights Catalina rubbed his sores with soothing balms. Not once did she complain. It was his eyes that she had been drawn to. Eyes that she told him were the blue of the sea, though he had yet to see it. Because sweat made his sores worse, Luis de Torres rarely exercised. The most he ever walked was beneath the shade of the cypress trees to the office of the governor where he'd worked as a translator until all of the troubles began. He walked to work at seven in the morning, then home for lunch.

Every day Catalina prepared a meal of noodles, flavored with tomatoes and herbs, fresh meat or fish, and the vegetables that were ripe in their garden. They never ate the same meal twice. She spent her mornings in the kitchen inventing new ways to please him, and every day she did. They drank wine that they kept in ceramic barrels in the dark cave beneath their house, where it aged for years. After lunch they would lie down together, resting in each other's arms. Often he made love to her, and they would sleep soundly for an hour or more. Then as the cool breezes of the late afternoon began to blow, he walked back to his office until evening. These were his days. This was his life. Until now.

He walks on, resting during the heat of the day. He gave too much of his water to the old woman. He must sip slowly to conserve his strength. He tries to walk in the evening, though he stumbles on the path. He rests only when the sun is at its highest and in the depths of night. He is grateful for the moon when it illumines his way.

At last he arrives at the port of Huelva where he confuses the sea with the sky. He has never seen the vastness of the water. As he sniffs the briny air, fear ripples through him. How could anyone cross this? He imagines that it goes on forever. Its blue stings his own blue eyes. Yet his sores begin to constrict. Soon they will start to heal. The docks are pungent with the odors of oily salted fish, and the ships are already full, loaded with Jews and Muslims, heading to Morocco where many will starve, or up the Dardanelles to parts unknown.

He asks a wizened quartermaster where he might find La Rábida monastery and the man tells him to go to Palos de la Frontera. It is another half-day's walk. At La Rábida the young Italian explorer is conferring with the Franciscan friars. He has finally convinced them that based on his readings of the Second Book of Esdras he can reach the Indies by sailing west. He believes that he will arrive at the Kingdom of the Great Khan and, with his letter of introduction from the king and queen of Spain, be shown the royal coffers. He will find the mines of silver and gold, and it will all be his for the taking. Then the old man points to the road south. "Keep walking," the quartermaster tells him. "Follow the sea."

Luis finished his last crust of bread the day before. The water bladder he'd carried with him is empty as well. He does not know if he can go on. His skin burns and his lips are parched and cracked. The sand scorches his feet; the salt air stings his sores. He walks for hours, dragging his feet. He thinks he will die before he ever sails from Spain and he will have left his wife and sons for nothing. He will die right there beside the sea. Then in the distance a rocky bluff, known as Saturn's Rock, juts into the sky. Upon it the whitewashed walls of the monastery rise, as bleached and blistering as the sunlight itself.

Nobody reaches La Rábida by accident. Perched so high above the sea, this is not a place you stumble upon. As he stares up at it, Luis understands that anyone who comes here comes by design. From this fortress, built centuries ago at the confluence of the Tinto and Odiel rivers, the Moors defended this entire coastline. Now it is a refuge of the Franciscan monks who pass their days raising bees and making sherry.

He begins the climb. The sun beats down on him and he longs for water. It seems that with each step he will collapse. He will never make it to the top of this cliff. His mouth is so dry. As he sweats, his wounds begin to ooze again, and he fears that the friars will take one look at him and turn him away for his trouble. Perhaps they will think that he has brought a pestilence with him. Just when it seems as if he'll never reach the monastery, after two more hours of climbing he does.

He stands in the dust and heat before the black iron door. He knocks but hears nothing. He knocks again and at last there is the shuffling of feet. The large door is opened and a small friar in a brown cassock, so thick for such a hot day, stands before him, bowing. Luis is about to speak but there is no need. The friar knows who he is. They have been expecting him. Without a word the friar steps aside. Luis follows him into the sudden coolness of the monastery. At first Luis can see nothing. For weeks his eyes have gazed into the glare of the sun. Here it is all shadows.

As his eyes adjust, he sees that he's come into a courtyard with twelve small doors. These are the rooms of the friars, one for each of the apostles. Without a word the friar leads Luis into a room where he is shown a place to relieve himself and to bathe his hands, his face, and his feet. He is given a cloth with which to dry. When he comes out into the small anteroom a hunk of crusty bread, a plate of cheese, and some fig jam await him along with a bladder of cold water and a goblet of sweet red wine. Mercifully there is no ham that he would have to force himself to swallow. He drinks the water, and then the wine. He eats voraciously until his hands are sticky with jam. Then he rinses his hands again.

Before the friar leads him upstairs, Luis stops in the chapel where he kneels before the Virgin of the Miracles and says his prayers to himself in Hebrew. When he rises, he follows the friar up a flight of stone stairs into a room in which several men sit around a long, dark wooden table and chairs. Despite the stifling heat the men wear high white collars and wool capes. As Luis steps forward, they gaze at this slightly built man, wearing only trousers and a soiled linen tunic. The room is large and filled with light and air. Its windows are flung open and a warm breeze blows through. Luis breathes in the brine of the sea.

As Luis de Torres approaches the table, a pale-skinned man with a shock of white hair and pale eyes rises to greet him. In front of him is a long tube of rolled parchment. Though he is not a friar, the man is dressed in a friar's robes. For an instant Luis takes him for a ghost, but the explorer is not surprised to see him. Christopher Columbus has received a message that a speaker of Hebrew would be asking to board his ships. Columbus does not look at Luis. He pays no attention to his soiled tunic, his knapsack, or the blisters that ooze on his arms and neck.

The Admiral of the Ocean Sea motions for Luis de Torres to sit down. "I am in need of a translator," Columbus says. "Someone who can speak the language of your dark race." Luis is surprised by his high-pitched voice. It is as if he is listening to a boy, not someone his own age. Columbus explains that when they reach the Orient, they will meet the Jewish traders—those who travel the silk route, importing slave girls and eunuchs, furs and swords, and bringing back cinnamon, musk, and camphor. The ones known as the Radanites, meaning "those who know the way."

"It is my intention," Columbus explains, "to find the sea route to the East. We will trade with your people in the goods I will require."

"I am a speaker of Hebrew, Arabic, Aramaic, Spanish, Latin, and Portuguese," Luis tells the young explorer. Columbus nods as he unrolls the parchment. It is large and covers the long, wooden table. Luis can barely hide his excitement as Columbus lays before him the portolan map that he has drawn.

"I have spent years thinking about this journey," Columbus tells him as he shows Luis his vision of the world. Columbus has read the journals of Marco Polo and studied the Book of the Splendor. He learned that Sardinia is known for its curative fountains, but if a rogue drinks from one he will go blind. In Cathay werewolves sacrifice humans and worship Mars. The tribes of Gelonne make saddles from the flesh of their enemies and an African tribe pledges friendship through the drinking of blood. The one-eyed Arismapes live in mountains inhabited by griffins. And in Lower Scitie the women go to war and the men do housework.

From all that he read Columbus drew this map, which he displays before Luis de Torres. He intends to use it to chart his journey. Luis leans closer for a better look. The map consists of two seemingly unrelated maps. To the far left is a map of the world surrounded by nine circles. The first seven are the spheres of the moon, Mercury, Venus, the sun, Mars, Jupiter, and Saturn. The eighth circle bears the signs of the Zodiac. The ninth sphere is empty.

To the right is the known world of the Mediterranean and the Atlantic. If he squints, for his eyes still burn from his walk to La Rábida, he can see that the map is cluttered with tiny drawings of towns. From the towns, minarets, ramparts, turrets, and churches with crosses, medieval towers, ancient domes rise with no particular rhyme or reason. There are churches in Madagascar, minarets in France. Over Africa the Portuguese flag flies and ostrich feathers grace the Sahara; ivory and civet from Senegambia, pepper from Guinea, parrots from Benin. In West Africa two black archers fill the void. Far to the north is Frixlandia.

Luis points and Columbus explains that Frixlandia is a land of ice and snow with high mountains and inhospitable terrain where six months out of the year the inhabitants dwell in mud hovels and live on frozen fish. Farther to the right are the fabled Isles of the Seven Cities whose shores, sailors claim, are made of pure gold. Below the Isles of the Seven Cities there is nothing but the open sea. Pointing to the empty space on the map, Columbus tells Luis, "This is the Unknown

World into which we will sail." And with that Luis understands that he has been hired for the voyage.

Then Columbus points to a tiny island off the coast of Asia. It is surrounded by rocks and seems to be at the very end of the world. Luis has to bend forward to see it more clearly and he reads the name of this island that Columbus has written in his own hand. He has called it Paradise. This journey is to take them to heaven. As Luis de Torres gazes at the map, it occurs to him that he may be sailing off with a madman.

Still the next day Luis rises before daybreak and kneels in front of the friars of the Rabida Monastery. He kisses the holy cross and becomes a Christian for the second time. He agrees to banish the dead laws of Moses from his spirit and not to consort with any who ascribes to the false doctrines of Mahamet. He swears his allegiance to the King and Queen of Spain and Jesus Christ and promises to help in the conversion of any heretics or pagans they meet along the way.

On the third day of August three ships sail out of Palos. Luis de Torres is on the *Santa María* with the Admiral of the Ocean Sea who now refers to himself as "Don." They head across the Atlantic, into the great unknown, believing they will come to a land of spices and gold that no white man has ever seen.

CHAPTER FOUR

✳

COLIBRI CANYON—1992

It is a day of hot dry winds and tumbleweeds. The kind when
poisonous creatures abound. Rattlesnakes coil on footpaths and
scorpions hide in shadows of the woodpile. Black widows spin
their webs while dung beetles cart turds away. The hideous twisted
cacti burst into giant scarlet flowers and for the time being Miguel can
forgive them their ugliness. For the past five days the heat has been
almost a hundred, too hot for this time of year, and Miguel is afraid
that his thin tires will explode on the asphalt. The car is a hand-me-
down from his father, an old Chevy Impala, and still has the souped-up
wheels and the flames painted on the hood. A classic, his father would
call it. A wreck, Miguel would reply. Still, he's never felt ashamed of it
before. But now he does.

As he drives down the highway south from Entrada, dogs that are
mostly wolves cross the road. Mexican grays have mated with these
wild dogs, producing the feral mutts that he and his friends take turns
firing potshots at on dull summer evenings, but the dogs are swift and
rarely struck. This is the closest Miguel has ever come to blood sport.
He drives quickly with his windows down. A rosary, green sponge dice,
and a pair of his baby shoes dangle from the rearview mirror. His father
insists on keeping the baby shoes and after all it's his car. Perhaps he
should have taken them down, but Miguel, like his father, is superstitious. Besides if you advertise for a babysitter in Entrada, this is what
you'll get.

He's showered and changed into a clean white T-shirt and jeans, but already he is sweating through. He wonders what kind of impression he will make on Mrs. Rothstein. In his mind he rehearses what he'll say to her. He can be a good babysitter. He is patient. He is an amateur astronomer and he spends hours watching the night sky. He's pretty sure he can convince her that he's sixteen and about to be a junior, not a sophomore. He looks older than his years. He will tell her that he plans to save his money for an even stronger telescope and, of course, for college. These are things that he assumes a rich white lady who lives out in Colibri Canyon will want to hear.

In fact he gives most of his money to his mother because his father is never going to make a killing on his airbrushed bike helmets. Miguel is fairly certain that he'll never get a store-bought telescope, let alone get out of that trailer. The only way he can go to college will be on a full scholarship, the way his aunt Elena did, but she was "exceptional." (That's what his father always says. She was exceptional.) So that probably won't happen. In fact Miguel is fairly sure that he'll never amount to much, but he'd like to help his mother out if he can. And he can use some cash if he ever wants to take a girl to the movies and out for an orange slushie—though he hasn't done so yet.

In the distance over the Sangres he sees the rain. Long, gray streaks running down from the clouds. But it is moving away, not toward him. At least he hopes it is. He doesn't want to get caught out in Colibri Canyon in a flash flood, or even a heavy rain. He doesn't have four-wheel drive and he remembers when he used to go out there and work with his father how thick the mud can be. But from the clouds and the wind it seems to be moving away, not toward Santa Fe. Forked lightning illumines the horizon off to his right. It is that unpredictable time of year.

He turns off the highway onto Colibri Canyon Road. It's a dirt road the way most roads are out here. One that twists and turns. He has an address though he knows it won't do much good. She's just told him to drive until he crosses two arroyos and a stone bridge, then look for a one-story white adobe about a mile and a half in. That is pretty much how you find places around here. The addresses are on the mailboxes but the mailboxes aren't always near the houses. You are just supposed to know where people live. This tends to keep strangers from your door.

As he makes his way along the road, his car bounces in the ruts. The road is lined in piñon, juniper, and sage, and the air smells of fresh pine. Miguel comes to the first arroyo. It's dry but there's a sign that warns "If There's Water, Turn Around. Don't Drown." He knows this is serious. Just last year a boy he went to school with was carried away in his father's gardening truck. He doesn't like to come down these canyon roads in the spring without four-wheel drive.

As he crosses the second arroyo, Miguel wonders if Mrs. Rothstein will hire him. It seems as if she already has, but he is sure she'll change her mind once she sees him. He wouldn't hire someone who drives a beat-up lowrider with a wolf and flames airbrushed on it. But this car is all he has for now. Maybe she'll let him drive hers. He bets she has a Porsche or a BMW. He'll drive it all over town. He is hoping for a convertible. He'll take it for a spin, maybe all the way to Entrada. He tries to imagine the look on his friends' faces when he shows up in a fancy car.

Miguel pulls into the dusty drive in front of what seems to be a small adobe house. But in Colibri Canyon looks can be deceiving. The canyon is named for the many emerald and ruby-throated humming-birds that flit among the cactus blooms, plunging their beaks into the flowers. There are also snakes, ready to inject their venom. Sometimes people get lost on these canyon roads, wandering out into the desert. A few years ago a toddler slipped out of his yard and was eaten by coyotes. Or maybe wild dogs. It is hard to tell. It is said that wolves have returned to the hills. Or, if you believe the natives, wolf spirits.

But the people who live out here come mostly from Texas or California. They never think much about such things. They are people with money. People with alarm systems and fancy cars and designer dogs. People who feel safe within their adobe walls and behind their automatic garage doors. Across the road he notices the work truck and men who appear to be drilling a well. They glance his way and he gives a wave. They wave back. It is what strangers do around here.

He slams the car door and walks up the path. But before he can knock, the door opens and Rachel Rothstein holds out her hand. "I heard you drive up. You always hear people drive up on this road." It seems like an odd thing to do but he shakes her hand. Her long red fingernails press into his palm. "So you're Manuel?" He nods, not bothering to correct her. He will next time.

He expected a thin blond woman. He has no idea why he thought she'd be that way. Maybe because he imagines most white women who have money and hire babysitters will be tiny with eating disorders and watery blue eyes, but she isn't. Rachel Rothstein is a fleshy woman with large hips and breasts. She has such dark hair and eyes that if he'd seen her in Entrada when she was posting her ad, he would have taken her for Hispanic. Maybe even someone related to him. Except that she is wearing black tights and high leather boots and a pale green blouse with a green cardigan sweater. Her dark hair is wrapped in a tight bun on the top of her head. No one in Entrada de Luna dresses like this. Not during the day. Maybe for a fiesta. But not at four o'clock in the afternoon in your own house. He wonders if she dressed up for him.

Despite how stylishly she is dressed, behind her he sees piles of Legos, trucks, train cars, stuffed animals, and plastic pistols and swords tossed all over the living-room floor. And he sees the huge picture window with a vista that looks out to the mountains and notices that the house has wings that jut out on either side. He is right. Looks are deceiving. Mrs. Rothstein pulls the door back to let Miguel in. But he has barely stepped inside when he is ambushed. A small boy, wearing a mask and cape and carrying a laser gun, latches on to his legs and tries to drag him to the floor. "I got you," the boy says.

Miguel raises his arms in surrender. "I come in peace," he says.

The boy eases his grip. "I'm Captain Chaos."

Miguel extends a hand. "I'm Captain Kirk. What is your mission?"

That seems to stump the boy. As he eyes Miguel, Mrs. Rothstein smiles. "Why do you want a job?" she asks.

Miguel looks at her oddly. What a stupid question. Why does anyone want a job? Because they need money, because their deadbeat father rarely comes around, but perhaps this woman does not understand that concept. "I'm working on a science project and I need to buy a telescope," he tells her.

"A telescope." She mulls over the word, and then smiles again. "This is Davie." She slips the mask off the little boy and a pair of deep blue eyes stare up at him. "And please call me Rachel." Miguel nods, biting his tongue. He's never called anyone more than five years older than himself anything other than Mr. or Mrs. or doctor or professor. Or officer on the occasions when he's had dealings with the police. He knows he'll never call her by her first name. "That's interesting," she says as she leads him into the kitchen. "Do you want to be an astronomer?"

Miguel shrugs as he follows her. He hasn't really thought that far ahead yet. "I just like to look at the stars," he replies. He follows her through the obstacle course that is the living room where an older boy with reddish hair and pale skin sits, glued to the TV. "That's Jeremy. Jeremy, say hello."

The boy waves a "hi" without looking up. A huge brown dog is flopped down beside him, which Miguel mistakes for a pillow until it wags its tail. "That's Baxter. Mostly he just sleeps." As Davie plunks himself down beside his brother, Jeremy gives him a pinch on the arm that Miguel catches a glimpse of. Tears in his eyes, Davie slides away, rubbing his arm.

Mrs. Rothstein doesn't seem to notice or, if she does, decides not to do anything about it. Perhaps she's already given up on some things. Miguel isn't sure as he traipses after her down a narrow corridor lined with huge windows that look out on to the desert. He is surprised that the house, which appears small and simple on the outside, seems to grow larger and more convoluted as he goes along. Indeed it is a veritable maze, perhaps good for extended games of hide-and-seek. Or just to get lost in.

In the kitchen buckets of water are lined up on the floor. Some of the water has sloshed onto the tiles. "Be careful," Mrs. Rothstein warns. "Don't slip." Miguel wonders if they have a leak. She points to the dishes in the sink. "They're working on the well across the way. That's why I can't do dishes. We haven't been able to take a bath for two days. We can barely flush . . ." Her hands flutter in the air. "Never mind. This just isn't, you know, normal." Looking around, Miguel wonders what normal is.

She begins opening cupboards. "Davie likes sweet snacks like ginger cookies or Froot Loops. But no dairy for Davie. Absolutely none. He has this condition. It's not pleasant. Just remember Davie, no dairy. That's how we remember it. Now Jeremy—" She hears them shouting in the other room. "Boys, cut that out." She turns back to Miguel. "Jeremy likes cheese and crackers. If Davie has a sweet, he has to have juice. But not Jeremy, if he has a sweet, he must have milk. Can you remember that?"

Miguel isn't sure he can remember any of this, but she goes on. "Jeremy can't handle double sweets. They get him all agitated. He shouldn't really have much sweets at all, but it's not worth the trouble arguing with him."

She opens a door that he assumes leads to a closet, but instead he finds himself staring into an enormous pantry that is stocked as well as the grocery store in Entrada de la Luna. Shelves teem with peanut butter, gingersnaps, boxes of cereal and granola, energy bars and Pop-Tarts. Tins of sardines, tuna fish, smoked oysters; jars of olives, pickles, catsup, mustard. Every possible variety of Annie's Shells—white cheddar, regular cheddar, Parmesan, dinosaurs, alphabets, the moon and stars. But with a label that reads in big red letters: "For Jeremy only." Mrs. Rothstein is prepared for an invasion. "You'll find most of what you want in here. You should help yourself too." Mrs. Rothstein continues, "Once a week or so you can take them out for pizza but soy cheese for Davie. Or you can order one but usually by the time they deliver here it's cold. Davie needs a nap just half an hour or so after school. And Jeremy, he needs quiet time. I'll be here some days but mostly I'll be working in my studio. I'm a sculptor." With a flick of her hand she points toward the back wall beyond which he assumes is her studio, but he can't see it. "I'll leave you the numbers. Either my husband or I will be home before six. Can you come three afternoons a week and sometimes on the weekend? I'll pay you ten dollars an hour. And your car? Is it safe?"

Miguel nods. He wants to say to her that he isn't really sure how safe his car is. He doesn't have his driver's license. He doesn't even have his learner's permit. He wants to tell her that she doesn't know him. She doesn't know anything about him. She hasn't asked if he has any experience with kids or if he has ever been convicted of a felony. Outside of his astronomy she hasn't asked who he is or what his father does for a living. When his father isn't too drunk to earn a living, that is. Or that his parents were barely married, then they split when his father's drinking got worse. He doesn't tell her that sign on the road heading to Lake Abiquiu ("Danger. Slow Down. Lake Ahead.") was put up after his father drove his car, filled with his friends, all insanely drunk, right into the lake one crazy Saturday night and that somehow all of them managed to survive. Instead he replies, "I'll be here at three on Monday."

"Wonderful," Mrs. Rothstein exclaims as she walks him back toward the living room where the boys are watching Road Runner and Coyote duking it out. "Boys—" she claps her hands but the only one startled is Miguel. "This is your new babysitter. He'll be here on Monday." Davie gives him a little smile, but the older boy doesn't even nod.

Mrs. Rothstein accompanies Miguel to the driveway. "Well, I'm glad that worked out. The boys need someone to distract them. And I think a boy your age . . ." She hesitates unsure of what she wants to say. "I think it's a good idea, don't you?"

Miguel nods as he gets into his car. "I'll be here Monday."

Mrs. Rothstein shouts, "Drive carefully." He's hoping she'll go inside, but she doesn't. He is embarrassed by the hepped-up sound his motor makes as he starts the engine. He tries to ignore the darkening sky, but as he drives away, a clap of thunder sounds. Mrs. Rothstein grows smaller in his rearview mirror. Above the mountains the sky is pitch-black.

He rounds the bends quickly, hoping to get ahead of the rain, but as he crosses the stone bridge, the skies open. Torrents pour down. There is another crash of thunder, much closer this time, as a lightning bolt splits the sky. Suddenly forked lightning shoots all around him. Miguel can see nothing in front of him. He knows these storms and he knows how they come quickly into the canyons, filling the dry riverbeds.

As he reaches the first arroyo, Miguel is relieved to find that it's still dry. He crosses it and speeds down the mud-slick road until he comes to the next one. He halts at the embankment. A river of brown water courses through it, but Miguel doesn't think it's that deep. And if he doesn't cross it now, he might not make it home tonight. He guns it, but halfway across his wheels start to spin, and he realizes his mistake. The water is already too deep and the current is tugging him along. He tries to gun it again, but his tires are slipping in the mud. The road recedes beneath him.

His car is being lifted, carried along as the water races through the canyon. It has come rushing down from the mountains, bringing a wall of mud. Now his car is shooting along as if he is on a water slide and there is nothing he can do to stop it. He sails along a trench of muck and mud. As his tires spin, he realizes that he was wrong about the storm as he often is about many things. It had been coming his way all along.

CHAPTER FIVE

THE WELL DRILLERS—1992

From her doorway Rachel Rothstein watches as the boy drives off. There is something about him that touches her. She believes that his coming is a sign, the way she believes most things are, but a sign of what she does not know. As her eyes follow the dust in his wake, she is trying to decide if hiring him was a good decision or a bad one. Lately she's been prone to bad decisions, moving to New Mexico being high on the list. She makes those mistakes because she lives with the illusion that life will be better if she changes something—if she buys a new sofa, if she loses weight or, at times, gains it, if the kids go to a different school, if they move to another state. And yet none of it ever seems to make a difference and certainly not for long.

Behind her the children are quarreling. She should go inside and stop them, but she is transfixed by the road and the swirl of dust that the boy has left behind. Though she can no longer see or hear his car, she sees the dust and her eyes follows it until he turns the bend about a mile down the road. Overhead black clouds appear. They seem to have come from nowhere. It occurs to her that the boy might be driving right into the storm. She wonders if he will be all right. She doesn't think he has four-wheel drive.

Davie and Jeremy huddle on the couch in opposite corners, Davie sniffling, watching cartoons. She looks out across the arroyo and wonders if the boy, whose name she cannot recall, made it safely to the highway. She ponders getting into her SUV and driving out to see, but it would mean throwing the boys into the car and what if she got stuck out there, so in the end she decides that he must be all right. He's from around here, isn't he? But still. She knows how these storms can take you by surprise.

Though they've only been living here for a few months, she is already familiar with how Colibri Canyon quickly turns to thick streams of mud. She has almost gotten stuck once or twice and is grateful that Nathan made them get four-wheel drive in both of their vehicles. Two Jeep Cherokees because he needs a car to go to the hospital and she has to shuttle the children back and forth. But now she wonders about the boy. What was his name—Manuel? How can you hire a boy to babysit your children and not remember his name?

Perhaps she should have told him more. Full disclosure, that is what her father always said. Should she have told him that Davie is hyperactive and that she is beginning to suspect that Jeremy, her sweet firstborn, is in the process of becoming a bully? Should she have warned him that she has difficulty putting a meal on the table, that she herself rarely eats but tends to pick at her food, that her husband, a doctor of some esteem, doesn't notice, and that despite her having hired a babysitter, it is unlikely she will get anything done. But if she tells this to the boy, then perhaps he will not come to work for her. And she desperately wants him to do so because, among other things, he is the only person who answered her ad.

Across the way the well drillers are staring into the well. It is what they've been doing for the past two days. As they stare down, she stares at them. Sometimes they shout into the well and a voice from deep inside the earth shouts back. This seems primitive to Rachel. You'd think they'd have some system in place for this sort of thing. She recalls years ago when she was a student traveling in Italy, and a boy with a faulty heart fell into a deserted, dried-up well. No one had ever bothered to seal it and the boy tumbled to the bottom.

For days they tried to dig him out. In the newspaper there were all kinds of images of the engineering problems the well presented and why they just can't go down and get the boy. The boy's mother spent days calling to him in the well, telling him that he will be rescued soon, that she loves him. Rachel shudders when she thinks about anyone being dropped down a well, let alone one of her children. The darkness, the wet, the cold. And you cannot get out. The moment you realize you are stuck. Of course the boy died before they could rescue him and in the end they closed up the well and left him forever. She has not thought about this boy in years, but now as she stares at the diggers, she thinks of him again.

Suddenly there is forked lightning all around them and the skies open. The well drillers rush into their truck as the storm moves closer. Thunder seems to be right over their heads and with a huge clap her boys start screaming.

+

Rachel Rothstein is not a happy woman. And she has not been happy for some time, though this isn't something she's been able to articulate. Recently she read that people with meaningful lives are healthier than people who claim to be happy. She is neither but prefers to err on the side of meaning, happiness having eluded her thus far. Still, most people, including her husband, wouldn't call Rachel unhappy. They call her scattered. A flake. A free spirit. A loose cannon. Restless. It is true that she can never get anything done—ever. Around her nothing is ever finished.

When she complains to Nathan that she can't finish things, he has little patience. "Imagine," he told her once, "if I paused to do the crossword puzzle instead of sewing my patient up." She has to admit that he has a point, but it doesn't seem to make a difference. Her life seems to be about incompletion. Half-made beds, unfinished projects. She makes meals in fits and starts. She'll have the pasta ready before she starts the sauce. There are many nights when she forgets to serve the salad.

The children's quarrel goes on, as they tend to do. She should stop it. At times it seems as if they are engaged in one endless feud. She should go in and tell them to cut it out. Of course it is probably Jeremy punching Davie for some minor infraction. She should go in and shout that they are brothers. They need to learn to love each other.

But at the moment she cannot bear to think of Jeremy's bullying and Davie's tears. And she can't move. Her head is about to explode. She is obsessed with the voice coming from inside the well. She wants to rescue him. She wants to rescue somebody. That would give her life meaning, wouldn't it? But the man in the well doesn't need rescuing. In fact just as the black clouds are about to open he climbs out of the hole in the ground and into the safety of his truck.

What began as a dull aching near the back of her reptilian brain is steadily inching forward. There is nothing she can do to stop it when one of these headaches is coming on. Soon it will engulf her entire brain. She should fix something for dinner, get the boys ready for bed. Instead she watches the storm clouds heading her way. As her headache comes on with its full force, the rains pour down. Rivulets of mud rush past, and Rachel Rothstein knows as surely as she knows anything that she is trapped.

She has only herself to blame. It was she, not Nathan, who wanted to move to the Southwest. She wanted a simpler life. And Nathan complied as he often does. He found a job with the pediatric unit of Mercy Hospital and took the New Mexico boards, which, of course, he passed. It's the way Nathan is. Things come easily to him. He slides from one to the next. He was only too happy to leave the rat race behind. And now here they are, and here she is. Two small boys who can't get along and a studio out back that she has hardly used, except to play solitaire on her computer, and a husband who always has a patient whose demands are always going to be more urgent than whatever hers might be.

Nathan is content saving the lives of children. He could be happy anywhere. He has a sense of purpose that Rachel knows she lacks. And he has a knack for looking on the bright side. He is always finding things to do. He likes to be busy. He has hobbies, interests. Once a year he volunteers for Doctors Without Borders. He goes to the most desolate places on Earth and saves lives. He weeps when mothers thank him. One brought him the family goat in gratitude. Once in the Sinai a tribe of bedouins set up an encampment and roasted a sheep to honor him for saving their chieftain's son. Where Nathan sees hope and possibility, Rachel sees despair. Sometimes when she looks at people's faces she imagines what they'll look like when they are dead. To Rachel death and calamity are just outside the door. She blames this on her mother, who always threw history—her history—into her daughter's face. Rachel envies her husband his sense of purpose. His ability to be content. Rachel thinks of herself as an amorphous creature like the blobfish. Something without cartilage or bone. Without a spine.

She doesn't want to be this way. She tries to have interests, but she has yet to find her sense of purpose. Her passion. The thing she believes she was put on the Earth to do. Because for better or worse Rachel thinks that people have their path and that path becomes their passion. She knows this is what Nathan would call touchy-feely. Various therapists have urged her to take medication, but she balks. She wants to feel whatever she is feeling—even if at times it means gloom and doom. And now she is here in the desert. She is surrounded by neighbors who wave when you drive by but won't invite you over for tea.

Across the way the well drillers are working again. They paused during the storm, but now they are back, standing beside the Lorca house in their hard hats and tool belts. Rachel and Nathan share the well with Julio Lorca, a famous Southwestern artist, and his girlfriend, who goes by the name of Cat, though Rachel has dubbed her Catastrophe because of the way she tears up and down the canyon road. Rachel has to be careful that the boys and Baxter never leave the yard. Lorca's prints of Indian women weaving baskets sell for tens of thousands of dollars. His enormous adobe house has a huge stone wall around it. They don't share the well with Lorca so much as have well privileges, and such privileges, as Nathan has made eminently clear, are delicate negotiations that can be broken in a heartbeat. As she stands in her doorway, Rachel Rothstein also knows that it cannot be a good sign if your excitement of the day is watching the well drillers return after a storm. The drill bit chews at the ground. The well has been turned off for two days, which has meant two days without bathing the children or flushing the toilet or rinsing the dishes without using cistern water or bottled water, and even then it isn't enough. The high point of Rachel's day—outside of hiring the Hispanic boy whom she hopes will run her kids ragged in the afternoons so that they'd tumble, exhausted, brows still sweaty, into their beds—is the fact that by six o'clock Lorca has promised that the well will be turned back on.

The well drillers are pulling out the bit and reattaching it to their truck. They reseal the hole. They're packing up and driving away. She'll miss them, but now the boys can take baths and they can flush the toilet. She'll wait for the housekeeper to come and do the dishes. She thinks about dinner. Heading into the kitchen Rachel opens the pantry. She'll do mac and cheese for Jeremy and a hamburger for Davie with green beans on the side. It is rare that the boys eat the same meal. She'll graze and she has no idea what time Nathan will be home. Will he have eaten?

She calls his office but gets his voice mail, as she knows she will at this hour. She can't call his emergency number and say, "Come home for macaroni." Though she's been known to page him for less. And it makes him angry. "Page me in an emergency," he tells her, "not to let me know when the movie's starting."

Rachel flicks on the TV in the kitchen so she can watch while she's making dinner. The local news is on. There's unrest on the Navajo reservation. Two people have been killed in protests surrounding the imprisonment of a former tribal council leader. And a court injunction has been filed by the Hopi Snake Society against Blaze Construction. The Hopi claim that Blaze Construction is disturbing the habitat of the rattlesnakes they use for ceremonial purposes. "Rattlesnakes," Rachel mutters as if she can't imagine such a thing.

+

The storm is over the way storms are around here, going as quickly as they come. The boys are staring at cartoons and Rachel thinks she'll go out to her studio for a few moments before dinner. Maybe she can get something done. It has been days since she's been in her studio. Weeks maybe. But perhaps now's as good a time as any to begin again. Gingerly she makes her way along the slick patio stones that pave the way from the house to the adobe shed where she's supposed to work. Inside it's musty and dark. Rachel flicks on the light and, for a moment, feels as if she has stumbled upon a crime scene.

The studio is littered with dismembered limbs—mainly hands. There are hands everywhere. Mannequins' hands. Dolls' hands. Hands from old sculptures. Plaster casts that she made of her own hands. Why all these hands? Nathan says it creeps him out. It used to be tiny heads. Well, actually one head, made over and over again. Her only subject. Her mother. In boxes she has dozens of these heads, all made of plaster, with different expressions, the permutations of her mother's frowns, grimaces, looks of disapproval and scorn, of affection and heartache.

She has captured her mother, sitting at her vanity table, looking at herself in a mirror, reading a book, walking into a crowded room. She has captured her as a young girl about to board a train for a place unknown. She has imagined her mother making love, giving birth. Expressions no child should ever see on a mother's face. These tiny sculptures resembled the shrunken head that her mother once brought back from a trip to Brazil, though it was, of course, a fake.

When she was younger, Rachel tried to understand her mother's dark story. It seemed as if somehow these heads would help her. Rachel knew what had happened to her grandparents during the war. But she couldn't help wondering if her mother was the way she was because of the war or if she'd always been that way. Growing up Rachel didn't know that her mother was a survivor. Rachel just knew that she had to do everything right. And that if she failed, she'd failed miserably. There was a moment, though she can't remember when, that Rachel gave up trying.

She had an exhibit of her mother's heads once in New York. She didn't tell her mother, of course. One critic called them "fascinating." Another said they were "disturbingly obsessive." But her mother learned of the exhibit. She went to see it and that evening Rachel received a call. "What is wrong with you?" her mother said. After that

Rachel gave up on the heads. She switched to hands. She doesn't know why. Hands to touch you, love you, slap you. Not only her mother's. Random hands. She's not sure if this was a step in the right direction.

Rachel slumps onto the wooden chair near her desk. She has no idea where to start. Perhaps she should begin by putting things away. But if she puts them away, it will mean she has to start something new.

+

She makes her way back to the house, slipping through the sliding doors. She's about to head to the kitchen to start dinner, but from the living room comes the familiar gasping sound, and she walks in in time to see Davie throwing up all over himself. Jeremy is shouting, "Mom, Mom, Davie's sick." She grabs a towel, races over to her five-year-old son. In an instant she takes in the scene. Jeremy is eating Cheetos and Davie must have eaten some. "Did you feed him Cheetos?" she yells at Jeremy.

"I didn't. He took some when I wasn't looking." She glares at Jeremy. "You know you're supposed to be more careful." She's wrapping Davie up in the towel. "Is that true, sweetheart? Did you take some Chee-tos?" But Davie is gasping, about to heave again. "Come on, pumpkin," she says, "Mommy's here. Mommy's going to take care of you. Let's get you into a nice warm bath." In that swift way that only mothers can manage, Rachel slips off his filthy T-shirt and pants, tosses them into the laundry-room sink, then carries her naked, whimpering child into the bathroom where she puts both of the spigots on full blast.

She lifts Davie up and is about to settle him into the water when she feels the steam rising and Davie starts to squirm out of her arms. She jerks him away from the water that laps at his feet. "On my god. That's hot," she says. "That's very hot." As she reaches down, her fingers are seared. The water is scalding. She turns off the hot water altogether and just lets the cold run, then tests it again, burning her fingers.

The cold water is boiling hot as well. She turns off the cold and turns on the hot, thinking that the pipes have gotten switched, but it too is boiling. "What the hell?" Rachel reaches for a towel that she damp-ens and then lets it cool. Gently she swabs Davie down. "No water, no tubby, no rubber ducky," she says, soothingly to her child. There is no cold water coming through the pipes.

Then Rachel fills the tub with hot water and closes the door. She will bathe them when the water cools. She plunks the boys in front of a cartoon and puts on a jacket over her stretch pants and T-shirt. "I'll be back in five minutes." She points a finger in their faces. "Do not move." The night is cooler after the storm and there is a breeze as she stomps across the dirt road. She rings Lorca's buzzer. It sounds more like a warning than a welcome. When no one answers, she buzzes again. A disembodied voice comes over the intercom. "Who is this?"

"It's your neighbor. From across the way."

There is a buzz and the gate opens. Rachel walks into the Spanish-style courtyard where a pickup truck and an SUV are parked. She walks up the gravel drive to the front porch. At last some lights come on. She hears the clomp of boots as someone comes to the door.

When the door opens a looming man with chiseled features stands before her. "What is it?" the man says.

"I'm your neighbor, Rachel Rothstein." He stares down at her. "I live over there." She points into the blackness. "We share the well." Rachel peers in behind him. She wants to get a glimpse of this house and now she can see his famous paintings on the walls, his ceramics on the glass tables, the carpets made from his designs on the floor.

"Yes," the man's voice is slow and she can hear his annoyance. People don't come ringing Julio Lorca's buzzer. Nathan has warned her to be careful about the well. He can take their rights away in a flash.

"Well, my son is sick. Actually he's allergic. To milk." The man just stares. "He threw up. And when I tried to bathe him . . ." She watches his features harden. He hates her. There is no doubt. He has just met her and already he hates her. He hates her because she is a newcomer, and she will always be a newcomer. And in the end what business does she have encroaching on his land. "Anyway there's no cold water coming through the pipes." He glares at her. "I think the men when they were working on the well . . . they must have clogged the cold-water pipes or something."

Julio Lorca stares down and Rachel feels herself growing very small.

Smaller than she's ever been. She is a beetle, a bug that he can crush with his cowboy boot. "And what do you want me to do about it?" he says.

She glances up at the sky. Overhead the moon is a narrow crescent, a sliver. Like a scythe. Something you can use to slit a throat. "Fix it," Rachel says. Then she turns on her heels and walks back across the dirt road.

＊

DEAD RECKONING—1492

Since the voyage began Luis has slept on the deck. He can't bear to stay below among the ripe odors of men, the stench of piss and shit and rotting meat and musty potatoes, and the rats nibbling at his toes. He can't drift off listening to the groans of men who touch themselves, or worse one another, in that dark, fetid hold. He prefers the wind and the blackness, the lull of the sea. He longs for the body of his wife, her smooth curves, her voluptuous breasts. The sea seems to mimic what he is missing the most. He makes love to it in his dreams.

This evening Luis's eyes are on the Admiral of the Ocean Sea. It seems as if Columbus has decided to forgo sleep. All night he paces. Or pauses by the railing, staring at the sky. He listens to the wind. Columbus can close his eyes and tell the direction from which it is coming. He calls the winds by their names as if they are his friends. Tramontane, Ostro, Sirocco, Gregale. He charts their course with the magnetic compass that his men do not trust. They don't believe that it will guide anyone to China.

From beneath the rigging Luis observes him. Back and forth the Admiral moves like a bear in a cage. Once more he crosses the stern castle, tilting his head. He eyes the sails as they take the wind. With his nocturlabe he measures the distance between the stars. Something is troubling the Admiral tonight. Even in the darkness Luis notes the worry on his face. Columbus does not know that he has miscalculated his direction by thousands of miles. Or that a continent and an ocean lie between him and his goal. In fact he will never know. At least he will never admit that he has been wrong. He resumes his pacing.

If Columbus sleeps at all, he dreams of silkworms spinning their cocoons. He envisions bolts of shiny green and crimson that he will bring to his king and queen. He dreams of palaces with a thousand rooms, women stretched out on couches to greet him. He sniffs the wild rhubarb growing in the mountains of Tangut and sees the cranes that fly over Changa-nor. He walks into the Forbidden City where he will enter hidden chambers, walls within walls, of the Lord of Lords, Sovereign of the Tartars. Kublai Khan will greet him with spices and silks, gems and gold. It does not occur to Columbus that the Great Khan is long dead, his empire in ruins. Or that he is leading his men not to Cathay but to islands of naked souls who have nothing to offer except parrots and mangoes and the human skulls in which they store their keepsakes.

When he does go to his cabin, it is rarely to sleep. It is to write in his log where almost each entry begins, "We continue west." When he is not writing, he is rereading the voyages of Marco Polo. He reads it over and over again, making careful notes in the margins. He looks for any hints of where he will find what he is searching for. He has to prove that his mission has value. He will find the gold and new trade routes that will make Spain the greatest empire that ever ruled. Never mind that Marco Polo told his story from a prison cell in Pisa to a romance writer from France who wrote the story as he saw fit. Never mind that Marco Polo never mentions eating with chopsticks or drinking tea, and some doubt that he's ever been to China at all. Columbus has based his journey on a fiction of a fiction, one that happened more than two centuries before he set sail.

Still he has memorized the passageways that lead to the private chambers where the treasures of the Great Khan are kept. Others that lead to the harem where he will find the slaves and concubines. Columbus doesn't care that Marco Polo writes of these rooms only from the rumors he heard whispered in the game parks and corridors of the palace. Only those closest to the Great Khan are allowed into the inner sanctums. It is in these chambers that the coffers of diamonds and pearls and gold overflow. Rooms filled to the ceiling with treasures no ordinary man has ever laid eyes on.

But Columbus is certain that he will. He spent more than a decade trying to convince the kings and queens of Europe to finance his voyage. He has presented his endless sea maps and charts and theories and drawings. He brought with him his knowledge of navigation and astronomy and mathematics. He explained his theories based on the almanac of Rabbi Abraham Zacuto. He spoke before the bewildered monarchs and archbishops and dukes who shook their heads. Few could understand the theories he spouted. King João of Portugal believed him to be deluded. Others have been even less kind. Behind Columbus's back they laughed at his demands. He will be Admiral of the Ocean Sea. He will claim every island as his own and for his king and queen. He will make his sovereigns, and himself, rich.

His men don't know their Admiral's dreams. If they did, they would turn around. As it is they are filled with fear. Most have never sailed away from the coast without land in sight. They don't know how to navigate without seeing the shore. The Unknown terrifies them. Their Admiral's night roaming disturbs them. His endless gazing at the stars. Among themselves they wonder if he hasn't lost his mind. Or perhaps never had it to begin with. At night when darkness falls, they can't bring themselves to look at the sea. Blackness surrounds them. During the days if clouds gather or if they are becalmed, they are even more afraid. They fear that the monsters of the deep will rise up, dragging them down. Meanwhile Columbus scans the sea. He searches the distance for a flickering light, though unsure of what that might be. A candle, a torch, an illusion. Even the most seasoned sailors see things that are not there.

Tonight something displeases the Admiral. Is it the direction of the wind, the movement of the waters? And though Luis is not schooled in the ways of the ocean, even he can see that above them, one by one, the stars are being obliterated. The rocking of the ship is different from before, more insistent, as if someone is knocking. Instead the blackest of clouds hover above them and in the morning the sun does not rise.

The Admiral never takes his eyes off the water. The steely gray ocean begins to roil. The men have never seen such darkness after dawn. Suddenly the sea seems to rise all around them. Caverns of water engulf them. The storm is as fierce as any of the seamen have ever known. They tie down the sails and let the waves carry the ship along. The bones of their boats ache. The wood stretches and creaks as if it will break in two.

Around Luis sailors are ill, vomiting into the sea, or they have gone below where the stench of their puke will hang thick in the air for days. Luis's stomach clutches as well as he stares into the black maelstrom. It is a darkness he has never known. He must get below or he will be tossed from the deck into that abyss, but he cannot let go of the rigging. He calculates in his head. It is ten paces to the hatch and he is about to make a run for it when a wave crashes over his head. All he can do is hold on for dear life or else he will slide over the railing and disappear into that roiling broth of a sea. He is certain they will go down. As the waves descend upon him, he does not think of the Christian prayers he has been made to memorize. He shouts the Kaddish, the Jewish prayer for the dead, into the eye of the storm instead.

Above the roar of the water, the darkness replies. "Shalom aleichem" is what he hears. "And peace be with you," Luis echoes back. But he believes that death is upon him and his ears are deceiving him. The voice seems to come from the sky, from the clouds. Has he heard the voice of God? Looking up, he expects to see the face of the Eternal shining through the storm, beckoning him, welcoming him. Instead he sees a sailor with olive skin and jet-black hair, strapped to the mainmast, peering down like an angel. Then another wave crashes upon them and Luis is sure that all is lost.

The storm continues to pummel them for days, until at last the black clouds break and blue sky, streaked with sunlight, appears. Sailors fall on their knees, crossing themselves. It is a miracle that they have survived. Luis turns away, pretending not to see as they thank God for getting them through this storm and pray that the next will be less fierce. That night the sea calms and the stars and moon return. Luis makes his bed on the sodden deck, but he is sure that he will not rest again on this voyage. He lies with his head against the rigging, watching as the stars return. It is then that he sees a shadow above him and a man stoops down.

"Are we both running away?" The man speaks to him in Ladino and Luis recognizes the voice from the storm.

"Who are you?" Luis asks. He stares into the face of a dark-skinned man with long black hair pulled back into a ponytail at the nape of his neck, a gold stud in his ear, and piercing green eyes. He is not tall, but he is strong with muscles that ripple down his arms and legs. For a moment Luis thinks that this must be one of the dangerous corsairs he's heard about, pirates who will ambush a boat, take every sword and piece of silver they can get their hands on, and then slit every throat even as brave men kneel, pleading for their lives. But if he is a pirate, he speaks the language of the Jews.

"Perhaps we are running to something." The man takes out a flask of wine and offers it to Luis.

"I was the translator for the governor of Murcia," Luis explains, taking a swig and handing it back.

Rodrigo de Triano is the son of a Moor, famous for his ceramics, and a Sephardic woman, known for her beauty. He is a man with olive skin and a fine, straight nose. "They hired me because I have a sharp eye," Rodrigo says. It is his task to remain on the mast and search for land. "Whoever finds land first," Rodrigo tells Luis, "is promised eight ounces of gold and a fine silk coat."

Luis laughs. "What will you do with that silk coat?"

"I will sell it and use it to help bring my wife and children to join me." He hands the flask back to Luis. "Unless we all die first."

Luis shakes his head. "I think our Admiral knows what he is doing. He is a fine navigator. Though he may be deranged. His mission is too grand."

"Yes, I think he may be mad as well. I left my little girls." Rodrigo shrugs.

Luis nods. "I left two boys, one just born." His eyes begin to well up. He glances at his finger that last caressed the lips of his young sons. He wants to sniff the sweat of their brows, their child smells, once more.

And his wife with her sultry eyes and the ripe odor of a woman about her. He breathes deeply. He will find a way to see them again. If he could, he would turn back now.

A shooting star blazes across the sky and the men smile. To both it means good luck. As the night grows cold and the moon begins to rise, they sip their wine. They speak in whispers of their children and their wives. They speak of the homes they have left, but soon these talks fill them with longing so they speak of what is around them. The height of the waves, the pewter gray of the sea, and the multitude of stars.

Rodrigo, who has been trained in celestial navigation, is less afraid of the vastness. He can name the planets and the stars. Betelgeuse, Polaris, Algol. Polaris is the one star that does not move. If you find it, you can set your course. With his finger he helps Luis connect the dots. He knows the constellations as well. The Plough, the Seven Sisters, the Hunter and his bow. Cassiopeia, the vain queen. Luis follows Rodrigo's finger and soon the patterns make sense to him as well. Suddenly there is less to fear. It is as if they are reading an ancient text, their fingers moving together across the page.

✳

CHAPTER SEVEN

LOWRIDERS—1992

Roberto Torres is crouched in his garage, trying not to die of the fumes. Then he races outside to take a gulp of air. Roberto has developed a way to hold his breath like a pearl diver when he is airbrushing. Sometimes he holds it for two or even three minutes at a time. He dashes outside only when he is about to faint. Now he stands, panting. He knows he should be wearing a mask, but when he wears a mask, he feels as if someone is trying to suffocate him. And Roberto's worst fear is being suffocated. He'd rather die in a fire than with a pillow pressed against his face.

The phone inside his trailer starts to ring, but he doesn't make a move to answer. He's got a few beers in him and some weed too. He's not sure he'd make much sense on the other end of a conversation. Roberto tries to decide who it might be. It could be MG, his ex, always wanting something—usually money he doesn't have. Or his probation officer, who checks in with him more than is mandated by the courts. His probation officer would like nothing more than to fling him back behind bars where he'd spent time after some drunk driving episodes. It could be Miguel, but the kid hardly ever calls. Or maybe a customer. But it's not a good moment to talk to a customer.

What can be so important that it can't wait an hour or so? Besides he wants to finish his work. But what if it's his sister, finally returning one of his calls? He doubts it. She never calls him back. She never answers his letters. Of course he can hardly blame her, but still he keeps trying. Finally the machine picks up. Vaguely he hears someone leaving a message. Roberto's arms start to itch, but he tries not to scratch. His eczema is festering and the fumes make it worse. He is glad that Miguel isn't plagued by this same condition. It seems to skip a generation. Maybe it makes him stronger—fighting this constant urge to scratch at his flesh. He takes a deep breath. In a moment he'll plunge back into the garage. For now he lights a cigarette and leans against an outside wall. His old El Camino sits rusting in the yard. He's got this idea of fixing it up for Miguel for his birthday in the fall. He keeps putting it off. The truck needs a lot of work. And he's got to handle his paying jobs first.

He's been airbrushing a coyote across the hood of Alberto Pinto's souped-up Chevy. The coyote with its fangs exposed, eyes aflame, is chasing a herd of deer along the sides of the car and onto the hood. In the center of the hood is a cross and Alberto's brother's name. Jaime was killed in a gunfight near Chimayó—probably over drugs. Roberto knows that most of the money he's paid to airbrush comes from the heroin trade. In fact Española where his client base lives has the distinction of being, along with the murder capital, the city in America with the most overdoses per capita. Roberto has done his best to stay clear of most drugs, except for some recreational enhancements now and then, but he is pleased to profit from its industry. Besides, alcohol is his drug of choice.

Roberto has been working on Alberto's car for a few weeks now. He is proud of the terrified look in the eyes of the deer as the coyote nips at their hooves. Roberto is known throughout Rio Arriba County for his fine work. His art isn't just decorative. He paints murals that tell a story. Seeing the coyote makes him think of Miguel. His wily son. It is almost six o'clock. He should be home from school by now. Perhaps he can catch up with him, maybe toss a ball around. Not that Miguel ever really likes to toss a ball with him.

At the thought of Miguel something darts in front of his eyes. A green flash. At first he thinks it is a hummingbird. At times Miguel comes to him like this. A flash, and it is always at these moments that Roberto knows that something is wrong. He needs me, Roberto thinks. And then the thought drifts away, lost in a haze of smoke and the five beers he's already had this afternoon. The day has grown dark. To the south, storm clouds seem to be heading his way. It must have rained over Santa Fe. It would be good to get some rain up here. Putting out his cigarette, he goes back inside to finish the coyote.

Before he starts up again, he pauses to admire his painting. His work is getting better and better. Everyone says so. Some of the creatures on his cars seem almost alive, as if they can pounce right off the hood and attack you. Roberto has more orders than he can handle. Everyone and his uncle, it seems, wants coyotes and wolves, flowers and flames on the sides and hoods of their cars. And on their bike helmets too. He's done volcanoes, tsunamis, dust storms. He's done too many RIPs and too many beautiful girls gone away.

On his own car, for instance, a 1964 Pontiac, he painted Morning Glory's image when they first got together and, despite her protests, despite the fact that she kicked him out almost five years ago, he still keeps her picture on the driver's door of his car. He likes to cruise around Entrada, tormenting her. Sometimes he drives by the trailer that had once been their love nest just so she can fling open the window and shout, "Loser."

Ever since they split he's been living in his late mother's trailer and using her garage out back as his airbrush studio. Actually his mother was alive when he first moved in. "It's temporary, right?" Rosa asked, and Roberto assured her that it was. But then she got sick and with Elena in New York (and even if she was right next door, who could count on Elena?) Roberto stayed on to take care of her. Before she died, she told him to keep the trailer and garage. He is probably more or less squatting on this property at this point because she rented it from old man Roybal who was her great-uncle by marriage and maybe also by blood, or something like that, but Roybal has never asked for rent money as far as Roberto can tell, so he figures he will just stay until someone decides to tell him to leave. But who can? Old man Roybal has probably forgotten that he is living here. And his sister, Elena? Hell will freeze over before Elena comes home.

He can't blame her. She got away, didn't she? After all she had the talent. That odd ability to stand on the tips of her toes. Even after she'd had the accident that shattered her ankle, she'd managed to stay away from Entrada and make a life for herself on the East Coast, and perhaps it was all for the best. There was a time that Roberto doesn't like to remember when the scent of his sister's shampoo threw him into an incestuous frenzy. He'd had so many girls clinging to his arm, but when he was young, it was Elena who set him on fire. The way she danced in the living room of their trailer in those leotards that fit so snugly around her breasts and thighs. Hers were the first breasts he'd dreamed of fondling. His sister was his first wet dream.

Then when they were still in their teens, that bad thing happened. That is how he refers to it. That bad thing. Something he didn't have anything to do with, not exactly, but still he blamed himself. And he is certain that his sister and his mother blamed him as well. He stoked the flames, didn't he? He didn't stand up for her. When the older boys made comments about his sister, those punks who'd dropped out of school and rode motorcycles, who used to come around and rough up the kids who went to White Pine High—especially ones who had a reputation of being odd, queer, fairies, not tough enough, not man enough, not hombres, no cojones. Then one night they laid eyes on Elena, and Roberto did nothing to stop them. He didn't say what a man is supposed to say: "You leave my sister alone." And he didn't go after them when he saw her getting into their car, drunk, her body limp. It had taken two boys to drag her.

But she didn't put up a struggle, so he assumed she'd wanted to go. She'd been dressed for trouble, hadn't she, the way she wore that tank top and those short shorts? Girls who dress like that are asking for it, aren't they? It is an invitation, right? At least that's what Roberto believed then. He didn't see those boys twisting her arm. He didn't see her trying to fight them off. He was down a six-pack already and laughing with his friends. "Look at that idiot sister of mine." He laughed and inside he was trembling, not from fear but from his own arousal.

He hoped that someone else would do the job for him. Someone else would be her first so that he could stop thinking about her the way he did. The way she walked around with a book balanced on her head. She danced through the trailer, stretching with her feet on the kitchen counter where his mother wouldn't let him leave a dish or his penknife.

He watched her in her black leotard and tights, her thick black hair pulled into a tiny bun on the top of her head. The way her body arched into a question mark. The way she spun on one toe, her gaze fixed on the oak tree on the hillside above the house. She had no idea that she'd entered her own brother's dreams, or that he lay hot and twisted in his sheets with thoughts of her.

She came home late that night. He heard her open the door. He heard her broken sobs, and before he could go to her, he saw their mother rushing to her daughter, for Rosa had been sitting up, waiting the way only a mother can who senses that something is wrong. He saw Elena with the bruises on her face and arms. And the blood crusted on her thighs.

But the worst was her sobbing. Tears that couldn't stop, that wouldn't go away.

It seemed as if she cried for months. She became La Llorona, the woman who cries because she has been betrayed and left alone. The woman whose voice you hear in the wind in the canyons and through the branches of the piñon. La Llorona who haunts the dry riverbeds, whose tears can bring on a flash flood.

That was what his sister became.

Then that dance teacher helped Elena apply for a scholarship to the American Ballet Extension School in Manhattan. Elena didn't expect to get it, but how many Hispanic dancers from New Mexico applied? How many good ballet dancers? Elena had been lucky in this one regard. A teacher with the ballet school in Santa Fe took her under her wing. She'd recognized Elena's talent when she was just nine years old. And now Elena would have her chance. She would forget Entrada and the boys who raped her. She would forget her home and their trailer and even their mother, and yes, she would forget her brother too.

It was for the best that she went away.

Then he had gone out and been with MG. He'd gotten her pregnant when they were both practically children and his sister was dancing with the New York City Ballet. He'd done the right thing as his mother said. He'd married her.

He doesn't know why he thinks of these things, dredging up the past. He shakes his head as if waking himself from a dream. He should not let his thoughts go there. He knows this, but sometimes he can't help himself. Sometimes his mind wanders and then he finds he is trapped inside of what he prefers not to recall. He turns back to his painting. The coyote has fire in its eyes. Roberto is proud of this. It seems to be glaring right at him, burning, almost alive. That is important. Nobody wants a coyote or a wolf with dull eyes. They want to see those flames, rising right off the hood.

But he is getting tired of spirit animals. He has ideas—some big ones in fact. His latest, but he needs a marketing person, is custom-made bike helmets. For forty dollars he figures he can airbrush anything onto a bike helmet. He wants to call it Hopes and Dreams Helmets and people will flock to him, he feels sure. But he needs a delivery system—a way to get the word out.

He has no idea how he learned to do what he does. In school he was always doodling, drawing. He decorated every notebook he ever had with stickers, collages, and paintings. He never handed in a paper that wasn't illustrated in some way. Though his teachers reprimanded him, he couldn't sit in class and not scribble. Mostly he drew patterns, strange elliptical patterns of curlicues, circles entwined with other circles and shapes.

Sometimes he drew people, but they never looked that much like the people they were supposed to be. His people resembled superheroes. Exaggerations. Often he just drew whatever came into his head. Drag-ons. Mermaids. Unicorns. Women with snakes coiled in their hair. He used to trap snakes and put them in his mother's casserole dishes (when she wasn't using them, of course). Then he'd draw all the details of their scaly spines and let them go. His mother would serve a tuna noodle casserole and never know that a diamondback had been living in her dish for the past two days.

The rain is pounding like gunfire on the tin roof, but the fresh air is a relief and for a day at least the dust will settle. Everyone will be able to open their windows and breathe again. Roberto steps back into the doorway. In a few moments the rain will let up. His coyote is done.

As he looks up, there is MG, getting soaked. She looks like an apparition, standing in the downpour. He runs to the open garage door and motions for her to get inside. "Miguel hasn't come home," she shouts, still standing in the driving rain. "I'm worried. Go and find him."

Roberto recalls that flash of green. His son was calling out to him. "Why didn't you call me?" he shouts.

"I did. You didn't pick up."

Roberto nods. It's true; he didn't. He's a little high. Time moves differently in this state of mind. "I'm sure he's fine." He doesn't know why he says this because he's not at all sure that he's fine, but Roberto has a habit of pushing bad thoughts out of his head.

MG stands there, drenched. "He always calls if he's going to be late."

It is a little after seven and there are only a few places where Miguel could be. Roberto gets into the jeep that he'd gotten secondhand and sets off in search of his son. It should be easy to find him. Miguel isn't like other kids his age—the ones who wander off after school with a gang, who hang out at the local fast-food joints or by the railroad tracks. The month in juvie cured him of that. Now he is more like an old man. He has his schedule, his routines. And he rarely varies. If he isn't in science lab after school, he is on his way home to start his homework. On weekends he is probably in the library. Or tinkering with that telescope of his. Roberto thinks it isn't normal. While his other friends are playing video games and chasing after girls, his son is trafficking in dark magic and charting the course of the stars.

Is it too much to want a kid with whom you can shoot a deer and throw back a few beers? Is it too much to ask that your son share a Sunday football game with you instead of reading every word in the Amateur Astronomer's newsletter? It hardly seems like a lot to ask and yet the universe is unable to deliver.

Many evenings Miguel doesn't come home until late. Those are the nights when he goes out to do his stargazing or whatever it is he does near the old cemetery. Who knows? Maybe he is divining spirits. Maybe he goes there to be with a girl. Or, god forbid, a boy. It occurs to Roberto from time to time that he has no idea if his son is into girls or boys. Not that he can't handle it if he is into boys, but he just wants to know. Most boys Miguel's age hide girlie magazines featuring big-breasted bombshells under their beds or in the back of their closets. Or they make some faint rumblings if a gorgeous thing walks by. Roberto certainly did when he was Miguel's age. And, of course, look where it got him. But still. Anyone who knew Roberto Torres years ago had no doubt that he was a boy who loved women. But they would be stunned to know who his first love was.

Roberto drives down the main road of Entrada, such as it is, looking for Miguel's car. It is easy enough to recognize. He airbrushed the flames on the hood himself. He cruises past the adobe houses with broken fences and auto parts on their front lawns. Some have vehicles piled up. Or refrigerators. Others have old metal chairs rusting on a broken-down porch. Some parts of Entrada, like over where the Roybals live, are nicer than this part, but they aren't what you'd call fancy. It is more a place you look at and think food stamps and welfare.

Nothing grows out here except beans. Scrawny animals graze. Mostly it is cottage industries. Women at home weaving blankets and making cheap jewelry for the tourist trade up in Taos (which he referred to as Tacos) and down in Santa Fe, men and women who worked in the hotels and restaurants as maids and busboys, on road crews or as nannies. There isn't any real industry unless you call auto repair an industry. Mike's shop on Riverside Drive has a sign that reads "Filling Station and Divorce," but that's because Mike is a notary too. He makes more money on divorces than on auto repair. For centuries his people have scratched out a living in this hot, dry place.

He wends his way around Entrada, searching for Miguel. If he is coming home from the cemetery, he'd be driving this way, but he isn't. Roberto goes past Roybal's store, and then slows down in the waning light under the old oak tree. No sign of him. He heads up by the school and traces the way Miguel drives home. He isn't there. He isn't anywhere. It is the first time he can remember hearing some actual concern in Morning Glory's voice. The boy should have been home. Roberto doesn't want to think about the two boys who went missing up in Mesa in the spring. Their bodies have never been found.

He circles back to their trailer. MG sits on the sofa on their porch. As he pulls in, she leaps up. "You see Miguel?"

"No, no sign of him."

MG gazes outside. It is growing dark. "I'm just remembering. I think he went down to Santa Fe about a job."

"What kind of job?"

MG shakes her head. But suddenly she seems to remember. "Babysitting. I never should have let him go."

"Babysitting," Roberto whispers under his breath. He can't imagine another kid Miguel's age who'd want a babysitting job. He looks out. The rain has stopped but rivulets run through the culverts. The arroyos can flood as well. "You know where?"

MG hangs her head. Her eyes and face look tired, beaten down, and her body slumped. Roberto recalls when her breasts were perky and firm, her ass nice and round, when there were no rolls around her middle and her jeans clung sweetly to her hips. She used to run like a deer. Now she barely walks down to the road to pick up her mail. She's just past thirty, but her dark hair is stringy and already flecked with gray. On the other hand he isn't looking so good himself, is he? He's definitely gone to pot. And he has the belly to prove it.

But she looks up at him with those penetrating eyes and he sees their old sparkle. Though she is no longer the girl he made love to when they were teenagers, he still gets a twinge for her. A flicker of longing. Or perhaps it is for them as they'd once been. He's been with other women—lots of them, in fact—but something keeps him coming back to the piney scent of her hair, though it has been months since she's let him get much more than a foot in the door.

"Out on some canyon road where you did a job once, I think."

Roberto nods. "Colibri Canyon?"

She nods. "Yes, I think that's it."

"Okay, I'll find him."

She manages to give him a little smile as he leaves. It is enough of a smile to encourage him. Maybe they can get something back again. It isn't too late. They aren't that old. They could even start another family. People do things like that all the time.

As Roberto drives out of Entrada and onto the highway, his heart is beating fast and his skin is itching. It always does when he is nervous. And now he's nervous. Shit happens out here, doesn't it? How does he know that this whole babysitting thing isn't some kind of a trap? As he grips the wheel, his palms are sweating. He wants a drink. He wishes he could stop for one, but he won't.

It is getting dark as he turns onto Colibri Canyon Road. As he suspected, the road is a bog after that heavy rain. He downshifts and makes his way. The jeep has four-wheel drive, though the car Miguel is driving doesn't, and this makes him worry all the more. He drives carefully so as not to slide off the road or get stuck in the muck. In the distance the lights of the adobe mansions that line this road shimmer. The storm is over and the sky clear. Stars are bright overhead and there's a flicker of moonlight to guide him.

CHAPTER EIGHT

✳

TIME CAPSULE—1992

Miguel lies stretched across the hood of his car. It's the clearest of nights, the storm long gone. The waters receded as quickly as they came, leaving Miguel and his car stuck in a muddy ditch. For the past two hours he has been trying to shove the car out of the gully where it settled in six inches of mud. Now, weary, he looks up at the stars that are beginning to brighten overhead.

He's a little bruised by the ride he took down the arroyo. Beyond his pride he's not really hurt, but he's angry with his father for not giving him a truck with four-wheel drive. Now Miguel is waiting for someone to rescue him. But because of the storm no one has come down this road in a while. He probably shouldn't have either.

Miguel considers walking back to Mrs. Rothstein's house but fears that he will arrive in the pitch-dark, covered in mud like the creature from your worst nightmare, and then he will be out of a job. There don't seem to be any other houses nearby. At least none that he can see. He doesn't want to go climbing out of this canyon in the fading light.

But it's not very safe inside his car in case there's another flash flood, which there easily could be. For now he rests on the hood, doing what he likes doing best. He's staring at the stars. With his finger he traces the constellations. He can name almost every one that he can see with the naked eye. He's already counted three shooting stars and made as many wishes. Lying on his back he wishes that he could see *Voyager*. He wonders where it's journeyed to now. More than eight billion miles from Earth, traveling one hundred thousand miles a day. Speed, time, and distance beyond anything mortals can imagine.

On the wall of his bedroom Miguel has a poster of *Voyager* as it passes Jupiter. On the poster is written "Keep on Going." Every night before he goes to sleep, Miguel gazes up at it. He thinks of the ship, hurtling through space, and its message. "Keep on Going." Never mind that he's stuck in the mud right now, somehow that message seems intended for him. On September 5, 1977, *Voyager 1* set off on its interstellar mission. Miguel knows the date very well. It's the day he was born. He couldn't believe it when he learned this in Mr. Garcia's science class. *Voyager* has been on its trajectory as long as Miguel has been alive.

The spaceship is on an endless mission. Destination unknown. It was a shot in the dark with only one real purpose: to find others like ourselves. Miguel chuckles at this notion. He assumes that the chances are one in a zillion that we'd find people like ourselves. Bacteria with brains is more like it. Many people thought this was a fool's errand, but after all isn't that how Polynesia was discovered? By men sailing from the coast of the Southern Hemisphere into the unknown. Didn't Columbus do the same, setting off on his quest for China? So what if he only got to Cuba.

Miguel knows all about *Voyager*. And that time capsule known as the Golden Record that's meant to last a billion years and has greetings in fifty-five languages, the music of Bach and Mozart, as well as Chuck Berry's "Johnny B. Goode." There are the sounds of volcanoes and earthquakes, thunder and rain, frogs croaking and an elephant's cry, wild dogs, footsteps, heartbeats, laughter, fire, Morse code, horses, crickets, and a human kiss. The songs of humpback whales. NASA wouldn't allow a naked human and so there are the only silhouettes of a man and a woman, including a fetus in the womb. What were they afraid of? That some alien would get off on Earth porn?

Sometimes Miguel thinks he's just like *Voyager*. Alone, wandering through space, destination unknown. He lies back with his hands under his head, counting the shooting stars. It's a crystal-clear night now. Somewhere out there *Voyager* continues on through the solar system. Eventually it will leave the Milky Way. It is expected to pass by the star Gliese 445 in the galaxy Camelopardalis in 17.6 light-years or 40,000 Earth years. No one knows for certain where *Voyager* will go. If the universe is infinite, it is possible that it will continue hurtling through space. Or if Einstein was correct, its journey could be circular and it will end up light-years from now back in the solar system where it began. Anyway, it is out there, moving at a greater speed than any object ever has before.

It's getting chilly in the high desert. If someone doesn't come and get him soon, Miguel will be spending the night. In his trunk he digs out an old dog blanket, for a dog long dead, and wraps it around his shoulders. If he has to sleep out here, this will have to do. Then he goes back inside his car and leans on the horn.

At the horizon he sees the red shine of Mars. His mother told him that when he was born, Mars was very close to Earth and they took him outside, all bundled up, so that he could see it for himself. Recently he'd heard that certain boulders and hills on the red planet are being named after the men from Columbus's first voyage. There is one that will be named for Pedro de Terreros, Columbus's lowly cabin boy. Miguel chuckles to himself. He bets that boy wasn't much older than he is right now. And yet he has a rock named after him in the sky.

Up ahead Miguel sees high beams and hears a souped-up engine making its way to where he sits entrenched in the mud. The horn sounds the opening bars of "Guantanamera" and he knows that his father is coming to save him.

CHAPTER NINE

✳

THE SCRIBE—1492

My dearest Catalina," Luis de Torres writes, "the days do not matter." He dips his quill into the inkwell, searching for his next sentence. "They blend into one." He pauses again. This is not his first attempt at writing to his wife, but he hopes that this will be more successful than the last. He has not been able to settle upon the words to tell her of his life at sea.

What can he say of his travels? How he avoids the dank quarters of the men and sleeps on the deck? He doesn't want to speak of the rancid meat that the cook boils to kill the maggots or the stagnant drops of water they sip each day. The alcohol they drink to assuage their thirst until they are all stumbling across the deck. It is a wonder no man has gone overboard. He doesn't want to share with her their tight quarters or the men who are going mad from gazing into the sea. Or their fears of the giant waves or sea monsters that might await them.

He wants to share his fears that he will never touch her skin again. That he will die far away and alone. That he will not live to see his sons grow up. Instead he tells her of the pewter sea and the sound the wind makes in the sails. Almost like a beating. How the ship rocks like a cradle. He tells her how stars shoot across the sky so brightly that he thinks they will crash into the water beyond the prow. Instead they burn out within seconds. "The seas are calm," he writes. "My skin smooth and healed." Though this is a lie. Then he runs out of things to say.

He tries to speak of his feelings. How his body longs for hers. And the heat that runs through his veins. He wants to tell her that he remembers the first time he saw her in the market of Murcia. She wore a blue mantilla and a long blue skirt. She was a girl, only fifteen years old, and he was almost twenty. She walked beside her mother with a basket in her hand and lowered her eyes when he gazed at her. Something was sealed between them on that day. He was patient, and he waited for her. When the time was right, he presented himself to her parents. They courted for a year but it was as if they were already husband and wife. He remembers the cool touch of her fingers on his brow and her flesh against his. He remembers every moment even as he fears that there will be no more to remember. But this does not come easily. How can you tell a woman you love her when you've never said those words before?

Though he intended to, it was always implied. Just never spoken. For an interpreter he'd never been very good with words. In the morning light he can see her, hand on her hip, head cocked, reading his letter. He can almost reach out and touch the softness of her cheek, smell the almond soap she washes in. Putting his pen down, he smiles. And she fades as all apparitions do and Luis is left with the pitch of the waves.

It is just daybreak, but for hours Luis has been hard at work. Whenever Columbus is on the deck, Luis uses the desk in his small cabin. The Admiral's desk is made of sturdy cherrywood. It is an old desk and Columbus used it to draw his maps and write his innumerable appeals to the kings and queens of Europe. At the back of the desk sits the rolled-up portolan map Columbus drew to make this voyage. From time to time he has seen the Admiral unroll it as he studies their course. At this desk Luis goes about his tasks of translating or copying documents. In his spare time he writes in his journal as well. One that he imagines he might publish someday. In his journal he is more honest than he is in his letters. He speaks of the unknowable sadness, of his fears of looking into the sea, afraid that the depth and darkness will swallow him.

Luis is also kept busy by the sailors who learned that he could write letters. And he had paper and ink. He knows the deepest secrets of every sailor's heart. If they love a woman they can never have. If they have betrayed their wives or long for their bodies. They tell their sons to grow up and be strong. They beg their fathers to be proud of them. He swears to each sailor that his secrets are safe. He copies their words onto paper and puts them in the pouch that will never reach home.

Luis wonders if he isn't involved in some fool's errand. Perhaps they are sailing to the end of the world. That is what Sepharad means, isn't it? The end of the world. For the Jews of Spain, Iberia had always been the end of their world. But that is no longer the case. Nor will it ever be again. It is possible that if Catalina ever reads a word he writes it will be after he is long gone. Still he admires Columbus. He navigates by the wind and the sun. He rarely sleeps. Few ever see him retire to his cabin for long. If he sleeps, it is more like a cat. Little naps, and then he is back on the prowl.

Already Luis's hand aches and the sun barely peeks through the porthole. He rises to stretch. It will be a clear day with a gentle wind and the sails are flying at full-staff. The ship moves with a lilt like a cradle. Luis has come to learn that there are good days at sea and bad days, just as there are on land, but somehow on the ship with nowhere to go it is more pronounced, and they seem much longer. Returning to the desk, his fingers touch the portolan map. Gently he unrolls it. He has not looked at it since they sailed, but now he sees once again Frixlandia to the north, Cathay, and the tiny island of Paradise. Perhaps the Admiral knows what he is doing. Perhaps they will arrive somewhere after all.

Now with the calm seas it is easier for him to write. Shaking out his hand, he sits back down. The Admiral has left him several documents to translate from the Latin. The work is tedious and Luis is surprised to find that his eyesight is not as strong as it once was. He had not come on this journey intending to be a scribe. But early in the voyage Columbus shared with him his most prized possession. Luis had no idea why one evening Columbus called him into his quarters. Perhaps because he is the only one besides the Admiral who can read or write.

"I have something to show you," Columbus said. He opened the strongbox in which he kept a letter of introduction, signed by the king and queen of Spain. It is addressed to His Supreme Preciousness. The name of the Great Khan has been left blank, to be filled in when they learn it at their journey's end. Luis stared at the document and then gazed into the pale, piercing eyes of the explorer. He hesitated to ask but wondered if Columbus had considered it. "With all respect, sir, but will the Great Khan be able to read Latin?"

Columbus seemed startled by the question. This had not occurred to him. "I don't know. Wouldn't he?" But what if the Great Khan can't read Latin? It is so obvious. Perhaps he can read other languages. It was then that Columbus made his request. "Can you translate the document into the languages you know?"

Luis nodded. "I can do that, sir." Luis began his labors with the documents in Latin. He translated them into Hebrew and Arabic, but then there were other letters and documents that Columbus needed. Luis became his scribe. While the Admiral keeps his own log, Luis translates the many letters and documents he carries with him. He copies them into Hebrew and Arabic so that the traders and the Great Khan will know who Columbus is and why he has come.

The sun is beginning to rise. When Luis looks up, shading his eyes from the glaring sun, he sees Rodrigo, no bigger than a bird, on the mast. Luis trembles. He could never climb a mast. It makes him dizzy just to think about it. He is sure he will faint from the heights, let alone a mast that juts out over the sea. He is a small, slight man used to the work of books and paper and pens. He worries that his friend might fall, toppling to the deck or into the sea. And then Luis will be alone in the founding of their settlement for the secret Jews. With each crash of a ladder or leap of a dolphin, Luis cringes, thinking that at last Rodrigo has been catapulted into the waters, but Rodrigo is as sure-footed as the goats that once grazed in the hills of Andalusia.

Once more Luis gazes at the map. Running his finger due west from Palos, Luis tries to imagine where they are right now. How much closer are they to China than when they set sail weeks ago. Are they ever going to really arrive?

Luis is staring out the porthole when there is a knock at the door. "Your breakfast, sir," the cabin boy calls. Without waiting for Luis to answer, Pedro de Terreros kicks open the cabin door, carrying in a tray of sea biscuits and salted beef. "Shall I put it on the desk?"

"Yes, Pedro. Thank you, that will be fine."

His hands trembling, the boy manages to put the tray down. Every morning Luis is certain that the boy will drop it. He seems too clumsy and ill-suited for this life at sea. Much the same as Luis feels ill-suited, but he is not asked to do chores such as carry trays across the deck in the unsteady seas. And when the boy does drop a tray, the cook gives him a sound beating. He is no more than fourteen, yet his parents sent him to sea.

The boy is a relative of the Pinzón brothers who own the other two ships that accompany them on this journey—the *Pinta* and the *Niña*. Perhaps they invited him on board. Or agreed to take him. Pedro is small, almost frail, but there is something naughty about him that Luis likes. He enjoys it when the boy is near. He likes the smell of him. His youth. It makes him think of his own small sons. Will they look this way one day—laughing with a toothy grin, a pimply face? Just the hint of a mustache on their lips?

Luis does not know that the boy has spent the first weeks weeping in his hammock for his mother or vomiting over the side in sickness. But he is the youngest of six children and his father forced him to leave. His father told him that when he returned, he would not be able to come home except to visit. He had to make his way in the world on his own. So he learned as quickly as he could. In a matter of weeks he got his sea legs. He learned the sails and the ropes. He knows the rigging and the lines. He scampers up the mast into the yards whenever the sails have to be trimmed. And during daylight he must turn the sandglass over every half hour.

Pedro de Terreros is responsible for time. In his brief fourteen years he'd never given much thought to time, but now he cannot do otherwise. It is right before his eyes. At each half hour, before the sand runs out, the glass must be turned, the bell rung, and the Admiral of the Ocean Sea takes his reading of the winds, the currents, and how far they have gone. This is how he sets their course. At first it was difficult for Pedro to remember, but soon the half hour became a part of him. He knows how many trays he can carry, dishes he can wash, ropes he can set before the sand runs through the glass. For the remainder of his long life Pedro de Terreros will do everything in snippets. He will eat a meal, make love to his wife, set a horseshoe—for he will become a blacksmith when he returns to Spain—all in brief increments of time.

Sometimes, when the weather is fair and the winds calm, the helmsman lets him try the wheel. Never alone. It is one of Columbus's main rules of the sea. The cabin boy can never take the wheel alone, but on fine days when the seas are calm, he can try his hand at the wheel, keeping the *Santa María* steady and on her course.

As Luis takes a bite of the cheese biscuit, the boy gazes at the paper he's writing. Luis pushes the page closer and the boy moves forward. "I can teach you if you like," Luis says. It occurs to him how much he would welcome this.

Pedro nods. He wants to learn. Perhaps one day he will be a ship's captain and keep a log the way the Admiral does. "Yes," Pedro replies, "I would like that very much." Then the boy scurries off because it is time for him to turn the glass.

+

The night is clear and calm as Luis and Rodrigo lay out their bedding on the deck. A few nights ago one of the sailors caught a glimpse of Luis covering Rodrigo with his blanket. Since then they make fun of them, calling them "lover boys." Luis and Rodrigo don't care. They have their wives and children at home. Their bond is not of their bodies. Not like some of the men whose coupling can be heard in the night. They share something deeper that the others cannot understand. They don't know if it is Tuesday or Thursday, but they sense when it is Friday night.

Rodrigo has brought some bread and a bladder of red wine he siphoned off one of the kegs below. They whisper the same blessings that their families are whispering thousands of miles away. So far away that they have no idea of how they might cross this ocean and return. Perhaps they will make a circle around the globe. "Unless we fall off of it," Rodrigo jokes.

While some think they are lovers, others believe they practice the dark arts of their race. Julio, the quartermaster, fears that they will come in the night and leach his blood. Julio asks Luis if what they say is true. Did the Jews kidnap that child, Dominguito del Val? Did they crucify him and drink his blood? Did they bring the plague to Seville?

There are rumors that Columbus himself is a Jew. That would explain his strange handwriting that appears to be almost backward, and his need to get away. But the sailors do not really care. They crave gold, and they have other concerns. They have gone through all the salted fish and dried fruit. They are living on rotting yams and hard cassava root. Some of them suffer from bruises that come from nowhere. They wake up in the morning with blood in their mouths. They have no more grain. The bread has worms. They try to lure fish out of the sea, but their nets do not go deep enough.

When the fresh water is gone, they pray for rain, but the storms come whipping out of nowhere, slashing their sails and then leaving them becalmed. Some men lose their minds. One keeps pointing to the horizon, muttering "land, land" until they put him in chains below. Others are sick all the time. The lower decks stink of vomit and shit, of sweat and piss. Rodrigo is certain that none of them will survive, and Luis is beginning to think he is right.

The wine is making them sleepy. "If we survive," Luis says, "let us find a safe place in the New World. We will bring our wives and children."

Rodrigo nods. "I have been thinking the same thing."

The two men hold out their hands and shake. They crawl into their bedding. Rodrigo drifts off. He sleeps the deep sleep of a child, but Luis barely shuts his eyes.

"I have made a friend," he will write to Catalina the next day. He does not dare write "another Jew." Instead he writes, "Perhaps we will all break bread together someday." She will understand. Luis finds comfort in the idea that they will bring their families to the Indies. They will make a new world for the Muslims who have been forced to relinquish Allah and the Jews who have been forced to convert, the ones who in secret still keep up the dead Law of Moses. He does not mention the cabin boy to Catalina. He cannot tell her that he wants to bring him home as well.

They continue west. Over the next few days there is no cloud cover and the sun bears down. Some strip off their tunics until the sun blisters their backs. They cannot bear the ropes of the hammocks at night. Luis seeks shelter in the Admiral's quarters, but Rodrigo stays on the mast until his lips are open sores, his face burned and cracked. There are no birds. From time to time a fish leaps into the air, and then it is swallowed again by the sea. A school of dolphins follows the boat and the men harpoon one. Though the flesh is tough and fatty, they still eat it.

Luis records all that he sees. Some of the men he does not trust. Nino, the helmsman of the *Santa María,* is a drunk who sneaks sips from the kegs at all times of the night when he thinks no one is looking. Luis watches him during his sleepless nights on deck. And he does not trust the boatswain either. At times Luis fears for his life. All the crew knows that he and Rodrigo are of the Hebrew race. Despite the fact that he writes letters for them, he has heard himself referred to simply as "the Jew."

Almost all of the men speak ill of the Admiral. They do not believe that he navigates by the sun and stars. They do not trust the magnetic compass that he uses from time to time. Some say that he navigates using the dark arts as well. They are foolish and superstitious—and mutinous—men. But Luis is fortunate in that they believe him to be harmless. Mostly they ignore him. They say whatever they want when he is near. They think he isn't listening as they plot to take command of the ships away from the Admiral and sail back the way they have come.

+

In the morning a bird appears. A large white creature with feet as red as blood soars overhead. It seems too enormous to fly. The sailors believe it is a vision. The bird perches on the mast, grasping hold with its bright red talons. Its feathers are as white as the Admiral's hair. The sailors look up and rejoice. Later they will think of it as the bird with blood on its hands.

That afternoon a log drifts by. It has a fresh green shoot growing from its trunk. Land is near. They keep their eyes glued to the horizon, searching for a dark rim that will signal land or a flicker of light. But then for days nothing. Just the endless rolling sea. Then at night from the stern castle something catches Columbus's eye. A flicker of light. A promise of land. It is close to midnight when he turns to his quartermaster and asks, "Do you see something there on the horizon?" Both Columbus and the quartermaster know that the sea can play tricks on you. It can convince you that you are sailing west when you are really sailing east. It can make you think that land is in sight.

To humor the Admiral the quartermaster replies, "I do, sir. I see a fire."

They don't see it again that night. But at dawn a great cry is heard from the crow's nest. Rodrigo has spotted a dark hump like a whale on the horizon. The faintest hint of land. Soon it grows larger. A piece of what looks like a hand-carved boat floats past. That evening they sail into a cove of turquoise waters with sandy beaches. On the island, palm trees sway in the wind. They anchor the *Pinta,* the *Niña,* and the *Santa María,* all three of which have survived the crossing. And not a single man has been lost. And they have discovered a western route to China. They have reached the shores of the Great Khan.

To celebrate they open kegs of red wine. They drink and dip their toes into the warm, salty sea. They dive off the boat and swim to shore, then lie exhausted in the sand. Some kneel, blessing the earth. Others who are ill from the relentless motion of the sea begin to heal themselves here. But the Admiral remains wary. He doesn't like the swirls in the water, the breaks in the waves. He fears the reefs and rocks that lie hidden. He will not allow his ships closer to the shore.

As night falls, Rodrigo goes to claim his prize. Columbus is in his cabin writing in his log and smiles at Rodrigo when he enters. But as Rodrigo explains that he had come to claim the silk coat and gold coins,

Columbus balks. "I spotted land myself last night," the Admiral says, returning to his log. "I did not shout out, but you can ask the quarter-master. He will tell you." Columbus claims the silk coat and gold coins for himself, while Rodrigo leaves the cabin seething and determined to get off this boat as soon as he can.

✳

CHAPTER TEN

CARAVAN—1992

As she walks the streets of Tangier, Elena Torres wants to change her shoes. The streets are packed with spice merchants and men grilling meat and women selling flip-flops. The air is redolent with jasmine, cinnamon, and smoking lamb. Moroccan men in pale pink and spearmint djellabas sip sweetened tea in nearby cafés. Elena and Derek had sailed that morning through the Strait of Gibraltar to arrive in Tangier. But all Elena can think about is her feet.

She had been a dancer for years and her feet have buckled and been distorted in the ways that she imagines the bound feet of Chinese women must have. And then there were the various injuries until the spin that shattered her ankle, effectively ending her career. The only solution she has found is shoes—different pairs of shoes. She needs to change them all the time. When she travels, she never worries about what shirts and jackets to pack. It is all about the shoes. She isn't someone who can get by with one or two pairs. She needs six. Or more.

She should probably be in sneakers, not sandals. It seems as if they've been walking for hours. Perhaps in circles, not getting any closer to their destination—a restaurant on the outskirts of the medina. Her bunions ache. With each step she feels the plantar fasciitis, collapsed arches, arthritis of the toes, along with the shaky, shattered ankle. It is early evening, but the medina is still packed. Outside of a social club, men sip tea and play dominoes. A donkey, burdened with bushels of grain, pushes past, almost pinning Elena against the wall. There is a sea of people—women in head scarves and caftans. Shopkeepers beckon.

Food stands selling souvlaki wrapped in pita. The smells are rich and meaty and they both want to eat and drink, then go to sleep.

They try to follow the map, but each street seems to wind its way into another like the roots of a tree. They are greeted and then harassed by "May I help you?" and "Can I take you somewhere?" They head down long dark alleys. Men in djellabas stand like sentries at the entrance to one street. A group of boys tells them that they are going down a dead end, and then laugh when they walk the other way.

"Let's turn back," Derek says. "We aren't getting anywhere."

Elena has her eyes in the guidebook. "But turn back how? We have no idea where we are." Indeed they seem caught inside this labyrinth and wonder how they'll ever find their way again. They continue through the souk and its maze of dark, winding streets, many of which like a coiled snake seem to lead back to where they began. Other routes take them deeper into the souk, and they all look more or less the same. Soon it is apparent that they have no idea where they are.

Perhaps they should have stayed in the hotel and ordered food. Can they even do that in Tangier? Elena doesn't know. They would have tumbled into each other's arms, made love, and fallen asleep. As Elena stands, hungry and tired in the middle of the souk, she longs for Derek's arms. His touch has always softened her, made her more real. It is a touch she finds she cannot do without. It has kept them together. Now she squeezes his arm. "I'm going in here."

Guidebook in hand, Elena steps into a souvenir shop. It is filled with miniature hand-carved camels, hookahs of all sizes, fezzes, teacups from which to drink sweetened tea, wrist and ankle baubles, scarves of all colors. Derek assumes she wants to ask directions, but instead she heads to the postcard rack. A blue-eyed bedouin on a camel stares out at her from one. Another is of sand dunes, another an oasis.

Turning the rack slowly, she looks at pictures of the Strait of Gibraltar, the North African coast, pyramids of spice in a marketplace. Then she comes to the fortress. It is a stone building, the color of sand, looming above the sea. It is taken from the ramparts of the old fortress from which Tangier defended itself against invaders. The soldiers could see boats coming all the way from Spain. Miguel will like the fortress. It is one of the first things she does on any trip. She buys Miguel his card. She doesn't want to forget to mail it. It is such a little thing, but it has become her habit everywhere she goes.

She planned to buy only the one card and the stamp to go with it, but the owner of the shop looks at her with dark, disgruntled eyes. She picks out a blue silk scarf and a set of silver ankle bells. Later she will dance with these in their room. Elena's travels are always about dance. In Spain she studied flamenco in the Gypsy caves of Granada. She has done belly dancing in Istanbul. She traveled to northern India to learn the dances of the nomadic bards of Jaipur. She brings home scarves and bells, castanets and ankle bracelets made of tortoiseshell. She teaches young dancers to twirl in long silk scarves, to gyrate to the tingle of the bells. In Morocco she hopes to find the Berber dancers of Fès. Tangier is only a stopover.

The shopkeeper smiles as he tallies her purchases on a sheet of thin white paper, and then holds it up so she can see. Elena pays him. She puts the stamp on the postcard and scribbles something the way she always does. When the shopkeeper offers to mail it for her, she does not refuse, though she wonders if it will ever reach Miguel. But then she wonders if any of the cards she sends ever reach him.

As they are leaving, Elena points to the guidebook. "Caravan?" she asks. The man nods and leads them into the alleyway. In French he tells them to go straight until they come to some stairs, climb them, and turn right. The restaurant will be down a side street. As they set out, Elena is already having difficulty remembering. She is one of those people who asks directions but never really listens to the answer. The passageway is barely shoulder width, and it is pitch-black. Ahead a shadow moves. A ghostlike man in a black djellaba walks toward them. They have to turn sideways for him to pass.

They come to the stairs as the man said they would. The steps are cobbled, and uneven. All along them merchants sell scarves, slippers, ceramics. Elena's ankles are weak and her balance isn't good. There is no railing so she clasps Derek's arm. Women wearing tiny slippers race around, grabbing the latest bargain. It is difficult to believe that they don't fall. A group of young men rush down the steps, shoving people aside. Elena clutches the pouch that contains her wallet and IDs.

At the top of the steps they reach a large square. Shopkeepers are closing their stands of trinkets and dresses, spices in bright orange, yellow, and red pyramids. Walking along the square, they peer down the narrow side streets. They are ready to eat anywhere, even from the street, when they come to a building with a set of stairs and a small light. Below the light a blue hand-painted sign reads "Caravan."

They climb the two flights and find themselves in a bright blue room where the clientele recline on pillows and sit on the floor. There is only one other couple seated near the back. "It's still early," Derek whispers.

Elena nods. Neither of them likes eating in empty restaurants. "I know. But I'm starved. Let's eat anyway."

The host seats them beside a raised platform where, as soon as they sit down, four musicians in red-and-white gowns and red fezzes appear. The lights dim. Before they even open their menus, the musicians begin to play. With the rattle of a tambourine and shaking of a gourd, an eerie melody begins. Despite herself, Elena's feet start to move. She can't control herself, but still she frowns. Elena is sure that this is only for the benefit of tourists—something she's spent years avoiding. She is proud that she has never been to the Eiffel Tower or Prague Castle. All those places are ruined as far as Elena is concerned. She has managed to live in New York and avoid the Statue of Liberty and the Empire State Building. In fact for years she thought it was the Umpire State Building and had to do with baseball.

Elena first went to New York when she was fourteen and moved there for good when she was seventeen. Despite her injured ankle, she never left. What Elena likes about New York is that most people have no past. It is as if they are the product of spontaneous regeneration—popping up from the soil without parents, siblings, hometowns, or the bad choices or rumors that followed them, the bullies who badgered them, and the lovers who betrayed them. Elena walked away from the world of drunken Hispanic boys with their lowriders, pregnant girlfriends, and debts, but in New York nobody knew any of that. No one knows who you are or where you've been. Everyone is in exile. It is a city of aliases and alibis. A city devoid of background checks. You are born the day you arrive.

She met Derek at a party in Tribeca and they've been together for almost three years. He worked for a tech startup that went bust, but he has a wild, cackling laugh and gray eyes like a fog she can get lost in. Now he does content for the website of a large insurance firm. It is just a job to pay the bills. Derek has other things that interest him. He belongs to a bluegrass band and plays the banjo often just so Elena will dance for him. Though she can no longer go on point, she swirls her body, twisting in ways that make him think of a serpent. She makes dips and turns that astonish him. Once or twice he invited her home to meet his mother who still lives outside of Bridgeport. It did not go well, but Derek says that he could have brought home the Duchess of Cambridge and his mother would not have approved.

Once, when Elena was returning to Entrada for her aunt's funeral, Derek asked if he could come with, but she said no. He wanted to be there for her. And he thought he'd understand her better if he experienced her in her natural habitat—a village where her family has lived for four hundred years since, as her deluded but endearing grandmother claimed, her ancestors traveled to New Spain with Coronado in search of the Seven Cities of Gold. In the end some of the conquistadors had had enough of conquest and decided to lay down roots. Some married native women and migrated into the hills of New Mexico. But Elena tries not to think about home. All she knows is that the farther away she gets from Entrada de la Luna, the better off she is.

A noisy party of eight—a whole family with grandparents, parents, children, including a toddler, celebrating something—comes in. They are laughing, scrambling for seats, arranging then rearranging themselves. A young boy holds a blue balloon that Elena feels certain will pop any second. They are given a long table near Elena and Derek. They speak loudly and point at one another. Derek squeezes Elena's hand. "What are you going to have?" He almost has to shout to make himself heard.

They are glancing at the menu when the waiter asks if they would like something to drink. Elena wonders if she dares and decides she does. She asks for a glass of wine but the waiter, smiling, shakes his head. "We do not serve alcohol. I'm very sorry, madame." Elena takes in a deep breath and Derek pats her hand.

"It's a Muslim country," he reminds her.

"I know." She sighs. Derek orders the chicken couscous and Elena the lamb stew with beans. They are going to share. They always do. Fifty-fifty, right down the middle. In everything, including money. The waiter, wearing a red fez, which annoys them both as some coy tourist attraction, takes their order, slowly scribbling onto a pad what seems to them fairly straightforward.

Nearby the party of eight is having a raucous time. It is clearly someone's birthday—maybe the little boy. They are shouting in Arabic, Elena assumes, then bursting out laughing again. Derek hasn't taken his eyes off her. "Do you want to go somewhere else?"

"Where?"

He furrows his brow the way he does when he is thinking. When she was growing up, Elena had a bloodhound that did the same thing when it was hunting and caught a scent. "Maybe there's a hotel around here with a bar."

"We're here. We're tired. Let's just eat."

But in fact she wishes she could leave. Elena has difficulty sitting in one place. She is constantly on the move. Perhaps it isn't for nothing that the butterfly is her totemic creature. "Bye byes" she called them when she was a child. Her father called her Flutterbye because she was always flitting from one thing to the next. Until she flitted thousands of miles away on a one-way ticket—unlikely to return to the world of scrub cactus and lowriders. But by then he was gone.

Elena has never felt good about leaving her mother to grow old alone. Sometimes she has offered to come home. Especially after her father died, drunk, driving off the highway into a canyon. Though they hadn't really lived together for years, still it had been a blow. A few times she'd invited her mother to come and live with her in New York, mainly because she knew she wouldn't, to which Rosa just laughed and said, "What will I do in New York?"

Yet her mother never complained. She never asked Elena to come home, not even for a visit. Not even for holidays. She let her daughter go free and pursue her dancing career in New York. Dutifully, Elena called her mother every Sunday and told her about her teachers and the classes she was taking and the girls she danced with—brief, perfunctory calls that always ended with her mother saying "I love you" and Elena replying "Me too."

She had her scholarship, of course. Otherwise how would she have gotten to New York? And she was good. For a time she was very good with those sinewy legs, that lithe body. One of her teachers, an older man who was famous and with whom she had a brief, insanely passionate affair, told her the sky was the limit. How could she explain to him that when he said the sky it meant to her that big blue sky that domed her village in northern New Mexico? How could she explain to anyone that place of Hispanics and hydraulic suspension, way too much booze, and a mother who raised two children alone, how can she explain what it was like to come from there? She did not go back. Even after she crushed the bone in her ankle, she returned for holidays and funerals, but never for more than a few days.

It was a routine spin. Her partner stood behind her, his hands on her waist. Something she'd done dozens of times, but this time when her body moved, her foot didn't. Perhaps he'd spun her too quickly or she'd resisted his move, but by the time Elena hit the floor her tibia was shattered. The minute she saw her twisted foot, she knew she'd never dance again. A racehorse, her surgeon told her, is put down for less. For a long time Elena thought the horse was lucky.

At last a tagine is placed before her. The waiter lifts the clay lid and the steam of the lamb stew fills Elena's lungs. As she breathes it in, she begins to swoon. The scent of cinnamon and ginger, turmeric and cumin rises to greet her like some genie that has come out of a bottle. Dipping in her spoon she tastes the sweetness of apricots, the savory of the broth. And there is a smell she recognizes. Cilantro. She gazes into the bowl of lamb, swimming in juices with chickpeas.

She closes her eyes and finds herself going away. She dips once more into the hot broth that burns her tongue. Blowing on the spoon, she waits for it to cool, then sips again. Suddenly she is crossing vast deserts and sailing across the sea. She is moving not only in space but also in time into a past she has never known. Where is this dish taking her? Elena thinks that she must be hallucinating. Or sampling an alchemist's brew. Or perhaps it is what barely sleeping for twenty-four hours does to you. Still it does not seem possible. No, it isn't impossible. Yet there it is. Elena almost drops her spoon, and then she catches her breath.

Derek glances at her, concerned. "Is it all right?"

Elena stares at him, a glazed-over look in her eyes as if she were just waking up from a long nap. "Yes," she says, "it's fine. May I taste your chicken?"

He makes a gesture with his hand. "Be my guest." She reaches over and samples his chicken couscous with its hint of turmeric and cumin, raisins and almonds. And mint. Then she puts her spoon down. This must be some form of déjà vu. Some temporal-lobe glitch. Her mind playing tricks on her. She's read that people with epilepsy sometimes experience a deep sense of euphoria just before a seizure. But she doesn't have epilepsy. Perhaps this is a mini-stroke. Or a psychotic break brought on by fatigue? Except for bringing her spoon to her mouth, Elena is certain that she cannot move. She doubts that she'll ever get up from this table.

The musicians are playing faster and faster. The drumbeat is quickening. They are shaking their gourds, blowing into their reed instruments. It is all too fast. Her mind is spinning like some dervish, endlessly twirling on a small stage. She is aware of families talking, laughing. Around her people are eating. Derek makes soft moaning sounds as he tastes the chicken that has fallen from the bones. Elena dips once more into her lamb with garbanzo, and then puts the spoon down.

It has been more than twenty years since she's tasted her grandmother's sweet lamb stew with garbanzos. After her grandmother passed away, it seemed as if the recipe died with her. It was one of the few things she yearned for the most when she left home. How is it possible that here in this North African restaurant hidden in a maze of streets she is tasting what she has been missing for so long? How can she even begin to understand what the Torres family, who live in an obscure valley called Entrada de la Luna, can have to do with desert nomads who settled in the medinas and souks of Tangier?

Finally she turns to Derek and says, "My grandmother made this stew."

He nods. "You mean she made some kind of lamb stew?"

Elena shakes her head. "No, actually, she made this stew."

Derek smiles, his gray eyes squinting. "What do you mean?"

"It's her recipe. It's very odd. I can't really explain it." Tears are welling up in her eyes. "I think I'm just very tired."

"Well, let's head back then." They finish their meal, pay the check, and walk slowly to the hotel. Somehow the way back is clearer than the way there and they don't get lost again, which disappoints Elena somewhat. Now she wants to lose herself because a part of her, it seems, is already lost. But the way back feels less ominous. They are exhausted as they trudge up the steep hill that leads to their hotel and enter the old Moorish structure with its decaying ceiling.

They climb the four floors to their room where Elena opens its French doors. The white lace curtains blow in the wind and the breeze is salty. It has been an incredibly long day and they are at last able to rest. Derek lies down, gives a great yawn, and stretches. Within moments he is asleep. But Elena will not sleep that night. She goes to the window. Below she can see the lights in the homes of Muslim families.

On rooftops caftans and djellabas and scarves flap in the breeze. In dimly lit windows, couples are bedding down for the night. Overhead a thin sliver of a moon, like a tiny cup, is rising. As the curtains rustle and the ocean laps not far below their window, Elena leans out on the small balcony with the distinct feeling that, despite herself, she has come home.

※

CHAPTER ELEVEN

THE THREE-BODY PROBLEM—1992

As he drives to his babysitting job, Miguel is thinking about the three-body problem. It has been on his mind for a while. How is it that the Earth, sun, and moon exert gravitational forces on one another? Sir Isaac Newton accepted the lunar theory. He believed that the movement of the moon was determined by the pull of the Earth and the sun. For the past few days, as he gazes into the sky, Miguel has been trying to determine if this explains the orbit and phases of the moon.

If the moon controls the tides, what else does it control? Of course Miguel has never seen the ocean. Few people he knows ever have. His parents certainly haven't, though his grandfather Rafael Torres, who died when Miguel was seven, did. His grandfather sailed across it when he went to fight in the war in Korea. He told Miguel many stories of when he was a medic. How he crawled on his belly through the mud to save the lives of wounded soldiers.

Miguel sat on his lap as his grandfather recounted how bullets flew over his head as he crawled through the muck and blood and shit. How he gave injections of morphine to dying men and dragged them from the battlefields. He raised his finger and went *pow pow pow* to show Miguel what it was like when the bullets came flying by, how it felt as if they were grazing his flesh.

But Miguel was more interested in what his grandfather told him about the ocean. How it had been icy blue and endless. How the waves had risen and fallen alongside the ship, sometimes soaring above their heads, crashing onto the deck. In those seas all the men had gone below and been sick for days. How day and night for weeks on end they could see nothing but water and sky. When his grandfather told this to Miguel, he rocked him back and forth on his knees so that Miguel could imagine what it was like to be at sea.

His grandfather read books about science, and he liked to talk to Miguel about the ocean. "Scientists know more about the universe than they know about the sea," his grandfather said to him not long before he died. "No one has ever been to the deepest part of the ocean. I know guys who were stationed in Guam. There's a place called Challenger Deep. It's in the Mariana Trench in the Pacific. It's only six miles deep but the pressure is too great. We can travel a million miles in space, but nothing on Earth has been able to reach that depth." His grandfather would just shake his head. "Try to imagine. You can never get to the bottom of it."

Still, even now, Miguel cannot imagine being in a place where all you see is water. Lake Abiquiu is the only body of water he's ever seen and he can see across it. He wonders if the ocean is like the desert. He's been to White Sands once, where there was nothing for miles except white sand that he and his father jumped into and rolled down as if it were a giant bed, but even in White Sands there are roads and places to get gas and buy a Coke, so it isn't the same as the ocean where there is nothing for weeks at a time. Is it like the sky? If it is so big, then the moon must be very powerful to exert any force on it at all.

Miguel knows from his science class that there are high tides and low tides and that at times the tide comes rushing in so that you have to be careful and at other times it goes so far out so quickly that fish are left flapping on the beach and you can walk among the tidal pools and pick up starfish that wiggle in your hand. He can imagine such things but he's never seen them. He's heard stories of people stranded on desert islands and spits of land. His teacher told them that Ireland used to be connected to the continent of Europe by a land bridge and the people went back and forth until one day the sea rose up and the people who were in Ireland were stuck there forever. That was how the Irish came to be. Miguel wonders if that is how his own people became stuck in this "godforsaken place," as his father likes to refer to Entrada. Is there some land bridge they crossed? Did a giant wave blot out their path of return?

He turns onto Colibri Canyon Road. He does this automatically, not even thinking. It just happens, the way many things happen in Miguel's life. Miguel often feels different pulls. There is the pull of his mother and of his father's world of airbrushes and booze and lowriders. The world in which Miguel is expected to remain. And then there is the tug of another world. The one Mrs. Rothstein inhabits. The one that is the few cities where he's traveled, like Albuquerque, when his father took him along on a job.

And the world beyond that his aunt Elena lives in. A world he knows only through postcards and some phone calls and a flurry of visits that never last more than a day or two, though his father keeps a picture of her framed above his workbench. She is in her ballerina costume and another dancer holds her high above his head. Her dark beauty haunts Miguel. A couple of times a year he receives a postcard—always from somewhere else. The last one came from Spain and on it she wrote, "Greetings from Granada." That is all she ever writes. Not "I rode a camel" or "We took a train." Not even "Dear Miguel." Sometimes she doesn't even scribble her name. But it is enough to draw him into her world.

There is a third tug in Miguel's life. He cannot see it, but he knows it is there. Like a black hole it exerts a strong pull. Miguel is not sure he is who he thinks he is. In those superhero movies, he always identifies with the hero who doesn't know he has special powers and only realizes it when suddenly he can see through the closed door or climb up the side of a building. Miguel wonders if such a secret is not his as well.

He passes houses he recognizes. Large adobes with thick walls set back against the arroyo. The houses he knows because on a job his father drove him through these winding canyon roads and pointed to the houses that belong to Hollywood stars and famous artists. People who are rich and sought the solitude of being alone. At last he comes to Mrs. Rothstein's house. He glances at the sky. He hopes it will not rain. He doesn't want to end up in another ditch. He doubts that he can keep this job if it rains. He doesn't dare think as far ahead as winter.

As he pulls up the drive, Mrs. Rothstein is waiting for him by the door. This sends a pang through him. It is rare that anyone ever waits for him like this. If his mother is at the door, it means that he is late or that he's done something wrong. Nobody ever waits because they want to see him arrive.

+

"So here's our list of emergency numbers." Mrs. Rothstein is showing him a greasy piece of paper with numbers typed on it, others scratched out and written over, taped to the refrigerator. "This is Nathan at the hospital. Here's the phone line out in the studio. Here's poison control. I should put your number up here as well." She starts riffling around for a pencil or pen but can't find one in the congestion of drawers she opens and closes. Drawers that seem filled with screwdrivers and tape and kitchen utensils and bandages. "I'll do it later. Anyway I'll pick the boys up today. You can come with me so you can see where the school is. Then we'll bring them home and if you can just play with them until six or so, that will be perfect." She stares up at him. "My god, you're tall."

"I'm almost six three."

"Well, you're a giant compared to me. Ha, that's funny. Davie and Goliath. You know the giant in the Bible . . . And you're taking care of Davie." Miguel stares at her with a puzzled expression. "Never mind. I bet you're still growing too. I don't think I grew an inch from the time I was twelve. I hope my boys take after their father. Not that Nathan is as tall as you are, but he's taller than me."

It seems to Miguel as if Rachel Rothstein never stops talking. A steady stream of words comes pouring out of her mouth. Miguel isn't sure he's ever heard anyone talk this much or this quickly. It is as if she has some kind of a battery and she is on high speed. And he has a feeling that she will just say anything that pops into her head. He makes a note to be careful what he tells her. And she does not seem relaxed. Quite the contrary; she seems very tightly wound.

When he was young and got into trouble, he'd talk a blue streak to try and get himself out of it. He'd just blah blah his excuses until his mother gave up. But what can she be in trouble for? She needs something to calm her down. Maybe she needs someone to screw her. He tries not to chuckle, imagining being in bed with a woman Mrs. Rothstein's age. His mother's age. The mere thought of it grosses him out. Yet he glances at her body. There's something buoyant about her. She's like a cloud. He can't help wondering if her husband loves her. Maybe she needs more to do.

"It's time to get the boys." Rachel motions for Miguel to follow her into the darkness of her garage where a red Jeep Cherokee is parked. He's disappointed. Not the fancy car he was hoping for. But she's got four-wheel drive. She flicks a switch and the garage door lifts. As they head out of the driveway, she points to a small adobe hut out back. "That's where I'm supposed to make art." She laughs under her breath. "When you're watching the kids."

"Supposed to?"

"I'm not sure what I'm supposed to do, Manuel, to be honest with you."

"It's Miguel," he says softly.

Rachel shakes her head and laughs. "I'm so bad with names." She flings her hands into the air in a way that makes him fear she'll lose control of her Jeep. "I'm supposed to be a sculptor, but at the moment, honestly, I have no idea what I am. I used to make all these little heads. Well, they were only of my mother. Some people liked them but other people thought they reminded them of those shrunken heads you used to get as tourist souvenirs in Borneo or some place like that. Lately I've been doing hands. You have nice hands. Maybe I'll do yours. Basically, I'm not really doing anything now, but I feel as if I'm getting ready to do something and that's a good thing, isn't it?"

Miguel nods. "Yeah. I guess so."

Without really looking, she makes a sharp right turn onto the highway, forcing Miguel to brace himself against the side of the car. An oncoming car has to brake and honks. Mrs. Rothstein makes a motion as if she's going to flip him the bird but catches herself. Miguel has never met anyone like Rachel Rothstein. The way her white hands and those long red nails flutter, the way she talks in one long stream of words. Though if he speaks, she listens intently as if what he is saying is the most important thing in the world.

Miguel turns to Mrs. Rothstein. "You should check out the sky this week. There's going to be a supermoon."

"What's that?"

"The moon is in perigee," he tells her. "It's the closest to Earth that it's been in a while and it's also going to be full. The boys will love it."

It is useful, Rachel thinks, to have someone around who knows something and will talk to her about it. Even if the thing they talk about—the universe—doesn't impact directly on their lives the way, say, the weather does. Rachel is surprised he doesn't talk about baseball or the things that she imagines other boys do.

They pull up in front of Magical Years and the boys come screaming out. Jeremy races ahead, holding a clay imprint of his hand that he then thrusts against the window of the car the way a hand is pressed to the glass in a murder mystery. Davie stumbles behind him, shouting, "Jeremy, wait up, wait up." He has his books clutched to his chest and there is something sad and cloying about the boy. Mrs. Rothstein gets out and holds them to her. She clutches her boys as if she has been separated from them for years, as if they are the victims of a custodial kidnapping and at last they are being reunited.

The boys pile in the backseat. "Buckle up," Mrs. Rothstein tells them. "Come on, Jeremy, seat belts." Even before they drive off, Miguel can hear the boys bickering. It grows louder until just as they are about to make the turn onto the highway heading home, Davie bursts out crying. "Oh, for god's sake, can't you two get along for five minutes?" She glares at them in the rearview mirror. "I mean it. Manuel won't be your babysitter if you are bad."

"It's Miguel. My name," he tells her, "is Miguel."

Rachel throws her hands into the air and off the wheel. "Of course, Miguel."

There is another scream from the backseat and once more Davie is in tears. Miguel turns to look. He assumed that Davie was just a cry-baby, but he sees Jeremy pinching the fleshy part of Davie's upper arm. Miguel gives Jeremy a look that can cut through kryptonite and the boy glares back at him.

Something in that seven-year-old's eyes stuns Miguel. They aren't like Davie's eyes, which are silvery blue. Despite his reddish hair Jeremy's eyes are opaque, dark as black holes. He has mean eyes. "Stop it, Jeremy," he says in a firm tone, under his breath, but the kid just stares back. He will break this boy, Miguel tells himself. Or at least he will teach the little one to protect himself. As Rachel Rothstein smiles and, for once, ceases her chatter, Miguel is clear as to his mission.

That evening as he drives back to Entrada, he has a strange feeling about his life. He can't explain it, but he knows that something is about to change. He drives north. The farther he drives, the fewer lights there are. And there isn't a cloud in the sky. As he gazes up, the sheath of the Milky Way looms overhead. On a night like this he can see ten thousand stars.

CHAPTER TWELVE

⁎

A JEW IN THE BAHAMAS—1492

They come in long boats carved out of wood, their paddles barely rippling the water. It is a strange silent procession. At first Luis de Torres thinks it's a herd of animals he's read about but never seen—mermaids or manatees—that is swimming toward them. Columbus joins him on the stern castle. He too has noticed the long boats from his cabin where he has been writing in his log, and he gazes toward the shore. He expects to see Chinamen dressed in the finest silk, with long black braids, yellow skin, and almond eyes. Instead what they see are men, naked from the waist up, their faces painted in red beetle juice and the green of banana leaves.

As they approach, Columbus fondles the key he wears on a chain around his neck. It is the key to the box where he keeps his documents, including his letter of introduction from the king and queen of Spain. Luis has translated it into all the languages he knows. Yet the space for the name of the Great Khan remains blank. Soon he will fill in the name. The men cannot imagine Columbus's thirst for gold and how it grows with each passing day. He will yearn for it all the more because it eludes him.

He turns to Luis de Torres. "Do you think they will speak Hebrew?"

Luis shakes his head. "I have no idea, sir." As the long boats tie up to their ship, Luis tries to greet them in Hebrew and Arabic. He tries Spanish and Portuguese. The natives keep smiling through their yellow-stained teeth, calling out in a language none of them has ever heard. In the end they use sign language. Columbus waves and they scramble aboard. They carry no weapons. No swords or arrows. They only bring with them squawking green parrots and colorful shells that they offer as gifts, and the white people give them in return the tiniest of hawk bells and beads of glass. Trinkets of no value.

It amuses Columbus and his men when the natives handle their swords. Clearly these are not a warrior people because they slice their skin on the sharpness of the blade. One almost chops off two fingers. The Taino are terrified of the blades and so Columbus and his men sheathe them. It seems that the only weapon they carry are the sharpened sticks they use to hunt the fish and fowl that they roast over open flames.

They have a leader with them, and through gestures he explains that the only enemy they have is another tribe that they call the Carib. "Carib," Luis says, showing that he understands. Their leader points to the sky. He acts out an elaborate scenario. The Carib people came from the moon, and once they reached Earth they had no way to return. At night they howl like dogs. They are filled with anger and longing. The Taino show Columbus the bite marks where the Carib have tried to eat them. They will defend themselves if need be, but it is rare. That night Columbus notes in his journal how gentle and docile the Taino are.

Luis tries to understand their language. He learns the words for boat, sea, and sky. Soon he will be fluent in their language, Arawak. For now it is all gestures. "Ask them to tell the Great Khan that we have come," Columbus tells Luis, who pantomimes what the Admiral has requested. That night in his cabin Columbus reads over the letter of introduction from the king and queen of Spain that he keeps locked in the box on his desk. It is October 1492 and Columbus believes he has landed on the coast of Asia. He is sure that this is a land of gold and pearls and soon he will be taken to the city of the Supreme Ruler. When the natives return to shore, Columbus tells his men that all they have to do now is wait. The news of their arrival will reach the halls of the Great Khan. Any day an invitation will come. They dream of the feasts that they will be served, the riches that will be showered upon them, the women that will be offered.

In the meantime they amuse themselves. They swim in the crystal-line waters and drink sweet milk from the huge brown nuts they find on the beaches and crack open on the rocks. They find whelk, as pink as their sunburned skin, and when they put their ear to it they hear the sea roaring back to them. One sailor collects one of every shell he finds. In his idle hours he lays them on the deck according to color and size. Rose, silver, mauve. He will weep when the pilot makes him hurl them overboard for the journey home.

But as the days go by they languish in the harbor. To keep his men occupied, Columbus orders them to clean and polish every inch of their ships. He wants his boats to shine when the emissaries arrive. He sends out small expeditions to hunt for game, but they return with scrawny rodents no bigger than rats and pigeons with no flesh on their bones. Some of the men dive for lobster and crabs. The salt water stings their blistered skin. The cook throws all the seafood into a boiling pot. They suck the juice from briny shells. Afterward they dive into the sea.

During the day the heat wraps itself around them and there is no escape. Even the water of the sea is too warm to cool them down. Some of the men try sleeping on the beach at night, where there are trees and a breeze. As they drift off, they hear the footsteps of giant lizards that they think are men. Bats tear above their heads. And, as the air grows still, mosquitoes and enormous green flies swarm. In the morning the men return to the boats, their skin speckled with bleeding sores. Some come down with fevers that make their teeth chatter and their lips turn blue. Still no one dies. Columbus considers this a miracle.

But no emissary comes. The Admiral waits for days and then a week for His Eminence to send for him, and when he does not receive word, he decides to send the Jew. The Jew will find the descendants of the Great Khan and the Ten Lost Tribes, and Columbus will begin to fill his coffers for the king and queen for whom he does all of this. He orders Luis de Torres and another sailor named Guillermo Jerez to make the first expedition inland. They are to follow the natives back to their leader. "I am certain they will bring you to the Jewish traders."

Even if it is dozens of leagues inland, Columbus is certain that he will reach the palaces he has spent years imagining.

"I would like Rodrigo to accompany me, sir."

"Guillermo is a good explorer," Columbus says.

"But, sir—"

Columbus holds up his hand. There is no use arguing with him. He has never liked Rodrigo. That afternoon Luis and Guillermo set off. They leave the beach and the waters behind. The jungles are thick and they have to chop their way with swords. Luis is unaccustomed to the heat and hard work. His thin pale hands are made for more delicate chores. He does not know how to slash his way through the thickets anymore than he knows how to hoist a mainsail.

Insects the size of fists buzz around them, and mosquitoes, thick in swarms, attack their faces and necks—anything that is exposed. Luis is grateful that he wears pantaloons and a long-sleeved tunic. Green iguanas that blend into the foliage scurry by, startling them. Land crabs scuttle on their claws and iridescent birds with blue tail feathers like a bridal train flutter past. Even as they hack their way through the brush, it seems to Luis as if it will close in around them as they walk by. As they trudge on, he is certain they will be lost in this maze of jungle forever and never find their way back to the sea again, but he says nothing. He marks the trees with deep gashes from his sword.

At last they come to a village of lean-tos with roofs made of palm fronds. The lean-tos have no doors. The women who greet them wear only short skirts. The men wear woven palm fronds. The children are barefoot and naked. The villagers are surprised to see such tall pale men wearing long pants and long-sleeved tunics with high collars. They point, laughing, wondering how these men can survive in the heat, covered in clothes. The villagers approach them, but the men are not afraid. Luis tries to find a language they speak in common. He tries Spanish and Portuguese, Arabic and Aramaic. He tries Hebrew in the hopes that Columbus is right and they are the descendants of the Lost Tribes. But they do not understand a word.

Luis has no idea where they have landed, but he doesn't think that these dark-skinned people are the Orientals Marco Polo described. Still, the natives welcome the visitors. They make solemn bows. Luis talks to them with his hands. He motions that they have come from far away, across the seas. He makes the movement of a boat on the water. He points to a boy and indicates that he has two, and then presses his hand across his chest. The natives nod, seeming to understand. Luis does not miss the irony. With all of his knowledge of languages he has come this far to speak with his hands.

They motion for the visitors to sit around a pit in which there is a small flame burning despite the heat. The fire is very smoky and smells like pine, and Luis thinks it must be to keep the insects away. The men stuff dried leaves into a pipe. They take deep puffs on the pipe and smoke appears. Neither Luis nor Guillermo has any idea what this is. The men hand the pipe to Luis and show him how to take the smoke into his lungs. Luis coughs and chokes. The natives laugh until tears run from their eyes. Guillermo chokes as well. Luis cannot imagine why anyone would want to draw smoke into his lungs.

They feed them bowls of sweet gruel served in coconut shells filled with fermented fruit juices that they sip until they grow sleepy. They are given a lean-to. Buckets of fresh water are drawn from a well so that they can sip and bathe. The water is cool and the men drink in great gulps. Mats of palm fronds are laid down on the forest floor. They sleep for hours and when they awake, a feast awaits them. Grilled turtle, the breasts of birds, cooked yams, and arrowroot. The food is as salty as the seawater they fish in. Enormous beige dogs roam among them, waiting for scraps. The breast of the bird is tender and juicy. They haven't eaten cooked food like this since they left home. Luis de Torres has never tasted fowl such as this. He points to the meat and the natives nod.

After they have eaten, one of the men taps Luis on the shoulder and indicates that he should follow. He isn't sure if he should be afraid, but he rises to go along. Guillermo stays behind. Luis follows the native down a path out of the village. The man moves stealthily. He is small and slim with gangly muscles. His feet are thick with calluses. He has no teeth. With a flick of his machete he cuts a path. They walk for several minutes in silence and Luis wonders where he is being taken. Overhead birds sing sweetly.

The man plucks a yellow fruit from a tree. He slices it in two, removes the skin, and places it in Luis's hands. Then he cuts another for himself and shows Luis how to eat it. He puts the mango into his mouth and sucks on the pulp, his hands covered in yellow slime. Luis grips the fruit that keeps slipping from his hands. At the first taste a sweetness fills his mouth. He never knew that the earth could produce something this succulent. For a moment he believes he has found something more important than the gateway to Asia or even gold. He has found paradise instead.

When they finish their mangoes, they wipe their hands on moist palm fronds and walk on. They walk for a long time until Luis is certain he is being led to his death. Perhaps he has been chosen as a sacrifice to appease their gods. He has heard of this. Natives sacrificing humans on high altars, surrounded by flames. He has heard that some are forced to lie down and have their hearts ripped out or that virgins are flung into the cones of bubbling volcanoes.

A shudder runs through him. Many times he has envisioned himself consigned to the flames. Still, what choice does he have? He must follow his guide who seems to be searching for something. At last the guide turns to him and puts his fingers to his lips. How is it possible that people who cannot speak the same language and have never laid eyes on each other before have the same signal for being quiet?

They come to a clearing. It is a meadow in the woods filled with wildflowers. In the middle is a flock of wild birds. They are big with fat breasts and brownish-red feathers that hide them in the dry grass. He points as if to ask the native what they are called and the man whispers back a word he cannot understand. Then the Taino raises his bow and arrow and shoots one square in the chest. That evening he shows Luis how to cook it over an open flame. Luis de Torres cannot think of a name for this bird so he calls it a *tukki* after the Hebrew word for parrot. It has a sweet taste. When they open the gullet, it is filled with wildflowers.

Four days later Luis and Guillermo return to their ship. They bring with them fillets of the fowl and the yellow fruit that surely is the nectar of the gods. The men feast, but Columbus is dissatisfied. He tells them to return to the forest and find those who live there and command that they bring gold. He is certain they are hiding it. He needs it to pay back his creditors, and if he does not pay them back, he will return a failure. And this will be his one and only voyage of discovery. Luis is to order the Taino to bring them gold and in return they will be given tags of worthless bronze to wear around their necks.

But there is no gold on the island, though the natives desperately search for it. They have no idea why these gold pebbles matter so much, but still they scavenge the riverbeds and along the shores for shiny yellow stones. They bring the tiniest glistening pebbles to Columbus, and if he accepts their offering, they are given the tag that they wear around their necks. Those who are found without tags have their hands cut off. Writhing they stumble, holding up what's left of an arm until they bleed to death. Others, terrified, race into the forests even as Columbus has his men run after them and murder as many as they can. It becomes nothing to slice off fingers, toes. Sometimes the men do it because they are bored. Luis can barely watch. One night he turns to Rodrigo, standing on the shore, a sea of blood surrounding them, and says, "I cannot go on. This man is insane."

When they do not find gold or spices or the palaces of the Great Khan, Columbus decides to sail. He takes with him the brightest green-and-blue parrots he can find, trinkets of gold, and several Indians. On the voyage home one of the parrots will fly off into the Atlantic as a sailor tries to get it to perch on his shoulder, never to be seen again. Most of the Indians will die in their own filth in the holds of ships. Those who survive the journey will be displayed in Lisbon and Barcelona as proof that Columbus has discovered the Indies. He will be hailed as a great man. His future expeditions will be funded because of the treasures he brings, though it will never be gold.

But some of the men grow weary of discovery and the bloodshed it brings. Luis is one of them. He feels the ocean breezes. He puts his toes into the sea that reminds him of the Mediterranean he left behind.

Then they sail on and leave this ruined island. One chief tells them about an island called Cipango. It promises cascades of gold, trees with rubies and emeralds for fruit. Lakes of diamonds. It seems as if the chief will do anything to get rid of these pale men. They set their sails due west for what the history books will one day call Japan.

The men are exuberant. Before they leave, they have a night of feasting and drinking. Columbus allows the wine to flow. In Cipango they will find the treasures that have eluded them for so long. The men drink until they are numb and then stumble down to their hammocks. At midnight they sail. Luis too has been reveling. He imagines his homecoming. How Catalina will greet him, stunned, and he will crush her in his arms. He will share with her the plan he has with Rodrigo. Together they will make their way to the New World.

Luis lies back on his bedding with Rodrigo already snoring beside him. Overhead is a night of shooting stars. He makes wishes. He does not see the Admiral of the Ocean Sea retire to his cabin where he will sleep for the first time in two days. He does not notice the drunken helmsman, Nino, turn the wheel over to the cabin boy and go below to sleep off his intoxicated stupor. Luis is too busy dreaming of home.

It is a clear night of smooth sailing as Pedro de Terreros steers the vessel. He has never been alone at the helm. If he holds the wheel at all, he has Nino beside him. But now the Admiral is asleep and Nino is dead drunk, and the sea is as smooth and calm as it can be. Surely on a night like this it will be safe. Still it is forbidden. The Admiral has said so many times. A shiver runs through Pedro. He takes a deep breath and gazes up at the profusion of stars. It is Christmas Eve. The night before the birth of baby Jesus, and Pedro de Terreros is alone with only the inky darkness before him.

His hands clasp the wheel. The tug is stronger than he remembers. The ship pulls at his hands as if she were a beast he's riding, not very wild but unpredictable nonetheless. But as he holds the wheel steady, Pedro has a vision. He was a boy, barely fourteen, when his father made him sign on. He cried night after night in his hammock. And now here he is, just months later. He has learned all the ropes and lines and rigging of this ship. He knows her masts and sails.

As he gazes out onto the black silky waters, he has a vision of his future. On the night before Christ was born, he steered the ship. This is the story he will tell. He too will make discoveries. When he returns to Spain, even the king and queen will honor him. Columbus will present him at court. "Here is my cabin boy who has become a man. He will be your next great explorer."

Just months ago he feared the life at sea, but now he would welcome it. He loves the feel of the boat in his hands. In the darkness he moves the tiller to the right. A gentle breeze catches the sails and they make the flapping sound that reminds him of the rise of wings. He tacks left and the ship obeys. Everything is before him. His whole future. For weeks he has been turning the sandglass every half hour. He has watched time slipping away. He never thought much about the passage of time before, but now he thinks he understands. Here he is at the helm of this ship that has discovered the western route to China. He will be a hero. Girls will flock to him. His father will praise him. His mother will weep at his return.

He hardly feels the bump as the hull drifts onto a sandbar. Perhaps only an experienced sailor would, and they are all in a drunken stupor, even the Admiral. At first Pedro thinks that one of the other ships has fired a canon. He only notices that the wind has left the sails. Their forward motion has slowed and now the wheel won't budge. It isn't at all what Pedro thought it would feel like. He expected the crunch of the slats, the piercing of the hull, not this easy settling into place. It is hard to imagine that this was how the *Santa María* would run aground.

In his cabin the Admiral of the Ocean Sea stirs and then sits up in his cot. He gazes out his porthole and rushes onto the deck as the cabin boy struggles to turn the wheel. "Nino," he shouts for his drunken helmsman. "Nino, where are you?"

Even as the helmsman staggers topside with the rest of the crew behind him, shoving the now sobbing boy out of the way, Columbus knows it is too late. Still he orders all cargo tossed overboard, all provisions, furniture, belongings, tables, chairs, anything to lighten the load. The horses, goats, sheep, cows, and chicken that remain are thrown into the water and swim frantically to shore. They will populate the New World, providing milk and cheese and fresh meat and turn these consumers of berries and roots and nuts into plump and lazy carnivores.

And when this still doesn't ease the ship off the sandbar, they hurl everything else, including the satchel with all the letters that Luis de Torres has written for the sailors. The epistles that contain their secrets and hopes and dreams fall with a single splash into the warm sea where the ink runs and all the words to the ones they love smear and vanish from the pages of parchment. All to no avail. On Christmas morning the ship sinks. In his cabin the great explorer weeps.

+

They name the place La Navidad, because it is the birthday of Jesus. It is here that Columbus orders his men to dismantle the *Santa María*. He suddenly sees this as an act of God's will. It is Christmas after all. God has sent them to this spot. Columbus will not punish the cabin boy. This is all part of the destiny. He manages to see the bright side. They will build a fort, a foothold in the New World. Out of the remains of his own ship the first building in the Americas will be constructed. There at La Navidad out of the bones of the *Santa María* the first Spanish settlement is born.

They break down the boat and salvage its wood. Luis de Torres, Rodrigo de Triano, and thirty-eight other men agree to stay and establish a settlement at La Navidad. Columbus will pick them up on his next voyage. Rodrigo has his plan. He will turn this settlement into a homeland for the Jews. They will get word back to their wives and children and to the other Jews who have fled, who will find a way to come to La Navidad, the birthplace, in the New World.

The cabin boy pleads with Columbus to let him to stay as well, but the Admiral refuses. "I cannot allow it," he says. "You are just a boy." And, Columbus does not add, a careless one at that. But Pedro knows that his dream of being a great explorer will never be realized. His fame will come in five hundred years when a boulder on Mars is named after him.

"But I will be a boy in the streets of Cádiz when we return."

Still Columbus won't let him stay. It breaks Luis's heart to see the boy go. It is as if he is leaving his own sons all over again, but he cannot show this to the boy. Instead, with the ink, stylus, and paper he managed to rescue before the ship went down, Luis drafts a final letter to his wife. "Tell them I am well," Luis says to Pedro before he leaves. "Ask my wife if she can house you. Tell her I will return as soon as I can. Or that I will send for her."

He hands the boy his address and the letter he has written to Catalina. It is the last letter he will write and the only one that will ever reach her. It contains all the things he's never been able to say. "Please," he whispers, "do this for me and when I return, I will do anything for you." Even as he says these words, Luis knows that he will never see the boy again. Perhaps Pedro knows this as well, for he does not look back when they sail away.

The forty men bring their few belongings, some provisions and trinkets to trade with the natives. They set up a small settlement near the beachhead where they eat guava and sweet mangoes and sleep under the stars. Luis dreams of Catalina. He wants to touch her soft flesh. He wants to smell the cinnamon in her hair, the ginger and turmeric of her nails. At night he is as tormented as the other men are—each longing for a woman to sleep at their side. They are tired of their own sweat and the piss of men who stand up against the trees. He is tired of their rough skin and beards. He wants softness. He wants a woman. And so do the others.

One night under the stealth of a half-moon they make their preparations. All except for Luis, who refuses to go. He remains inside his lean-to and when his eyes catch those of his friend, he looks upon him in scorn. Rodrigo looks away, but his eyes seem to say that the ocean is too big and perhaps they will never return. That night they sneak through the forest. They know where to find them. At night they see the light of their fires and hear their drums.

The Spaniards have learned to walk like Indians. They make no noise. They don't let the branches snap as they slip by. They crouch behind fallen trees. It is at the moment of the deepest slumber that they strike. Children who scream have their throats cut. Men who reach for their machetes have their heads lopped off or an arm severed. Hands are cupped swiftly over the mouths of struggling women as the Spaniards carry them back to their settlement. One woman fights Rodrigo even as he grasps her by her hair. He has never injured a woman before. Until now he has always been the most gentle of men, but now he drags her behind him. He slaps her. He believes that in time she will come to want him. He strikes her with his fist until he silences her.

Back in the settlement each man takes his woman into a tent. The ones who have not gotten a woman must wait their turn. They are ravenous. They have been trapped in the hold of the ships with only men and have longed for warm bodies to satisfy them. In his tent Rodrigo holds the screaming woman down. He tries to silence her but then he gives up. He is upon her. Even when he is finished, he does not share her with the other men but keeps her for himself.

Eventually she stops whimpering. She lies curled into a ball and as he reaches for her again he sees that she is hardly a woman. She is a child. The hair between her legs has only begun to sprout. The breasts to bud. And the blood that pours from between her legs is his doing. He gives her a rag and motions for her to clean herself, but she does not move. Her eyes are dark and fixed. They stare at him as if she is already dead. She uses the rag to cover her breasts. The blood dries and cakes, but that doesn't stop him from taking her again.

Luis sits in his lean-to, staring out at the sky. He tries to trace the constellations. Orion, Andromeda, Pleiades, but without his friend, he loses the way. He wonders if Catalina sees the same stars he does and if he will ever find his path home. He mutters the Hebrew prayers under his breath. He tries not to listen to the women's cries, the men's deep groans. He tries not to blame them. In silence he recites the Kaddish, the prayer for the dead. At some point he shuts his eyes.

꙳

CHAPTER THIRTEEN

THE PALE BLUE DOT—1992

Miguel stands under the oak tree with his telescope aimed at the outer edge of the solar system. Above him the tree looms. It is hard for him to believe that it has stood here for four hundred years—as long as his ancestors have been in Entrada. And yet at times it feels as if he knows more about this tree than he does about himself. And more about the universe than he knows about any of it. There are as many stars in the sky as neurons in the brain, and we know even less about the brain. How is it that humans have managed to be here at all?

Miguel has come to observe the supermoon. He doesn't really need his telescope, but he likes to gaze into the craters. It was Galileo who first used the word *crater* to describe these depressions. When he turned his telescope to the moon, he gave them the Greek word for vessels that contain wine. Perhaps he imagined that some day he would sip from these. It was only later that these craters came to be named after deceased scientists. Copernicus, Tycho, Janssen, Humboldt, Fra Mauro, Picard.

But as Miguel moves his telescope along the uneven ground, it's not the moon he's thinking about. It's *Voyager* that comes to mind. He knows that *Voyager* is now almost six billion miles away from Earth. He wishes he could see it. Or at least chart the radio waves it is transmitting back to Earth. Though he realizes it is a spaceship, it is hard for Miguel not to think of it as being lonely.

Most boys Miguel's age only care about girls, booze, cars, tattoos, smokes, their muscles, drugs, sports, and occasionally school. Unlike them, Miguel struggles to understand his place in the universe. *Voyager* is his touchstone. Ever since he learned that the spaceship was launched on his birthday, he's been charting its course. When he went into juvenile detention, *Voyager* was sailing past Neptune. Just before it left the solar system, Carl Sagan asked the NASA engineers to turn *Voyager*'s cameras around. He wanted one last glimpse, and the spacecraft obliged. It took the Solar System Family Portrait: a snapshot of the planets as they rotated around the sun. In the family portrait, Earth is a pale blue dot.

Miguel wonders what his family portrait would look like? Just MG and his dad. When his dad left, his mom cut him out of half the pictures they had together. In some she just cut out his head so that there's a blank circle where his father should be. Miguel has some cousins on his mother's side whom he rarely sees. He had an aunt and uncle who were killed in a car crash when they were drunk. There is his aunt Elena who shows up once every few years for a funeral. He doesn't think he could pick her out of a lineup. Miguel laughs to himself. That's a phrase he remembers from juvie.

On the wall of his room, across from his poster of *Voyager,* Miguel has a poster of the pale blue dot. *Voyager* took the snapshot on February 14, 1990. Valentine's Day. The poster is of a sunbeam and in its midst, barely a pixel, the tiniest of blue dots. It is on this dot that all people have lived, all animals have been born and perished. Battles have been fought and won, and lost, generations upon generations of humans have lived and struggled and died. Everyone who has ever loved or cried or lost or hoped or dreamed, every creature that has ever fought for its survival or watched it come to an end. All the life we have ever known has been lived on the pale blue dot that sits in the middle of a sunbeam.

He's read that Carl Sagan and Ann Druyan, his lover and, later, his wife, had asteroids named after them. They are in an orbit around each other for eternity. He thinks of Carl Sagan believing that somewhere in the universe other forms of life exist. Perhaps not just like us, but intelligent life all the same. This is how Miguel thinks about his family. Surely they are out there somewhere. But he has no idea where. Or what form they might take.

After *Voyager* took this final picture, its cameras were turned off and the ship continued on its dark, solitary journey toward the edge of the Milky Way. Miguel estimates that he will be almost forty—a number that is incomprehensible to him—when *Voyager* leaves the Milky Way and crosses into interstellar space. And by then he will be an old man.

✳

CHAPTER FOURTEEN

SUPERMOON—1992

Rachel Rothstein can't sleep. She sits in her living room, staring out the large picture window. She should have known there was a full moon when her restlessness settled in. The boy told her that it would happen this week, but she forgot. Normally she's so tired or has had so much to drink that she just drops into bed. Passes out, Nathan will say. Nathan never has trouble sleeping. His circadian rhythms are inordinately intact. He sleeps the guiltless sleep of children. Even her own children, especially Davie, toss and turn more than Nathan does.

But for Rachel it's different. It isn't that she's tossing and turning. It's that she will wake for no reason in the middle of the night as if she's slept for eight hours. Her sleep is more like a long nap. But tonight she's just awake. When she finally came out of their bedroom, leaving Nathan snoring in his deep REM sleep, she found the living room bathed in a shimmering blue light. It was as if a spaceship had landed in their driveway. Something that would not really surprise her in this desolate landscape in which she has, for reasons that at the moment escape her, decided to live.

She goes to the window to see if ET is standing in the shrubs, but instead she sees the enormous moon. It is a supermoon. She recalls that Miguel told her that. He seems to be into such things. The full moon is in perigee, he told her, the closest it ever comes to Earth. *Perigee,* she likes that word. Like pedigree. It implies something important. And now it is fourteen percent bigger than a regular full moon. This is just one of the reasons why Rachel cannot sleep. For years she's tried to practice good sleep hygiene. No late-night television. No caffeine and as little alcohol as she can manage. She's tried to use the bed only for purposes of sleep or intimacy—neither of which seems available to her at the moment. Still she is awake.

She glances at the digital clock in the kitchen. It is 3:47. She's been sitting up since 2:17. She contemplated taking half an Ambien, but the boys will be up at 6:30, and she'd be out cold. She could take a bath, maybe that would relax her. It took a few days but Julio Lorca did get the well drillers back. They had clogged up the cold-water pipe and they unclogged it. She left Lorca a box of oatmeal cookies and a thank-you note, but he never responded. Nathan worries that he's going to take their well rights away. She decides against a bath. It might wake the boys.

Instead she pours herself three fingers of Scotch to which she adds an equal amount of half-and-half and a spoonful of honey. She sticks the concoction into the microwave for forty-five seconds. Moose milk. It was once a surefire remedy to get her back to sleep, though as she sips it the impact it's having is to make her feel drunk but not tired. All her life the moon has interfered with her sleep. It makes sense, doesn't it, that some people have circadian rhythms and others are governed by circalunar rhythms? Coral reefs, she read somewhere, reproduce once a year after the full moon.

As a young girl, she'd wander sleepless through her parents' house or tug on her mother's nightgown sleeve until she woke, looked out the window, and said, "Oh, it must be the moon." But then her mother, who was usually drunk, would tumble back into whatever stupor she lay. But at least in this her mother was consistent. Studies have shown that sleep isn't as deep when the moon is full, nor is it as long. Minutes are shaved off the night; dreams are troubled and seem never to end. Some people, even those who dwell in dark places like basement rooms or windowless cells, still can't sleep. It is not because of its light but because of its pull.

And of course the moon meant other things. When she was a teenager and became impossible, hysterical, when she binged and vomited and drank until she took herself to AA, her father called her "the lunatic." She'd overhear him as he and her mother stood outside of her bedroom, arguing. Now, in this household full of men with their love of blood sports and propensity for sound sleep, Rachel has no doubt that she is governed by the moon. She touches her aching breasts and feels the stiffness in her back. Her period will come soon. And when it does, it is always a relief, a letting go. It happens every twenty-eight days like clockwork. Her whole body is governed by the moon.

As she sits up, staring at the blue curtain of light that filters down into the room, a brightness that seems otherworldly, she wonders what her next move should be. What will it take for something to occupy her enough that it will make her actually get tired? The three miles she runs every day doesn't do it. The running after the boys, the picking up and dropping off, the crossword puzzles, the attempts at modeling in clay, the long phone calls with her mother and friends back in New York who imply every so often that it might be time to reconsider her move to, as her mother calls it, the middle of nowhere. None of this can make her lie down and close her eyes.

Sex used to do the trick. For a time it was Rachel's cure for everything. It had long been her drug of choice. She'd meet men in libraries, on the bus, in bars. Sex plus vodka worked very well for a time. And then she met Nathan and sex was how she put herself to sleep with him as well. Until something changed. Maybe it was her hormones after two babies. Or maybe it was the sex itself. But instead of putting her to sleep, it keeps her awake. If they make love at night, she'll be as awake as if she's had a double espresso—something she doesn't dare drink after ten in the morning. Though sex in the early morning does still put her to sleep.

She could go into the bedroom and wake Nathan. Probably if she tried hard enough, he would comply. And perhaps at this point it would make her sleep. But she doesn't want to risk it. And besides the moose milk is settling in. She feels warmth growing inside of her. Not sleep, exactly, but cozy, which is almost as good.

They came here for a reason, didn't they? They wanted a better life.

You need to learn how to hold on to the good, her therapist would say. But where is her therapist now? Perhaps Rachel is just lost in one of those moments in life where everyone finds herself from time to time. Isn't that how Dante begins his *Divine Comedy*? About being in the middle of the woods where the right way is lost? Or something like that.

Rachel can't explain this to anyone—not to her husband or her closest friends or her family—but she believes deep down that things happen for a reason. That people's lives have paths—destinies, if you will—that will take them eventually where they need to go. Rachel believes, for instance, that she was destined to meet Nathan on that kibbutz in Israel. That their lives together were intended for a reason the way she believes most things are intended. Of course this theory falls apart if you are in Germany in 1938 or a mudslide in Peru. Her belief in the inevitable cannot alter the hand of history, but in some sense there is such a thing as destiny. It is as if there is an invisible map that you have to find and then you will know your way.

As a girl she used to have dreams. She could be in the mountains in a blizzard or on a jungle path and all of sudden the mountains would recede, the snow stop, the jungle disappear, and she'd be walking up her front steps. She'd be coming home. But where would home be now? Is this home? The moon is rising higher and higher, and brighter, into the sky. She will not sleep tonight. She can take pills or drink whiskey or do push-ups all night and still she will be awake. Now she recalls that she felt like this at another time in her life, a time that seems so long ago—when she was pregnant with Jeremy. She couldn't sleep. He was due in July and it was only June, but she was wide awake.

She cleaned cabinets and scrubbed floors. She shelved books that had been lying in piles and threw out clothing she'd meant to toss months before. In the morning Nathan woke and found neat packages of shoes and coats and sweaters to give away, books to send down to the Strand. He wondered if she was out of her mind.

She mentioned her sleeplessness in passing to a neighbor in the building and the neighbor said with a knowing look in her eye, "Your baby's coming now."

"But he's not due for another month."

The neighbor just smiled as she wandered by. "No, he's coming now."

Two nights later her water broke and Jeremy was born, perfect, fully formed, four weeks before his due date. The doctor told her he'd heard of women about to give birth who also found themselves wide awake. There is no medical explanation, the doctor said. Perhaps it is a shift in the hormones. Perhaps nesting is in the genes. For whatever reason women about to give birth often find themselves unable to sleep. But she isn't giving birth to anything right now.

Perhaps she should try for another child. But what if it is another boy? She doesn't think she can actually handle it. She wanted a little girl. Someone with whom to get her nails done and to see Broadway musicals. She doesn't think she can handle any more all-day weekend soccer games or Sunday football. She wants a girl to curl up with in their pajamas and paint their toes. Perhaps she should look into adopting a little girl from China. Or perhaps she should volunteer for something or take a class in desert ecology. As she ponders the moon, staring into its brilliant, blue face, Rachel Rothstein wonders what it will take to make her yawn, stretch, and go to sleep.

Someone is staring at her, and she knows it is Nathan. She feels the eyes burning into her. The boys wouldn't have hesitated to jump into her lap, but Nathan stands in the doorway. She doesn't need to turn from the window to see that he has that look she's seen when he's about to give a patient a bad prognosis. Years ago she found this held-back, assessing-the-situation stare appealing, even sexy. It is what makes him a good doctor. His diagnostic abilities. The way he can stand back and appraise. There is no emotion, no weakness in him at all. It makes him an outstanding pediatric cardiologist. And a cold husband. And he learned this from his own father, didn't he? That judgmental man. If only Nathan didn't feel as if he had to prove something all the time.

She stares back at him. "What?"

"Why are you up?" It isn't so much a question as an accusation. It is the way he always says things. Is that what you're going to wear? Is that what's for dinner? Didn't you invite the Adelmans? Because he already knows the answer to all the questions he asks. In fact Nathan never asks a question, it seems to Rachel, to which he doesn't already know the answer.

"I am up because I can't sleep." Isn't that why most people are up at this hour, she wants to add. But she pauses, thinking that she should get up and soothe him. She can take away the fears that plague him— whatever they are. She can touch him and say, "I am not going any- where. I am not leaving you." Because he has been left. He has been alone. He tries to pretend that it doesn't haunt him. The way his father walked out one day when he was twelve. The annual birthday card he received with a check, always for fifty dollars, until his father died. The things he won't talk about. She had tried, for years, to love his hurt away, but this wall stands between them and at times it seems as if it grows thicker and more solid. She fears he has become impenetrable. "I am awake . . ." she hesitates, "because of the moon."

"The moon?"

She pats the space beside her. "Come," she says. "Sit down."

"I have a procedure at six a.m." He frowns. "I need to get some sleep."

Rachel nods. All the more reason to sit down, she wants to say, but instead she replies, "Just for a moment." She always feels guilty for tak- ing up his time. As if these few minutes she wants will make the dif- ference whether a child survives or doesn't. She can't bear the burden that places on him. And still. What if there is only this moment during which they will say the things they need to say to each other? What if this supermoon enables them to be honest with each other the way they once were so many years ago? She wants to lie in the blue light beside him and tell him the truth and have him do the same—whatever the truth is.

Nathan moves across the room, his eyes not yet adjusted to the dark. He holds his hand out like a blind man, afraid he will bump into the corners of tables or step on the dog. As he approaches the sofa she holds out her hand. "Here. Sit next to me."

With a sigh Nathan sits down beside her but not so they touch. There is a space between them. Rachel is more and more aware of this. The small space that has grown larger, into a crevasse. It will be a canyon soon. She thinks of the lyrics to that Leonard Cohen song. The one about the light coming through the cracks. What song is it? She used to know them all. Every song. Every lyric. Now they elude her.

"Our new babysitter, Miguel. He tells me that there is scientific proof that the full moon impacts our sleep cycles."

"Miguel?"

"Yes, he wants to be an astronomer." Actually Miguel hasn't told her this. It is an ambition that Rachel has given to him. She wants Miguel to succeed. She wants him to become a famous astronomer and thank her when he wins a national science prize. That is one thing Rachel likes to do. She likes to make people believe they can succeed—even if she suspects they cannot.

Nathan shakes his head. It is the first time he's heard the name of the new babysitter. In fact it is the first time he's heard that she's hired a babysitter. "Where did you find him?"

She can't tell him the truth. She can't tell him that she drove out of Santa Fe into the pueblos and the Hispanic villages where she put up her ad in gas stations and general stores. She didn't move her family out here for her boys to have the same nannies as they had on Madison Avenue. She wants them to be different from everyone else. She wants them to be surprised by life and all that it has to offer. "He saw my ad at the Santa Fe Public Library. He's working on a project that I don't quite understand. It's very scientific."

There is a pause, silence.

"And he comes highly recommended."

Nathan doesn't ask by whom. He breathes another heavy sigh. "Are you happy here? Are you happy with your decision?" She waits until she is sure he is finished. "Because this was your decision."

She pats his hand. "No, it was our decision . . ."

Nathan gently pulls his hand away. "No, not really. It's what you wanted. I was fine to go along. Because I wanted you to be happy." A quiet comes over the two of them because they both realize he is speaking in the past tense. "I want you to be happy."

She glances over at him in the moonlight and a feeling goes through her. Something she hasn't honestly felt in a while. She curls closely against his side. "Of course I'm happy. Why wouldn't I be?" She runs her finger along his arm, making a circular motion, a swirl that seems to deepen and deepen. If she stops, the moment will be gone so she keeps at it. She leans into him more closely. She wants him to kiss her. It is that simple. A kiss.

Nathan sighs, leaning back. "Shall we try and get some sleep?" He catches her fingers in his own like a web. Then he tugs her from the couch and leads her into their room.

✳

CHAPTER FIFTEEN

THE STREET OF THE DEAD—1492

Inez Cordero stands outside her father's study. She's bringing him his supper as she does every evening at this time. A plate of cheese, fig jam, bread, and tea. A cooked egg. She's holding his tray and hoping he won't notice that her hands are trembling. Inez pauses, trying to catch her breath. She prays that he won't detain her. Javier is waiting for her. It's all she can think about. Every day she can barely wait for his touch. Every evening she burns for it. Soon she can slip away.

Inez pushes open the door. Her father is hunched over the paper he is writing, dipping his stylus into the inkwell. He's been studying a document that is causing him distress. At first he is unhappy with this intrusion. But as she settles the tray at the end of his desk, he looks up. Diego Cordero sees that it is his daughter. His beloved daughter. It is difficult for him to grasp how beautiful she has become.

It seems as if just weeks ago she was a little girl, sitting on his lap as he concocted tales of dragons and unicorns, mermaids and pirates. She liked the pirate stories best. Accounts of swaggering men who went to sea and found adventures there. He invented sea monsters to frighten her and mermaids to beguile her. Now here is this woman with a thin waist and gentle curves, creamy skin and jet-black hair. So like the way her mother had once been. It is as if Diego is falling in love all over again.

Unfortunately it has begun to occur to him that she is beautiful to others as well. Daily, it seems, suitors are coming to the door. Young men who glimpse her praying in the cathedral or buying tomatoes at the market with her maid. She turns so many away that Diego imagines a river of tears trailing from his house. But there is more to Inez than her beauty. She has a brain. A very good brain. He taught her to read and write himself. But he never imagined that every morning she would sneak one book from his shelves and replace it by the end of the day. It amuses him to find the space in his library where the book is missing and try to guess its contents. And she has a good heart. Once she nursed the tiniest sparrow back to health with drops of warm milk and gruel. Diego never imagined the love that could fill his heart until his daughter was born. He loves his wife, but Inez occupies his whole being.

As she arranges the tray beside him, he clasps her arm. "Thank you, my dear."

She kisses his hand. "It is my pleasure, Father, to bring you whatever you need. Is there anything else I can do for you?" Every night she asks this question, knowing that he'll tell her that it is enough. He does not notice the impatience in her voice or see how longingly she looks toward the door.

"If you can greet my guests when they arrive. I am having a meeting here tonight." Inez breathes a heavy sigh. She doesn't think she can wait a moment longer and yet she will have to wait at least another half an hour until the men arrive. She will not be able to leave before then. She is glad that her father is preoccupied because he does not notice the flush to her cheeks, the faint hint of rouge on her lips or smell the almond soap with which she bathes, the lavender drops that she has placed behind each ear, in the bed of her elbows, and on her breasts. He does not notice that she has let her hair down instead of wearing it up as she does most days. He is thinking about the meeting at his house.

Diego Cordero is angered that the Inquisition continues to persecute even the converted Jews and exacts such a heavy price. Didn't he receive the sacraments of the church, as did all of his converso friends? So what if they have converted only in name. The authorities don't really know that. Still they are taxed and persecuted more than any other group. Their money is used to wage war on the Muslims—all in the name of unifying Spain. And still they must submit to the ridiculous curfew that the authorities claim is for their own good.

"Yes, I will wait until they are here." She lets her hand rest on her father's shoulder. "But you work too hard. You need to rest."

"I will," he says, "after some things are settled." He nods wearily, rubbing his eyes. It is true. He does need to rest. He puts down the magnifying glass that he uses to read. But rest is something he cannot afford. There is a meeting tonight in this very room. In a short while Pedro Fernández de Benadeva, who serves as the cathedral's butler, and Adolfo Piera, a wealthy merchant, will be coming to the house. These secret meetings have been going on for weeks. Inez is weary of them. She sees how much strain it puts on her father. She doesn't understand what it is that upsets them so much except it seems as if it has something to do with taxes. Why would taxes bring her father so much distress? And why should this matter to her? All she can think of is Javier, who is waiting for her.

Inez sits on a bench in the courtyard, gazing up at the stars. It is a clear, warm night of early spring. In a few months the city will be blazing with heat, but now the air is soothing. She sniffs the scent of jasmine already in the air. And yet she is anxious. Javier waits for her at the end of the Street of the Dead where she lives in the heart of the ghetto. This had once been the street of the coffin makers and has kept its grim name. He will be waiting as he does every evening until she can get away. How long will he wait? She smiles. She knows the answer. He will wait until she comes. Neither of them can stay away.

They have known each other since they were children. They met at the cathedral where their parents worshipped side by side. But it was only in the past year that Javier began to look at her differently. She was fifteen after all. He noticed how she had changed. She was no longer a girl. She had blossomed into a beautiful woman. At first he came to the house and they walked together with her mother or her chaperone, but as their passion grew, they began to meet in secret as they do now almost every night at eight o'clock and say goodbye to each other at ten just before the gates of the ghetto close.

But it is already after eight and still she cannot leave. The moments seem endless. Her mother has retired for the evening so Inez must wait to greet their guests. At last there is a knock on the door and she rushes to open it. Pedro Fernández and Adolfo Piera stand at the door with worried looks on their faces. She brings glasses for sherry and trays of cheese and sweets. She slips out. As soon as she hears the muffled voices in her father's study, Inez knows that she will no longer be needed. She grabs her rose-colored mantilla, the one that brightens her features and sets off her dark hair, the one that Javier likes to lift gently from her head as he kisses her. She tiptoes to the front door, undoes the latch, and slips out into the warm spring evening.

Inez races through the winding streets of the ghetto of Seville. She knows all the shortcuts. The tunnels and secret passageways, all the paths that the Jews use to escape when their persecutors come to punish them, and now she uses them to race to her lover. She wishes her family no longer lived in the ghetto. They had been planning to move for years since her parents' conversion just before she was born. Inez has no memory of being anything other than a New Christian. She was baptized into the church days after she was born. Her father, a successful merchant and trader in pepper and spices, had no trouble leaving his Jewish life behind. He was as indifferent to being a Jew as he is to being a Christian. It is a matter of expediency. Whatever enables him and his family to live with the most comfort and ease. It is not that he is gluttonous or without beliefs. He believes in life and he believes in his love for his fellow man. For Diego Cordero, what a man believes about his god is only the business of that man.

After the massacres and the forced conversions, it had been easy for Diego Cordero and his wife, Olivia, to convert. They had kept the Law of Moses out of convention. It was easy for them to let go of many of the rituals—though Diego had never resigned himself to the eating of pork. And they still kept the Sabbath as they had before. But for years now they have been good Christians. They follow the teachings of the Catholic Church. They go to mass. They kneel. They take communion and ask for absolution for their sins.

Still they have not moved away from the ghetto. Her mother loves the old stone walls of their house, the coolness of its inner courtyard filled with plants and flowers. She loves the insularity of their home, and so each time when moving is discussed, Olivia has said no. "This is my home. No matter where we worship and what we believe." So Javier, who is from an aristocratic Old Christian family, comes to meet Inez in the ghetto. It is easier for him to bribe the gatekeeper after curfew to let him out than it would be for Inez to bribe the gatekeeper to let her in. It is easier to be an Old Christian in Andalusia than a converted Jew.

She grips her shawl around her chin as she runs. It is dark and she is very late. They will have so little time together. And what if tonight he has left, thinking she might not come? But as she rounds the corner at the Gate of the Butchers there he is. He leans against the wall, watching the street. Even from a distance his dark eyes are flashing. His thick slicked-back black hair shines in the moonlight, as does his silky green tunic. It is as if he were a dragon, spewing fire. "Inez," he whispers as low as the wind, as soft as a kiss, so that at times she wonders if he really said it, if he is even there and not just some vision she has conjured. When she hesitates for an instant, he calls to her again, louder and more insistent. "Inez, I thought you would never get here."

Without a word she runs to him and he catches her in his arms. She drops her shawl, and he kisses her neck, her throat, her mouth. Then he pauses, whispering into her ear, "I was so afraid you weren't coming."

She holds his hands in hers as he moves them toward her breasts. "I couldn't get away." She falls against him as if he is a wall she can lean on. He envelops her in his cape and leads her into the shadows.

"The important thing," he says, his breath hot against her throat, "is that you are here." He takes her into one of the narrowest alleyways where his hands reach between her thighs. "I want you," he says, leading her farther into the darkness. They have a place they go to. There is a stone seat by a narrow wall where gently he lies her down and hoists up her skirts. She never refuses him.

His touch ripples through her flesh. His slightest caress sends a quiver. He knows how to touch her and where. Tonight he lets his fingers linger inside of her, then his tongue. He is never rushed, never in a hurry. As he licks her, Inez stares at the sky, and her body seems to blend into the stone seat she lies on and out into the whole world. And then he is inside of her, moving slowly at first as she opens to him. He takes his time. It is a feeling that never ceases to amaze her. It is a pleasure she has never imagined. And now they are one. They are in unison. This, Inez Cordero decides, though she is barely fifteen years old, must be love. What else could it be?

Afterward she lies in his arms, his moisture between her legs, the stickiness of him upon her. "I'm sorry," she whispers, "that we didn't have more time. My father had one of his meetings, and I had to greet the guests."

"His meetings?" Javier's breath is warm on her throat. "What kind of meetings?"

"I never know. They come and they talk for hours." Inez doesn't know exactly why the men meet or what for. What she does know makes little sense to her. All she knows is that the men are disgruntled. "I think it is about taxes."

"Taxes?" Javier says with a laugh. "Why would they meet about taxes?"

Inez shrugs. She doesn't know and she doesn't care. Even when she can overhear their muffled voices rising in anger and when she hears the name of the mayor of Seville uttered, it doesn't matter to her. Her only thought when she is not with Javier is how soon she can be with him. "I don't know. Would you like me to ask?"

"No, I would like you to listen. You are New Christians and we are Old Christians. My father will want to be sure that you keep the rules of Christ."

"Of course we do." Inez pulls away. "Those are the only rules we have ever kept."

Javier sighs. "I know that, but to the rest of the world you are still Jews." Above them the church bell rings. It is almost ten o'clock. A shiver runs through Inez. Soon Javier will slip away. "I want to know everything about you and your family. We can have no secrets between us."

She kisses him on the forehead and on the lips. "And I want to know everything about you." She coils her fingers around his.

"I will ask your father for your hand before the week's end." He takes his hand, placing it on her pounding heart. "I'll be here tomorrow night as always."

As Inez hurries home along the Street of the Dead, she is surprised at the chill that has come into the air. Perhaps it is later than she thinks. She wraps her mantilla around herself and dashes up the street. But as she slips into the courtyard she hears the men still talking in her father's library. One of them is raising his voice, and it occurs to her that they are arguing. She sighs, her body shaking. She had expected her father to be in bed by now. What if he had caught her out at this hour? What lie could she tell him? Putting her fears aside, she leans against the door. They never stay this late. They will meet and talk and sometimes argue, but never like this for hours. Now their voices are louder than ever. This cannot be only about taxes.

And then she overhears what Pedro Fernández says. Someone has informed on him. He does not know whom as informants are never identified. Anyone can inform on a converso. Anyone who wants your land or envies you your business or your home or your wife can say that you are practicing the dead Law of Moses. They can claim that you keep Jewish rituals, that you do not light fires on the Sabbath, that you will not accept money on the Sabbath. You refuse to ride in a carriage. You will not eat pork. You wrap your dead in white linen and bury them before sunset. Anyone can say this, and you will never know who it is.

Pedro Fernández has been called before the Inquisition. He has been ordered to confess his sins. Already they have confiscated all his property, and he has not yet been accused of a crime. Any day now he will be arrested. Now Inez hears her father's voice. "They cannot keep doing this to us. They don't care about our beliefs. They only want our wealth. They are envious of our gold and our success. They are murderers and thieves."

Inez trembles outside the door of her father's study. She has never heard him speak in this way. She is frightened. Frightened for her father and frightened for herself. If he does anything, Javier will not marry her. His family would never allow it. She wants to plead with her father not to do whatever it is that he has planned.

The next day at noon she brings her father his tray. The cook has made the soup with vegetables and guinea fowl that he likes. She brings a bowl for herself as she sits in his study. "Your meeting went late, Father," she says.

He nods. "There is much to discuss."

"Yes, I overheard some of it. Señor Fernández was very upset."

Her father's face reddens, not because his daughter has listened to what was said but because he cannot contain his anger. "They continue to persecute us. We worship in their churches. We loan them money. We do their bidding. And still they tax us, but much worse they inform on us. They make up stories, anything they want. It has happened to Pedro and it can happen to us. This must be stopped."

Inez has never seen her father so enraged. "Stopped how, Father?"

Before he finishes his soup, he pushes it away. "We will make a new government. One with new laws. The Inquisition cannot rule us in Seville."

Inez listens, not entirely understanding what he means. Will there be an election, a battle? How will the new government come to be? How can they get rid of the Inquisition in Seville? The inquisitor has free rein here. That night she is able to get away early. She runs to their secret place where Javier waits for her. Before she can speak, his hands are on her back, her breasts, her buttocks, under her skirt. She has never felt his passion this strong, this intense.

As he opens her, she can hardly breathe. Slowly he brings his pleasure to her. Inez will never question it. Never wonder how he learned to do such things. She is merely grateful that he has and that it is all for her. Though once he is inside of her, he is less gentle. He is like an animal, a beast that has awakened, but this arouses her all the more. He pushes into her more sharply than he ever has and puts his hand over her mouth to stifle her cry that comes not only from her pleasure but from the force of his strong, sharp thrusts. Afterward she lies in his arms.

"We have no secrets, do we, my love?"

"None," she says drowsily. Between her legs she is throbbing. How she wants to fall asleep, drift off. How she wants to be able to doze night after night in these arms. There are so many nights when she finds that she cannot sleep but she knows that in Javier's embrace she will sleep as if he has given her a soothing drug.

"Did you learn what the men are meeting about?"

"Yes, they are upset over the treatment of the conversos. It seems that one of my father's friends has been informed upon though he has no idea why or by whom. All of his wealth has been taken. And he has been told that if he does not repent and confess, he will be relaxed to the flames."

Javier nods, holding her all the more tightly. "That is a terrible thing. I am very sorry. I am so glad it has not happened to your father."

Inez gasps. "Oh no, it cannot happen to him." Tears come to her eyes. She cannot bear the thought. What if someone does inform on him? "He and his friends are planning to do something to gain control of the government." Even as she tells him, Inez isn't sure what all of this means.

"What are they planning?"

Inez shakes her head. "I don't know, but he says it will protect us when it does."

Javier kisses her as he always does when it is time for her to leave. "I will wait for you tomorrow."

All through the next day Inez dreams of when she will meet her lover, but once again the men come to her father's house and she has to wait until they have their sherry and sweets. It is after eight thirty when she dashes out to meet Javier, but when she gets to their place, he is not there. Perhaps he grew impatient and left. But he has never done so before. He has always been here when she arrives. Perhaps he was detained. But who or what could have kept him away when nothing and no one has before.

She waits. Each time she hears a footstep, the clomp of a horse's hooves, she leaps up, hoping it is he, but each time she is disappointed. The air grows chilly and she tightens her shawl around her. Soon in the corner by the ghetto wall she starts to shiver. By ten the gates of the ghetto are locked, and still he has not come.

She returns the next night and the next, but he is not there. She worries that he is ill. That something terrible has befallen him. At night she weeps. During the day she refuses to leave her room. She writes letters, imploring him. She gives these to her servant who delivers them each day and returns empty-handed. Inez ignores her parents' pleas that she join them to eat. She will not budge until her lover appears.

On the third day at dusk there is a knock on the door and Inez knows. Javier has arrived at last to ask for her hand in marriage. Perhaps he has brought his father with him in order to make it official. She breathes a sigh of relief as she runs to the door and unlatches it. Instead she finds four men: a bailiff, two soldiers, and man in a leather mask. Inez shouts as they push her aside.

"Where is your father?"

"My father, what do you want with my father?" One of the men slaps her across the face and she screams again. "My father is not—"

"Inez," her father calls, "what is it?" He stands in the doorway, a book in his hands. But when he sees the men, he knows. "How dare you come into my house?" he says as the man in the leather mask smashes a fist into his jaw. There is the crunch of cartilage and bone. Blood splatters everywhere. His glasses fly. Even as he falls, the man continues to strike him and then, as he lies writhing on the ground, kicks him in the ribs. Inez hears the bones break. Then they chain his hands behind his back. Her father shouts something to her, but she cannot understand if what he says is a blessing or a curse. All she sees is blood and broken teeth as they drag him away.

"It's my fault," Inez cries, "take me instead," but the soldiers shove her away.

Dona Olivia grabs her by the shoulders. "Whom did you talk to? Who did you tell?" She shakes her daughter until Dona Olivia crumbles, writhing, to the ground.

Inez races after the carriage that takes her father away. She dashes out of the ghetto and when she can no longer run after it, she pauses. She can barely breathe, and she presses her hand to her chest as she sobs. She will go to Javier. She has never gone to his house, but she knows where he lives. She will go and plead with her lover and his father to intercede. Surely there is a mistake. At the house of Javier's family she bangs on the door. Upstairs a curtain is drawn back, and then closes. No one comes to the door.

That night she leaves her mother, whose sobs wrack the house, and goes to where she meets her lover every night. She will tell him what has happened. She is certain that he can use his influence to get her father out of jail. Certainly he or his father can attest to the fact that her father is a righteous man who practices the teachings of the Holy Church and not the dead Law of Moses. It is not possible that Javier has informed on her father. Perhaps he has spoken to the wrong person or he hasn't been prudent with his words.

She waits for him as she always does. And when he does not appear, she goes the next night and the next. She will keep coming here every night because of course he will come. Or he will find a way to contact her. Perhaps he is in trouble. She learns the fine art of waiting. She stares at stones in the moonlight. She watches shadows passing by. She tells herself that if his is not the fourth shadow she will leave. Then the fifth. The sixth. Until one day she goes to the market, for they must go on living, and she sees Javier parading around on his gray horse, riding down the main street of Seville. He is laughing with a friend. He stops to touch a young woman on the cheek. He has caressed Inez this way dozens of times.

Still every night she returns to their meeting place. She knows he will not come, but she waits. She looks up at each footstep. She leaps at any voice. Some nights she is certain she hears his voice, calling her name. It is that same sultry voice he used when he first saw her in the shadows, when she ran to him. She hears her name whispered in the wind as it blows past her into the trees. She goes every night, listening for him, until the verdict comes down upon her father. He and his co-conspirators are consigned to the flames. Inez goes to the gates of the prison and stands there until she is turned away. She goes to her lover's villa where the doors do not open. Her mother will not speak to her. Inez lives in her own home as if she lives alone.

The day of the auto-da-fé is festive. The whole town comes out, wearing their finest dresses and cloaks, their jewels and mantillas. Musicians play and people dance. When the penitents are brought in, dressed in their yellow sanbenitos and dunce caps, Inez's mother faints. When her father is given one more chance to repent and kiss the cross, he recites the Sh'ma. As the flames are lit, his screams rise. As his ashes are carried by the wind across Seville and along the flat, dry plains of Andalusia, Inez Cordero breathes her father in.

✳

CHAPTER SIXTEEN

SOLSTICE—1992

The car is packed and ready to go. In her mind Rachel rattles off her checklist. Drinking water, bug spray, fried chicken, salad, wine, corkscrew, watermelon slices. It seems as if this has been weeks in the planning, though they only decided a few days ago. At Rachel's urging they are going to get away for the weekend. Overnight at least. She's hired a friend's nanny who can spend the night. She would have asked Miguel but she doubts that Nathan would have accepted that. But now Rachel can breathe a sigh of relief. They are about to leave.

Nathan is going over his own list. Sleeping bags, tent, flashlight, batteries, blow-up mattress, air pump, small stove. He's in charge of equipment. Rachel's responsible for food. Nathan borrowed some camping gear from one of his colleagues at work. "Hey, if we have fun," he tells Rachel, "we'll get some gear of our own."

It's all set. "Okay," Nathan says, "let's roll."

They kiss the boys goodbye and give the babysitter last-minute instructions. "Davie, no dairy" and they are off. Nathan's driving and Rachel puts some Native American wolf spirit music into the tape deck. She leans her head back. The gentle sound of the flute lulls her almost to sleep while the rhythmic beat of the drum reverberates through the car. Outside, the mesas, the red clay mountains, sage, and juniper all rush by. They are heading west. Just the two of them. Farther than they've been since they moved here. She can't really remember the last time.

And it's been so long since they've been close. Since they've even touched. Rachel envisions them at their campsite, resting in each other's arms under the stars. Their steady breathing. Nathan's gentle doctor's touch. They'll make love. She laughs to herself at the notion of making love in a tent on the hard ground, but a part of her is stirred. She is ready for him.

Rachel reaches across, touching Nathan's arm. "I've always wanted to see Chaco Canyon," Rachel says. He is still the handsome man she married. He has his head of dark curls that she loved to run her fingers through when they were first together. And those pale blue eyes that Davie inherited. It's true that he's heavier than when they first met whereas she hasn't gained a pound. But he's still strong. He still does his sixty sit-ups every night before bed. Not much has changed beyond two children, the move to New Mexico, and all the years. But the core of it, what started it all, that remains.

"I can't remember when we last went camping." Nathan clasps her fingers, then makes his turn onto the highway heading west. Piñons line the dry, desert road. Rachel rolls down her window and smells the pine.

Rachel laughs. "I'm not sure we ever have."

"Oh, we must have. But maybe that was some other girl." A large truck passes and she rolls her window up. Nathan gives her a playful wink.

"Maybe," she says, running her fingers through his thick, dark curls. As they drive along Rachel starts talking about the boys. At school they are studying Columbus. It is the anniversary of his discovery. Five hundred years, the quincentennial, and their curriculum is all about Columbus—discovery, navigation, and geography. In art class they are making cardboard boats. They are designing Columbus coins. She turns to Nathan. "Why are they making a big deal out of that? He committed genocide. Why don't they learn about that?"

Nathan shrugs. "He discovered America."

"No, there were native people here before Columbus. But he killed them. Millions of them."

"I think it was smallpox that killed them."

Rachel nodded. "But we gave them smallpox."

"And they gave us syphilis."

Rachel stares at Nathan, about to laugh. "Seriously? I didn't know that."

"Yes. The sailors brought it back to Spain with them."

They stop at a roadside diner for lunch. The graffiti on the side of the building catches Rachel's eye. ALLWAYS BE YOURSHELF. Inside the diner she spots an old poster. "Tommy Macaione for governor. Vote for the Mutual Happiness Party." His platform promoted art, agriculture, disarmament, and free school lunches. "I'd vote for him," Rachel muses. "I Shot the Sheriff" is playing on the radio. They order eggs with green tomato salad, tortillas, and beans. It is a delicious meal, and as they gobble it down, Nathan reaches across the table and holds her hand. "I'm glad we're getting away."

Rachel squeezes his too. "So am I and look, we did it. We got out of the house."

Nathan laughs. "Yes, that is an accomplishment."

Rachel has been wanting to see Chaco Canyon since they moved to New Mexico. It is one of the oldest sites of the ancient Pueblo people, and its buildings and structures are believed to be more than a thousand years old. She did some research and learned that they can camp on the grounds. Rachel thought about making a camping reservation but Nathan said, "What for? Let's wing it. Besides that's just if you've got a Winnebago or something like that."

So they are going to wing it. The way they used to when they first met. Backpacking around Europe. Busing it through Latin America, never sure of where they were going from one stop to the next. It was an adventure. And neither of them could recall the last time they'd been on one—though, of course, as Rachel likes to remind Nathan, moving to the Southwest is an adventure, isn't it? Not what anyone expected them to do.

They drive through miles of desert. Brilliant sunshine filters down. The pure light. That's what they call it around here. Because of the altitude and the dryness the light is as clear and pure as anywhere in the world. Rachel closes her eyes. Listening to the wolf spirit music soothes her. For the first time since she can remember, certainly since they moved to the Southwest, she can relax. Perhaps she dozes off. She isn't sure, but suddenly she is jerked awake. She looks around. Ahead dark storm clouds loom. Rachel points to the sky. "Look at those clouds."

Nathan nods. "Don't worry. They're moving the other way."

Rachel stares at the black clouds. "How do you know?"

"From the way the wind is blowing," Nathan says.

They pass a motel. "Maybe we should just grab a motel room for the night."

Nathan shakes his head. "Rach, it's going to be fine. I didn't spend all this time getting camping gear together for us to check into a motel."

She squeezes his arm. "You're right. And the clouds probably are moving the other way." Though it seems to Rachel that the sky is darkening even more. She gazes at her husband. His sharp nose and pale blue eyes, his round face. They should get out more. Go hiking. When the boys get a little older, they'll do that. But for now it is just them. And she is glad.

As they reach the turnoff to Chaco Canyon, a sign reads, CAMP-GROUND FULL.

Rachel plucks Nathan on the arm. "Nathan, it says that the campground is full."

Nathan laughs, shaking his head. "They always say that. They don't want too many people camping here at night."

"But why would they make that up?"

"Honey, would you please stop worrying? We'll be fine."

They drive for thirteen miles at a snail's pace down the pitted road, bumping along, and when they reach the campground, it is full. Every space is taken. Rachel stares straight ahead, not wanting to say anything, but she's thinking about that cozy motel room with clean sheets. They drive around in circles. Finally two men—a father and son—motion for them. "There's some space here if you want it."

The space is at the edge of a sandy mound. It's not really a space, but it's enough for them to park the car and set up their tent. And there's a picnic table nearby. "Thank you," Nathan says. "Much obliged. Hey, why is it so crowded tonight?"

"Oh, it's the night of the summer solstice. A lot of people have come out to, you know, worship the sun. Enjoy the stars." That's when Rachel realizes that the men have a telescope set up.

"Are you here to stargaze?"

The son, who is probably in his early twenties, nods. "Chaco Canyon is one of the darkest places on Earth. And one of the best places to see the stars." Rachel thinks about that for a moment. She'll have to tell Miguel. Maybe he'd like to come here sometime. Maybe they could all come together to go camping as a family. He could bring his telescope and show them what he knows of the stars. Rachel can't help but notice that overhead the skies are darkening. "Maybe we should set up camp."

Nathan agrees. "I'll put up the tent. Why don't you get dinner on the table?"

Rachel has Tupperware, neatly stacked, filled with chicken that she fried herself, deviled eggs, pasta salad, and fruit. She puts them on the table along with a bottle of red wine and a bottle opener. She's just taken the lid off the food when the wind picks up, blowing sand everywhere. "Oh, my god." Quickly she's covering the food, racing it to the car. Just then the skies open. She sees Nathan struggling with the tent stakes. It's only about six inches off the ground. "Nathan, let's put the tent up. We can eat inside."

Nathan who is getting drenched steps back. "It is up," he shouts.

Rachel can't see how this is possible. It's barely above the ground. "What do you mean it is up?"

"I guess I borrowed a pup tent." Nathan shrugs as the rain pelts his shoulders. "It's not what I expected."

"Me either." Rachel tries to laugh it off, but as she looks at the army-issue pup tent, she sees any hopes for a romantic night sliding away. It occurs to her as she watches Nathan pounding the tent stakes deeper into the ground that he doesn't put much effort into things when it comes to her and the boys. He doesn't try very hard for them at all. If he really cared about her, and about being with her, wouldn't he have found a tent they could cuddle up in? "Let's get in the car," Rachel shouts and they rush into the car as the rain pours down. They rip off their wet clothes and throw on dry T-shirts and sweatpants. They eat in silence, watching the rivulets of rain rush down, pooling around their tent.

The chicken has the gritty taste of sand. In her mind Rachel calculates. How long would it take them to drive back along the pitted road to that motel. And what if it's full now? Rachel looks around. She sees all the well-appointed camp sites. The tents with the rain covers. The tents in which she can see entire families eating dinner at folding tables. Hurricane lights turned on. One family is playing cards. Another has a generator and a portable TV.

It is only eight o'clock. "What should we do?" Rachel asks. She'd imagined a moonlit walk among the ruins. Romantic caresses. Shooting stars. Instead they are sitting in the bucket seats of their SUV, eating their picnic out of Tupperware tubs. And they can't even joke about it. She remembers when a friend had an outdoor wedding and during the ceremony the neighbor's dog ate their wedding cake. And the bride and groom just laughed about it. Why can't they be like that couple? Rachel touches his sleeve. "Can we talk about this?"

"What's there to talk about?" She wonders why he's so stubborn. Why can't he just admit that they should have stayed in the motel? They should have checked to see that they had actual camping equipment. They should have turned back when the sign said that the campground was full. Why can't he ever say, "I made a mistake. I'm sorry."

They eat in silence, staring at the torrents cascading down their windshield. Rachel wipes her hands and picks up a guidebook to the Southwest that she proceeds to leaf through. She learns that Chaco Canyon is believed to be a place of special powers. The Pueblo people lived here for hundreds of years and then, about a thousand years ago, they abandoned it. No one knows why.

Nathan, who is reading a medical journal about advances in the artificial heart, yawns. The rain has let up. "Shall we try going to bed?"

Rachel gazes at the sodden ground. "Maybe we should sleep in the car?" But he shakes his head. He takes the air mattress and puts it inside the tent. There's no point blowing it up because it wouldn't fit inside, so he lays it flat on the ground to keep the water from seeping into their sleeping bags, which he then unrolls. They crawl into the tent and into their respective sleeping bags. Then they just lie there.

After a while, Rachel says, "I'm going to read."

"Me too," Nathan says. They try to prop the flashlights on their chests, but the lights keep falling over. They agree that it's futile. Shutting off their lights, they decide to sleep. Rachel thinks about zipping the sleeping bags together, but Nathan hasn't suggested it, and really what is the point? She lies there, not touching her husband. In the dark Rachel turns to Nathan, "You know they just abandoned this place."

"Who did?" Nathan asks.

"The Pueblo people. They lived here for thousands of years until about 1250 and then they just left. They completely abandoned it. No one knows why. Isn't that interesting?" But he doesn't answer her. His breathing grows heavy. Outside the rain continues to fall. The rhythmic pattern it makes on the tent roof is soothing. Soon she is starting to drift off as well. In the morning this will be over and they can begin their adventure again. They will walk among the ruins. They will learn the ancient ways. Then she hears the drums.

At first she is not sure what she's hearing. It might be rain or thunder but it doesn't stop. It just goes on and on. Finally Rachel gets up. "Nathan, do you hear that?" But he is fast asleep. The rain has let up as Rachel crawls out of the tent onto their muddy campsite. When she stands, she trips over the tent rope, almost falling. "Damn it," she says under her breath. Around her are people in their campers, drinking beer and grilling on their hibachis. Others recline in lounge chairs in their nicely lit tents, complete with mosquito netting, listening to the *Late Show*. Or reading. It's like a little village. Now she can hear the drumming louder and she follows the sound until she comes to a group of about twenty people sitting in a circle, banging on bongos, tambourines, plastic garbage cans, toy drums. A man standing outside the circle sways to the rhythm. "What is this?" Rachel asks.

"It's the summer solstice," the man informs her. "We're with the California Summer Solstice Society."

"And the drumming?"

He smiles at her through luminous white teeth. "We're honoring the sun."

Rachel looks up at the pitch-black sky. "But it's hours until dawn."

"We greet that dawn. It's our tradition. We do it twice a year." There is something strange about this man. It almost seems to Rachel that he is glowing in the dark. It starts to rain again as she makes her way back to their tent. She crawls in. Her sweatpants, her socks are wet. Nathan is breathing heavily, burrowed into his bag. Damp and exhausted, she slips into her sleeping bag and lies awake all night, listening to the drums.

⁕

THE SILENT WHORE—1494

Columbus is returning to find his men. The ones he left behind to build the fort he named La Navidad. In fact he left them so that he would have an excuse to return. It had taken months to convince the king and queen that he needed to return. Now he is back with seventeen ships. But as they anchor in quiet harbors, he sees things that haunt him. Skulls used to hold trinkets, long bones boiling in cauldrons. One young man shows Columbus his back where the flesh has been bitten away. Young boys whom the cannibals have castrated are presented to him. Castration makes them more tender. Columbus cringes before these ghastly stories. Then goes on to perpetrate some of his own.

They come upon the encampment. The wood from the *Santa María* has been burned to ash. Bones are scattered among the lean-tos his men built. Heads sit on wooden spikes. It is clear that he is too late. He hears that the Carib killed everyone at La Navidad. Or that his own men stole women from a nearby village and the villagers killed them. Another rumor hints that they fought among themselves until they were all dead.

Except for one. There is one, the Indians say, who survived. They did not kill him because of his red hair and piercing blue eyes. They believed he was not a real man but a ghost man, a shadow, a god. They tell Columbus that this one preached against the Spanish God. He cursed the place called La Navidad. Some say he escaped into the jungle, taking a wife, and is living in a hut on the shore. Others say he has gone to Cuba and is founding a colony of his own kind. Luis de Torres has been spared. He has been killed. He has been captured and eaten by the Carib. He is living in Cuba with wives and tobacco and gems.

This bothers Columbus more than his men can know. Everyone supposes that Ferdinand and Isabella have financed this second voyage, but in fact the Duke of Seville financed it with the money he confiscated from the Jews of Seville before they were all exiled or killed. What if the first citizen of the New World is a Jew? What a curse this would be. Columbus thinks fondly of his scribe with the delicate white hands and mottled skin. It saddens him that he was left behind and he missed him on his return voyage. But that does not mean that he wants him to be the first settler to survive in the New World.

In his despair he sails on. Columbus loses track of the coves they drift into, the harbors where they seek to anchor but can't because the reefs are too sharp or the sea worms will bore holes into the hulls and sink his ships in a matter of days. He cannot recall all the places where they don't stop. He loses track of the natives who greet him, of the hawk bells and glass beads he hands out, the flowers he has sniffed, the fruits whose sweetness he has never imagined, and the buoyant breasts of the women who climb aboard or wave at them from the shore.

He cannot recall the name of the large nuts filled with sweet milk that he sips after the natives slash them with sharp knives. He cannot remember all of the women who kiss his hands and the gold studs he sees in their noses and ears, the promises made, the treasures that elude him. He is weary of the wonders he has seen. The parrots that speak the same language as the natives who let them perch on their shoulders. The mermaids whom he found ugly and pearls that he believes come from dew raining on the shells of oysters. He passes up bitter leaves that the natives light and draw the smoke into their lungs. All he wants, all that matters to him, and that has ever mattered, is gold. And the men he left behind. His heart aches for them. But there is nothing he can do except journey on.

As Columbus sails through the Caribbean on his endless search for China and silk and gold, the itinerant Jew taunts him. Will the Jew be the one who finds his way to the coffers of the Great Khan? How can Luis de Torres have survived when the others perished? Though in his heart he believes that the Jew is dead, his doubts gnaw at him, keeping him awake at night, pacing the decks so that the crew wonders if he hasn't finally gone mad. They catch glimpses of him staring at the sky as if charting new courses. Columbus knows everything through his instincts. He knows where to sail because he feels it in the wind and the movements of the water. He reads it in the flight of a bird. And just as he knows this, he is sure that the Jew is dead along with all the others left behind. He is as sure of this as he is that he has discovered China.

And yet there are doubts.

He cannot find the palaces of the Great Khan, the men and women with long braids, dressed in silk. It is just this endless sailing. When it is safe, they drop anchor but mostly they keep moving. The reefs are too dangerous, the shore too shallow. Or he spies sea worms, wiggling in the turquoise ocean. When they do stop and go onto the pristine sandy beaches, or when the natives sail to greet them, he asks where the gold can be found. He has no interest in the pearls or the tobacco they bring in their trembling hands.

In his rages he has ears severed, hands chopped off. He has a man's nose cut off to prove that he can. Soon he will be roasting them alive. He will teach them not to lie. Or deny him his precious gold. He will hang anyone who defies him, including his own men. He will force the natives to take him to the Great Khan. But on this second voyage he has another goal besides the gold and the discovery of China and bringing new Christians into the fold.

This voyage is different from his first. This time he has many ships. And there are women on board. Columbus only refers to them in his logs as "the ladies of Castile." Their names do not appear on the passenger or crew manifest. It is not as if they are wives or lovers. Women are bad luck to the sailors, but these he found on the docks at Palos. They are here to keep the men at bay. Their skin is still smooth and they smell of lavender and clove. He knows nothing of them except that they have each agreed to pleasure his men. There are never two women on the same ship at the same time. They only see one another in passing. They are rotated between the ships so that no man grows attached.

But there is one woman who is different from the rest. She does not have the cold, calculating ways of the others. She does not drink or make jokes. One of the women laughed at a sailor's penis and the other sailors had to stop him from slitting her throat and tossing her overboard. Even then she laughed. But this one is possessed with a strange, dark beauty. And silence.

She does not speak. She nods her head and agrees to what is offered. She is not deaf. The sound of plates clattering to the floor makes her jump. But she is silent. Some of the men thought her tongue had been cut out and they pried open her lips, but her tongue was there and ready to welcome them. When they have sex with her, she groans, not with pleasure but in some anguish they cannot understand. So the men know that she has vocal cords. It becomes a game at times. They try to frighten her by jumping out at her in the dark. They try to make her laugh. One puts a knife to her throat and draws a thimbleful of blood, but still she doesn't say a word. And then the sailor, thinking she is a saint, tosses his knife aside and, on his knees, pleads for her forgiveness.

The fact is Inez Cordero does not speak because if she did the truth would come out. And the truth is unspeakable. So her life has become a vicious circle of silence. It is not only that she has caused her father's death but also that she has betrayed him and herself. She banished herself before her family had the chance to banish her. No one knows that she comes from a wealthy family who dealt in books and rare maps, who traded in spices throughout the Mediterranean world. Her father was a man who could take a whiff of stew and know if it was seasoned with cinnamon or cardamom, turmeric or saffron.

But her father is dead. The day after she breathed in his ashes, she took herself to Palos where she earned her living in the ports and on the ships ready to take on a worthless girl. She heard that her mother had made it out of Seville and was living in Lisbon, but she had not gone to look for her. She would never have let her in. For two years Inez had stayed around the docks. Then she found this ship, heading for the New World, and they hired her. At least she would have a bed to sleep in and food to eat. It is odd that she doesn't speak, but it puts her at a slight advantage. Though most men want her for her body, some just want to talk. And because she does not reply, they trust her with their secrets and some even leave her body alone.

Her silence is matched only by her beauty. Her long black hair, her olive skin. Those green eyes. And a body that is full, that men love to cup and knead. A body made for the taking. After Javier, hands did not matter. Men did not matter. In silence she bears her pain. It drives some of the men mad. They taunt her. They try to trick her into speech. But most make silent love to her, then tell her their darkest secrets that they will share only with their confessors. Some of these men she drives mad. Even Columbus enjoys her, and her silence makes him want her all the more. But what entices him the most is that he can tell her anything, and he knows she will not betray him. Columbus does not trust many of his men, but he has come to trust this silent whore. She is the only one he doesn't rotate among his other ships.

When they anchor off the coast of Hispaniola, Columbus brings Inez to his cabin. He offers her a basin of water where she may wash and a comb with which to untangle her matted hair. From his bed he observes her. He is drawn to her green eyes, her lush hair. He pours her a glass of sherry, and as she sips it he begins to confide in her. He shares his fears that he might not find gold. It is possible that he has not reached China. He never writes about this in his journals, but he tells Inez. In his journals he is always on course. He keeps his doubts for himself and his silent whore. He will force his mapmaker and crew to swear that Cuba is not an island but a peninsula of the mainland. He will make it part of Cathay. But he cannot invent gold. What can he bring back of value that will satisfy the king and queen?

When he finally touches her, he is gentle and slow. No one has touched her with such tenderness in years, and though she feels no pleasure, she isn't repulsed either. She does not mind resting in his arms in the softness of a bed and sheets. His skin is smooth, almost hairless and pale, and he smells of the sea. Late into the night, he continues his monologue that is filled with his doubts and his need to return from this voyage with something of value. Night after night after they make love, he confides in her.

Somehow in talking to Inez, Columbus discovers the solution to his dilemma. Though she has never spoken to him, it is as if she has. Looking around one afternoon, he finds his answer. He considers it another sign. He observes the gentle Taino who bring them wild birds and rodents that they roast. Who methodically, futilely search for gold. He gazes at their brown naked bodies and knows what he can bring to his king and queen. He will bring slaves.

After all he has seventeen ships. Surely one can be used to carry the captives. Slaves are as good as gold, aren't they? He orders his men to capture as many Taino and Carib as they are able. For three days they raid villages, putting as many as they can into chains. Those who struggle or try to flee are slashed to pieces. An arm, a foot is chopped off as they run into the jungle where they will bleed to death. Others cower. Children are left behind to starve. But the women are taken. How else can they populate Spain with more slaves?

His men capture five hundred and chain them into the hold of the ship. The prisoners cry and shriek as the ship sails. They do not stop shrieking until the sailors slit two throats. In a matter of days the captives grow ill. They develop skin ulcers that will not heal. They clasp their guts in pain. They cough blood. Half die on the voyage and their bodies are tossed into the sea. The rest perish shortly after they reach Spain. But Columbus will only learn of this failure upon his return. Once he has captured the slaves and sent the ship, heading for home, Columbus believes he has at last succeeded.

He is ready to leave this desolate place, but something catches his eye. Over by the river he sees something moving. A tiny creature crouches by the banks, drinking and bathing itself. At first Columbus thinks it is an animal and perhaps they will kill it for food. But the creature hears the men and toddles toward them on short, stubby legs. It is a child of no more than two, a naked fair-skinned little boy who smiles as he walks in their direction. Columbus looks and sees that the encampment is deserted. No one is here to care for this boy, but somehow he has survived. The child totters toward Columbus, curious, without fear, and then smiling, gazes up at the Admiral of the Ocean Sea with the bluest of eyes.

Inez is also at the river's edge where she has come to bathe, and Columbus shouts to her. When she sees the little boy, she stifles a cry and scoops him into her arms, covering him with her shawl. "I will care for him," Inez says in a clear, crisp voice. These are the first words anyone has heard her speak since the voyage began.

Columbus is not sure what to do with the boy, but Inez convinces him. "Look at his eyes and his fair skin. He is the child of one of ours." While among the men there is speculation about whose child this might be, Inez knows right away. It is not his eyes that tell her. The boy is circumcised, and when she bathes him she sees that it has been done with a swift, sure hand.

Inez takes the boy into her cabin where he nestles against her in her bed. When he grabs at her blouse, she lets him find comfort at her breast, and before they reach Lisbon, her milk begins to flow.

❋

CHAPTER EIGHTEEN

FIXED POINT—1992

Since she's been back in New York, Elena can't get lamb with garbanzo beans out of her mind. She barely remembers the Berber dancers in Fès, the drummers in Jemaa el Fna in Marrakech, the camel trek into the Sahara. Since she and Derek have returned from Morocco, she can only think about the lamb stew. Elena rarely thinks about food, but now she thinks about it all the time.

It is a warm summer day and, even as she walks to the class she is about to teach at the Ballet Extension School, the savory dish is on her mind. They've been back for weeks, but she recalls little of their ten-day jaunt beyond the swirls of spices like a genie rising from the tagine, the aromas of turmeric and ginger, cumin and cardamom that filled her head. The salt of the lamb, the sweetness of the apricot. It seems impossible to her. How many times had visitors begged her grandmother for the recipe to her lamb with garbanzos? Or her chicken that falls off the bone?

She'd seen guests in their home, their mouths watering at the flavors, begging to know. How many times had her grandmother laughed in their faces? Maybe if someone put her feet to a fire she'd tell. How can the family's secret recipe that her grandmother guarded with her life—and the recipe that everyone believes died with her—be served in a Moroccan restaurant that they'd stumbled upon in a maze of dark alleyways and narrow streets in Tangier?

Elena cannot understand. Throughout their trip through Morocco, to Fès, down to Merzouga and the Sahara where the sand covered the

roads and got into their teeth, across the Atlas Mountains and finally
to Marrakech, Elena had been obsessed with this one fact. And now it
is the only thing she remembers of their entire journey. Not the wild
love they made in Malaga, not the ferry crossing past Gibraltar or that
strange giant circle around the moon their last night in the desert,
none of it made a lasting impression on Elena except for her first taste
of that lamb stew.

And now wherever she is—at Gristedes getting groceries, at Lincoln Center at the ballet, in bed with Derek—the past comes streaming back. Moments she has long ago forgotten or put into a vault inside
her brain that she hadn't intended to open. Memories and secrets that
she sealed away to such an extent that it seemed as if they happened to
someone else. All of this comes roaring like a locomotive through her
mind.

On the corner of Eighth Avenue, Elena lights a cigarette. She has a
few moments to smoke before she reaches the school, which is located
on Fifty-Seventh Street and Ninth Avenue in an old loft building that
had once been a millinery factory. It is a large room, really, with mirrors
on one side and ballet barres along the wall. There is a dressing room
and a small office. A former ballet dancer who had a semi-illustrious
career opened this studio for young dancers. All of the teachers are
former members of the ballet corps.

Crushing out her cigarette in front of the building where dozens of
other butts lie, she goes inside. She's already a few minutes late. This
isn't unusual. She's been warned about being late before. Perhaps it's
just a matter of time before she'll lose this last link she has to the world
of dance.

Taking off her coat, Elena hangs it up in the dressing room. She is
already wearing her black tights and leotard. She slips off her sneakers
and puts on her ballet shoes. She used to spend so many hours sewing
and gluing her shoes herself, putting in padding just where she needed
it, replacing the ribbons. Now they are worn down, frayed, another
sign of her diminishing life. Flexing both of her feet, for they ache as
usual, she walks into the room. Eleven girls and two boys, aged twelve

to fifteen, are in various poses of stretching. Some have a leg on the barre; others are bent forward. A few are on the ground, legs spread. Most wear leg warmers.

As she walks into the studio, there is a flurry of "Good morning, Ms. Torres" and "Hello, Ms. Torres." Elena smiles, and then claps her hands.

"Against the wall," she says, "in second position. Now pick a spot and hold it. Heads up." She walks past them, raising a chin, straightening a spine. It is hard not to look at these children and have a glimpse of what lies ahead. She examines the turnout of their hips and legs. The lift of their chins. In the next two years half will drop out. Others will begin to experience problems with their feet and spines. One might make it to the ballet corps. In her years of teaching, Elena has only had two students go on to dance with major companies. She looks at these children's faces and feels as if she is selling snake oil.

Tilly Wilson stands, arms out, feet splayed like a crooked cross. And poor Sterling Anderson. His nervous mother sits, plucking lint off her dress. She stays for his lessons on the excuse that it will be too short a time for her to go home. Sara Murphy is flapping her arms like wings. All that girl can do is pretend she is Odette in *Swan Lake.*

Most of them saw *Swan Lake* and maybe the *Nutcracker* and decided they were going to be dancers. Others, like Elena, had a different trajectory. She didn't even know what a ballet was when she began to dance. She just twirled around in her family's trailer, spinning on one foot. She fell in love with the movement of her body. She flowed through rooms. She soared on roads on the way to school until it began to occur to her that she could spin right out of this life and into another.

As Elena's legs grew longer, her gym teacher thought that she might like to dance. There were classes in Santa Fe about forty minutes from Entrada, and dutifully every Tuesday and Thursday afternoon her mother, Rosa, drove her down once she'd finished her shift cleaning rooms in the Taos hotel.

Elena was only nine when her lessons at Miss Marilyn's Dance Studio began. She had no idea if she wanted to be a dancer. She didn't even know what that meant. But she knew she wanted to dance. Then Miss Marilyn took her to see *Giselle* when it played at the Santa Fe Opera. Elena was twelve at the time and she spent the two hours riveted by the story of the peasant girl with a weak heart and a passion for dance who sacrifices all for love. From that moment on, for Elena there was no going back.

Now as she looks over her roomful of students, Elena thinks back to the first time, when she'd come to spend her summer in New York. She was only fourteen, a wisp of a girl, as if hands could break her, her father used to say. When she was seventeen she'd come back for a year that has extended itself into the rest of her life, except for a brief return to pack up her things and those occasional sojourns home.

Her father drove her to Albuquerque where the School of American Ballet was hosting auditions. Though he drove in silence, he had tears in his eyes the whole way. "You are my little girl," Rafael Torres told his daughter even as she was drifting away from him. It was as if by making this simple drive down from the mountains, the rest of his life and hers were all mapped out, and in a way, they were. Her dance instructor arranged for Elena to have a shot. "She's a natural," Miss Marilyn, as all her students called her, said. Miss Marilyn had once danced with the New York City Ballet, and then she had a baby and moved to Santa Fe where she raised her daughter alone. Years later Elena heard rumors that the daughter was Balanchine's child.

Elena had been so nervous she'd thrown up twice the night before her audition. She'd stretched all night long until she could lay completely flat, legs in a split, on the floor, but now her muscles ached. She'd slept in her leotard. She'd been up at four though they didn't have to be there until ten. She made her father drive at first light and he'd driven at a snail's pace because there was ice on the road.

When they arrived, her father waited in the hallway with the other parents. "I'll be right here," he told her. Taking a deep breath, Elena walked into the stark room where Miss Marilyn and a man and a woman she'd never seen before sat on folding chairs. Elena was still sick to her stomach.

There were four other children in the room. One girl she recognized from her ballet class. A nice girl with a toothy grin and, Elena thought, rather floppy arms, but perhaps she was just jealous as she often was of other girls who received Miss Marilyn's praise. Since she'd first seen Miss Marilyn in that burgundy velvet tutu with her pink tights and toe shoes, a costume she'd worn when she danced in *Giselle,* Elena wanted to be her daughter. Miss Marilyn always came to class wearing a lovely tutu and tights. Some days she looked like a black swan. Some days she was a Spanish dancer. Elena was amazed at how easily it was to turn into something else just by changing your clothes.

Elena was expecting a piece of music. Instead they asked her to stand before them. The man, who wore a gray suit and looked like a school principal, examined her turnout and ran his fingers down her long legs. He asked her to rise on her toes and bend so that he could see the flex in her feet. He spent a long time on her neck. Elena was glad that she'd pinned up her hair that morning.

Then he asked them to assume second position and raise a leg. As they stood, legs raised, the man walked around. When he came to Elena, he pushed her leg up farther than she thought it could go, but she did not lose her balance. He turned her to the left and right, still holding her leg in the air. He touched his finger to her chin, raising it slightly. The man walked away from her and she held the pose. After a few moments he looked at her again and she put her leg down. He did the same with them all, and then he asked a boy and a girl to leave. The girl burst into tears. The boy seemed relieved. He dashed out as if none of this had ever been his idea.

The remaining three included the girl with the toothy grin. She didn't want that girl to get the scholarship to go to New York. She hoped the girl would smile and show her buckteeth, but the girl had long ago stopped smiling when things mattered.

While the man told them what to do, the woman, who wore black slacks and very red lipstick, was making notes. From time to time she nodded at the man or the man nodded at her. Miss Marilyn sat with her spine erect, as she always did. She'd injured her spine years ago. But

Miss Marilyn regretted nothing. Not even when her daughter moved back to New York to study piano. "You are all my little girls," Miss Marilyn liked to say.

The man in the suit told the third girl to go and she left, stone-faced. Now it was just Elena and the toothy girl who wouldn't smile. He sent them to the barre where they performed various movements. It was so easy Elena almost forgot she was doing something important. After a few more minutes the man stepped back and thanked them. "You'll get a letter from us," he said. As they were leaving, Miss Marilyn smiled but, because they were both her students, Elena couldn't tell who she was smiling at.

Outside her father waited and they drove home, but this time he wanted to talk. He asked her questions, but Elena was silent. Nothing was what she'd expected and the whole experience made her sad and made her feel as if her life was going to be sad and as if it belonged to someone else. Three weeks later a letter arrived offering her a summer scholarship to study at the School of American Ballet. The toothy girl didn't get accepted and soon afterward stopped going to Miss Marilyn's, but now Miss Marilyn worked with Elena all the more fiercely. "Hold your head up," Miss Marilyn said to her ten times in every class. "Show everyone your beautiful neck." Miss Marilyn ran her finger slowly along the front of Elena's throat just to remind her of how long it was.

+

"All right," Elena says, "we're going to work on spotting for spins." She moves around the room, or rather glides. It is how she always moves. The way Miss Marilyn taught her. Head up, feet sliding along the floor. Never move your torso. Just your arms. When it is Tilly's turn to cross the room, Elena follows close behind. "Chin up. Eyes straight forward. *En pointe.* Be very straight, Tilly, very tall." Tilly's eyes flutter, the way they always do when Elena is behind her, as if she is going to cry. But Elena doesn't care. She pushes Tilly the hardest.

Now she wraps her hands around the girl's tiny waist. "All right, spin, head forward. Spin, head forward." The girl spins like a top.

Of all of them, Tilly has the most promise. She has that long black hair, those long legs, and an excellent extension. Everything about her feels like a dancer. It is the odd thing about a dancer. You never look at someone and think, "Oh, that's a teacher or that's a doctor." But a dancer always looks like a dancer. Of course it is in her body, isn't it? But it is more than that. It is also the way the gaze is always set at some distant point in space. It is one of the first things a dancer learns to do when spinning. To have a fixed point in the distance so that you don't fall. Even years later, many of them, herself included, can't stop looking at that spot.

+

Patterns, paths, destinies, song lines. Elena once believed that dance was her destiny. As a girl she danced in sneakers during the powwows at Taos Pueblo, leaping up from the sidelines, her feet beating the earth, her body hunched into the form of a rabbit, rising into that of an antelope. She found the place inside of herself that could not be separated from her. She is the dance. The dance is she. It is her spirit path.

But she hadn't needed to find her destiny. It was already in her feet, her arms. As a girl at the powwows she couldn't sit still, as a scholarship student at Miss Marilyn's Dance Studio, and later in New York, she danced because it was the only thing she was meant to do. The only thing she really could do. At times from the hilltops near her family's trailer she watched eagles circle, and she'd spread her arms and twirl and dip. It was as if she could fly. And why couldn't she? Why couldn't she soar?

When she was a child, Elena had dreams that she could fly. She could see herself gazing down at the deserts and oceans, rain forests and grasslands. Sometimes the dreams were very specific. She was flying over the Gobi or the Amazon. But she couldn't get lost because in her belly button she had navigational redial. She just had to press a finger to her stomach, and it would take her home.

Now nothing brings her home. Not even Miguel. Nothing except perhaps lamb tagine. It's all changed. Her life had one direction and now it has another. She's surrounded by ghosts. In Morocco her grandmother caught up with her. This was the first time her grandmother came to her, though Elena often sees her mother. Once in a dream (or was it a dream?) she woke to find her mother sitting at the edge of her bed, stroking her hand. Her mother came to tell her something, but what could it be?

+

After class she heads along Broadway. She is vaguely hungry. But for Elena, hunger is always vague. She has to remember to eat. It is like someone who has to remember to breathe. She stops at a restaurant near Lincoln Center where she orders a Caesar salad without looking at the menu. "And water. Tap water." The waiter nods and the salad seems to come too quickly as if it has already been made. For a few moments she pushes the lettuce around on her plate. She takes a few bites, then shoves it away.

The busboy comes by. "Are you finished?" he asks. He has a slight accent. He is Hispanic, tall and lanky. He looks at her with pleading eyes. Somehow he is hoping she isn't finished. He is hoping that she will eat more. She is bone-thin, fragile, as breakable as a young bird. The boy looks at her with concern. "Yes," she says, "I'm done."

When she gets home there is one message on her machine. Her brother's voice speaks to her. "Hey sis, I still haven't heard from you about that bicycle helmet. I really want to make you one. Just tell me your secret wish and I'll put it right on your helmet. Free of charge. Just a little regalo from your hermano."

Roberto is wooing her. Trying to win her back. It has never worked before and it won't work now. Roberto is an airbrush artist who paints anything anybody wants on the hoods and doors and trunks of their cars, and he makes a killing every spring. He's done well with cars but now has the idea of making a fortune with airbrushed bike helmets. He believes that soon everyone will be wearing bike helmets. America is so safety conscious. That is his theory. Look at what happened with seat belts. It's against the law not to wear one now. Soon it will be that way with bike helmets.

Elena laughs at the notion of seat belts. Given everything that has happened in her life, the protection of a seat belt is an afterthought. Helmets for bicycles and motorcycles. Roberto thinks he'll get rich by customizing them. That will be his big thing. He knows that Elena likes to ride her bicycle around Central Park so he sent her pictures of his samples. She has yet to order one. He wants to put her hopes and dreams on her helmet. But what would they be? Ballet slippers, toe shoes? A butterfly. A migrating monarch. Or some darker images. A shattered ankle. Broken dreams. A girl with blood between her thighs. Secrets never shared.

Roberto taunts her in the phone messages he leaves and the notes he writes. She fears that he'll find a way to worm back into her heart and make her miss the place she's spent so many years trying to get away from. She never answers the notes he writes and she never returns his calls. Nothing he does will ever change anything. Nothing will ever make things right. All Elena knows is that the farther she gets from Entrada de la Luna, the better off she is.

As her brother rambles on, Elena stares at the only picture she brought with her to New York. It is a portrait of her father when he was stationed in Korea, years before she was born, before the booze and bad luck got to him. He's a man she barely recognizes, smiling from ear to ear, with Rita Moreno on his arm. The picture is signed, "To Rafael, with love, from Rita." Her father used to hint that there had been something between him and Rita Moreno, but with her father one never knew.

At last her brother finishes his message. Elena shakes her head. That's the thing about her brother. He's a dreamer too. Then she pushes the button and a recording says, "To delete all old messages, please press delete." She hits delete and pours her first glass of wine.

CHAPTER NINETEEN

THE GOLDILOCKS ZONE—1992

M iguel is in the Goldilocks Zone. In astronomy the Goldilocks Zone is the area within a star's orbit in which it
might be possible for life to be sustained. It can be neither
too hot nor too cold. It has to have just the right mix of life-sustaining
gases. Like Goldilocks sampling porridge and slipping in and out of
beds, it has to be just right. And that is how things are for Miguel right
now. He has a good job. It pays him well. He likes Mrs. Rothstein and
even enjoys the boys. School is good. He has found the place where he
wants to be.

He has gotten into his routine, and it is an easy one for him. After
school he drives his lowrider to pick up Jeremy and Davie at Magical
Years. He's got an old booster seat for Davie, and he makes Jeremy
put on his seat belt. He drives slowly and carefully because if the cops
stop him, he's finished. They may as well put him away for life. Their
mother is usually out back when he gets there, in her studio, doing
whatever she does, but she leaves a plate of Pillsbury cookies that she
sticks in the oven herself.

As he pulls up in front of Magical Years, the boys are in the yard.
They rush to him. Jeremy attacks Miguel's leg and Davie tries to leap
on his back. "Okay, okay," Miguel calls out, laughing as he peels the boys
off his body. "What're we going to be today? Ninjas or Spacewalkers?"

They thrust their fists into the air. "Ninjas," Davie shouts. "No *Star
Trek*," Jeremy proclaims, his dark eyes darting, that angry look in his
face. He gives Davie a punch in the arm like an exclamation point.

Miguel sees the tears well up in Davie's eyes, tears he holds back as Miguel often has. Miguel holds up his finger. "Do not do that, Jeremy, or we won't do anything today except your multiplication tables." He stares the boy down. His eyes are X-rays. Once he has them in his power, he shakes the car keys in his hand. "Okay, let's go."

And they race to the car, punching and kicking each other, but playfully this time, as Miguel gets into the driver's seat. Even with the boys' quarreling in the backseat, he likes the drive to Colibri Canyon. The roads are winding as they head up toward the mountains. The sky is blue—that big New Mexico sky—and everything seems right in the world. As he pulls up in front of the house, he turns to the boys and tells them to go play in the yard. He'll get them some drinks and be outside soon.

+

When he walks into the kitchen, he finds Mrs. Rothstein at the sink in an orange bikini. She is squeezing lemons into a large pitcher filled with ice. He stops dead in his tracks. For a moment he thinks she is naked, she is so scantily clad and the color of the bikini seems to blend into her bronzed skin. He braces himself as she turns to greet him. "Ah, here you are," she says. Miguel steps away. The bikini barely covers her ample breasts. The bottom is just a thin triangle of cloth. His eyes trace the scar across her belly. Her skin is smooth and slathered in cream. He is so close he can smell her. She smells as tart as a lemon. Yet oily too. He's about to swoon. "Snack time," she says, smiling. "I'm making lemonade."

She's been sunbathing, perhaps all afternoon. She has raccoon circles around her eyes, from wearing glasses he assumes. She is at least twice his age but he finds himself staring at the crease between her buoyant breasts. She is fit and muscular as if she once trained for a weight-lifting contest. Her athletic build, the whiff of almond soap, and her sweat surprise him. And the scent of lemons is everywhere.

He takes the iced glass that she offers. It is cold to the touch, and his fingers tremble. "So what's the plan?" Mrs. Rothstein asks.

The plan? With the boys? "I'm not sure. They're fighting about it.

I came for tinfoil. We're making swords." She points to a drawer. "I think they'll be Ninjas today." Mrs. Rothstein nods, but Miguel is fairly certain she has no idea what he is talking about. "And cardboard?"

"In the garage. I'm going to take a shower," and she disappears down the corridor, her buttocks rocking as she walks away. Miguel has to catch his breath. This is not normal, he tells himself. It isn't normal that she should be waiting for him almost naked. He has a hard-on, but he can't bring himself to look down. In fact he wants to go into the bathroom and jerk off. Or just get into his car and drive away. It seems to him that there is something unnatural here and that he needs to be careful from now on.

He wonders if he isn't here for more than babysitting. Has he walked into some weird trap? Something he'll have to pay for later? He begins to sweat, then goes outside to make swords. They settle on Ninjas. Jeremy is Leonardo and Davie is Michelangelo. Miguel is the rat sensei, Master Splinter, trained in the art of ninjutsu. As they are fashioning swords out of cardboard and aluminum foil, Miguel can feel her watching him. Or is he just imagining it. Once or twice he looks toward the bedroom curtains and sees them flutter. Just as he and the boys are about to do battle, Rachel appears with a tray of lemonade and gingersnaps and a glass of milk for Jeremy, which she places on the ground. She is dressed now in jeans and a T-shirt. Her nipples spring forward. Miguel gasps, trying to shift his gaze.

As Rachel turns to go, she says, "Would you like to stay for dinner? It's Friday night and we all eat together. Nathan should be home soon."

Miguel isn't sure what to say. Normally he eats dinner on Friday night with his mother, but he really wants to stay, if only to be near Mrs. Rothstein. "I need to call my mother. She's expecting me."

"Of course. You can always use the phone. We'll eat as soon as my husband gets home."

Miguel picks up the wall phone in the kitchen. At first his mother objects, but then he convinces her. It's for his job, after all, and he assumes he'll be paid. "It's fine," he tells Mrs. Rothstein, "I can stay."

For the few weeks he's been working for the Rothsteins, he has yet to meet Dr. Rothstein. It seems odd because sometimes he stays until seven or even eight o'clock, doing his homework while the boys get ready for bed. He has seen Mrs. Rothstein whisper on the phone to her husband. He has seen her put the boys on the phone to say good night to their father. Then she will get back on and speak more sharply in a high-pitched voice that seems troubled or just tired.

He wonders about Dr. Rothstein. What kind of a doctor is he? A pediatrician? An orthopedist? Is he handsome? Miguel can't envision Dr. Rothstein at all. He has no idea what kind of man he might be. He has seen no pictures of him in the house. No snapshots of them all fishing somewhere, going camping. Even his mother has kept some pictures of Miguel with his father and there is even one of the three of them together for Miguel's first communion. He wonders what kind of time, if any, Dr. Rothstein spends with his boys.

An hour goes by and then another. The boys sit glued to the TV. It is getting late and Miguel is hungry. He wants to go home and eat his mother's Friday-night stew. He wants to leave, but he said he'd stay. It is hard for Miguel to know what to do. The phone rings. Once more he hears Mrs. Rothstein talking. There is an angry lilt to her voice this time.

After a few moments she hangs up and comes into the living room. "Turn off the TV," Mrs. Rothstein says. "We'll eat without Daddy." The boys moan. Jeremy hurls a softball across the room, and then curls up like a roly-poly bug when it's poked. "Come on. Let's eat," she calls. They clomp into the dining room where the table has been set with china, placemats, and flowers. Mrs. Rothstein takes out a match and prepares to light the candles. She closes her eyes, whispering what Miguel assumes must be a prayer.

Miguel is surprised. "Do you light candles every night?" he asks her, though he'd never seen her do so before.

Mrs. Rothstein shakes her head. "No, only on Friday."

Miguel laughs under his breath. "That's funny. My mother does too."

Rachel looks at him oddly. "And why is that?"

Miguel shrugs. "I don't know. We just do. Why do you light candles on Friday?"

And she keeps staring at Miguel, "Because we are Jews. And you?"
Miguel shakes his head. "It's just what everyone in my town does."

Rachel nods as she serves him a plate of roast chicken and rice with
steamed vegetables. It is buttery and delicious. He gobbles it down and
is pleased when she offers him more. "Here," she says, "there's plenty."
When she serves him, she leaves little for her husband to eat when he
gets home. Miguel wonders if he is going to be eating out that night. He
is a doctor. Doctors have emergencies all the time, don't they? Things
that keep them from coming home.

+

It is dark as he heads back to Entrada, but the sky is filled with clouds.
He expects that it will rain tonight. That is good. They need the rain.
But Miguel doesn't like a night when he can't see the stars. He drives
up the road with his radio on. Normally he'd gaze at the sky, but now
he just keeps his eyes on the road. It is late when he pulls into Entrada
and he decides to stop at Roybal's to pick up some milk and bananas
for breakfast, and a can of beer if he can convince the old man that it
is for his mother.

As he walks in, the old man is at the cash register, smoking and
drinking a beer himself. He is staring at his old and tattered family tree
and looks up, startled. He hacks, trying to catch his breath. Then he
wags a finger at Miguel. "I've got something for you."

The old man goes into the back and comes out with the mail. Half of
Entrada gets their mail at Roybal's store. Nobody really has addresses
so it is easier for the postman to drop most of it off here. A lot of the
inhabitants want to avoid the mail anyway. It is usually a bill that won't
get paid or a notice for deadbeat dads to appear in court. Or a bank
that's about to foreclose on your land. He hands Miguel an electric
bill marked "Final Notice" and Miguel knows that the electricity will
probably be turned off again. There is some junk mail that he riffles
through.

Stuck between a flyer for funeral insurance and one for low-cost
car insurance is a postcard. It falls out of the small stack and onto the
counter. It is addressed to him and Miguel sees the foreign stamp. The

image is a fortress, golden in the moonlight. Behind it is the glistening sea. "Greetings from Morocco" with a big letter "E."

He wonders why she bothers. She never calls and he never sees her, but she sends him these cards. She hardly says a word. She sends monuments, statues, rolling hills. A vineyard. The sea. But never any people. It is as if she goes to places where no one lives. Maybe where somebody has dropped a neutron bomb. She has never sent him a single face.

When he gets home, his mother is asleep on the couch. He goes into his room and puts the postcard into the shoebox he keeps under his bed. It is where he keeps all of her postcards. He flips through them like a dealer with a deck of cards. In the morning he'll find out where Morocco is.

That night Miguel has his first wet dream about Mrs. Rothstein. She is in her orange bikini and turns, falling into his arms. Her skin, her hair are filled with the scent of lemons. Even though he thinks that you can't smell in your dreams, he smells the lemons.

CHAPTER TWENTY

LISBON—1496

It is good to have the streets beneath her feet, the cobblestones, and the winding paths as she walks from the river into the narrow streets of the Alfama. She is glad not to be on the ship with the stench of sailors, reaching for her, touching her. These streets are not familiar the way the streets of Seville once were and she is lost in the maze. She has the address for her uncle's house and assumes he will take her in. Around her neck she carries the pouch with the gold she's earned for her trouble. In her arms she carries the child.

Benjamin nestles against her breasts. She knows he will not wake in her arms. He wakes only if she puts him down. It seems to Inez that if she holds him, he will just sleep. As she scurries along, passersby glance her way. A man with a cart lets her pass in front of him. An old woman smiles. They see that she cradles a child. No one doubts that he is hers. And once they hear her story, they will not doubt it at all. Everyone knows that the women who sailed with explorers, unless they were the captain's wife, did not go as cooks or chambermaids. There is only one reason why a sailor would tolerate bringing bad luck on board.

Inez laughs to herself as she makes her way along the streets. After all the men who have touched her, raped her, sodomized her, come inside of her, not one has left her with a child. It's true she had been careful, counting her days with the moon. She never let a sailor touch her during the new moon and she always rinsed with a vinegar douche. And she made sure that no man left himself inside her, though once or twice she feared someone had. Her first month at sea she did not bleed.

After that she bled as she always had. This was her penance—to be touched by many and mother to none. Until now. As she makes her way through the streets of Lisbon, Inez Cordero vows that no other man, except for her son, Benjamin, will ever touch her again. She will devote herself to the boy she found orphaned on a beach and to her God. This is more than she deserves.

She stops to ask a woman for directions and learns that the street she is looking for isn't in the Alfama. She must climb one of the hills of the city, heading into the wealthier, higher neighborhoods. It is there where the Jews make their homes. Her uncle, who left Spain before the expulsion, has obviously done well. But it is an old address and, for a moment, she wonders if he or his family still live there. Then she begins her climb. The hill is steep. Around her black slaves push carts laden with food from the markets up to the homes of their masters. One slip and they will slide back down the hill along with their carts. Many citizens of Lisbon have died in this way—being struck by runaway carts.

From windows above, chamber pots are emptied into the streets and the cobbled walks are slick with their filth. The heat and stench almost overwhelm her. At last in the darkness she comes to an inn. The Three Cocks Inn. She laughs again. Fitting place for a slut. She will spend her first night here where she will bathe and eat, then continue on her way to where she is headed. At the door she raises the large knocker. The innkeeper takes one look at her and shakes his head. He does not want a woman who is alone to stay in his lodgings. Then she shows him the child. "We have just returned from a long journey." She touches her hair, her skirts. "I would like to bathe."

The room is small but efficient, and the innkeeper finds an old crib that he dusts off. She is so touched by the gesture that she almost weeps. He tells her that he is heating the water for her bath. He hands her a gray cloth and a bar of soap. He leads her into the kitchen where a large tub stands off to the side. Steam rises from the water. There is a screen placed in front of it. And a linen cloth with which to dry herself and the child. "No one will bother you here." Inez dips her finger into the water. It is too hot for the child. She will bathe first, then the boy.

Besides, Benjamin is asleep. There is no point in waking him. She looks around her. The door is closed and a curtain drawn. No one can see her. The water is scalding hot, but she doesn't mind. Her flesh burns, but she takes on whatever pain she can.

As Inez sinks into the water, and the heat rises; her skin is aflame. She takes the bar of coarse soap and begins to scrub. As she scrubs, she feels the hands of Javier when he first touched her flesh. Those loving touches that made her alive, and made her open up, and then left her alone with her unspeakable crime. The men on the ship grabbing her, the oily hands that tugged at her flanks, the dirty hands that caressed her thighs, the rough hands, the calloused hands, the salty hands, the smelly hands. The hands that stank of fish and the sea, others that smelled as sweet as the wind. In the dark she knows the men by their fleshy palms, their sweaty skin, their fetid smells, their dankness, their dryness, their softness, their harshness. Their names are irrelevant, their faces unknown. What she knows of them is their hands.

As Inez washes, she scrubs them away. The rough touches, the pinches, the tugs, the fingernails, the cruel jabs, the hair pulled, the nipples squeezed. She works the soap deep into her flesh until she thinks she will emerge raw, red as a cooked lobster, but bathes until Benjamin wakes. Then she takes him and gently dips him into the water that has now cooled. With the soap on her hands, not the rough bar the innkeeper has given her, she slides her fingers over his limbs that have grown plump on her milk, his blond baby curls. He stares up at her with his steady blue eyes, his small carefully pruned penis, his buttocks where there has been a persistent rash, his little nails and snotty nose and dirty ears.

He has never had a warm bath. He has only been washed in the cold brine of the sea. Now his little body relaxes. He gives himself over to her. His will be the last hands that will ever touch her, the last lips that will ever suckle at her nipples. The final pleasure she will feel. No man will ever put his hands on her body again. She bathes every inch of him and when she is done, she dries them both, and is surprised at what it feels like to be clean once again.

That night she feeds Benjamin rice cooked in sweetened milk and looks at the delight in his eyes. The innkeeper's wife has prepared for her a mutton chop with a potato and a mug of red wine. She has forgotten what kindness is. In her bed that night she cannot stop weeping. In the morning at first light she is on her way. She does not have far to travel, only a few streets more and her journey is done.

The mezuzah on the doorpost surprises her. She assumed they were done with such things. But there it is. When she knocks, she expects a servant to open the door, but the woman who answers looks at Inez and gasps. At first Inez doesn't recognize her because she has aged in a few short years, but her mother recognizes her. Without a word she slams the door in her daughter's face. Inez waits, trying to catch her breath, and then knocks again.

This time her mother flings open the door and shouts at her. She calls her a murderess and a whore. She's about to slam the door again when Inez opens her shawl, revealing the child and the purse filled with ducats of gold.

+

Without a word Inez settles in. Her mother has her only servant, Amelia, lead them to two dark, windowless rooms off the courtyard where her uncle, a merchant, stored the spices that were his trade. It is Amelia who explains to Inez that her uncle slit his own throat rather than worship the Christian god and that his family fled to Antwerp on a ship laden with pepper and clove. In the past few years her mother has remained here, in seclusion and alone. Dona Olivia never asks about Benjamin's origins or who his father is. But though she can't acknowledge her daughter, she accepts this child as her grandson. Still Dona Olivia will not permit her daughter to inhabit the upstairs rooms where she dwells in solitude, but Inez doesn't mind. She is grateful for the storage rooms and glad that she hasn't been put out onto the street.

Inez sweeps out her rooms with a hard straw broom. She finds old bedding that isn't being used. She sets up a small table with a lamp for herself. In a storage cellar she finds an old cradle that she cleans and polishes and stuffs into it a pillow she makes of goose down. She sleeps on a bed that smells of cinnamon with her son at her side. Then she begins to take charge of the house. In the kitchen she discovers bins filled with potatoes and rotting fruit. She throws most of it away. She goes to the market and brings home baskets of rice, tomatoes, and squash. She teaches Amelia how to roast a chicken in a pot with saffron and rice.

On Fridays she does the laundry by hand. She changes the sheets. She bathes herself and her son. At dusk every Friday she turns the portrait of the Virgin to the wall and follows her mother down the five steps—one for each book of the Torah—into her uncle's secret cellar. Here the two women light the candles and say their prayers. It is often the only time that they are in the same room during the entire week. Beyond their prayers they never say a word.

Inez rarely talks to anyone and certainly not to her own mother. Her mother only speaks to her in curses. Or addresses her in the third person as if she isn't in the room. Otherwise Dona Olivia will have nothing to do with the daughter who was dead to her four years ago as she watched her husband consigned to the flames. They live in a war of wills, locked in a hatred for which Inez does not blame her mother. But the silence between them does not bother Inez either. She has grown accustomed to silence in the years since her lover's betrayal and her father's fiery death. It is speech that is foreign to her.

In her mother's house Inez devotes herself to one thing only: the raising of her son. His childhood is confined to the walled courtyard of the house. Inez knows what happened to the children of the Spanish Jews when they entered Portugal in 1492. How they were torn from their parents, dosed with holy water, and taken by ships to Africa. How the virgin girls were sold to the Arabs in Morocco, and the boys became slaves in Cape Verde. She's heard tales of Jewish children shipped off to the island of São Tomé where they are left to languish or be swallowed by giant lizards that roam its hillsides. Housemaids warn Inez that when the children reach the age of four the soldiers come knocking on the houses of anyone they suspect to be practicing Jews. And that child will never be seen again.

She keeps Benjamin hidden in the inner rooms of the courtyard. During the day she plays games with him and when they both weary of this, she gets him a small, wiry puppy that they name Fury. Benjamin can spend hours running through the house with Fury nipping at his heels. Inez bribes Amelia not to mention the child to anyone. He spends most of his time in the kitchen, watching his mother preparing meals. Once a day he is allowed into the courtyard to play and be in the sun, then he is shuttled back into the darkness of their rooms.

When he turns three, she can barely contain her fear. For almost a year Inez struggles to decide. At night she tosses and turns, wondering when the soldiers will come. Though she never speaks of this to her mother, for they remain in their silent battle, they both know what she must do. Inez tries to prepare for the day. She goes to church. She prays. She begs for guidance. And then forgiveness. Because she does not know her son's birthday, she has given it the date when she found him on the island, alone in the New World.

On his fourth birthday Inez gives him his bath. She makes it warm so that it reminds him of the first bath she ever gave him, and he grows sleepy. She adds almond milk to make his skin and hair soft. She dresses him in her favorite blue suit to set off his eyes. She makes the special cake he loves—custard with cinnamon in a fluffy pastry shell. She delights as he devours his cake—piece after piece, his fingers sticky with pudding. She does not tell him to stop or that he has had enough. When it is time, Dona Olivia kisses the boy good night, tears flowing down her cheeks. Then Inez takes Benjamin up to their room. She dims the lights and says her prayers. She holds him in her arms and rocks him as she sings his favorite lullabies. His little body grows warm and sleepy in her arms. She lays her head against his sweaty brow as tears slide down her face.

Then she places a pillow against her belly and eases him facedown onto the pillow. "Hug Mommy," she tells him. As Benjamin wraps his little arms around her, she presses him to her, gently at first, then more tightly, until she is crushing his face into the pillow. Tears stream down her face as he begins to struggle in her final embrace. He tries to push away. With his tiny fists he pounds her arms. She hugs him more tightly even as he kicks and slaps her. She is stunned by the life force contained in this tiny frame.

And then, still weeping, she lets him go. She cannot do this. She cannot kill this spirit, no matter what fate awaits them. She will keep him at home. She will hide him. She will find whatever ways she can to keep him safe. He is limp, sobbing as she releases him, laying him back upon the bed. "Mami," he says, touching her face, "I couldn't breathe."

"I know, m'hijo. I hugged you too hard." She tells him she is sorry. It won't happen again. In the morning she finds her mother, sobbing in a parlor chair. Inez leads the boy into the room with her, shaking her head. "I could not," she says, some of the few words she and her mother have exchanged since Inez and Benjamin arrived. And, relieved, Dona Olivia looks away.

That afternoon Inez has the mezuzah removed from the doorpost of the house. The space it leaves is covered in cement. Everything that identifies them as Jews is put into a sack. A pair of candlesticks Dona Olivia brought with her from Seville, Diego Cordero's old tefillin. For the next several years, Benjamin will not go outside. And Inez will rarely let him out of her sight until the day he buries her. All of her son's tutors, his doctors when he needs one, which is rarely, for he is a very healthy boy, even his fencing teacher, come to the house. She monitors all of his lessons. Before he is ten he is fluent in French and Portuguese as well as Spanish. He reads Latin and Greek and understands higher mathematics. He can identify all the plants in the garden and the birds in the air. He takes a passing interest in the solar system and learns what is known of the moon and the stars. And she teaches him the secrets of chocolate.

Inez Cordero brought back with her from the New World a bag of these beans along with the knowledge of how to roast them and grind them into a fine powder. Columbus served them to the king and queen of Spain, who were unimpressed with the bitter brew. But Inez experimented. She added honey but found it too viscous. She tried guava juice, but it tasted strange. Then she added warm, sweetened milk to the concoction and brought it to her mother, whose eyes widened as she sipped. Every night from then on her mother could not go to sleep without it.

On market days Inez goes to the docks and purchases sacks of raw cacao. When Benjamin is older, she will bring him with her, teaching him to haggle for the best cacao seeds. And he will watch, amazed, that his mother can argue with the most hardened merchant. She teaches Benjamin what she knows of these beans that grow only in the warmest, wettest climates. She teaches him how to melt the fine powder in hot water and how to make it into a creamy paste. How to add nuts and cherries. How to put it into pastry shells. And she tells her son that he will become a rich man one day if he can import these beans. Already she's heard that the Jews of Bayonne are making chocolate in France.

Inez loses track of time. The only way time seems to move isn't through clocks but through her son. She watches as he grows taller. His eyes seem to become more piercingly blue. The years fly by. A thin mustache darkens his upper lip. He begins to sprout hair between his legs. Everything that her son does enthralls her. Inez thought she could never love anyone more than she once loved Javier. She didn't think that love could run deeper than that, but now she has loved a hundred times more. Though she hasn't thought of Javier in years, she recalls how her body shook with pleasure when he made love to her. How it had all seemed like a dream, being in love, being loved in that way. For a time it seemed as if she was made for love. And then for betrayal.

When Inez boarded the ship where the sailors would do whatever pleased them and she would do nothing to stop them, she never felt pleasure. She thought she would never feel the pleasure of being touched again. Then she took this child to her breast. And nothing has ever been the same.

+

The cows are taking over Lisbon. More than two hundred wander the streets, thirsty and confused. It is believed that they will absorb the spores that carry the Black Death. Instead they only add to the filth and misery of the streets. Inez must avoid the manure of the donkeys that carry the carts up and down the hills and the cod-oil slick on the paving stones and now the cows. She wraps her mantilla around her face. She has never gotten used to the stench of these streets and the raw sewage that runs along their gutters. Amelia, their only servant, trails behind.

It is a hot, dry April morning. Lisbon hasn't seen rain for eleven weeks. King Manuel and the nobles have left the city for their villas in the hills. They have left the heat and the stink, the illness and desperation. Peasants whose fields wither in the sun roam the streets like the cows—disoriented, without purpose, and thirsty for rain. It seems as if Lisbon has been infected with the plagues of Moses. But today feels like a respite from all of that. For Inez Cordero, who now spells her name with an "s" when she must sign a document so that she'll be less likely to be taken for a Spanish Jew, it is the time of Passover. At home her mother is dusting the house with a feather.

Despite the heat, Inez is enjoying her morning stroll. She has been cooped up for so long. She is content, walking down the sun-dappled streets. Never mind that the white-and-black-patterned cobblestones are thick with muck and slime. She is happy to be making her way along the winding alleyways of the Alfama to market. It is the first night of Passover and she must buy a spring lamb, salted cod, apples, honey, and walnuts, plus some sweet red wine. They are Christians in name only. But as always on the Jewish holidays they must pretend that it is like any other night. They must not open the door for Elijah. If the neighbors see their doors open, they will tell the authorities. As New Christians they always attend mass. But in the secret of their homes, in the basements and storage rooms where no one can see, they recite the Hebrew prayers.

At last Inez reaches the market but the streets are eerily calm. She hadn't noticed as she was walking but she's hardly passed any carts leaving the market. And certainly none are heading up to the Barrio Alto where the wealthy New Christians live. For a moment Inez wonders if it is the Christian Sabbath. If she has mistaken the day. Gazing up she is surprised to see so many of the houses shuttered and so many of the stalls not open, even though it is already ten o'clock in the morning.

The old man who sells dried fruits and nuts isn't there. Neither is

Mr. Samuels who sells spices. Still the butcher is open, and she can buy her spring lamb. Inside the stall many are hanging upside down, bleeding, their throats cut. Though they aren't kosher, this will have to do. As Inez makes her purchase, there is an acrid smell in the air. It stings her nostrils and brings with it a swirl of memory. It has been many years since she smelled anything like it, and at first she doesn't remember when or where. Gazing up she sees smoke swirling from the direction of the Rossio. She turns to the old butcher and asks, "What is that smell?"

And the man with his filthy hands and bristly chin hairs leans in to whisper, "They are burning the Jews." Inez feels as if a knife pierces her chest. Now she knows that smell. Tears well up in her eyes but she struggles not to cry. She cannot bear recalling the day that her father was consigned to the flames.

Inez steps back in horror. "What do you mean?"

"You haven't heard?" the butcher says. "They're making a bonfire of the Jews."

"Why?" Inez can hardly believe what she is hearing.

"To cleanse their flesh and redeem their souls," the old butcher says.

Inez pays for her lamb and clasps Amelia by the hand. As they walk out of the market, Inez notices what shops are closed. Samson, the goldsmith who can shape the tiniest leaves. Eli, the tailor who makes every fabric like new. Simon, who sells honey that tastes like a field of flowers. Nothing would keep Samson from opening up his shop. Not even the Sabbath. On the outskirts of the market a cow has been slaughtered and is being sliced into pieces by the hungry peasants who seize whatever flesh they can.

Ahead of her Inez sees the smoke rising. Huge black swirls darken the sky. She turns to Amelia. "Go home," she orders her. "I will follow." Amelia stares at her, tears welling in her eyes as Inez heads toward the Rossio. She cannot believe what the butcher told her. Why would they be burning the Jews? But along the road Inez passes severed limbs. Hands and feet. A jeering boy races past holding a bloody head by the hair. By the side of the road an old man writhes, holding his guts in his hand. A child lies with its head smashed in. As she approaches the

Rossio, flames are rising. An endless line of Jews with their hands tied behind their backs are being shoved and kicked toward the pyres. A pregnant woman, a neighbor from her street, clasps her belly, screaming, "My child, my child." For an instant she and Inez make eye contact. Then the woman is shoved closer to the fires.

The vision of her own father swirls in her brain. She sees him being led into the plaza, refusing to kiss the cross, and being tied to the stake. It is as if it is happening all over again and she is, and always will be, to blame. Sickened and terrified, Inez turns. She does not run. If she runs, she will betray herself. She walks toward home, her shawl wrapped around her face, tears streaming. All the way she smells the burning flesh.

In the courtyard her mother waits for her with Benjamin sobbing in her arms. They are certain that she will never return. When she arrives, Inez collapses on the ground. "There is no time," her mother tells her, dragging her to her feet. "You must go down into the cellar. Bolt the lock. I will hide you there until the danger has passed." These are more words than her mother has said to her in years.

"But what about you?" Inez asks. "You must come as well."

But her mother shakes her head. "I am an old woman. I will tell them that you have left Lisbon. If I am not here, they will tear the place apart. This is the only way to save you." Inez knows what this means. She knows that her mother might easily be struck down with a sword or tied up and dragged to the Rossio.

"I can't let you," Inez says but her mother puts her finger to her lips. "There is no discussion. You will do this for me."

Inez can barely stand. "And Amelia?"

"I have sent her away."

Inez protests again. "I cannot leave you . . ."

But her mother is already pulling back the carpet that covers the trapdoor. "There is no time to argue." And Dona Olivia opens the door to the secret basement.

Benjamin makes his way down the five steps into her uncle's secret place of worship. Inez follows. They carry with them bread and hard cheese, a bucket for water and an empty bucket in which to relieve themselves. Dona Olivia hands them blankets. Once they are settled, Inez calls up to her mother who closes the trapdoor, which Inez bolts shut from the inside. Inez hears the carpet as her mother pulls it over the door to conceal their hiding place. Then she and Benjamin are alone in the darkness.

Her son trembles beside her. Within moments his flesh turns cold. It is as if ice has been injected into his veins. Inez reaches for him as she once did when he was a baby, and he falls into her arms. In the dark she holds him and for the first time since he was four years old and she tried to squeeze the life out of him, he lets himself be held.

✳

TOPOGRAPHY—1992

Vincent Roybal stands in the archives of the New Mexico History Museum, talking to Pascual, who is buried in the cemetery in Chimayó. He is asking if he should give up his search. Vincent sifts through the stacks of folders listed under land deeds and topographical maps, hoping to stumble upon something he doesn't even know exists. The answer to why he cannot leave Entrada, to what makes him stay. It is as if he suffers from some rare form of dementia. He has been searching for something and has no idea what it might be. As he stands, riffling through the files, Pascual says to him, "Hey, old man, what do you think you're going to find here?"

"Shut up," he tells his son.

He hears Pascual laugh. Most often it is what he hears. His son's laughter, defying him, taunting him, but today it is different. "Keep on looking. You're getting warmer." It was the game Vincent used to play with Pascual when he couldn't find something. *You're getting warmer, you're getting colder.* Maybe things would have been different if he'd just told Pascual where the damn thing was.

Vincent is unable to move. He has come to the archives as he always does hoping that this will be the day when he finds if not the answer, at least an elusive clue, to whom his people are and why they settled in Entrada. Instead he stands perfectly still among the musty documents and yellowing parchment and dusty shelves. For weeks now he has been thinking about the day that Pascual died. It was a year to the day that he'd stopped speaking to his son. A year that they had lived together in the same house, eating the same meals in silence. A silence joined by Esmeralda, who in protest stopped speaking to her husband as well. But Vincent Roybal was a principled man, and he had only asked Pascual once, "What happened that night?"

And he had replied, "What night?" looking Vincent square in the eyes. Whenever Pascual lied to his father, he looked at him that way.

"I will speak to you again when you tell me the truth," and that was the last time Vincent Roybal said a word to his son. It was surprising to Vincent because even though he'd tried to quit many things in his uneventful life—cigarettes, alcohol, the women he dallied with when his children were small—the only thing he'd ever successfully quit was speaking to Pascual. It was as if he was born into this stubbornness—as if it tapped a vein he didn't know existed.

Even as they slept within the same four walls, ate their meals together, watched baseball in front of the same small black-and-white TV, they did so without sharing so much as a "hello" or "pass the salt." Pascual could never figure out how his father knew that Elena Torres was found sobbing in front of her mother's trailer, and that his son had something to do with it, but you don't sell beer and cigarettes and condoms in a town like Entrada and not hear things. And Vincent had heard that something had happened to that Torres girl. And some of the local boys were involved. And whenever local boys were involved, Pascual was among them.

At first Esmeralda tolerated their silence because she assumed it was temporary. She let it go on for a week, then another, because she knew how stubborn her husband could be, but then it went on too long and she began pleading with him. She reminded him that Pascual was his youngest child. That he'd been born early and was as scrawny as a chicken. That all he'd ever wanted was his father's love and approval. She reminded him that he had been hard on the boy and he had expected too much. And then as the weeks dragged on Vincent stopped speaking to her as well until they all moved through the house like a family of ghosts. As the wedge grew deeper, Pascual took to being out of the house more. He drank and often came home drunk. His father could not begin to divine the torments that lived within his son. A boy who had wanted to please a man he could never please and then had decided to please no one, least of all himself.

Pascual could not bear his father's scorn. Before the incident, he could do nothing right. He did not study the way his sister, Katrina, had studied, and he was not a good athlete like his older brother, Tomas, who had gone to the University of New Mexico on a football scholarship, then moved to Dallas and never came back except for Christmas. Everything Pascual did was wrong. Even the first time he smoked a cigarette he lit the filter. And when he told his father, Vincent replied, "You can't even do a bad thing right, can you?"

So at one point Pascual gave up trying. Since he was so good at doing things wrong, he began doing them wrong all the time. But at least he'd gone to church. At least he'd confessed his sins and his priest had absolved him. Wasn't it enough if he said his Hail Marys and Our Fathers and the priest said he was free of sin and could take communion again? And he had begged his father's forgiveness over and over. But Pascual would not, he could not, answer his father's question that was ringing in his ears even as he downed his nightly six-pack, even as he drove his motorcycle blindly around the bends, then flipped over into oncoming traffic on a moonless night. *What happened that night?*

When Vincent got the call that there was an accident and his son was dead, he'd cried inconsolable, bitter tears until his wife said, "He is dead because of you." Vincent did not argue with her—because he knew she was right. He stopped crying and went out to the place on the road to Chimayó where he'd hammered the white cross he'd made into the ground. He strung the wreath of plastic flowers and on the cross he painted in black block letters: PASCUAL ROYBAL. Then he walked away from the roadside memorial and began talking to his son.

Though Vincent stopped speaking to Pascual when he was alive, he has spoken to him almost nonstop since he's been dead. He asks his advice on matters great and small. Should he carry more varieties of beef jerky? Should he sell cigarettes to fourteen-year-olds? (He shouldn't, but he does.) He asks if he should sell the store or diversify. Carry video cassettes and magazines. He tells Pascual about the aches in his legs and his back. He complains about Esmeralda—though Pascual won't say anything bad about his mother. He complains about how the young people are leaving Entrada, how soon it will be a town of old ghosts. He imagines a life for Pascual. He has a wife, two kids, his own auto-repair shop, like Roberto Torres. Vincent asks how they are doing. If they are sick, he offers the remedies to make them well.

Despite his refusal to speak to his son during his last year of life, Vincent can find a wealth of topics to address to him now. He avoids the topic that drove them apart. He does not ask about what really happened to Elena Torres. He does not refer to the way Pascual came home, drunk and stinking of vomit, smoke, semen, and blood. What good would it do him to know about it now?

As he riffles through a folder, a piece of tattered yellow parchment catches his eye. He pulls out a topographical map and puts it on the table before him. It takes him a moment to register what he is looking at, but then he does. He lays it out flat on a nearby table. It is the original plan for the old hacienda that was first built here. He sees the width and breadth of the land—thousands of acres that over the past four hundred years have dwindled away and been sold off to pay for taxes, gambling debts, children who never amounted to much, luxuries that are never paid off, Indians who won land claims until what was left are the five dry acres upon which Vincent Roybal has his own house and his store and on which he tries to keep a patch of land watered enough so that it provides tomatoes, corn, and beans during the few warm months of the year.

It is as if he is peering down at his land from an airplane. He has an aerial view of the old courtyard where the circle drive is now, and the store was the stable where the milk cow, laying hens, and goats for cheese were kept. The other livestock—sheep and cattle and more goats—were housed in a barn farther down in the valley. Along with the plan for the house, someone has recorded in careful script all the livestock and their numbers. There were fifteen head of cattle, twenty-seven goats, fourteen sheep that were mainly kept for their wool, dozens of chickens and ducks, and seven horses, including a brood mare. There are also eight servants listed as property. The house servants: Clara, Maria, Bernadine, and Angela. And four field hands: Pablo, Enrique, Hector, and Oscar.

Vincent stands, stunned, before this sheet of paper. They owned slaves. It had never occurred to Vincent that his ancestors had enslaved the native people. He also notices something strange. There were no pigs. It is an odd thing. There were slaves, but no pigs. Vincent has never really thought about this before, but there are still no pigs in Entrada and as far as he can tell there never have been. In his store he sells beef jerky and beef hot dogs, turkey bacon and chicken cutlets. But he does not sell pork, not bacon or sausage links or sliced ham or chorizo or salami for sandwiches. And no one ever asks for it either. He doesn't even know why he doesn't. He just never has. These are the unanswered questions that keep Vincent Roybal up at night. He is made sleepless by the stories of people he's never known and who died long before he was born. And now it seems that there were slaves.

As Vincent holds the topographical map, he feels a cold breath on his neck and hears a voice that says to him, "See, old man. I told you if you keep looking, you'll find something."

✳

CHAPTER TWENTY-TWO

MAN VERY EARLY MAKES JARS—1992

The sun is rising over the hills. In the cool morning air Rachel Rothstein shivers and pulls her jacket tightly around her. She did not anticipate this morning chill. In the distance she hears the drums. In a moment the deer will come bounding over rises of the hills. She has no idea what to expect, but soon she sees the tips of their antlers, festooned in leaves and fur, as they prance silently toward her. There is an eerie stillness to them as if they are not moving at all, yet they are getting closer. Now the sunlight glows through their antlers.

It is the feast day at one of the pueblos, and Rachel has come to witness the traditional dances. She knows these events are mainly for tourists as the tour buses in the parking area attest, but she wanted to see them anyway. She shouldn't be here, really, but Nathan encouraged her to go. He even offered to get the kids to school. In fact he was so accommodating it almost made her suspicious. But Nathan said he'd relish some time alone with the boys. Rachel wanted to come no matter what. After all they'd hardly done anything since they got here except for their visit to Chaco Canyon, which hadn't turned out very well.

She wanted to bring the boys with her, but it is Davie's birthday. He is turning six, and Rachel is in charge of his party at school. She must pick up the volcano ice-cream cake, made with dairy-free coconut ice cream, which Davie requested. Lately he is into volcanoes. He likes the idea that they erupt. Rachel doesn't know why, but it is good to be curious. It was her idea to do the strawberry lava flow and the baker thought that was a great idea. She ordered the cake from the only bakery in town that can make a completely non-dairy cake. It cost almost a hundred dollars, but what does Rachel care? How often do you turn six anyway? All she has to do is pick up the cake, grab the party hats and paper plates, and be at his school for their ten thirty snack time. She promised that she'd show up at his school with the party. Besides, this is her first visit to a Pueblo feast day. She will bring the boys with her the next time.

Nathan told her to go ahead. He'd take care of the morning shift. The boys were elated. "Can we have pancakes?" Jeremy shouted.

"Pancakes," Davie echoed. So Nathan said he would make pancakes.

"With soy," Rachel said. She wasn't certain if he'd ever made pancakes in his life, but this morning he said he would. It pained Rachel to see how happy they were that their father would take them to school. This is, of course, what she wants. Still it caused her some pain. She left when they were all still sleeping. She kissed their foreheads as if she would not see them for a long time and headed out the door.

The dancers move closer. Now they are shaking, tossing their antlers. They are cautious and alert as if a coyote were near, as they prance down the hillside in the morning light. The drums pound and around her the Pueblo people chant. In a circle their moccasins pound the earth. The bells they wear on their ankles and strapped to their knees tingle to the beat of the drums. They dance on one foot and then another. They spin in circles, their bodies hunched, antlers down, chanting. It is an unreal sound. Around them dust swirls. As the sun rises she sees their faces more clearly. Many are just boys.

At last as they clear the ridge, they enter the main square of the pueblo. Here the people join in. They dance and hoot. They cheer and sing. The tourists are snapping pictures. But Rachel isn't a tourist. She has no intention of being an outsider. She can't help herself. She comes forward and joins them. Soon she finds herself stomping her feet in the dust, twirling with the deer. No one seems to mind that she is there.

When the dance is over, she is about to leave. She wishes she could stay for the buffalo and corn dances, but she wants to give herself plenty of time to pick up Davie's cake and get to school. But as she is heading to her car, a dancer, still wearing his antlers, approaches. He hands her two long strands of rawhide with feathers and beads at the end. Rachel takes them in her hands. "Are they for me?" The man nods and motions for her to put on the earrings. She slips them into her piercings. The feathers dangle around her neck, tickling her skin. She is so touched by this offering she doesn't know what to do so she puts her hands together in a "namaste" blessing even though she realizes this may mean nothing to this man. He points toward a tent. "There is food and drink and you are welcome."

Rachel is about to ask him why he chose her. No one has ever chosen her for anything. She has never won a raffle or a contest in her life but the dancer is already heading toward the tent and fading into the rest of the herd. Rachel believes that everything happens for a reason. She believes that there is some plan even if it is not clear to us. She wants to tap into the energy that she is sure dwells in the earth, the skies. So for some reason the dancer chose her. It is a sign, but of what? To be more welcoming? That she is on the right path? But we don't always know what that path is, do we? Still she believes it is her destiny to follow it. Of course she knows that there are other destinies. There is her mother and her own dark history. "Look what happened to the Jews," her mother would say. "Was that our destiny?"

But the dancer chose her and she cannot ignore it. In the tent coffee and fry bread are being served. Rachel wears her earrings and they treat her as one of them. A little girl cries when she spills her juice and Rachel wipes her hands and pours her another. She munches on the hot, greasy fry bread and sips the strong coffee. She cannot remember when anything tasted so good. She helps pour coffee. She clears the table when plates are left. The native women smile and thank her.

She wants to stay longer, but suddenly she looks at her watch. It is almost ten o'clock as Rachel races to her car and drives like a wild person down the hill from the pueblo toward Santa Fe. She speeds to the bakery where the baker hands her the cake. It looks just like a volcano with strawberry lava made from cinnamon sprinkles pouring out of the crater and white ash frosting along the sides. She zips over to the grocery store where she grabs a half gallon of apple cider and paper goods. Plates, hats, napkins. Then she flies over to the school.

She's ten minutes late. When she arrives, the children are all sitting at their long red tables. Some of them are pounding on the wood. Others are crying. The teacher glares at Rachel as she quickly presents the cake. Dashing around she hands out plates, party hats, cups. "Look at this," Rachel says, displaying the cake. "It's a volcano. It's about to erupt!"

There are some oohs and aahs, but mainly she is greeted with impatient, hungry looks. She lights the candles and they all sing. "I'll cut the cake," she tells the teacher, "if you'll pour the cider."

Ms. Johnson bristles in disbelief. "Cider? They can't have cider. That's double sugar. No double sugar!"

Rachel shakes her head, dismayed. "Right. Double sugar."

The teacher races to the fridge where she grabs a half gallon of milk and begins pouring that instead.

"Not for Davie," Rachel shouts but Ms. Johnson just shakes her head.

"I know," she says as she pours cider into Davie's cup.

The children scarf down the cake, then race outside. Just as Davie is about to follow, he erupts into projectile vomit. "Oh no," Rachel shouts. "It's a non-dairy cake." He vomits one more time and she cleans him up, and then wipes off the table. In an instant Davie is better and races outside to join his friends.

When Rachel looks up, the room is empty. All the children are running around outside, screaming. She slumps in the chair that is only big enough to hold a child. It seems as if she cannot get anything right—not even cake and ice cream. She's going to have to go and yell at that baker. She can see her mother saying that to her. On the table beside Rachel the volcano is melting.

+

"I didn't do it," Jeremy says later that afternoon when Miguel picks them up after school, and Davie comes crying to the car. He has snot running down his face, blood in the corners of his nose.

Miguel gets down on his knees. "Hey, buddy, what happened to you?" He clasps Davie by the hands but Davie can't stop gulping, hiccupping. He can barely catch his breath. "Okay now, breathe. Hey, it's your birthday. You shouldn't be crying. Tell me what happened."

But Davie can't catch his breath and Miguel is aware of Jeremy standing back, rubbing his foot in the dirt, churning up a little dust devil. "It isn't my fault." Jeremy folds his arms across his chest.

Miguel sighs. "Jeremy, what happened?" Jeremy begins a long rambling story that has to do with older boys with whom Jeremy was playing who wanted a ball that Davie had, but Davie didn't want to give it to them even though Jeremy told him that he should. On and on it goes—this narrative of how innocent Jeremy is in the face of the boys who want to hurt his baby brother. Miguel doesn't believe a word of it, but all the same Davie says nothing to alter the story and just keeps bobbing his head up and down in agreement as if this were the true version. It makes Miguel feel the way he felt when he and his friends were arrested, each one covering for the other until they all ended up in juvie for a month.

Still, no matter what the truth is, and he is fairly certain that Jeremy isn't telling it, Davie is small for his age. It is one thing that Miguel has been spared for he has always been big. In fact Miguel has no memory of being little. He always towered over his father and mother, over his friends. For as long as Miguel can remember he's had to duck when going through doorways. He has no idea how many times he's hit his head; he wouldn't be surprised if he hasn't had half a dozen concussions by now.

But nobody ever picked on him. No one dared. And Davie is always going to get picked on unless he learns to fight back. In the car, he has Davie sit in the front seat. They stop along the way to get slushies, but he makes Jeremy stay in the car. Jeremy needs to know, no matter what, who is boss. And Davie needs to learn how to fight.

When they get home, Mrs. Rothstein is nowhere to be seen. "Jeremy, you go watch cartoons." Miguel takes Davie into the bathroom where he washes his face and wipes his nose. Then he stoops down and takes a good look at Davie's face. "It's not so bad," he says. "Come with me."

As they walk into the yard through the sliding glass doors, Miguel tries to remember what his father taught him when he was Davie's age. His father was an amateur welterweight, and though he'd taught Miguel very little, he had shown him how to hold up his fists. "Okay, it's your birthday and I'm going to give you this present." In the yard Miguel assumes a stance. "Davie, look at me." He holds his fists in front of his face. Davie mimics him. "Dukes up. That's all you have to remember." Miguel punches into the air, bringing them back to his face. "Okay, keep those fists in front of your face. Punch from there." He takes the tetherball by the string and holds it up. "Now punch this ball." Davie assumes a stance, a fierce look on his face. Then he slugs the ball. "Bring those fists back. That's right. One, two, three . . ."

Davie begins slamming the tetherball, hitting it harder and harder as if months, years of rage are flying out of his hands. Miguel is surprised at how much power he has. "Wow, that's enough. Now here, try it with me."

Miguel gets down on his knees and holds up his forearms. "Now hit my forearms. Give it all you've got."

Davie shakes his head. "I'll hurt you."

. "Nah, don't worry. I'll be fine." At first Davie hesitates. But then he lashes out. He starts swinging like a crazy person, and Miguel can barely deflect his strikes. Miguel is stunned at the fury Davie manages to find as he lets those fists fly.

+

It is homework time when Miguel is ready to bring Davie inside. Miguel has his own homework to do as well. He's back in school now. His sophomore year. He has more math homework and science than he's ever had before. And that whole Columbus curriculum to learn. But Davie doesn't want to come in. He wants to keep pounding the tetherball until Miguel shakes him out of it. "Come on, it's time." In the living room Jeremy is glued to the television with Baxter flung across his lap. "Okay," Miguel says, switching it off. "That's enough TV for one day."

Jeremy shouts. "That's my favorite show."

"Well, not today it isn't. We're going to do something else." He decides to teach them how he learned the order of the planets in the solar system the way Mr. Garcia taught him. Man Very Early Makes Jars Stand Up Nearly Perpendicular. Miguel thinks that he can go through his entire life and never forget this one phrase.

He'll teach Davie at least. He's still curious. But maybe not Jeremy. Something happened to that boy. Perhaps Davie doesn't care that his father is never around. But Jeremy does. Miguel always has his father. Even after Roberto moved out, he's there every day for him. Never mind that he's often drunk, that he earns a living by airbrushing cars. Miguel doesn't have a yard with a picture window that looks out over the mesa. He doesn't have a big room of his own to play in or a swing set in a fenced-in yard. But he has a father who comes looking for him when he drives his car off the road.

In fact, for most of his childhood Miguel only had a cot in the living room. His parents' bedroom door was made of cheap wood and it was as if there was no separation between Miguel and his parents' marriage. He may as well have been right in the room with them. In his early years he was a keen observer of his parents' marriage. He overheard their lovemaking, their drunken fights over his father's infidelities. He watched and listened, blow by blow, to their shouting, the hurling of objects, and ultimately to the demise of their union. He watched his mother go from the cute, pixieish woman she was into the heavy, flat-faced woman she became. It was as if Miguel in his short life had already been married, divorced, and grown old.

Rachel comes into the living room. She is about to ask Miguel if he wants some ice cream and cake, but he is imparting a lesson to the boys. "Do you know," Miguel tells them, "that our brains are like the universe? We have as many neurons in our brains as the universe has stars. In fact the brain and the universe resemble each other."

"What are neurons?" Davie asks.

Miguel is trying to figure out how to answer that when Rachel says, "I didn't know that. It's very interesting."

Miguel nods. "And we know less about the human brain than we do about the universe."

Rachel stares at him, not blinking.

"It's as if each one of us is a universe unto ourselves."

"Where do you go to look at the stars?" Rachel asks.

"I have a place near where I live."

"Will you take me sometime?"

Miguel feels his throat catch. She doesn't say, *Will you take me and the boys?* She is asking him to take her. Why would she do that? Where is her husband? Why is he never here? Why has Miguel never met him? He knows that something is wrong between them and he cannot help but feel as if he is a stand-in, and not a very good one. And yet here he is, going along, because the truth is she turns him on. And he senses that she, for whatever reason, has some kind of a thing for him.

"If you like," Miguel tells her. "In a couple of weeks when there's a new moon. That's when the sky should be the clearest."

"I'll get a sitter. How far is it?" As he sits on the couch beside her, Rachel wonders what it would be like to be with this boy. She could just slip into his arms and let him hold her. She is awed at his sense of wonder. The way he sees the world with a child's eyes. She is touched by his kindness. She gazes into his green eyes, struck by the depth of them. A whole universe lies inside of those eyes. *Galaxies lie in the bottom of thimbles.* Who is the poet who said that? She could be his mother, and yet what she wants right now is to curl up inside of those long, dark arms, to pull him around her like a blanket and find some rest. Instead she stands up, willing herself away.

"It's almost an hour's drive." He doesn't look at her. His gaze is straight ahead. "We can find a closer spot."

"No," she says emphatically as she turns to leave the room. "I want you to show me where you go to see the sky."

+

As Miguel makes his way back to Entrada, he is aware of a banging in his engine and feels a drag as he shifts into gear going uphill. He decides to detour over to his father's trailer. Instead of making his turn, he stays on the road north. This will be a good excuse to see his dad. Not that he needs an excuse, though he rarely just pops in for a visit.

In fact, Miguel wants to see his father. He is hoping that he can find a way to talk to him. Man to man. Because Miguel is bothered, no, it is more than that, he is obsessed with Rachel Rothstein. He finds himself thinking about her all the time. He can't wait until after school when he goes to her house to babysit her kids. At night before bed he grows hard just thinking of her and has to jerk off. He wakes up in a sweat, dreaming of her in that orange bikini, smelling of sunscreen and lemons.

This can't be normal. Miguel is still a virgin. He hasn't been with a girl yet, though he's done his share of fooling around, but he is drawn to this woman in a way that he doesn't think is entirely natural. He is almost fifteen and she is really old. At least thirty. Maybe more. But none of the girls his own age turn him on the way Rachel Rothstein does. Miguel doesn't believe in sin, but this seems sinful. He wishes he could talk to his mother, but how could he? How do you explain to your mother that you are having wet dreams about a woman who is almost her age?

As he clangs up the hill, he sees his dad standing in his garage, cans of spray paint all around him, and wearing a mask. He is putting the finishing touches on a wolf on someone's truck. His overalls are filthy and covered in paint as is the whole garage. His father looks as if he's putting on weight. His gut is sticking way out. He is probably drinking again. Roberto only looks that way when he drinks. He remembers his father from his boxing days, when he was a model welterweight, trim and healthy. Now he is soft as dough with a hacking cough.

Roberto sees him coming. Flicking off his mask, he steps outside the garage. "To what do I owe the pleasure of this visit?" Roberto says in a fake British accent. Yes, Miguel thinks, he's been drinking.

"There's a banging in my engine. Can you check it out?"

But Roberto can tell his dad has already been listening. As he gets out of the car his father says, "Yeah, you probably need a new radiator and you've got a leak in the exhaust pipe." His father points to the driveway where a small pool of dark liquid is already forming.

"You could tell that just from the sound?" His father throws him a fake punch and Miguel ducks, pretending it is going to hit him. It seems as if they always go through this routine. His dad throwing a punch, Miguel ducking. His father gives him a hug, patting him on the back, the way athletes do after a game when one team has won and the other lost. The loser gets that pat.

"Yep, but I'll check it out. I assume that's why you've come by."

Miguel shrugs. "Well, if you've got a sec."

"Hey, for you, kid, I've got nothing but time."

"Dad . . ."

His father turns his back to him. "Don't worry. I can handle this." Like a doctor Roberto checks out the car's vital signs. He throws open the hood. Checks the oil, the fan belt. He bends down to look at the muffler and gives each of the tires a kick, though Miguel feels that this is more bravado than anything else.

"So how ya been?" Miguel asks.

"You know. Hanging in there." Roberto drags the creeper he made from a piece of plywood and the wheels of an old pair of roller skates out from a corner of the garage and slides under the car. With a wrench he bangs at the bottom. Miguel waits for his father to ask him how he is, but he doesn't. Instead he slides out and starts jacking up the car. "Hey, Dad, use the jack stands." Miguel points to the metal stands in the corner of the garage.

"Jack stands are for sissies." He gives the car a kick. "She'll hold." Then he lies back down on the creeper and disappears under the car, first his head and then his torso. Miguel can't imagine the dark places where his father goes.

Miguel loves to watch his father work. The way he can take apart an engine and put it back together again. The way he can lie under a car or a truck and find what's wrong. His father has always had a fascination with machines—motorcycles, radios, toasters. It doesn't matter. If anything is broken, he'll fix it. He'll lay all the pieces down until he figures out exactly what's wrong. He does this sometimes even if a gadget isn't broken just to see how things work.

Miguel has little interest when it comes to machines. He has built his own telescope, but to him it isn't the same. He only wants the telescope in order to see the stars. But his father actually loves to figure out how things work. Not Miguel. He has no knowledge of electrical currents or brakes. He doesn't understand how an image comes on the TV, how a telephone rings. Miguel lives as if the world is a magical place. Presto. Things happen, appear, disappear, and he has no idea how. But his father actually knows how they work. And he isn't afraid to slip into small places—behind a refrigerator, under a car. He doesn't mind pipes that go to places Miguel doesn't want to think about. He's seen his father climb into a septic tank to clean it out. He's seen him hold two wires together to see which one is live.

Lying on the creeper, his legs and belly sticking out, Roberto resembles a dead bug. Beneath the car he grunts about the exhaust pipe. "It's all rusted out. I gotta replace this. And you should get a new radiator. I'll have to get parts." He whistles through his teeth. It sounds like a crow flying overhead.

Miguel wishes he knew something about cars. If he gets stuck on the road at night, he can't even change a tire. And if he were interested in cars, it would give them something to talk about. His father could tell him about cool hubcaps or horsepower. He wishes his father cared about the sky. It doesn't matter to Roberto that black holes can suck anything into them. Or that there are stars flickering in the sky that died a billion years ago. Miguel wants to show his father the constellations he's tracked in the Milky Way. The moons he can see with the telescope he made. But all that seems to matter to Roberto are machines, and mostly cars. His father talks about them as if they are women. He admires their smooth lines, their shiny façades. He complains about the way they let you down. He grows despondent when he has to trade one in.

"Hand me the wrench," his father's disembodied voice says. Miguel looks at the tools spread out on the ground like on a tray at the dentist's office. He picks up what he assumes is the wrench his father wants and places it in the hand that reaches for it from under the car. It's weird, seeing his father like this. That hand like the ghost story about the monkey's paw that terrified him as a child. "I'm going to have to replace this. You don't want a rusted-out exhaust pipe." His voice comes from a distant place.

At last Roberto slides out. "Well, it'll take me a couple of days to do this. When do you need it?"

Miguel stares into his father's eyes. They are familiar. They are mirrors. He knows that at least this is one place where he belongs. "When do I need it?" Miguel laughs. "Like yesterday. You know I've got that job." Now, Miguel thinks, he can bring it up. He can ask his father, man to man, if it's normal to be thinking all the time about a woman old enough to be his mother.

Roberto ruffles his son's hair. "Right, you're babysitting." His father laughs, and Miguel knows that this isn't the time to bring up his love life. He fears he'll be made fun of. "I'll work on it tonight. It'll at least be safe to drive tomorrow."

Roberto smiles, then stares back in that blank way he sometimes has, as if he has no idea who Miguel is. And at other times he looks at Miguel with his lips pursed in a way that makes Miguel feel as if his father has something he wants to tell him but he never does. A big question looms between them like a wall. It is as if they are double agents, unsure of whom they can trust.

"And I'm going to start getting that truck in shape for you." His father points to the old El Camino that sits in the dirt. Miguel looks at the pickup that's been rusting in his father's yard for more than a year now. He looks back at his father.

"Well, I was going to get it done for your birthday, but I guess it'll be your early Christmas present instead."

Miguel chuckles. "Sure, Dad. That'd be great." He's fairly certain he won't be driving that truck anytime soon.

"Get in the car before your mother starts to worry about you. I'll drop you off, then bring it back in the morning." Miguel jumps into the driver's side of his father's truck.

"You know, I got a postcard from Aunt Elena," Miguel says as they drive.

Roberto nods, looking straight ahead. "Oh yeah? How's she doing?"

Miguel shrugs. "I don't know. She never says."

"Where was she this time?"

"Morocco."

Roberto nods again, not looking at his son. "Where the hell is Morocco?"

"It's in North Africa," Miguel answers. "I looked it up."

Roberto shrugs. "That's a long way from here." They drive the rest of the way in silence.

When they pull into the driveway, Miguel gets out. "You wanna come inside?"

But his father shakes his head. "Better if I don't." And he drives off into the night.

✳

CHAPTER TWENTY-THREE

BEATRICE DE LUNA—1535

Throughout her son's childhood, Inez Cordero told him a story that he thought was a fairy tale. Benjamin loved this story so much that he made her repeat it night after night. She told him that once she'd found a naked boy at a river's edge, feeding himself on raw fish and ripened fruit that had fallen from trees. She'd cradled him on a long voyage and he became her own. With each telling the story grew. The boy was a feral child, raised by whatever beasts roamed the island. A tortoise taught him how to fish. He rode on the backs of dolphins. Mermaids suckled him at their breasts.

But it wasn't until her death, when he was almost a man, that Benjamin Cordero understood this wasn't a story at all; it was his life. He held Inez's hands and wept as she told him from her deathbed that most of the fairy tale—minus mythological creatures and friendly animals—was true. She told him that she believed he was the child of the interpreter who sailed with Columbus. A man who may have gone to Cuba and become rich or who may have been killed. No one knew much about him or his fate, except that he was a Jew. Benjamin had only to go piss against a tree to see that this was true. And then she left him alone in this world.

For weeks he rumbled around his house alone. His grandmother was long dead and Amelia, their servant, let go. In the night he sat in the courtyard, staring at the sky. How many days had he played alone within these walls? Benjamin lost himself in the darkness. He ate sporadically and even then it was only random things he found in the cupboards: an egg, a chunk of moldy cheese, the remnants of a chocolate bar. He had managed to survive before and so he would survive now. He just was not sure how. He wallowed in his loneliness. After all, he was accustomed to it. He had grown up with barely anyone around him, but now his mother's absence left a gaping wound in his heart. He was stunned at the depth of his grief and by the many questions that plagued him.

When she died, her secrets died with her. He had planned to ask her why she had sailed on that ship. What had brought her to him? And why did her own mother despise her? His mother would never talk of such things. She would only say, "Because that is how it was." He thought he'd have more time. There were mysteries hidden within his bones and now he would have no way to solve them. He had to accept amid the solitude of these walls that there were some things he would never know.

It was at the moment of his deepest despair that Francisco Mendes knocked on his door. Benjamin was surprised to find a short, stocky man standing there in his brown leggings and cape. "May I come in?" Francisco Mendes asked. He was one of the brothers of the great House of Mendes—conversos from Spain who, when the Jews were expelled, had brought their expertise with them to Portugal. Francisco ran the daily workings of the Mendes spice-trading business from Lisbon, while his older brother, Diogo, who lived in Amsterdam, imported pepper and other spices to northern Europe—spices that had made them wealthy men.

"Of course," Benjamin replied. He was stunned out of his misery. Around him he saw the filth and squalor he'd been living in, but Francisco didn't bat an eye as they walked into Benjamin's living quarters. "I have nothing to offer you," Benjamin said.

"Oh," Francisco replied, "I believe you do." He settled himself on the corner of an unmade bed. "I understand your circumstances. I will only bother you for a moment." Francisco had heard of Inez's death, and he knew that she had schooled Benjamin in the art of chocolate. In recent years Francisco had observed Benjamin on the docks, waiting for the ships to come in, haggling with the merchants, and buying what was required to make chocolate. Francisco was also aware that just across the border in France, converso Jews were teaching the French how to make chocolate bars, pan au chocolat and chocolate truffles, stuffed with cherries and rum. "You have a nose for this business," Francisco said and he offered Benjamin a position as expediter when his ships came in.

This was nearly twenty years ago, and Benjamin has worked as an expediter for the House of Mendes ever since. Now he is one of Francisco's most trusted workers. It is Benjamin who convinced Francisco to rent the large warehouse on Rua de Lava Cabecas. For almost two decades Benjamin Cordero has stood at the docks. Only Benjamin was trusted to put his fists into the sacks of pepper and clove and sniff the spices to determine if they are fit to be sold by the House of Mendes. Only Benjamin signs the papers that send the ships on to Antwerp and beyond.

Now Benjamin is making his way to Francisco Mendes's town house on the Rua Nova dos Mercadores. Francisco's wife, Beatrice de Luna, summoned Benjamin from the docks just as a ship filled with curry leaves came in, and Benjamin understood that there was only one reason why Beatrice would call him at this time. Francisco is about to die. Benjamin sends word to his young wife, Leonora, that he will not be home for lunch. Then he moves quickly past the silk workshops, the bookstalls and shoemakers, the tailors and haberdasheries and apothecaries—almost all of which are owned and run by conversos. People who for the past four years—since the Inquisition became official in Portugal—have feared once again for their lives.

As Benjamin wends his way, he wonders what Beatrice will ask of him. He knows that Francisco cannot have much time. And he also knows that soon Beatrice will be widowed and alone.

+

Beatrice de Luna sits in a silk armchair beside their bed, watching her husband die. He has been ill for months with a pain that began in his stomach and soon took over his entire body. All the elixirs that the doctors provided could not quell it. His skin is yellow and painful to the touch. The tinctures of milk thistle have done nothing to quell the vomit of green bile and blood. Death would be a blessing.

Soon she will have to call the priest to administer the last rites, but she is waiting for Benjamin to arrive. He will help her do what needs to be done now. He will help her husband die as a Jew. At the moment Beatrice is numb and afraid. It seems as if she has only just come to love Francisco and now she is about to lose him. And she relies on him for a million things. But her future is mapped out for her and she doubts that she'll be able to overcome its darkness. Were it not for her little daughter, Ana, who clings to her skirts, Beatrice would be in utter despair.

Beatrice was only eighteen when her father agreed to allow her to marry her mother's brother. Beatrice begged her father not to force her to do this—not only because Francisco was her uncle (many daughters married their blood relatives in order to keep the family estates intact) but also because he was more than twice her age. Indeed to her he was an old man, but the House of Mendes was too rich and powerful for her father to decline.

At first Beatrice shuddered at her husband's touch. On their wedding night she felt ill when he raised the skirt of her nightgown. She could not bear his caresses. His kiss revolted her. After all he was her uncle, and she had grown up playing at his feet. And he was not what she'd imagined for herself. He was large, almost portly, with a head of thinning gray hair. And she wondered why he had not married until now, though it was clear that he'd had women before her. He knew where to touch her and how. He knew that his tongue would bring her pleasure. But she resisted him.

Night after night she stayed in her room with her door bolted. During the first weeks of their marriage he didn't bother asking if he might visit her again. It was clear that he wasn't welcome. But he was a patient man. He waited for her in the mornings before he ate his bread and cheese, before he sipped his hot chocolate. He was never in a hurry when it came to her, even listening to her chatter. He never forced himself on her and with time she grew accustomed to his caresses. The way he brushed his hand over her hair, the way he touched the small of her back when leading her into the dining room. Eventually she opened her door. And with time she came to want him. The way his lips found her nipples, the way his finger moved between her legs. He awakened in her something she'd never known existed, and for this alone she was grateful. Even on the rare nights when he did not visit, she could pleasure herself. She had found comfort in his arms. She never slept better than she did with her head on Francisco's chest. He held her in the most gentle of ways, as if she were a gift, wrapped for the giving. She had grown used to him in her bed, and now they shared this child, their Ana. The proof that she had come to love him in her own way.

They settled into married life. Though he was one of the richest and most powerful men in all of Europe, he was kind. He treated their servants and workers well. He never raised his voice to her. He bought her this beautiful home on the Rua Nova dos Mercadores and set up his offices on the ground floor. They'd had every meal together since they'd married eight years ago.

She had come to love him. She was surprised when she began to anticipate their nights together. Once she unlocked her door, she rarely bolted it again. Even when she bled and in the early stages of her pregnancy, she allowed him into her chamber. And when she grew larger with the child, he came at night to hold her. She had been stunned by the comfort that a man's arms could bring. And now she was preparing to say goodbye.

She sits in her armchair, the red velvet curtains of her room drawn. She will not allow the sun to shine today. She will not allow time to move on. In the courtyard she hears the house bell ring. Benjamin has received her summons. Beatrice knows that Benjamin will do anything for her. Though she wonders if he will do what she is about to ask.

+

As Benjamin enters the room, he is stunned by the putrid smell of death and by Francisco, so diminished, so pale and thin—this once enormous and powerful man. Yet even from his deathbed he has managed to revamp his will. He has had half of his estate transferred to his brother in Antwerp. Of the remaining half he has allotted a third to his wife, a third to his daughter, and a third to cover the costs of his funeral because Francisco has at last made peace with his death and with the fact that in public he must die a Catholic, but in his heart he will die a Jew.

He has left careful instructions for his funeral procession. Exactly how many carriages and horses will be required. How many men in uniform to accompany his coffin. The money that must be paid to the priests and to the great cathedral, not to mention the contributions to the papacy and various charities in order to maintain the semblance of a good Christian life. And finally he had secured the secret funds for which his wife will continue their work of enabling conversos to leave Portugal and establish lives for themselves elsewhere in the world.

As the stench of death almost overwhelms him, Benjamin takes in the room. Beatrice, her head bowed, sits holding her husband's hand, his nurses and doctor at his side. His banker is waiting with more papers to sign. Beatrice signals for them all to leave. Now Benjamin approaches and kneels before her in respect, kissing her hand. "I came as quickly as I could."

Beatrice motions for him to stand. "Yes, I knew you would. I need you to do something, Benjamin. I need you to do one last thing for him and it would mean the world to me."

"You know I will do anything for you and your family."

"Yes, that is why I sent for you. In a little while I must call the priest to come and administer last rites."

As Benjamin listens, he gazes at her trembling white hands, her soft round face. But it is those dark, demanding eyes that he can't turn away from. Eyes that compel him to do whatever she desires, as he has done since she was a girl when he first came to work for the House of Mendes. "What is it that you wish?"

"Francisco cannot be alive when the priest arrives. He must die now as a Jew."

He wishes he could wrap his arms around her and hold her. He thinks of the comfort he could bring her. And bring himself. He is wondering if this is the moment when he betrays his wife and declares his love for Beatrice. He has loved her for years. But he does not think he is capable of doing what she is asking. He stands before her shaking his head. "I cannot."

Beatrice de Luna grips his arm. "If you do, I will get you and your family safely out of Portugal. I will protect you, and I will make certain that you never want for anything. You may go anywhere you wish. I can make this happen."

Benjamin nods. He knows that this is not idle talk. She can do what she says. For years now Beatrice and Francisco have watched over a vast escape network for conversos throughout Spain and Portugal. When the Inquisition came to Portugal, the first thing the king did was prevent the Jews from leaving. In this way they could not take their great wealth and commerce with them.

But the House of Mendes had thus far been spared. Just days before the papal bull that authorized the Inquisition in Portugal, Francisco Mendes and his family were granted a personal exemption by the pope himself. But who knows once Francisco is gone how long this exemption will remain? Benjamin thinks of his own wife and small son, Balthazar, and another child on the way. He has long lived in fear of being betrayed. For his wife, Leonora, is also a converso, and in the secrecy of their home they light candles and whisper their Hebrew prayers.

Benjamin understands what she is asking. It is a known practice among the secret Jews to kill the dying just before the priest arrives and to turn the body to the wall to ensure that they will depart this world as Jews.

She clasps his hands between her own. "Please."

At last Benjamin nods. "I will do this for you."

Beatrice gasps. "Thank you." She turns to her husband whose rasping breath has become a rattle. She stoops down and kisses him on his forehead, whispering into his ear. Benjamin knows what she is saying. She is assuring him that she is carrying out his final instructions and wishing him a safe journey. She slips a coin between her husband's lips to pay the way for his soul to travel into the next world. "I will send for the priest," she says, lowering her voice. Then she leaves the room.

When she is gone, Benjamin sits beside his patron. He too has loved Francisco. Francisco gave him work and has been like a father to him. Benjamin reaches for the pillow and raises it. A strange flutter passes through his mind like a memory that he is not even sure he remembers. And just as suddenly the memory is gone. With all the strength and tenderness he can muster he presses the pillow to Francisco's face. Francisco grabs Benjamin by the arms, but Benjamin holds firm. Still Francisco fights but soon he weakens. Within moments his benefactor is gone. Then he turns Francisco Mendes's body to the wall and silently recites the prayer for the dead.

That night Benjamin stays awake beside his wife. Her breathing is heavy as she lies on her back. This pregnancy seems more difficult than the first. Leonora has been ill and the baby is pinching her spine. They have not been married that long and though he admires her, he cannot say he loves her. He has loved another woman for too long. One he now knows he will never have. Once he had believed that Beatrice felt something for him as well. The way her dark eyes seemed to pierce him. She seemed to know him in ways that he did not even know himself. He had watched her emerge from a child into a young woman. She had become not a beauty but a woman with a powerful will. But today he realized that what he had hoped for would never come to be. She was now a wealthy widow, perhaps one of the wealthiest women in the world. Why would she want to give that up for a man, even a lover, who might lay claim to her freedom and fortune?

Beatrice of the Moon.

Luna was the name of the town her family came from in northern Spain. It was not uncommon for conversos to take on the last name of the town from which they'd been expelled. But to Benjamin it was as if she came from the moon itself. She has long been the light that shines in his darkness.

Beside him Leonora shifts her weight. The new child will be born soon. He must think of his family first. It is strange for him to feel that what happened today was the deepest secret he will ever have to bear. Deeper even than the prayers he whispers and the candles he lights.

+

Beatrice de Luna, who will soon go by her Hebrew name, Dona Gracia Nasi, sits up in her room, cradling Ana in her arms. She will not sleep tonight. Within the hour she will return to her place beside her husband's body. She has seen to it that his body has been washed in cool water, his nails trimmed. She watched the servants wrap him in white linen cloth. And she has ordered one of them to sit with his body until her return so that he will not be alone. If the servants whisper to the priests, she does not care. At least for now the exemption from the pope will remain. Neither the Vatican nor the king can afford to live without the subsidies from the House of Mendes.

But she must come up with a plan. She must decide what is best for Ana and herself. How long will the pope continue to protect her and her family? And what about the other conversos who depend on her to secure their safe passage elsewhere. The king will do whatever he can to prevent the Jews from leaving until he has at least had a chance to confiscate their belongings upon arrest because "everything they have must be given back to the true God."

Beatrice leans back onto the bed where her husband often visited her. She can still smell him on her pillow. Tears slide down her face. She has never felt so utterly alone. She takes a sip of the hot chocolate that grows tepid at the side of her bed. Ana breathes heavily beside her. Her forehead is hot the way a child's forehead tends to be when they sleep, but Beatrice panics. What if her daughter grows ill too? What if she has caught her father's fever? But she cannot allow herself to think of such things.

Instead, lying there in her bed Beatrice knows that she must get used to this—her widowhood. She cannot ever marry again for she will give up all of her holdings. And she cannot take a lover, or even have a dalliance, for fear of blackmail. Beatrice de Luna is twenty-five years old and her bed will be a cold and empty one for the rest of her life.

Three days later the grand procession weaves its way through the streets of Lisbon. The funeral carriage is led by six sleek black horses and accompanied by a dozen soldiers dressed in white, riding pure white horses on either side. Dressed in the finest black silk, Beatrice de Luna and Ana follow in their carriage. Along the way, jugglers, clowns, fire-eaters, flute players, carts selling sausage and chickens roasting on spits, and throngs of spectators line the road. All of Lisbon has come out to see Francisco Mendes make his final journey to the great cathedral where he will be given a true Christian burial. Almost thirty years later Beatrice de Luna will keep the promise she whispered to her husband on his deathbed. She will have his bones disinterred and brought to Jerusalem where he will be buried as a Jew.

Not long after the funeral Beatrice receives a letter from the king's emissary, making a generous offer. The king requests that Ana be sent to the palace to be raised like royalty by the queen herself and with the promise of an advantageous marriage for her in the future. Stunned by this request, Beatrice contemplates what she must do. She realizes that Ana has already become a pawn in a game she has no intention of playing. She replies that she would be honored to have Ana raised at the palace but first they must go to Antwerp on business and she will send Ana to the queen upon her return.

Beatrice knows that she must act swiftly and in stealth. She packs whatever they might need for a short journey. The rest of her clothing and possessions she will leave behind. She sends word to Diogo in Antwerp that he must arrange safe passage for her and Ana to London via Calais, and then they will travel overland. It is the only safe way to go. A week before she is to leave, she sends word to Benjamin to come and see her.

He arrives as soon as he hears from her and is let right in. He finds her sitting in the shadows of her room. Beatrice is dressed all in black and seems paler and thinner than he remembers when he last saw her the night Francisco died. He cannot bear the reminder of Francisco, fighting back. That feeling as the life left his body. And a strange memory that will not leave him as if once someone had tried to smother him as well. Benjamin would give anything to banish such thoughts forever from his head.

"You asked to see me?"

Beatrice nods. "I did. I am going to tell you something and I trust you will keep it to yourself."

"Of course. I have always given you my full loyalty." He trembles slightly but tries not to show her.

"I am leaving Lisbon in a week's time. You must tell no one. I can arrange for you and your family to come with us to Antwerp. You will have work there for the rest of your days." She looks tired and already worn by the demands made upon her.

He can't begin to imagine all that she must bear. He will never know of the thousands she will help escape. How many she will aid in their passage to Antwerp, across the treacherous Alps where many will die, to Venice where boats will carry those who survive to the Ottoman Empire and a place called Tiberias where they will be free. If he goes with her, he will never be free. He will always love her. He will spend his life wanting her. His marriage will be loveless. He does not think that he can bear to be near her for the rest of his days and not make love to her. He would be her loyal servant, but nothing more. And his life would be wasted.

Instead he makes his decision right then and there. Ever since his mother brought the sweetened liquid to his lips he has been fascinated with cacao. He was born in that part of the world where the cacao trees grow. The sea is in his blood. He does not want to travel north. He believes that there is a future for him in chocolate. While Beatrice de Luna prepares to leave Lisbon, never to return, Benjamin Cordero makes his plans to travel to the New World.

CHAPTER TWENTY-FOUR

❋

ATONEMENT—1992

W**e're going to be late," Nathan says. He always says that. It doesn't matter where they need to be. A movie, dinner, an outdoor barbecue on a lazy summer day. Even the beach. Nathan hates to be late. Rachel knows this, and at times she wonders if she isn't late on purpose, if she doesn't do it just to get under his skin. That is one of the things about her that drives him crazy. As a pediatric cardiologist, Nathan has to be precise.

But it seems to Rachel as if she always has a million things to do. Just this week she has to help Jeremy build a cardboard boat for the Columbus quincentennial celebration on Monday. Five hundred years since Columbus discovered America. Davie needs a costume for the reenactment. Jeremy is supposed to build the *Pinta* along with two of his friends, and Rachel hasn't even looked at the design, though she's had the cardboard from the refrigerator they purchased in the garage for months now.

This drives Nathan mad. He can't tolerate the chaos in their lives— the piles of laundry that never seem to get into the hampers, let alone into the washer, the things that need to be fixed that never get fixed. Small things that it would be easy enough for Rachel to do. A lightbulb, for god's sake. The meals that don't get prepared, the groceries that never make it from the shopping lists into their cupboards and shelves. Rachel can come home with smoked salmon, pesto, and pumpkin ravioli, but forget the coffee, butter, milk for cereal. Nathan will say to her, "Can't you remember the staples?" She'll stare at him blankly. "You know," he'll explain, "the things we need every day?"

"I'm coming, I'm coming," Rachel shouts as she kisses the boys good-bye on the tops of their heads and gives Miguel last-minute instructions about what they can and cannot watch and where they can and cannot go. She totters in the doorway in her black sleeveless blouse, her pencil skirt and heels, a shawl thrown over her arm. Miguel wonders if they are going to a funeral.

"Rachel," Nathan calls again.

She signals with her fingers: two minutes. Even though Rachel and Nathan are fasting, she can't expect two little boys to fast as well. They'd thought of bringing the boys with them. There is, after all, the playgroup, but it means the boys will be stuck there all day and, given Davie's ADHD and Jeremy's tendencies to what she has to admit to herself is borderline bullying, it just seems better if they stay home rather than having to go through the trouble of introducing them into a new playgroup with strange kids.

As they pull off their dirt road and onto the highway, Nathan says. "You sure you can trust that kid with our boys?" Today is one of the few times he has seen Miguel and it is always in passing.

"Oh, he's spent a lot of time alone with them," she lies. In fact most afternoons Rachel is home.

Nathan shakes his head. "He drives a lowrider with flames painted on the door and you're okay with that? Rachel, what do you really know about him?"

Rachel stares straight ahead at the mountains, the city of Santa Fe appearing just over the crest of the hill. "I know enough," she says. It is a day of fasting; of making the world right. Tikkun, it is called. Putting the pieces back together. It is what Rachel tries to do. She often fails, but she does try to make the world a better place. She doesn't understand how people can be so callous and cruel. She practices kindness whenever she can. "He's a good kid, Nathan," Rachel goes on. "The boys like him." Nathan purses his lips in that way that makes Rachel uneasy. He is practiced at making her doubt herself. He makes her start to put question marks at the ends of her sentences. *He is a good kid, isn't he? And the boys like him a lot, don't they?*

It is packed in the shul and hot. Very hot for October. It wasn't this warm last night for Kol Nidre (when they had brought the boys with them), but that was because the desert breeze blew. Now it is the heat of the day. The High Holy Days usually come earlier, but this year they are late. Still the heat is unusual. Rachel can make no sense out of the Jewish calendar. All she knows is that now they are stifling. When she enters the synagogue, she keeps her shawl around her arms, but as the large room fills with perhaps five hundred people, atoning for their sins, she drops her shawl. Nathan takes off his jacket. Then he looks around at the other men and takes off his tie.

The service has already begun. The prayers, the recitation of sins, the beating of breasts. And then the Torah portion, but Rachel's mind drifts back to Rosh Hashanah—the sacrifice of Isaac. And the rabbi's endless sermon, "What Sacrifice Will You Make?" Rachel always wonders why God asks Abraham to kill his own son. What is God testing? On the holy days, they are asked to make a sacrifice. How much would you give up for God? What if God asks for your son? Anyway it didn't go over very well with Isaac. He never spoke to his father again.

But at last the Torah portion is done and the rabbi's talk, and then comes the haftorah, and that recitation seems endless as well. It takes so long that Nathan leans over and whispers, "It feels more like the full Torah to me."

Rachel stifles a giggle, putting her hand over her mouth. She is glad that her husband said something funny. That he whispered into her ear. He seems happier, his mood lighter of late. "That is good," she whispers back, her lips grazing his ear. She has a sense that perhaps now, at last, things will be better. Perhaps even all right. Today is a day of tikkun, isn't it?

Someone is opening the large sanctuary windows, letting the hot breeze in. And the doors, they too are wedged open, but still it is boiling inside. No one can remember it being this hot for the holidays. Suddenly there is a bustling. People moving around her quickly. Behind her she can see that someone, an old man perhaps, is slumped over. A hush comes over the room. The rabbi ceases his prayers. Someone calls out, "Is there a doctor in the house?"

About thirty men stand and rush to the back of the room. So it's not just a joke about Jewish doctors. The room is full of them. She turns to say something to Nathan but he has slipped from her side. She doesn't even feel him sliding away from her into the sea of doctors. Her eyes scan the room until she sees that it is Nathan who is tending to the man. It makes sense, of course. Nathan is a cardiologist—for children, it is true, but still. From the chair where she sits she can see her husband holding the man's hand. Gently he bends over the man, asking him questions as he checks his vitals. He takes his pulse. He prods the man's chest, his throat. He examines his eyes. Water is brought and Nathan cradles the man's head so that he can sip. She sees the look of concern in her husband's face.

She studies Nathan's every movement because it occurs to her that he hasn't touched her, in a very long time, as tenderly, as patiently as he is touching that elderly man. It has been months since he has stared at her with those same, focused eyes.

+

Back in Colibri Canyon it is hot in the house and the natives are restless. They'd gone through at least three rounds on the Game Boy. They'd watched all the Looney Tunes that Miguel can find on the TV and a DVD of Dumbo and Snow White, which Jeremy described as "idiotic." What a smartass seven-year-old to call something idiotic. He's idiotic. But Miguel can't tell him that. He will learn it himself soon enough. But Miguel doesn't like the way Jeremy pushes his brother around, and Davie still won't fight back. Just an hour ago Jeremy got a wild look in his eyes just before he hit Davie over the head with a Wiffle ball bat. It is plastic, but still it made Davie cry his eyes out and run around like crazy. Jeremy had a mean look in his eyes that chills Miguel to the bone.

Miguel stands in the long corridor, staring out through the yard and into the desert beyond. This day he knows is a special one for the Rothsteins. He doesn't entirely understand it, but he knows that it is a holiday and that he is being asked to spend the day with the boys— something he's never done before. And now he's at a loss with what to do with them. At the edge of the property there is an arroyo and beyond that he's seen a trail that appears to head off into the desert. He hears the shouting from the living room. These boys need to burn off some steam, and Miguel decides that they should go for a hike. He wouldn't mind getting out of the confines of the house as well.

He goes back into the living room where Jeremy is flipping channels and Davie keeps saying, "Let's watch this one. Let's watch that."

"Boys," Miguel says, getting their attention. "I have an idea. Let's go for a hike."

They look up at him, bewildered. "What's a hike?" Davie asks. And Jeremy nods. He's only heard the word used once before when another babysitter told him to go take a hike, but he'd never learned what it meant.

Miguel stares down in disbelief. "It's when you go for a long walk outside."

"We've never been on a hike," Jeremy says. Miguel looks out the window at the vast expanse of desert and mountains, a picture window onto the Southwest. They've lived here for six months and they've never been on a hike. He wants to ask if their father has ever taken them anywhere, but he is pretty sure he knows the answer. "Well, you're going on one now."

Miguel hesitates for only a moment. Mrs. Rothstein has never said that he can take the boys beyond the yard but she's never said he can't either, and they will all be climbing the walls soon if they don't get out. The house has a small fenced-in yard with a swing set and slide, the kind you pick up at Home Depot and assemble in an afternoon. He thinks a doctor can afford a better swing set and probably even a bigger yard, but no matter.

He helps the boys put on long pants and sneakers. Jeremy complains that it is too hot for long pants, but it is a warm day and snakes can be active. Miguel finds a stick that will serve as a walking stick, but also in case he needs it to prod or poke something. He also carries his pocket-knife with him as always. It has a four-inch blade.

"Can we bring Baxter?"

Miguel shakes his head. "No, no dog." It is enough to take care of the boys without being responsible for a dog as well. This is a good plan. Miguel likes it. He'll take them for a half-hour hike, no longer, but it will get them tired out. And then they'll be exhausted all afternoon. "We're on a mission," Miguel says, "so it is very important that you follow my instructions exactly."

Davie jumps up and down. "What mission? What mission?"

Jeremy shakes his head. "There's no mission, dummy."

"Yes there is," Miguel says. "I've just received a message. There's a missing ship and we've been asked to find it."

Davie leans toward him. "What kind of a ship?"

"An intergalactic spaceship," Miguel whispers into his ear.

Jeremy shakes his head. "I'm staying here."

"No," Miguel replies. "You are my second-in-command."

He knows that this will all be lost on Jeremy, who has long ago taken a deep dislike to him, but he doesn't care. Miguel goes into the kitchen where he fills two water bottles and grabs snack packages of Fig Newtons. He puts baseball caps on the boys and slathers them in sunscreen, especially Jeremy who is so pale. He doesn't bother putting sunscreen on himself. He's lived in the desert all of his life. Besides he is dark-skinned. All that happens to him in the sun is that he grows darker.

At last they are ready. As they step out, they are greeted by the blistering sun. A wave of heat. Jeremy shakes his head, turning to go back inside but Miguel turns him around. "Come on. You'll get used to it. Okay, you're both going to follow me and stay on the trail. Jeremy, you bring up the rear. Single file—Indian style."

So the boys set out on their first hike into their new world. They've never headed out along Colibri Canyon Road let alone into the desert. They walk down the driveway to the side of house, and then follow the fence that contains their yard. Miguel can feel their excitement. They won't go for long. Just long enough to get them good and tired.

It is one of those broiling hot desert days. The kind when you can scramble eggs on the canyon roads, as his father likes to say. No wind comes down from the Sangre de Cristos. There isn't a cloud in the sky and the sun beats down on them. Still the boys walk ahead at a good pace. This is something new. An adventure. Overhead a hawk glides. And in the distance vultures circle over the crest of a hill, probably above a dead deer or coyote. Maybe even a dog.

They make their way down the arroyo. The riverbed is bone-dry. Tumbleweeds blow past them. Only the piñon and juniper grow here. The boys seem awed at how big the world is, at how much space they could have to play in. Suddenly Jeremy is racing ahead and Davie takes off after him. "No running." The boys race on a little farther, then come to a sudden halt. Miguel catches up with them. Off to the side of the trail he sees what Jeremy has seen. An old diamondback rattlesnake lies coiled, basking in the sun. Miguel clasps the boys by the arms. "It's not a problem," Miguel says, taking each boy by the hand. "We just step around them here." Gingerly they make a wide berth around the snake. Miguel breathes a sigh of relief. He's so glad that he decided not to bring the dog. "If you hear the rattle," Miguel tells them, "then it's a problem. But for now let's let this old guy take his nap."

He can teach these boys things. Things they'd never learn without him. He knows how to extract water from a cactus when you are dying of thirst and how to move logs in the woodpiles where scorpions hide. He knows that tarantulas don't hurt you if you know how to handle them and that they even make good pets. And that in the spring during the melt these arroyos and canyons can bring on flash floods that you'll never hear until they are upon you. Rattlesnakes are dormant in winter so you never have to worry about a snakebite at that time of year and now in the heat of the day this snake is just sunning itself. Even though diamondbacks are very poisonous, he can tell by the thickness of the body that it is an older snake. The young are more dangerous because they don't know how to conserve their venom, but an older snake won't bite unless you mess with it. An older snake saves its venom for its kills. Its bite might not release any venom at all. If the boys are going to live here, he'll have to teach them what he knows.

Now the boys are curious. Jeremy finds a dead lizard and pokes at it with a stick. Because of the rains the chamisa are in bloom and they pause to admire the yellow flowers. A ruby-throated hummingbird buzzes around the chamisa blooms, and the boys watch as it sinks its beak into the petals. Overhead a raven cries. Using his hand as a visor, Miguel searches for it in the sky. Though he can hear the raven, he can't see it. It is hard in the desert to gauge distances. Perhaps it is farther away than he thinks. Still, from its sharp cry it seems as if it is right overhead. He scans the skies, letting his gaze drift toward the mountains. Perhaps one day, if Mrs. Rothstein will let him, he'll show the boys Entrada.

In the middle of the trail Miguel comes to a pile of fresh horse manure. Some riders have been by here not long ago. Normally Miguel wouldn't stop and look at a manure pile, but the dung beetles are all over it. They are marching in a straight line toward the manure, and then they are walking backward, pulling their spoils in the same straight line. Pausing to observe their fecal foraging, he wonders why they are doing that. It's what Mr. Garcia always told him to ask: Why? Perhaps he will show this to the boys. They'd probably find it gross but he finds it interesting. He squats down, looking more closely at the beetles. He prods the manure pile with his walking stick, but the beetles right themselves and continue on their way. Miguel turns his head, gazing up toward the blinding sun. Then he looks back at the beetles.

He is distracted for only an instant when he hears the cry a few feet behind him. He turns to see Jeremy punching Davie hard in the arm. And Davie raises his fist and punches him back. Miguel can't help but smile. Still he doesn't want them fighting out here. "Stop that," Miguel shouts, but before he can intervene Jeremy hits Davie square in the face. Blood splatters from the little boy's nose and sobs rise that Davie makes no attempt to hold back. "I hate you," Davie shouts at his brother, his little fists flying. "I hate you."

"Jeremy," Miguel shouts. "What's wrong with you?"

Miguel runs to where the brothers are fighting, but Davie has already taken off back down the trail, away from his brother, away from

Miguel. "Davie," Miguel shouts, "Stop." He chases after Davie, heading back to the house, calling out to Davie to wait for him. That is when he sees it. The snake, no longer coiled off to the side in the sun, is making its way across the path. Miguel raises his walking stick. "Davie, don't move. Stop," Miguel calls out just as Davie puts his sneaker down on the back of the snake, and it rises up to meet him.

Ten miles away as Rachel Rothstein sits in the heat of the temple, listening to the rabbi drone on, a shiver runs through her, and she wonders if she too isn't about to faint.

+

"I thought it would never end," Nathan says, wiping the sweat off his brow, his jacket slung over his shoulder as they are heading to their car. He unlocks the car and turns his beeper back on. He had turned it off during the service. He wasn't on call so it shouldn't matter. But now he gets several beeps. "I need to call the hospital." Nathan frowns. There should be plenty of doctors on call who can stand in for him.

Rachel gives him an impatient look. They have been fasting, and she's anxious to get home. And it seems to her as if there's always something that gets in the way. If he calls now, he may not even go home. And Nathan is tired and hungry as well. "I'll do it when we get back," he says.

"It was a long service, wasn't it?" Rachel says as they are driving. "But then you saved that man's life right in the middle of it." Rachel touches his arm.

Nathan shrugs as if he does this every day, which of course he does. "I don't know if I saved his life."

"Well, his wife certainly thinks so." It is the day to welcome the stranger, and Rachel has decided that she will invite Miguel to break the fast with them. But is he really a stranger? She has known Miguel for almost four months. He spends three afternoons a week with her boys. She leaves plates of cookies and pitchers of lemonade out for them. Yet Miguel has never eaten with them all together, not as a family. It only seems right that he should join them tonight.

Riding beside her husband and lover of almost a decade, Rachel

Rothstein wonders who the real stranger is. Even now, staring straight ahead, she is trying to think of something to say to him. She has no idea what Nathan does all day long. She has no idea whom he sees or talks to. She doesn't know if he has a sandwich for lunch or a slice of pizza. He makes a joke in synagogue and she wonders if he is really a funny man. Does he keep the OR laughing, making jokes as he's sewing up a child's aorta? She doesn't know. All of these details of her husband's life are unknown to her.

She has moved them far from family and friends and now they only have each other. It is as if she has been marooned on an island with a person she's never met. "What was I thinking?" she asks herself. It is so odd, so hard to understand and yet she feels as if she knows their Hispanic babysitter better than she knows her own spouse. And she wants to share the trays of smoked salmon and bagels, creamed herring and pickled beets with him.

They're having a feast—enough to feed her entire extended family (who collectively think they were insane to leave New York and move to the middle of nowhere). So she will ask Miguel to stay. And then, because she has thought this through, afterward, when the kids are in bed and the dishes done, she will put on that purple nightgown she hasn't worn yet. She will reach for her husband and bring him into her arms. Smiling, she reaches over and squeezes his thigh. And to her surprise he takes a hand off the wheel and clasps her hand.

Something has been made right after all. That shiver that went through her, it is only that. A wisp of the wind. A chill that sometimes comes to you on a hot day. No, this is tikkun. She will invite Miguel to dinner and somehow Nathan will see why they are here and he will want to make love to her as he used to. And yet as they wind their way up Colibri Canyon Road, Rachel knows that nothing can be this simple. Nothing can so easily turn things around. She is having one of her strange feelings. Something that is difficult to describe. And yet as they swerve along the road, everything is eerily still. It is as if the world has slowed down.

When they pull up to the house, Rachel knows something isn't right.

"His car isn't here," Rachel says, almost to herself.

"What do you mean?"

"Miguel should be here."

Nathan shrugs. "Maybe he took the boys somewhere."

But Rachel shakes her head. "Why would he? He never has before."

"Well, there's always a first time. Let's get inside."

Before he even stops the car Rachel is dashing to the house. As she approaches, Baxter is barking. Outside of the dog the house is quiet and dark. No TV on, no lights. "Davie, Jeremy, we're home," she shouts, and then goes to the picture window. Probably they're in the yard, playing. She expects to see them banging the tetherball or on the swings, but except for a tumbleweed blowing across the yard, nothing moves. She begins running from room to room, calling their names, Baxter at her heels. Is this some creepy form of hide-and-seek? At some let's-surprise-Mommy moment they'll jump out of a closet in unison. But there is no surprise. No shout intended to startle her. The house is as empty as the yard.

Then the darkest thoughts come to her. Has he kidnapped her boys? Is he involved with some drug dealer and they've taken them away? She really doesn't know Miguel that well, does she? She hadn't asked for references. She'd just gone on instinct. Her gut. And now her children are gone. Was this a big plot in the first place? A bad TV show? At any moment she expects the ransom call with those specific instructions. *Do not call the police. Assemble a million dollars in unmarked, nonsequential bills. Your husband is a doctor. Of course you can get that much cash.* Then you hear your kids, screaming in the background. Wasn't it that Italian billionaire who kept getting parts of his son in the mail until he paid whatever the kidnappers required?

She knows nothing about Miguel. Nathan is right. Everyone is right. Her boys are gone. She is trying not to panic. Trying to hold it together. She needs to think, catch her breath. Surely there is an explanation. That is when she notices the light of the answering machine. It is blinking with one message. Her family wouldn't call on Yom Kippur. They are all in temple atoning for their sins. Miguel just called to say that they went somewhere for ice cream and ran out of gas or something like that. And she'll laugh and everything will be forgiven.

But as she listens, she can barely make out what Miguel is saying, but then she does. Not the specifics, but at least she knows where they are. That's when she turns and sees Nathan standing at the door. "There's been an accident." Rachel races outside shouting at Nathan. "Quick. Drive. To the hospital."

Even as he speeds around the turns, Rachel can feel those pursed lips, those judgmental stares. "Oh god," she thinks, "please let them be all right." And then: "Oh god, Nathan will kill me if anything happens to those boys."

"Did he say what happened?" Nathan asks in that cold voice she can barely stand. She envisions dozens of things. The boys were fighting and one of them fell. Perhaps off the couch, twisting a wrist, an ankle. Or one of those sword fights with those cardboard-and-tinfoil swords. Some stupid childhood thing. The kind you dine out on years from now. How much damage can a cardboard sword cause? Can you lose an eye? Why not scribble a note? What can be so serious that you can't leave a note on the kitchen counter.

"Just drive," she answers. And Nathan speeds along. As they are rushing to the hospital, Rachel does something she's never done before. She prays. She prays to God that her sons are all right. She makes promises. *I will be a better mother. I will be more attentive to my sons and my husband. I will do volunteer work to help the less advantaged. I will complete tasks I have begun. I'll be a loving wife. I will make any bargain I can, but please let my sons be all right. Please God, don't let any harm come to them. It is still the Day of Atonement, isn't it, so after all it is a day when one can beg forgiveness and ask for pardon.*

They tear into the parking lot at Mercy Hospital, and Nathan pulls into his reserved spot. Rachel dashes out of the car, racing through the double doors of the emergency room entrance. All those antiseptic smells and other smells, the smells no one wants to think about, hitting her at once. There in the waiting room Miguel sits, slumped, his head in his hands and Jeremy, surprisingly quiet, is kicking his legs back and forth against the chair as she races up to them. When Jeremy sees her, he springs up, tears pouring down his face. "Mommy, Mommy, Davie stepped on a snake."

"A snake?" Though she never has before, she thinks she will faint. "There was a snake in the yard?" That's why they built a fence, wasn't it? To keep danger away. The coyotes and snakes and whatever else might threaten her children. That's what the fence was for.

Nathan arrives, panting behind her. Tears pouring down his face, Miguel tries to explain. "It's my fault," Miguel says, "I took them for a hike."

"A hike?" Nathan is yelling and Rachel is trying to calm him down. "Who told you to take them for a hike. Who the hell—"

"It was very hot inside and the boys needed to get out—"

"Get out? We have a yard. We have a swing set. Who says they needed to get out into the desert?"

"Nathan, please, let's just see about Davie." Even as she runs to her son, Rachel doesn't blame Miguel. No, she tells herself, no matter what happened, and she prays to God it is nothing terrible, it's not his fault. This isn't his fault. Dashing through the ER, she goes from bed to bed. Doctors look up at her, patients think she is a nurse.

"May I help you?" a doctor asks.

"I'm looking for my son," she gasps.

In one of the beds she finds him. He is pale, his skin bone white. His eyes are closed, and there is a droplet of spittle in the corner of his mouth. His ankle is packed in ice, and an IV goes through his arm. The attending physician is with him and a nurse is checking his vitals. "Dr. Rothstein," the attending says, extending his hand. "Mrs. Rothstein." He pats Davie on the head, and Davie opens his eyes. When he sees his parents standing there, he smiles. Rachel bursts into tears, hugging Davie, who seems surprisingly not upset. "He's not out of the woods yet, but I think this young man is going to be fine. It was what we call 'a dry bite.'"

Suddenly she feels a sense of relief. "What is a dry bite?"

"The snake was being defensive. It wasn't trying to really hurt or kill your little boy. It released very little venom. He's had a scare, but he's very brave." The doctor smiles at Davie. "Mostly I think he's in shock." He takes Rachel and Nathan aside. "You know, your babysitter, he did everything right. He tied a tourniquet. He carried Davie to the car, made him stay calm, and kept his leg elevated."

Rachel nods. "Yes," she says, "I am sure he would."

"He even told the ER that it was an old snake and it probably didn't release much venom." The doctor smiles at them through watery blue eyes. "And he was right about that."

Again Rachel nods. "He's smart. He would know." She is still trembling, but Nathan seems calmer. "I'll go tell him. And I'll get Jeremy."

When she gets to the waiting room, she finds Jeremy sipping apple juice and sitting with a nurse. The nurse stands up. "You must be Rachel," the nurse says. For an instant Rachel wonders. *How does she know my name?* Rachel glances at her name tag. "Dawn." Is this significant, Rachel wonders? Dawn. The start of a new day.

Rachel takes Jeremy by the hand and looks for Miguel. But Miguel is gone.

✳

CHAPTER TWENTY-FIVE

EL ILLUMINADO—1569

When Alejandro Cordero emerged from the mines of Taxco, covered in a fine silver dust, it was as if in a matter of days he had turned into an old man. Perhaps in some ways he had. Though he is barely thirty years old, his pallor and white hair startled those who encountered him. They gave him safe passage as if he were a ghost. Yet it was not only the whiteness of the dust that surprised but also the translucent blue eyes that peered from its paleness. No one had ever seen eyes quite like his before. Certainly not in the hills of Taxco. Alejandro traveled by night down from the hills with only one mission in mind. He had to go to his mother. He'd been told that they would be next.

Now he makes his way in the darkness. The city is a puzzle to him. For all of his abilities, Alejandro has no sense of direction. Despite the fact that his grandfather sailed with Columbus, Alejandro does not know north from south, left from right. He can never remember if he's been down one street or another. He carries no internal map. But it seems to be a family trait. More than once he'd run into his own father, walking home the wrong way.

It is pitch-black with no lights to guide him. The cobblestones are wet and slippery from an afternoon rain. Alejandro is careful to avoid the rivulets of sewage that flow through the drainage ditches by the side of the roads. He also must keep his eyes on the upper windows, for at any moment someone could toss down a bucket of dishwater or a chamber pot of slop. In the night these streets are rife with murderers and thieves. Yet there are much greater things to fear.

His brother, Simon, had gotten word to him. He was being searched for in Taxco, where he oversaw his family's silver mines. It did not surprise him to learn that there was a price on his head. Two months ago his older sister, Magdalena, was arrested and no one had heard a word from her since. She had always been the most outspoken and careless of the siblings. She refused to eat a pork stew at a neighbor's house and wore clean clothes on the Sabbath for all to see. Alejandro has been more discreet, but now it doesn't matter. Magdalena has put them all at risk.

He rode slowly down from Taxco through the hills to the city that was once ruled by Montezuma. Now it is in the hands of Spanish bureaucrats, whose only purpose seems to be to protect the pure blood of Spain. He longs to see Sofia. If he can, he will find a way. It has been months since he has been with her, but he is not sure if he can risk it. It is enough that he is going to see his mother. He fears he will compromise Sofia and her family as well.

Yet it is so difficult for him to come to Mexico City and not see her. For years she was only his little cousin, the daughter of his mother's sister—a child given to luring birds to eat out of her hand and who plucked wildflowers wherever they grew. One day she began to tame wild dogs. Dogs that bit the ankles of horses riding by, that snapped the meat from the butcher's hands. These wild dogs roamed the streets, terrifying everyone except Sofia. She carried fatty scraps in her pockets and they followed her like lambs, lying at her feet when she commanded, handing her a paw when she asked.

When she was only fourteen and Alejandro was just turning twenty, he ran into her coming down the street with her pack of dogs, her dark hair hanging loose in the wind, and he recognized her for the magnificent, feral creature that she was. He too began to follow her, though he refused to be tamed. This was the only way he would win her over and he did. One rain-sodden night he approached her and declared his love. "We are first cousins," she said as if he needed to be reminded. "But I will marry no one else but you."

For years they have had to steal moments to be together, meeting when they can sneak away. Since he has been in exile, he dreams of her every night. When he can, he sends her messages, and when she is able, she replies. She will wait for him. When he is ready to leave Mexico, which will be as soon as he puts some of his affairs in order, she will accompany him wherever he decides to go. He will try, but only if it is safe. Otherwise he must stay away.

As he follows the canals, Alejandro covers his face with his cape so he will not have to breathe the ripe air. The Spanish use these once teeming waterways as garbage dumps. Thirty years ago when his father, Benjamin Cordero, arrived in New Spain, the canals were lined with orange and lemon and palm trees. The petals of hibiscus filled the banks while gondolas drifted past. His father saw the monuments and pyramids of the great Tenochtitlan upon whose ruins houses and government buildings now stand. Alejandro gasps. The canals are rife with the stench of rotting meat, fetid fruit, and human waste. Normally he arrives at his mother's house in a carriage or on horseback. He never walks along the canals. But tonight there is no other way.

He has not seen his mother in almost a year, since his father died. But now he is coming to warn her, though he also brings danger to her door. He is almost there, but he will not knock. He will find another way to make his presence known. A knock will send terror through his family. Every Jew has come to fear the knock on the door. When he reaches the house, he goes around to the back where he can peer into the kitchen. Julia, the cook, stirs something on the stove. She is speaking with someone he cannot see, but he can make out the smile on Julia's face and he can hear her laughter.

After a few moments he taps at the window and Julia looks his way. Julia does not seem surprised to see him. Since his sister's arrest they have anticipated his return. She lets him in with a hug and tears in her eyes. "You've come. We knew you would."

He hugs the old cook who has worked for the family since he was a boy. Now he looks at her companion. It is Bernadine, Julia's daughter. Alejandro can't believe his good luck. Bernadine works for his aunt and uncle. She is also Sofia's maid. He turns to Bernadine. "How is she?"

Bernadine gives him a shrug. "As good as any of us. She waits for you."

Alejandro nods. "Tell her I've come." He cannot resist. "I'll see her soon."

Bernadine smiles, for she likes Alejandro and she also likes taking messages between the two as she has been doing for years. Bernadine goes back and forth between the houses, carrying food and linens along with notes and small packages. Bird feathers, lockets, a snippet of hair. Bernadine is the only one who knows for certain of the secret love that Sofia bears for her cousin and he for her. Being a go-between makes Bernadine feel indispensable, as if she were the center of some intrigue, which she is, though their families have long ago suspected that the two cousins are in love and also long ago agreed that it would never be consecrated.

Bernadine slips her shawl over her head and kisses her mother goodbye. "I must be going."

Julia turns to Alejandro. "Your mother is in the dining room."

Alejandro slips down the corridor, where he finds his mother, poised like a mannequin, in the black dress and veil of her mourning, at the head of the table where his father once sat. Before her is a plate of lamb with apricots that she has barely touched. His heart breaks at the sight of her. He has never seen his mother alone at the long wooden table surrounded by empty chairs made from the finest Spanish cane. Before there were never less than half a dozen people—his parents and siblings, cousins or friends—at a meal and they were all so busy, chattering about their days, laughing at whatever silliness had occurred, arguing over the differences they might have. And now his mother sits in her solitude. It occurs to him that she has been eating like this for months.

It seemed like yesterday that his father had his thriving import and export business. Cacao, pepper, and spices that he shipped from Veracruz to Lisbon and Antwerp. When he came to the New World, he specialized in cacao. His own mother had taught him how to mix the milk and sugar to make the cocoa sweet. And he had sold his beans all over Europe. In New Spain Benjamin had branched off into spices and textiles. Later he invested in the silver mines in Taxco. But that thriving business had also diminished. Fewer and fewer people came to their home and now Leonora eats alone. But it is not only because Benjamin is gone. It is also because he was bathed, then wrapped in linen and buried in a plain casket according to the Law of Moses.

It was a year ago that Alejandro had helped his father whose body was fetid and oozing, turn his face to the wall and leave this world. Alejandro was there to comfort him in his pain. He was with him as he drew his last breath. Alejandro abided by his father's wishes. He stayed with his body to enable his soul's journey from this world. He ordered the servants to bathe him in cold water and wrap his body in a white linen shroud. He ordered the plain casket with three holes drilled in the bottom so that the soul might pass through. Alejandro cut his father's nails and his hair. He said the prayers for the dead. Any one of these servants could have betrayed his family and they would never know. For months they mourned. But now they have an even greater sadness to bear.

His mother looked up and, seeing her youngest son, her dark, troubled eyes fill with tears. "So you've come."

Alejandro nods. "I had to see if you are all right."

"I am not all right," she says in a cold, dry voice. "They've taken Magdalena." And she adds in barely a whisper, "To the Flat House."

"I've heard." His mother doesn't have to explain to him what this means. Everyone knows that the Flat House is not the Royal Prison where you might be given the courtesy of a trial and have a lawyer for your defense, where you might receive visitors and be brought food. The Flat House is the prison of the Inquisition where you are put into one of the secret cells. You are kept for as long as the proceedings against you take. Days, months, even years. You are presumed guilty unless proven innocent. All your worldly goods are confiscated. You might never know who has informed against you or what the charges are, besides heresy. If you do not confess to practicing the dark Law of Moses and repent, you will be tortured until you die. Or you will be broken and made to confess not only to your own heresies but also to those of your family and friends and perhaps even to those of strangers.

Julia slips into the room with a plate of lamb with garbanzos that she places in front of Alejandro, who is now seated beside his mother. It is his favorite dish, one that his mother brought with her from the old country, a dish once famous among the Jews of Córdoba and Seville, so sweet with apricots and so savory with cumin and turmeric. It is as if she knew he would be returning that night.

"Have you seen Simon? Balthazar has written to me. He is in Rome. He wants us to join him," his mother says.

Alejandro nods. "Yes, it is Simon who told me. And I will write to Balthazar. We will all join him. I am going to put our affairs in order so that we may leave." He gazes upon his mother more closely. Her face is pale. She has aged in the months since he last saw her. His eyes are drawn to the necklace she wears. Its chain disappears into her bodice. Gently Alejandro reaches for it, pulling out a crucifix. "Why are you wearing this?" he asks.

"I have sworn allegiance to Jesus Christ, our Lord." She makes the sign of the cross.

"You cannot be serious. We are Jews."

"I will not burn in hell," his mother says.

"I will burn at the stake," her son retorts, "but not in hell."

His mother lowers her eyes. "It is the only way."

"This so-called Inquisition is more about filling the purses of the king and queen than saving souls from damnation."

"Be that as it may, I am now a true believer in Jesus Christ, our Lord."

Alejandro is stunned. He has come all this way to find his mother a true Christian. He doubts her every word. "You do not mean what you say. I know that. I will not submit to their tyranny."

With that he pushes himself away from the table and goes to his room. He lies down on his bed but does not undress. In the morning he will go and see Sofia, and he will tell her that he is leaving and he wants her to join him. He knows that she will come. He will urge his aunt and uncle to leave as well. If nothing else he is hoping that this will be the catalyst that will allow his mother and Sofia's parents to grant them permission to marry.

For years they kept their love a secret. At family occasions they low-ered their eyes. They tried not to look at each other, but in the end they could not help themselves. With his dark skin, shiny black hair, and blue eyes, Alejandro was not a man whom women could ignore, but he had only loved one—his cousin Sofia. It seems to him as if he has loved her his entire life and perhaps in some way he has. But both fami-lies have refused to allow them to marry. And Sofia's mother will barely let her see him. Sofia has vowed to go into a nunnery if she cannot marry Alejandro. And so far her parents' efforts to find suitors and marry her off have been thwarted.

Alejandro spends a sleepless night tossing in his bed, planning for when and how they will leave. Yet even as he thinks about Sofia, a sense of dread fills him. It is almost dawn when the knock comes at the door. The alguacil and his henchmen clomp up the stairs. As Ale-jandro protests, they beat him with truncheons and when he cries out, they stuff a metal gag into his mouth. They tighten its screws until Alejandro thinks his jaw will break. His mother rushes out of her bed-room and cries out as well, but they slap her until she lies whimpering in a corner. Then they force his hands behind his back and drag him away.

+

A decade ago none of this would have happened. Until Alejandro Cor-dero was thirteen, he did not know a thing about his family's past. He was a teenage boy who cared only for the small world that surrounded him and a housemaid named Lily, who at times slipped into his bed to comfort him. He never questioned his family's strange practices of refusing to eat shellfish even when they went to the sea or the grimace on his mother's face when the butcher offered her a choice cut of pork butt, which she purchased though rarely served unless Spanish officials were coming to dine. Mostly she gave the pork to the servants. These things meant nothing to him until the day when his father, Benjamin Cordero, took him aside and explained as gently as he could that they were Jews.

His father told him the strangest story he'd ever heard. Alejandro thought that it was a story that grown-ups like to convince children is true. His father told him that he had been found on an island in the New World by a woman named Inez Cordero who raised him and that he was descended from the translator who accompanied Columbus on his first voyage. His father explained that both he and Alejandro's mother were Jews. At first Alejandro did not believe his father. How could it be that he had lived his life one way and now suddenly had to live it another? Why would they hide this from him? None of it made sense and yet it must be true.

He was determined. If he were a Jew, he would live as a Jew. He would not hide who he is. He began to study. He sought out a teacher, a secret Jew, who taught him the Hebrew alphabet. He studied the letters late into the night until they swirled in his head. Through the letters he found his gateway to God. Within weeks Alejandro was able to read the Torah. He learned that Abraham made his covenant with God at the age of ninety-nine by cutting off his own foreskin.

That night in his room in the hacienda where he had lived his entire childhood as a Catholic on the outskirts of Mexico City, Alejandro examined his member. Up until this moment he had enjoyed the pleasure of his own flesh. His large, pulsating cock had served his boyhood needs, bringing him dreams that left him soaked and spent. It had responded well in the hands of Lily, who was soon afterward let go. Alejandro was struck by its considerable size. Even his own mother admired it. Once in front of his father she pulled it out and said, "Look at this son of yours—he's hung like a bull." But now he would make his covenant with God as Abraham had.

The next day Alejandro went to the river, where on a chilly fall morning he removed his clothes and stood naked on the banks. He entered the frigid water and stayed until his body was blue and shivering. Here he whispered a prayer, asking for strength for what he was about to do. Then he left the river and dried himself off. He took out the barber's razor he'd brought with him in a leather rucksack and began to slice off his foreskin. The pain was excruciating, but still he cut. Blood coursed from his groin, down his thighs. He thought he would faint or even die of the pain. When he was done, he tossed his foreskin into the waters. He wrapped his penis with a cloth that was soon soaked in blood. Then he collapsed.

When he woke, the blood still flowed down his legs. It occurred to him that he was bleeding to death. Besides this, what was left of his member was the size of a newborn lamb. Delirious, he staggered home and when he saw his mother, fell into her arms. She feared that a bee had stung him for he was allergic to bees and once she'd had to breathe air into his throat. Then she saw the blood dripping down his thighs.

"Oh, my God," she said. "What have you done?" She unwrapped the cloth and gasped. Now her son would be marked for life. Later he will think that his member, which he had once admired and which had brought him so much pleasure, resembled a rooster with its ruffled red cock's comb, and for years he would avoid the intimate touches of women because of the pain it would cause and the laughter it would bring. Indeed, despite his good looks and considerable charms, Alejandro Cordero was certain that he would die a virgin and a martyr. But then he fell in love with Sofia. And while they have touched and caressed, they have never been together—not as a man and woman should be. He has braced himself for the day when in their marital bed he will have to reveal to her his mutilated member and she will love and embrace him without batting an eye. At least this was how he imagined his life would be.

+

At the Flat House they yank the metal bulb from Alejandro's mouth. He spits out his front teeth. Blood spurts from his lips; the corners of his mouth have been ripped open by the gag. He gasps and then sobs. A man in dark robes sits at a desk, writing down his name, his age, the address where he last lived. The seven reales he has on him are also confiscated. "We will open an account in your name. You must sign here." Trembling, Alejandro takes the pen with which he opens his account. It will pay for his room and board, and his trial and torments and any other expenses he might incur, including his own execution. There is a fixed price for everything.

Without another word he is taken downstairs and stripped of his clothes. He stands naked, shivering, and afraid. Then he is taken to his cell. His heart sinks when he sees the windowless room with a wooden door. On the floor is a bed of urine-soaked straw and a bucket in which to relieve himself. There is no blanket to keep him warm. He is given a candle and a bowl of thin gruel. "May I have a Bible? Something to read," Alejandro asks his jailer as he takes the bowl away.

"You are entitled to nothing," his jailer replies, taking his candle away as well. Alejandro lies on his pallet, shivering, gasping. In the darkness he cannot even make out the walls, but he hears the sounds of creatures scurrying. He hears the sound of crying. It sounds like women's voices, coming from the next cell. He calls out "Is anyone here?" but receives no reply. Only the thinnest line of light from beneath the door lets him know that it is still day.

+

He is brought to a room that has black curtains on the walls. In the center is a table covered in a black cloth. He has lost all sense of time, but through the slim opening of the curtains it seems that the light is beginning to fade. Soon he will spend his first night in the Flat House. Still Alejandro is fortunate. Some people wait months to be called. He has had to wait only a matter of hours for his first questioning.

At the table sits the priest in a hooded cloak. Alejandro cannot see his face, let alone his eyes. He has been given sackcloth to present himself in before his inquisitor. "Why not save yourself from the flames," the priest says. "You have nothing to do but confess." The priest puts a sheet of paper on the table before Alejandro. "And tell us the names of others who are practicing the dead Law of Moses."

"But, Honorable Sir, how can I confess if I do not know of what I am accused?" Alejandro knows what awaits him if he confesses. All his property and worldly goods will be confiscated. He will have to wear the sanbenito, the yellow holy cloth of the repentant, for at least two years or until the inquisitor determines that he is fully rehabilitated into the church. And then his sanbenito will hang in the church for all to see. All he has to do is kiss the cross and admit that he has been practicing the dead Law of Moses. If he does not, what awaits him is torture and death.

Even as he stands before the inquisitor, his mouth throbbing, his hands numb, his thoughts turn to Sofia. As he contemplates the torments that lie ahead, he knows that he can never utter her name. He can call out the names of those who have already fled New Spain, such as his brother Balthazar, or those already dead who will be burned in effigy. If his bones are being broken or his flesh ripped, he can say the name of Magdalena because she is already in this hell house. But he cannot implicate his beloved cousin or her family. In fact he can never see her or utter her name again.

His inquisitor passes a sheet toward him. It is his confession. All he has to do is sign it and implicate the members of his family and friends who are Judaizers. And then testify against them. And he can go free. Without bothering to look at it, Alejandro pushes the paper back. The inquisitor raises his eyes at a man who stands in the shadows. The man who wears a leather mask grabs Alejandro by the arm and leads him away.

He is taken to a room that has no light, but Alejandro can make out the glittering of the metal shackles, the rope hung over the rafters that will pull him up once his hands are secured behind his back. He cannot find the words to reach his God. Instead Alejandro begins to cry, pleading for mercy as he had not since he was a child. He thinks he will faint as they yank his arms behind his back and hoist him up by the wrists. As he screams and screams, they leave him dangling inches off the ground. His hooded inquisitor is in the room, asking the same question over and over: "Tell me who else is guilty of your sins, and you will be free."

And Alejandro, gasping for breath, responds in kind: "Unless I know my sins, how may I accuse others?" Afterward he sits in his dark, dank cell, his arms hanging uselessly at his sides.

+

Hours go by. Or is it days? The passing of time is told by a faint flickering of light. The shuffle of his jailer's feet. The clanging of the slop buckets being emptied at dawn and then again at dusk. In the nearby cells he can hear sobs, and once or twice he heard his name. At first he thought he was imagining it, but in the night it came to him more clearly. His mother and his sister are in cells nearby. In the night when the jailers are asleep, he calls back to them. Or with a stone he taps the refrain of the Sh'ma and listens as they tap a sad, faint reply.

Every few days the hooded inquisitor takes him into a room, ties him to a plank, and pours ewers of water down his throat. They ask him the same thing, over and over again. "Tell us who else is guilty of your sins and you will be free." They pour more and more water until he is certain he will drown. And he always answers in the same way. "Please tell me my sins so that I may answer your question."

When they are done with him, they toss him back into his cell where the straw he lies upon itches his skin. It smells of his own piss. He is certain that insects have burrowed into his flesh. He feels them, moving beneath the surface. Or is it his nerves? How long has he been here? For a time he etched the days on the wall of his cell. When the light came through the cracks, he made his mark. But then he began to forget if he had marked a day or not. And soon he doesn't even notice the light.

Has he been here a week? A month? He is certain that a season has passed because when he arrived he was so cold, and now he is beginning to feel the warmth. The sound of scurrying feet makes him tremble. He fears the rats that come at night. He has seen prisoners with their toes and ears nibbled away. The guards joke that the rats work for the grand inquisitor. But Alejandro will not let them feast on his flesh. He has collected a small arsenal of pebbles that he culls from his crumbling walls. At night he hurls these into the darkness. Many nights he stays up until the first crack of light, hurling stones at whatever sound he hears, even if it is only inside his head.

Alejandro dreads the darkness. It is his greatest tormenter. He can't bear that time of day when the tiniest shard of light that comes through a crack in the ceiling above begins to fade. It's a flame of hope extinguished inside of him. In the darkness his solitude is complete. There is no sound of his jailers shuffling from cell to cell with trays of thin gruel and crusts of stale bread, a bucket of water or another to pick up their slops. Not even the terrible sounds of men and women being dragged off to meet their interrogators, to suffer the endless sessions of tortures. Or to be taken on their final walk to the flames or, if the interrogator shows mercy or if the prisoner confesses his sins, the garrote. These entertainments are reserved for the day. Now it is only the blackness of night, the silence, or perhaps the faintest hint of weeping.

Like a blind person he learns to distinguish the cries. He can tell his mother's from Magdalena's. His mother's are silent gulps of air whereas Magdalena sobs loudly, not even trying to stifle them. Only a wall of thick stone stands between them. Still they cannot talk; they cannot speak to one another. Not even in the quietest of whispers or their suffering will be worse. Though it brings him some comfort to know that they are there, he cannot bear to think that their suffering matches his.

He ponders the flames. He cannot imagine what it will be like as his flesh burns. But the pain bothers him less than the abomination. For a Jew is intended to have his flesh returned to the earth, not blown as ash into the wind. He cannot bear the fact that his body will not be bathed and wrapped in white linen, that he will not be placed into a plain pine box, left open for the worms. No one will accompany his soul as it passes from this world to the next. No one will be there to guide him except his enemies. More than anything he worries that his soul will not reach his God.

Of course Alejandro is guilty of his crime. He knows that. He could easily confess. Hadn't he turned his father's face to the wall, washed his dead body in cold water, and trimmed his hair and nails? Doesn't he refrain from eating pork and continue to keep the Sabbath? And hasn't he, with a barber's razor, removed his own foreskin when he learned he was a Jew? But his mother? What has she done? To Alejandro her only sin has been to embrace Christ.

The only thing that interrupts his monotony are the parcels of food that Sofia leaves for him with the guards. If there is a note, he never sees it, but he is given a tin of stew or handful of fruit from time to time that has been brought to him by the sad, dark-eyed girl, as Gaspar, his jailer, refers to her. One morning Gaspar brings Alejandro an alligator pear that Sofia left for him. It is soft and green and creamy. Alejandro fondles its flesh. In the hint of light, he examines the green pulp. "You may share this if you like," Gaspar says. Alejandro has no idea what he means, but he eats only half of it, then summons his jailer and asks him to give the other half to his sister and mother. The next day the jailer brings him another alligator pear of even softer flesh. The natives call it an avocado. It is so green and fleshy and Alejandro wants to devour it in one bite. Instead, he eats a quarter of it and scrawls with a piece of stone he has sharpened a note to his mother on what remains. "Te Quiero, Mama."

The jailer takes it to her, and on the portion she does not devour she writes, with her hairpin, "Yo tambien." Every day Gaspar brings Alejandro an alligator pear that Sofia leaves, and on its green flesh Alejandro speaks with his mother and sister. Day after day, despite their hunger, they pass the pear between them with their messages inscribed.

On the day that will be his last, Alejandro Cordero inscribes one final note. He writes in the smallest letters he can: "This is the road to paradise. There is none other. It is a better journey than the one back to Castile."

✳

CHAPTER TWENTY-SIX

THE VISITOR FROM THE MOON—1992

A fter her last class Elena decides to walk home. It is a crisp fall day and she wants to be out in it, to stroll and think. If she can, she'd like to avoid seeing Derek for at least another hour. He is making her nervous. He seems to be hovering, watching her every move. She has been on the brink of leaving him so many times, but now it feels as if she will. It is difficult for Elena to stay with a man for more than a few years. It is almost as if once they get close, once they actually think they know her, she breaks away. Except that this time part of her wants to stay. She would like to think that this is the man with whom she will grow old, but it is hard for her to imagine. Whenever Elena thinks of herself in the future, she is always alone.

She likes walking along Central Park West. She loves the huge apartment buildings and tries to envision the people who live inside. The wealthy New Yorkers who have their doorman hail a cab, whose dry cleaning and groceries are delivered to their door. Elena wonders when, if ever, she'll feel like a real New Yorker. She's lived in the city for almost fifteen years. She danced with its premier ballet company. She eats in its restaurants, gets drunk in its clubs. She wears black. She pushes people out of the way to get on the subway. So when will she start to feel as if she is actually from here? Soon? Never? But aren't most real New Yorkers from away? Men still find her exotic. She does have a slight Spanish accent when she speaks. She walks with her feet turned out the way dancers do. At parties people like to guess where she is from. Mexico? Spain? Argentina? Once when she told a man she was from New Mexico, he asked what kind of visa she had.

The sun comes peering through the trees, the foliage turning to orange and gold like the aspen in the mountains where she is from. It is always this time of year when she thinks of home. When the leaves are turning and there is that crispness in the air. She never knew spring or summer the way it is here. That sweet smell of daffodils and tulips. Or those hot, humid summer days. And winter is too gray. But if anything makes her homesick, it is the fall. Though until her accident five years ago, she almost never thought of home. Except when her mother called, it was as if that place had been somewhere she'd dreamed about, not a real place, and certainly not one where she'd grown up. That was then and this, this city, this life, was ahead of her. But now on a brisk fall day with the leaves turning, her thoughts are of home. And Miguel.

She tries not to think of him, but sometimes she can't help it. She's kept only one photo of him that Roberto has sent over the years. Miguel as a toddler, learning to walk, his arms outstretched, holding on to someone's hands. Elena often wondered whose hands those were that helped him take his first steps. He is dark the way she is and smiling the way she once did. In his letters that always go unanswered, Roberto tells her about him. How he has grown tall and lanky. How he is interested in the sky. And now he has built his own telescope.

These thoughts make her happy. But they also make her wonder. She wants to know what he is like as a person. Does he have a girl? Has he made love to her yet? Does he know how to treat her? She hopes he does. She hopes he will treat a girl well. Still she barely knows Miguel. And she assumes she never will. But more than anything she wants him to be happy.

Elena wanders through the park. There are mothers out with strollers, kids playing ball. She comes to Strawberry Fields where she pauses to pay her respects. She often lingers here because it is a quiet zone, but today an out-of-tune musician is singing "I Want to Hold Your Hand." A sign reads, "No Music." Still, would-be musicians come here all the time to pick up some cash. Then the tourists come as well.

There are a dozen, snapping pictures. A young woman in tight green pants with red streaks in her dark hair kneels on the mosaic, inside a ring of rose petals, her hand touching IMAGINE as someone clicks her picture. Elena had moved to New York a few years before John Lennon was killed. The whole city had mourned. She wondered what it would be like—to have a whole city, a whole world, mourning your passing. It occurs to Elena that if she dies tomorrow, no one will mourn for her.

She walks on, past the artist selling his watercolors of John Lennon with a sign that reads "Feel Free to Look." If she looks, he'll try and convince her to buy, so she continues on, taking the path that leads her into the park. Rowers are in their boats on the lake and others sit basking on the rocks. Squirrels are foraging, burying their nuts. A woman on the rocks is doing yoga. Another man, half-naked, basks in the sun. In one of the pagodas, people are sitting, reading. Still as she descends on the lower path, the darker side of the city emerges. A used condom, flung into the bushes, hangs from a branch and needles and vials line the path.

Elena knows about that dark side. It seems as if her life is made up of mistakes, accidents that become turning points. One night in particular. The night when everything changed. The one when she numbed herself with booze and drugs, and once with turning, twirling, leaping. It is a foggy picture, something at times she can barely recall. At other times it seems as if she can think of nothing else. A cool spring evening, hanging out with the gang that managed to buy fifths of Scotch from old man Roybal who knew better than to sell to the kids, but what the hell. There weren't exactly any policemen in Entrada—except those who drove down from Taos or up from Santa Fe. Or the occasional state trooper who stopped on his way back from some domestic disturbance in Española.

They'd all been hanging out, even Roberto was there, her brother, just a year and change younger than she was, so close in age that people asked if they were twins. Irish twins, people joked. Especially the year when Roberto is held back, but by the end of that year Elena was gone. There had been four or five of them. The numbers blur as did the faces and the hands and the bodies. Tommy Aguilar was there because he had egged them on. And Juan Ramirez. And maybe the Hernandez brothers, who were both friends with Roberto. And Pascual Roybal, that tall high-school senior. The football hero. The one they looked up to. She had a crush on him. She wanted to impress him with her taut dancer's body, the way she could glide through rooms, slip easily into a boy's arms. Was she asking for it? The way some people said?

Maybe someone slipped something into her drink. Or maybe it was just the heat and the whiskey—stronger than what she was used to. Because she was a tiny girl. A lithe dancer, barely sixteen. She'd known these boys since grade school. She knew their mothers. They all went to the same church, listened to the same tired priest chant the prayers. She was friends with their sisters. And they were having a good time, weren't they? All laughing, joking. Punching one another in the arm. It was all in good fun.

They led her toward Pascual's car under what excuse? She couldn't be sure. Were they going out for burgers? Were they taking her home? But when she didn't want to go, they dragged her. She struggled, tried to pull away. And maybe she shouted. When she called out, she caught a glimpse of her brother, looking her way, a smile on his face. Her brother, who never came to her aid. "I thought you wanted to go," he'd say to her later.

They were drunk and joking around. They had a bottle of whiskey in the trunk that Pascual had stolen from his father's store. So they took her down to the arroyo where rocks and even cactus spines dug into her flesh as she'd thrashed and tried to pull away, but she couldn't because there were too many of them. Too many hands. Too many boys. "You want it, don't you, Elena?" they whispered into her ear. "You're just asking for it." She tried to remember, but she lost count. All she knew was the bleeding, the feeling that she was being broken in two. And when they were done, they loaded her back into the car and dropped her off somewhere near her mother's trailer.

It was Roberto who heard her crying. She was glad it was he because she wanted him to hear her crying for the rest of his life. Her brother who had done nothing to stop them. Who had watched them take her to that car and drive away. And it was her mother who, when she received the School of American Ballet scholarship, didn't hesitate. Her mother who put her hand on Elena's cheek and told her, "Go."

She leaves the park at 79th Street and cuts across to the Museum of Natural History where she finds herself drifting over to the side entrance to the planetarium. When Elena first came to New York, she made a point to go to every museum, see every show she could afford, learn where every bookstore was located. This was part of her mission to become a New Yorker. But she's never been to the planetarium. She doesn't know why. Perhaps because she'd lived long enough beneath the big western sky. Why would you need a planetarium when you lived inside of one? But now she goes in and buys a ticket. She walks past the huge Willamette meteorite that fell to Earth in the Pacific Northwest thousands of years ago. The Clackamas tribe worshipped it as a spiritual being and called it Tomanowos, "Visitor from the Moon." In the early twentieth century, treasure hunters stole it from them. They have been fighting for decades to get it back.

Elena pauses at Tomanowos. Her hands touch the hollows that mottle the meteorite's surface. It looks as if it has been melted and perhaps it was. Some extraordinary collision knocked it out of the sky. Then it burned as it entered Earth's atmosphere. No one knows where it landed but glaciers carried it to Oregon where the native people discovered it and claimed it as their heavenly visitor.

As she walks into the main hall, Elena notices that a laser show is starting in a moment, featuring Pink Floyd's *Dark Side of the Moon*. But she's heard you have to be pretty stoned to enjoy it. She heads to the Hall of Meteorites instead, and along the way comes to the History of Man. Here there are skeletons of early man, some diminutive, some with huge chests, others with simian features. In a glass case she pauses at a facsimile of two tiny hominids, walking side by side, his arm draped over her shoulder. The footprints of hominids were discovered in Africa. They were so close together that paleontologists determined they could only be walking like that if they were touching.

At the Hall of Meteorites she watches a brief film that tells how meteorites are the Rosetta stone of outer space, how they enable us to grasp the wonders of the world. There are pictures of the wilderness in Siberia where in Tunguska a giant fireball struck the Earth and caused brush fires to burn for two decades. She walks around the small meteorites that line the room. They all have names. Gibeon, Guffey, Knowles, Diablo.

Then in the middle of the room is Ahnighito, the greatest meteorite of them all. Weighing thirty-four tons it struck Greenland ten thousand years ago. The Inuit believe it was hurled to Earth by the gods. Its name means the Tent. There are two other meteorites that were once part of Ahnighito. They are called the Woman and the Dog. The tent, the woman, the dog—all that is required for a happy life.

One night in New Mexico when she was just a girl she stood outside with her father as an enormous flash of light came shooting across the sky. Not like a shooting star but a fireball. Her father pointed to the sky. "That's a bolide," he told her for he had read about such things. He explained that a meteorite had entered the atmosphere where it might burn out or might strike the Earth. It was rare to see one.

Once it seemed to Elena that her father knew everything and that he had read everything, when in fact he had only learned such things when he was stationed in Korea in the dental unit. The soldiers were afraid of the dentist so her father had a lot of time on his hands. There was a shelf in the mess hall where soldiers left the books they'd finished and he read as many as he could. "Almost no one ever sees a bolide," he told her. "You'll have luck in your life, m'hija." As Elena strolls, she misses her father. She thinks about how big the universe is and how little we know. Perhaps if she hadn't crushed her ankle, she would be dancing her way to the stars. But anything can strike us at any time. On her way out of the museum Elena ponders the simple things. The tent, the woman, the dog. Footprints so close you'd have to be touching.

She hesitates at the gift shop. In another one of his letters Roberto told her that at night Miguel goes to the old cemetery to look at the sky. She'd gone there herself many times as a girl. She liked to sit under the old oak tree among the crumbling stones with the strange lettering on them. The nights were as black as any she's ever seen and the Milky

Way stretched across the sky. She stood on that hill, waiting for another bolide to shoot out of the sky.

She is browsing among the constellation ties and scarves, the books, the night-sky star kits. Then she comes to a row of telescopes. Some are small and compact. Others are large and bulky. Labels describe their focal lengths and apertures. One says that it has the most reduced chromatic aberration. Elena has no idea what any of it means. But she peers through one lens and finds she can read a street sign that is more than a mile away.

She goes up to the saleswoman. "I'm looking for a telescope for a boy who is interested in astronomy." The woman shows her two or three that might be appropriate. Elena picks a slim blue one that seems lightweight and portable. The saleswoman suggests a tripod, and Elena takes one of those as well. "Can you mail this to New Mexico?" she asks.

"We mail anywhere," the woman replies. "Would you like to include a gift card?"

Elena hesitates for a moment. It was his birthday last month after all. "I would," she says.

The woman hands Elena a card. On it is a comet, shooting across the sky. On a practice piece of paper she scribbles. "I heard from your dad that you are into the stars." She doesn't like this. It is too personal. She rewrites it to read, "I hear that you are into the stars. Hope you enjoy this. Tía E." Should she put xs at the bottom? Is that too personal? Is this too impersonal? In the end she just signs her name. It is more than she has ever written to him. And even it feels like too much.

She only held him once as a baby. Then she put him in her mother's arms and walked away. As she watches the saleswoman packing the telescope, she wonders if she should be sending him a gift at all. But this is something she can do for him. As long as he never knows that he is hers. And that she left him behind long ago.

✳

CHAPTER TWENTY-SEVEN

WHY?—1992

Two weeks after the snake bit Davie, Mr. Garcia asks Miguel to see him after class. They are in the middle of a biology lesson on the anatomy of frogs. They have just pithed two frogs and one lies splayed on Miguel's desk, its legs wiggling, when Mr. Garcia leans over and tells him to "wait up" when they're done. Miguel nods as he stares down at his frog. It's writhing with a pin through its neck. His stomach clenches the way it has been clenching since Davie was bitten, and a cold shiver runs down his spine. Why would Mr. Garcia ask to see him?

As Mr. Garcia walks away, heading down the rows, glancing at the dissection of frogs, Miguel thinks he will be sick. He is certain that what he'd come to fear the most—that the police will arrest him for endangering the welfare of a child—is about to happen. He knows about child endangerment because he watches so many crime shows and courtroom procedurals on TV with his mother. It is one of the few things they enjoy doing together. Not speaking, silently staring at the screen.

What if Dr. Rothstein has decided to press charges? From what little he's seen of the doctor he wouldn't put it past him. And Miguel already has a record, doesn't he? Just for disorderly conduct and reckless endangerment, but it put him in juvie for a month. His court-appointed lawyer had gone to the trouble of trying to get it expunged from his record. "Just three boys playing chicken on a country road, Your Honor." But the judge would hear nothing of it. So if Dr. Rothstein comes after him, Miguel can be looking at prison for what—six months, a year?

He scratches at the stubble of his beard and fingers a pimple on his chin. His skin has turned oily in recent weeks and pimples are popping up all over its once smooth surface. Even his mother has noticed. "It's puberty," she says. As he watches his frog, its legs twitching, and Mr. Garcia ambling in the aisles, he wonders what else his favorite teacher could possibly have to say. He could come up with an excuse. He has to go to the bathroom. And then he'll get into his car, drive away, and keep driving.

He's been driving around lately. Right after the snakebite happened, Miguel rushed Davie to the hospital. And after Dr. Rothstein yelled at him, he left. He didn't know where he was going, he just drove around aimlessly. Eventually he went home, but then he began calling the hospital. He called every hour until he was sure that Davie was all right. He kept calling even after the hospital assured him that Davie had gone home.

Then he started driving by the school to make certain. He saw Davie on the jungle gym, but he was always alone. Not really playing with anyone, just sitting. He wanted to park, get out, and ask him if he was all right. He wanted to say "Sorry." He wanted to ask Davie how he was doing and if he was still working on his right hook. And he wanted to tell Davie how brave he'd been. But if Miguel was seen standing by the school fence talking to a six-year-old, they'd arrest him in a heartbeat. And probably jail him as a sex offender.

Every day he goes to school in a state of panic and every afternoon he returns home more or less in the same state. He is sure the patrol car will be waiting for him in front of the trailer. He envisions scenes in which police officers take him away. He can imagine his mother crying, "But he's a good boy. He's never hurt anyone. Not on purpose anyway." He envisions the squad car, the officer putting his hand on his head the way they do on TV so that he doesn't bump it as he gets into the car.

Miguel is a loser. He knows that. If he'd doubted it before, it is now officially confirmed. He has a knack, almost a skill, for not doing things right. If someone hands him a precious keepsake, he'll lose it. If he gets a puppy, he'll drop it. A girl. He'll ruin it. A job. He'll blow it. The losses keep piling up like one of those baseball teams (those Cubs) who can never win or like that Boston infielder who let the World Series slip between his legs in a bungled grounder. So he takes two boys for a walk and one of them gets bitten by a rattlesnake. These things don't just happen to anyone, do they?

Miguel is looking to see if he can make his getaway, but Mr. Garcia keeps his eyes on him. Mr. Garcia is old, but not that old, like forty. Older than his mom which is already pretty old to Miguel. He always wears a tie and sometimes colorful ones. During different sports seasons he wears special ties. Football, baseball, basketball. He has a Santa Claus tie for Christmas and a turkey tie for Thanksgiving. Miguel thinks it is pretty silly, the way Mr. Garcia always wants to get along and blend in. He is always glad-handing the kids, giving them high fives. Trying to be too cool. But what Mr. Garcia is very good at is science.

It is Mr. Garcia who taught Miguel to question everything. Over his desk Mr. Garcia has a single word in white against a black backdrop: WHY? Whenever anything happens, Mr. Garcia makes the kids ask themselves why. When Miguel's ink-distilling experiment exploded last year, Mr. Garcia wasn't mad, even though the ink went all over the place. He looked Miguel square in the eye and said, "Okay, now ask yourself: Why did the ink-distilling experiment explode?"

Since Mr. Garcia has been his teacher, he's asked himself why a million times. And then he applies it to things outside of science. Why did Mrs. Rothstein hire me? Why did the snake have to bite Davie? Why is Jeremy a bully? Why does Mr. Garcia want him to stay after school? Sweat pours down his back. There is no reason. All of Miguel's homework is in. His test scores are good. He hasn't been playing hooky. So there is no reason except that the police are coming to arrest him and Mr. Garcia is here to make certain that he goes peacefully. Isn't that what they do in the movies?

"Are you all right, Miguel?" Mr. Garcia asks as the others are filing out of the classroom and the school and back into their normal lives of afternoon sports and smoking joints and beer and girls and maybe homework. But not Miguel. No, his life is about to irrevocably change.

"I'm fine, sir," Miguel replies, not looking up.

"You look a little pale."

"I'm fine, sir."

"Well," Mr. Garcia sits on the edge of his desk, his dark eyes piercing. "You've been quiet lately. Usually you talk more in class."

"I'm just tired. I've got a job," Miguel replies, "out in the mall." He has no idea why he lies, especially to Mr. Garcia whom he likes and respects.

"That's good," Mr. Garcia says, clapping his hands together. Miguel looks up and sees that Mr. Garcia is wearing a tie with pumpkins all over it. Is it already Halloween? How has so much time gone by? This is something Miguel wonders about. Does time always take up as much time? What makes time move more quickly at certain times than others? This is what Miguel likes about Mr. Garcia. He taught him how to ask questions. The question, Mr. Garcia believes, is often more important than the answer. "I hope you're saving up for college."

Miguel shrugs. "I've got other things to pay for."

Mr. Garcia nods, a look of understanding sweeping over his round, almost pudgy face. "Well, that's what I want to talk to you about." Miguel looks at Mr. Garcia for the first time since he told him he wants to speak to him. "I want to nominate you for something."

A grin breaks across Miguel's face. "Nominate me?" He points to himself as if to make certain Mr. Garcia means him.

"Yes. For a National Science Foundation Scholarship." So this isn't about the snakebite. Maybe he isn't going to be led away in handcuffs. Not today anyway. "All you have to do is come up with a project proposal. I'll help you. We can work on that together. Maybe one of your astronomy ideas? Don't you have that idea about one of Jupiter's moons having water on it?"

"A frozen sea. Yes, but it's nothing I can prove. The Lowell Observatory can't even prove it."

"Well, we don't have to decide now. Why don't you come up with a few ideas? We can talk them over. Take it from there."

Ideas? Miguel shakes his head. His mind is a blank. He tries to remember when he last had an idea. Normally he is just full of them but in the past couple of weeks, he hasn't had any ideas except how to get the hell out of Entrada before the police come after him. In fact he's only barely looked at the stars in weeks and then it is because he is having a smoke and once to make out briefly with a girl who dropped out of high school last year. He certainly doesn't think he is in a good position to prove that there is life on Mars. Or even microbes in that frozen sea on Europa. "I'll try and think of something, sir."

"Look, here are the forms. Let's put our heads together and come up with a cracker-jack proposal. I bet you can get an NSF scholarship and then"—Mr. Garcia raises his arms into the air as if he were going to float away—"the sky's the limit."

Miguel thanks his teacher and takes the forms. He flings his backpack over his shoulder and heads toward his car. Halfway there Miguel pauses to light a cigarette, which he smokes all the way to the filter. Then he gets into his car, stuffs the forms into the glove compartment where he keeps dozens of little things he plans to never look at again, such as traffic violations and bad report cards, and drives away.

On his way home he stops at Roybal's to pick up the mail, grab a chocolate bar, and buy a pack of cigarettes, ostensibly for his mother. "You've got a package," Vincent Roybal says. The old man shuffles into the back of the store and comes out with a large box that he puts on the counter. Miguel glances at the return address: Hayden Planetarium, New York. He takes it, puts it in his car, and heads home, where he opens it on the kitchen counter. Inside is a telescope. Slim and blue. State-of-the-art telescope with a three-inch aperture and a seven hundred millimeter focal length. It is three times more powerful than the one Miguel built and has a tripod too.

He takes it out of its wrapping. There's a card from his aunt Elena. His father must have told her that he was interested in the stars. Later that evening before his mother gets home, he takes the telescope outside and plants it on the tripod. He adjusts the lens and starts to pan the sky. It is as if he's a person who needed glasses and hasn't realized it until now. The whole sky comes into focus. He can see the craters on the moon as if they were canyons nearby. He pans to the planets. He sharpens his focus on the rings of Saturn. The colors are startling. Then on to Jupiter. Miguel thinks of Galileo trying to solve the problem of longitude by using the moons of Jupiter. With this new telescope Miguel can make out those moons. Perhaps he will even find one of his own.

Except Miguel knows that he will never amount to anything. He knows that he has failed at everything he's ever tried to do. So he folds the tripod and puts the telescope back into the box. He slides it under his bed and proceeds to forget that it ever existed.

※

CHAPTER TWENTY-EIGHT

AN OLD MAN IN NEW SPAIN—1599

F ederico de Torres wakes as he does every morning with sores in his mouth. They are also on his hands and his neck. And yet even as he begins his morning ablutions of astringents and salts, he does not curse his illness. Instead, he recalls that had his father not discovered that the only real relief for his son's symptoms was an ointment of aloe laced with gold, he would never have come to the viceroyalty of New Spain and probably would not be alive. He is alive because his father believed what the sailors who returned from New Spain told him. That the streets of Montezuma's empire were paved in pure gold and his son would never want for his cure. At the same time, his father knew that his son carried within him the dark family secret. The renowned Dr. Eduardo de Torres of Córdoba was a scientific man, and he knew that the disease from which his son suffered was very rare, often fatal, and only found among the race that called themselves Jews.

Federico gazes in the mirror. He has seen himself look better, and he has seen himself look worse. At any rate he is long past the concerns of vanity. All he seeks now is comfort in his old age. He begins his preparation of warm salt water, which he splashes onto his face and neck. Salt water has always soothed his wounds. Once the stinging stops and his flesh is dry, he takes the jar of ointment and dabs the gold flecks on his hands and neck. He touches it to the sores inside his mouth and on his gums. People who do not understand this cure are stunned when he speaks to them and they are coated in gold.

Sofia is still asleep, her brow furrowed. He doesn't like to see that worried look on his wife's face. The night before she had pleaded with him. "Don't go into the field tomorrow. Stay home with me." He'd laughed at her concern.

"Is this one of your premonitions?" he teased her, for he didn't believe in such things. But she'd shaken her head.

"Just stay home," she said.

Federico sits beside her and gently rubs her brow. At the foot of their bed one of her two dogs stirs. He will not allow her to keep all the dogs in their room for they would take up every inch of space. Nor will he allow her to witness the ritual of cleansings he performs every day. He never lets her see his naked flesh in the light of day for fear that he will repulse her. During the two decades of their marriage, she has never seen his body except in darkness. Not that she would mind. Federico knows only too well that his wife adores him. At least she has come to love him.

This wasn't always the case. She had loved another before him— someone she will not talk about. Perhaps someone who jilted her. She was almost thirty when they married, but he won her over. Looking at her, he chuckles. Almost twenty years ago he had been tentative with her when she came to him on their wedding night, dressed in the long white gown that tied around her wrists, neck, and ankles, and with the cross-shaped triangle near the groin where Federico understood he was to penetrate her.

He kissed her as he burrowed through the narrow opening that barely allowed him in. Night after night he tried to enter that hole in her gown, and each night he grew flaccid in his efforts until finally one night when he could bear it no more he untied all the strings, pulled the linen gown over her head, and then made his way up and down her body with his fingers, his mouth, and finally his member. And as she responded to his touch, as she grew more and more suppliant and aroused, he knew that he was not her first, but he would be her last. He placed his tongue on her nipples, between her thighs until she cried out, and in this way he won her over. It was a gentle love of foot mas-

sages and head rubs, followed by moments of bone-deep satisfaction—
the kind that would last a lifetime.

Federico has come to believe that even if he had the scales of a rep-
tile, which at times he wonders if he does, she wouldn't turn him away.
Still, he is so ashamed of the sores and scabs that at times cover his
entire body so that he looks as if he has survived a fire. That is when
he has to be covered from head to toe in the ointment of aloe and
gold that his father had made for him—the father he never saw again
after he sailed to the New World. When his skin is blistering like that,
Federico allows no one to tend to him except Bernadine, the old cook,
who worked for his wife's family in New Spain and traveled with them
when he brought Sofia north into these hills where they have made
their home. Bernadine is a mestizo who was indentured to Sofia's family and who, for all practical purposes, they owned though they never
thought of her in this way.

When he was younger, there were moments when Bernadine's touch
stirred his flesh. She rubbed his wounds the way no one else could.
At times when she massaged the salve into his skin in gentle swirling
motions, he was tempted by her. Especially just before their last child
was born when Sofia had taken to her bed for months. Federico could
not bear the loneliness of his flesh. One night she came to him in her
nightdress with her lush black hair hanging down and declared her love
for him, but he refused. After a while they settled back into their routine, and Bernadine had remained in their service. He had always been
true to his wife. And they had lived in these hills for all these years.

Sofia's mother sobbed when he told her that they were moving
north from Mexico City. She pleaded with him not to take away her
only daughter, but Federico would not give in. He felt that they would
be safer in the northern territories. Sofia was a New Christian after all
and Federico had suspicions that he was a converted Jew as well. In the
end Sofia's mother relented. She was plagued by the memory of her
nephew, Alejandro, who was burned at the stake, and her own sister,
Leonora, who never emerged from the Flat House. She let Sofia bring
Bernadine, her maid, with her. Bernadine had been with Sofia since
she was born and her mother could not bear the thought of her not

having the Mexican girl to braid her hair at night and prepare her hot chocolate in the morning. And once a year in the cool months, Federico allowed his wife and three children to travel south to visit.

Federico glances outside. It is not yet dawn. He always rises when it is still dark. In the sky there is a full moon at the horizon. It is about to slip behind the western hills. To the east he sees the thin line of purple light as the sun is rising. It is a beautiful morning. He can't imagine why Sofia had wanted him to stay home. In a few minutes he'll head out into the hills where he will join two of his sons who work the garbanzo fields with him and the Pueblo Indians, whom they have indentured.

Sofia is stirring. No matter how tired she is, he never leaves without her waking to see him off. Now she sits up and stretches. "You're going?" she whispers. It is as if each morning she knows when she can open her eyes. When her husband is ready to receive her.

It is still first light and dawn is breaking in shades of violet across the high-desert terrain. At times like this Federico longs for Spain. He longs to return to his mother and father's home, even though they left this world years ago. The memory of his childhood on that purple plain ripples through him. As he watches Sofia resting in their bed, he thinks how much he loves the soft curve of her neck, her warm breath against his cheek. He cannot imagine leaving her the way his grandfather left his grandmother. Federico aches when he imagines walking away from Sofia and their children. It is beyond his imagining.

Federico sits down beside his wife. As he strokes her back, his fingers caressing her flesh, he thinks of how she loves him. How he loves her is not a wonder, but her love for him comes to him each day as a blessing and a surprise.

Opening her sleepy eyes, Sofia looks at him. "Stay with me," she pleads with him again.

"I will see you for supper," he promises. He kneels in front of the cross that hangs at the small shrine in their bedroom, says his morning prayers, crosses himself in the name of the Father, and heads into the kitchen where Bernadine has prepared a strong coffee with thick cream, a fresh bun, and two poached eggs.

+

Federico Cordero de Torres knows that he is a fortunate man. He was still a boy when he came to the viceroyalty of New Spain with money his father gave him. Money that his father hoped would buy him as much gold as he needed to mix with his ointments. Instead he marched with Coronado in search of the Seven Cities of Gold. He was with him when they camped in these very hills. It was here that Coronado had gazed up at the thin crescent rising from between the mountains and declared this place to be Entrada de la Luna. It was also Coronado's gateway into America.

Federico went west until he stood at the rim of a canyon that stretched as far as the eye could see and the river that roared through it far below and thought that this must be what God intended heaven to be. And he journeyed east into the region known as Kansa where a Wichita Indian, whom Coronado dubbed the Turk, led them away from the dwellings of the pueblos and brought them to Apache land. The Turk promised more gold than they had ever seen, but all they saw were a million buffalo and prairie grass and land so flat that they could see the sky between the buffalo's legs. While Coronado had the Turk garroted for his treachery, Federico turned away from the vast plain and headed back along the Camino Real to the place where he had encamped with Coronado for a time.

He found the place where the moon had slipped between the mountains. Here Federico would make his home. Instead of buying gold as his father had commissioned him, he used his money to make a land claim and on that land he planted the bags of seeds he brought from home. Federico never saw his father again, but he knew that the distinguished doctor would be displeased that after all of his education and all of his money Federico married a converso girl whom he loved and became a grower of garbanzo beans.

But he doubted it would matter. His father was always displeased with him. Federico had never been the son his father dreamed of. It was perhaps why he agreed to make this journey in the first place. He could not bear the disappointment in his father's eyes nor the sadness in his mother's. His father—who insisted that everyone refer to him as Dr. Torres and his only son address him as sir—was a man of science. He was versed in all the latest theories of the universe. Messengers brought him books and papers from all over Europe. He read about how Copernicus had proven that the universe was heliocentric and how Tycho Brahe was measuring the distance between planets and stars.

Eduardo de Torres lectured him about the mysteries of the universe, but his son had no interest in the planets or the stars. He did not share his father's fascination with the placement of the sun. Federico was interested in plants. From an early age he tended his mother's garden. He was interested in color and shapes, not in classifications. He didn't care for the names or species. He liked soil. He liked the feel of the earth in his hands. Just with his fingertips he could tell acidic soil from alkaline. He knew if hydrangeas would bloom pink or blue from the texture or taste of the earth. He knew instinctively how much sun a plant might need and how plants, like people, showed sadness when they were not in happy places.

But he did not want to be a botanist and no matter how much his father tried to interest him in the biological world, given that he could not interest him in the greater world that surrounded them, Federico did not have the curiosity of a scientist or the mind of a philosopher. What he did possess was an innate ability to make things grow. He knew how to create flowing borders with delicate blue lobelia and bright orange and yellow nasturtium, where to add jasmine and irises for a sweet and sudden scent, and how to build the backs of gardens with flowering shrubs. He knew when plants needed to be moved or cut back. He did not want to be a student of anything besides life. Books and theories and studies took him into the shadows, where his mind would drift and his sores fester. Federico shunned the important work for which his father had groomed him.

Though Eduardo de Torres and his wife produced three daughters, including one who would go on to make important contributions to the study of diseases of the blood, it was his son who mattered. It was his son who kept Eduardo de Torres up at night, smoking his pipe into the late hours, worrying over what would become of the boy whose greatest pleasure was to bring an armload of cut flowers into the house and help his mother arrange them in vases. When Eduardo de Torres called Federico into his study to show him some new papers that arrived from Italy or France in which Copernicus posed his heliocentric theories, his son broke into a sweat and began to tremble. As he lectured his son, Federico's gaze drifted off toward the window, out into the garden and the fields and beyond. The boy had no attention span. And at last Eduardo de Torres concluded that Federico had no curiosity. And that, for Eduardo de Torres, was the greatest sin.

Then, of course, there was his skin. The hideous lesions that his father spent years tending to, searching for cures. At times Eduardo de Torres stayed up nights in his laboratory, mixing bitter potions for Federico to drink, which had him spewing out his guts for days, or burning salves to pour onto his skin, which left his son rawer than he was before. For Eduardo de Torres's ostensible contempt for his son came from his deep love and the fury that he could not cure him or even help him. And this made him think that, despite his belief in science and reason, his son was cursed in his soul.

It was only when the lesions were the worst that his father allowed Federico to go into the fields. To Eduardo de Torres this was a defeat, but to his son it was a blessing. It seemed as if only the sun could assuage his sores. And only for a while. Then his father discovered what seemed to be a miracle cure—an ointment of aloe and gold—and when he heard that a ship with a new patron was to sail for New Spain, Eduardo de Torres made certain that his only son was on it. He gave him only two instructions upon his departure: He was to discover gold, and he was to search for his grandfather who decades ago had sailed to the New World with the explorer Columbus, never to be heard from again.

Federico was only too happy to leave. He would at last do something that made his father proud and his mother less sad. His journey across the sea took four months, in part because of strong storms that drove them back toward Spain, and Federico spent most of it above deck. While the other sailors thought they would go mad from the briny air and the constant wind, Federico welcomed it. It was the only time he was not plagued by the relentless itch and anguish of his skin, a reprieve that would end as soon as they disembarked. But in New Spain he met Coronado and found a man who did not look upon him with scorn. He did not seem to notice the sores and pustules of his skin. Years later Federico would come to feel that Coronado was the only man whom he regarded as a son should regard his father—even though the great explorer was only twenty-five years old at the time.

+

As he is heading to the fields, Federico glances at his grandfather's clock. His father gave it to him when he was about to sail for the New World. It was an odd thing to give his only son who was crossing the sea. And somehow it survived the journey. It is an ancient clock without numbers, having instead strange letters that his father told him came from the Phoenicians. It has been in the family for generations. And the hands of the clock go backward. No one knows why. No clock-maker who'd ever seen it could explain, but the clock tells time just as well as those that go forward and Federico has learned to tell time in this way. He can't even read other clocks. It is almost six a.m. Time to go to the fields. The day already feels warm. He glances once more toward their bedroom. As soon as he is gone, she'll rise and stretch, and the business of running their house and farm will begin. By noon the heat will be unbearable, and Federico and his workers will pause from their work to eat bread and cheese and sleep in the shade of the trees. He will try to slip back to the house and lie down with Sofia for a time.

As he steps onto the porch, the air smells of dung and hay. He pauses, taking in his land, his barns, his house, and the fields beyond. The heat hits him like a furnace. He is a man accustomed to the heat and normally he does not suffer from it, but this morning he does. It is the dry heat of the high desert, and as he walks through the paddock toward the fields, he drags his feet. It is as if he is walking uphill, except he isn't. Heaviness weighs on his chest as if water has settled there.

He has not felt this uneasy since he stepped off the ship and began his search for gold and his itinerant grandfather who disappeared so long ago. Instead he found this valley where garbanzo beans grew in abundance and from where they are shipped and sold across two continents. He has loved a woman and had three sons with her. He has claimed this land and this valley as his own.

Federico smiles even as he walks to the fields. He hardly ever thinks about his voyage across the sea, but today he does.

As he walks toward his workers who are already pruning the stalks and harvesting the ripened beans, he remembers that morning when he was boarding the ship that brought him here. There is something about this dawn that feels like a new beginning. Something in the light and the hot wind that makes him feel as if he were embarking upon another journey into yet another new world.

✳

CHAPTER TWENTY-NINE

GROUND ZERO—1992

A tarantula scuttles across the road, and Rachel swerves to miss it. "Oh my god," she says, "look at that." Jeremy turns, but Davie stares straight ahead. "Did you see that, honey?" Rachel pulls off to the side of the road. "C'mon," she says to her boys, "let's go see it." The tarantula is still making its way across the hot asphalt. The sun is beating down on the desert. They are two hundred miles south of Santa Fe. Rachel has brought them on an outing while Nathan is at a conference in San Francisco.

"Look at that." She takes Jeremy by the hand and picks up Davie who really is too heavy for her to carry and they walk back to where the tarantula is. It is a large, hairy black spider but Rachel isn't afraid of it. She knows that they aren't really poisonous, and she thinks it might be good for Davie to try and reacquaint himself with the natural world. Jeremy is curious and bends down, but Davie squirms in her arms. He is afraid of the spider. Since his snakebite, he's been afraid of everything.

"Isn't that an interesting spider." Rachel stands in her thin sneakers on the warm pavement. She's wearing a T-shirt and shorts and she can feel the sun searing her skin. Somewhere in her bag there must be sunscreen. She should slather it on all three of them.

"I want to go home," Davie says, crying.

"We're going to have some fun." Rachel kisses the top of his head. "Come on, let's go." She gets into the car and puts on the radio full blast. "Galveston" is playing as she gets back on the highway and drives on. They are heading to Alamogordo and White Sands National Monument. It is also near Trinity Site, the place where the first nuclear bomb was detonated in 1945. "Now I am become death, the destroyer of worlds," J. Robert Oppenheimer is said to have muttered to himself when he saw the explosion, quoting the *Bhagavad Gita*. Rachel read this as she planned the outing.

Rachel didn't bother telling Nathan that she was taking the boys on a field trip. It just seemed like a good thing to do. She had heard that White Sands is like a giant mattress where you can jump up and down and slide for hundreds of feet down the dunes. It will be good for the kids. It will be especially good for Davie. Anyway, does she really owe her husband an explanation? For months now, he's always been late. Getting home even after she's gone to bed. He barely sees the kids. Their phone conversations last for five minutes. Rachel can't remember when they'd last had a meal together as a family. He is punishing her. He hasn't forgiven her for letting their son get bitten by a snake, and perhaps he never will. But it began before this, didn't it? Rachel tries to remember how long she's been feeling that her marriage is in free fall.

When they approach the entrance of White Sands, the gate is closed. There is no one at the ranger station. "Shit," she hisses under her breath. She has driven more than two hundred miles only to have come at a time when it's closed.

"Don't swear," Jeremy tells her.

"I'll swear if I want to," she snaps at her son. She's not sure what to do. Maybe there's a Dairy Queen nearby. Maybe she can figure out a way to salvage this trip. As she makes her way down the highway, cursing under her breath, she notices something by the side of the road. There's fencing all along the highway, enclosing White Sands, but at one spot three or four cars are pulled off to the side of the road. Rachel pulls over as well. She can see why they have stopped here. Along the four-foot fence the sands have drifted, and it's easy to climb over. "C'mon, we're going to be bandits."

Jeremy groans but Davie perks up. "Bandits," Davie shouts, raising his fist in the air. Rachel takes the boys out of the car and holds their hands as they scramble up the dune and climb over the wooden fence. "Oh my god," Rachel says, "this is so much fun." But now with nothing but sand before them Davie's eyes scour the ground.

"I want to go back to the car," he tells her. He is about to cry again.

"Nothing is going to hurt you," Rachel says and hugs him, "I promise," but still he starts to whimper. It's about the snake, of course. My snake, he calls it. He tells her about it dozens of times—how it came upon him, how it tracked him down, how it was after him all along. Davie long ago stopped stepping on it. Instead he has his snake chasing him down the path. "It was after me," he says. Night after night it's lurking under his bed, in his closet. It is in the toilet, in the tub. He has stopped going into the backyard—not for a tetherball game with her, not for a plate of sugar sandwiches with Ovaltine, made with soy milk, that she prepares just for him. Lately he throws a fuss if he has to go outside at all because his snake could be anywhere—in the driveway, on the playground. When they go to school, she practically has to carry him from the car, and when he comes home, he races back into the house.

Rachel assumed that after a while it would fade from his memory the way most things fade in a child's mind, but instead his snake is getting bigger, thicker, longer. It rises up five, six feet into the air. Its rattle sounds like a jet engine. And its strike. He remembers the searing pain as if someone set him on fire. Except this fire comes from inside. She cannot bear the thought of what will become of her son. Through his whole life, when he is disappointed in love or fails to get into med school (where he never belonged in the first place), he will feel his snake coming around the bend, waiting for him in the dark corners that house every one of his fears. If Miguel were here, Rachel thinks, he'd coax Davie outside. He'd show him how not to be afraid. He'd tell him how brave he was. Miguel made a mistake, it's true, but it was a mistake, nothing more. He is just a boy like her own, flawed but well meaning.

She thought he would return. She anticipated his call. Or perhaps he'd just show up. But in the weeks since the incident he has not made an attempt to contact her. And she has looked everywhere for his number. She only had to call him once—that first time he came to the house. She should have scribbled it on the refrigerator door where she keeps important numbers. But she didn't. She forgot. And now she has no way of reaching him unless he comes to them.

It was better for the boys when Miguel was around. Better for her too. He provided company for them all. And the boys miss him. Davie especially wonders about Miguel and where he is. "Did he forget about me?" he asked one night as she tucked him in.

"Oh no, he'll never forget about you. He just has to study harder now so he can get into a good school."

Jeremy has raced ahead and Rachel takes Davie by the hand. "We're going to do this," she says. "Remember, we're bandits." She manages to drag him to the top of the pure white dunes. They stand at the crest, peering down. Below they can see the others who've climbed the fence as well, racing, rolling, flying down the sandy slopes that are as soft as any bed she can remember. Taking Davie by the hand, Rachel runs. They catch up to Jeremy and she clasps his hand too. "Get ready. On your mark. Get set. Go!" Rachel runs and they have no choice but to run beside her. They race across the glistening sand to the crest of the dune, and then she leaps. She flies into the air, pulling her boys with her. And suddenly the three of them are flying. As their feet touch the sand, she releases them and they roll, tumbling head over heels down the soft white dune, a softness she's never dreamed of. The world has become a pillow.

At the bottom they come to a halt, their feet deep in sand, and Rachel hears what she first assumes is Davie crying. But turning, she sees something she hasn't seen in weeks. He is laughing. Hysterical belly laughs, the kind when you might pee in your pants. She wants to cry. Her eyes well with tears. "Let's do it again," she shouts. She turns and starts to scramble back up the dunes. "Race you to the top." And now both boys are laughing, scrambling after her, and of course she lets them win. And before she even gets near the ridge of the dune,

Davie is flinging himself down again, somersaulting his way past her outstretched arms.

For lunch they stop at a Dairy Queen where they all order burgers, sodas, and fries. Just no cheese for Davie. They sit at a picnic table and Rachel distributes their food. "Wow," Jeremy says, taking a huge bite, "this is the best burger I've ever had."

"It is, isn't it, Davie?" Rachel says.

And Davie, his mouth full of food, just grins. Then he picks up his straw and blows the paper end at his brother and Jeremy blows his back and soon they are all laughing again, then hurling French fries, and Rachel doesn't stop them because it's good to have a food fight after you've spent the morning flying down sand dunes. And they're on the road again, driving past innumerable gas stations. Rainbow Pawnshop and Cash. Lines of government tract housing in the middle of nowhere. Fast-food joints and cut-rate motels. Stores with steel grates, all abandoned as, is Herman's Filling Station. There's an "Injured? I Sue Drunk Drivers" sign on the highway, except the sign is facing the wrong direction, going against the traffic. Rachel can't help but wonder if this is for people driving on the highway the wrong way. In the middle of a red clay mesa a giant refinery looms like something out of *Star Wars*.

Then Rachel sees the sign for "Trading Post." She pulls into the parking lot. They've never stopped at a real trading post before. "Okay, everybody can get a souvenir." The boys dash inside and find what resembles Santa's workshop if it were set in the Southwest. It's a hodgepodge of everything. Owls made from rocks, "rock" concerts, fool's gold, statues of prospectors, petrified wood with small carved animals on top, carved figures of coyotes and bears and wolves and eagles, dream catchers, tomahawks, imitation Kachina dolls, faux Navajo rugs, cowboy hats, boots, saddlebags, fake saddles, real saddles, hobbyhorses. There's a rack with every kind of beef jerky in the world: teriyaki, hot pepper, Cajun, sweet and sour, sausage, salmon, shrimp.

It's a tourist trap but the kids are entranced at the aisles packed with junk. Jeremy is cradling an amethyst geode. He's trying on rings of turquoise. Davie has gravitated toward the polished stones that are being sold as dinosaur eggs. Rachel is reading the back of a package of soil conditioner for cacti when she hears the scream.

Racing around the corner she sees Davie, hand raised to his face, pointing, shrieking. It is a shelf of snakes made into key chains, toilet seats, wall hangings, and the one that he is pointing at—a stuffed diamondback, poised and ready to strike.

"It's all right," she says to him, cradling him in her arms, pulling him away. "It's not real. And I'm right here." But Davie stands, hands over his eyes, screaming his head off. It's not until long after they are on the highway heading home that Davie cries himself out, crumples onto the seat, and sleeps.

+

Later that night the boys are watching cartoons. Davie seems to have forgotten the incident at the trading post, but Rachel can't get it out of her mind. She sits at the kitchen table, drumming her fingers on the granite countertop. She should get dinner going. She'll give the boys mac and soy cheese, and throw in a little diced chicken. She'll nibble from their plates. Maybe she'll cut up some broccoli and toss it into the macaroni water. She tries to give them balanced meals. And without Nathan at home why can't they just eat like that every night? What difference does it make?

My son is afraid of the world.

At moments like this Rachel wonders if she isn't losing it. If she isn't becoming her own mother, something she decided long ago that she would never be. She really wants a drink. She is very careful not to drink in front of the boys. She waits until they are asleep. But right now she wants a drink. She'd love a couple of fingers of Scotch. She would love to numb herself to this pain.

As she starts to boil the water, it comes to her. "It began with an *E*." The town he came from. It started with an *E*. How many towns beginning with an *E* can there be in northern New Mexico? Leaving the water on, meaning that it will boil down and she will have to begin again, Rachel goes out to her car. Opening the glove compartment, she takes out the map of New Mexico and brings it back inside. Laying it out on the kitchen table, with her finger she traces a trajectory north until it lands on Española. "That's it," Rachel says. And there at her kitchen table, Rachel Rothstein makes the first clear decision she has made in a very long time. She will find Miguel.

CHAPTER THIRTY

THE MOTHER OF THE MOON—1992

Four and a half billion years ago two planets hurtled through space. When they collided, they became one. The dust that rose from their collision formed a ball, and that ball became our moon. One of those planets was Earth. The other became known as Theia. In Greek mythology Theia is the mother of the goddess of the moon, Selene. If you want to know what became of Theia, you just need to step outside. You'll be standing on her. We know that the moon comes from the Earth. When Neil Armstrong walked on the moon, he took soil samples. And the composition of those samples is identical to the stones found here."

As Mr. Garcia lectures, Miguel sits in the back of the class, pondering the facts. He is nothing. We are all nothing. Since Mr. Garcia told Miguel he wanted to nominate him for a science scholarship, Miguel has scrupulously avoided his teacher. There is no project. Miguel's only purpose right now is to stay one step ahead of the law. He's trying to imagine all the things he might go to jail for that certainly go beyond driving without a license. And then there's kidnapping. That carries a mandatory life sentence, doesn't it?

As class ends, Mr. Garcia looks up at Miguel as if a thought has crossed his mind. He's about to say something when Miguel slips out the door. He decides to skip his last-period class. He gets in his car and drives. He's told his mother that now he's going to his job every day after school so she never expects him before six. Instead he just drives around. Mostly aimlessly. Sometimes he stops in Española, but there is always some kind of trouble going on there. You can hardly ever stop in Española and not hear about another shooting. Mostly he drives farther north, toward Taos, though he has to be careful about gas because since he left his job at Mrs. Rothstein's he isn't making any money.

He thinks about the boys, especially Davie. He misses him. He betrayed him. He let danger come his way when all he wanted was to make him stronger, to teach him how to fight back. And he misses Mrs. Rothstein. He thinks about her at odd moments. In the science lab, on the ball field. She comes to him with a strange force. He wants to be rid of her. He wants her to go away. He dreams about her. Not the weird, kinky dreams he had for a while but just dreams where she's walking or leaning against a wall, watching him, waiting for him to say something. Anyway, obviously she doesn't want him looking after the boys again. If she did, she would have called by now.

Miguel turns onto the highway to Santa Fe. He can be there in forty minutes if he steps on it. Which he does. He pocket drives, almost daring a cop to stop him, but no one does. He drives through the center of town, then turns up Canyon Road until he's about a block from Magical Years. He pauses to smoke a cigarette, and then he gets out and walks. It's almost three o'clock. And like clockwork the doors of the school open and kids come flying out in the playground where their mothers and nannies and fathers are waiting for them. There's the usual shrieking and chatter and hugs and off they go.

He spots Jeremy, racing out, surrounded by some friends. Though it's only been a few weeks, Jeremy seems bigger to him, more grown-up. It's the way it was with Miguel once. He was a child, and then suddenly he shot up. Jeremy is going around, giving his friends high fives. Then Davie comes out, walking slowly, eyes to the ground as if he's looking for a marble he lost. He resembles a zombie pretending to be a boy. Miguel shakes his head. But suddenly Davie's eyes light up and he rushes to the gate where his mother awaits him.

Rachel Rothstein stands on the curb, leaning against her car. She is thinner than he recalls and her features look almost hollowed. There are dark circles under her eyes. He wonders if she's getting any sleep. He wants to go up and give her a hug. He wants to tell her he is sorry for what happened. But what good would that do now? They will go on without him. So he gives them all a little wave and heads back to his car. He has said his goodbyes.

Miguel gets back on the highway and drives to his father's place. When he sees that Roberto's truck is gone, Miguel pulls into the driveway and parks. He opens the garage door with the remote his father keeps hidden inside an old tire. He keeps it there in case Miguel gets kicked out one night or just can't make it home. He is always welcome at his father's place. As the garage opens, Miguel is struck by the fumes of spray paint. He doesn't know why this stuff doesn't kill his dad.

He walks to the back of the garage where his father keeps empty cans filled with lug nuts, bolts, nails, screws, old spark plugs, wire, cables. He also keeps loose change. Once every week or so Miguel comes by and helps himself to whatever he can put in his pockets. So far his father hasn't seemed to notice. He doesn't want to ask his parents for money because they think he is working and he doesn't want to have to go into a long explanation about why he isn't.

He manages to cobble together five dollars in change. It will give him a few gallons of gas—enough to last him a day or so. He will leave Entrada. He will get away. He has no idea where he will go or what he will do, but that isn't what Miguel is thinking about. All he wants to do is disappear. But first he stops at his mother's trailer. She won't be home for hours so he's not worried that she'll catch him as he's filling a duffel with a pair of jeans, sneakers, and a few T-shirts. He takes his telescope. Not the one Aunt Elena gave him but the one he made himself. He's heard that the space shuttle *Discovery* has taken a telescope into space where it will remain for years, photographing the solar system and sending pictures back to Earth. He grabs the last forty dollars that he's saved from when he worked for the Rothsteins. He thinks about leaving a note for his mother but decides against it. He'll call her once he gets somewhere—wherever that might be.

On his way out of town he decides to swing by the old cemetery one more time to say goodbye to this place as well. Old man Roybal is standing on his porch, smoking a cigarette, and he gives Miguel a wave as he drives by. He wishes the old man hadn't seen him but there's nothing he can do about that now. Usually he walks but today he is in a hurry. It's already getting dark. He doesn't want to change his mind if he's going to get on the highway and disappear. He parks near the top of the hill and climbs the rest of the way. It is dusk as he is standing among the tombstones, looking out across the dry scrub valley that he has called home. He feels no particular attachment to this place and yet it will be difficult to move on.

He sits looking out across the Sangre de Cristo Mountains down into the desolate valley where he is from. Some cows have been up on this hill. That's all that ever comes here. Cows and Miguel. The cows leave their pies behind. Miguel laughs to himself. That's more than he's leaving behind. As he sits, he looks down at the ground. Dozens of dung beetles are making their way to the cow pie. This is not a good memory for Miguel. It was these beetles that distracted him and caused Davie to be bitten by that old rattlesnake. What was it that intrigued him anyway? He can't remember, but he was right about the snake. It conserved its venom. Its intent was to protect itself, not to kill. Still it struck. And this changed everything. Now a boy walks like a zombie, afraid of all the snakes that will bite him. And Miguel can no longer live in the place he calls home. He hates these vile beetles and he wants to crush them, murder them all. Instead he watches.

They walk a straight line forward toward the manure, as he'd seen them do the day Davie was bitten. They gather their little pile of dung and then walk backward, exactly as they had come. Forward and backward, one after the other. Always in a straight line.

Why do they do that?

Miguel looks up and sees that the stars are starting to come out, twinkling along the horizon. For a long time he looks at the sky, then back at the beetles. Then he goes to his car where he finds an old Coke bottle. He takes a sniff. It is dry and with the tip of his knife blade he gathers up half a dozen of the beetles. He drops them one at a time into the bottle. And then he has a more unpleasant task to do. There is a small shovel, along with a bucket of sand in his trunk, something his dad gave him for the next time he had to dig himself out of a ditch until his four-wheel drive is ready. He dumps the sand on the ground and fills the bucket with manure. Then he heads back to his father's place.

His father still isn't home. And Miguel senses he won't be back for a while. Maybe he's got a job or he's on a binge. Maybe he has a woman somewhere. Miguel hopes that he does. He'd like his father to find someone new and have a life—the way Miguel is about to have one. Miguel thinks about what he'll miss when he leaves Entrada. He will miss his father and his mother. He will miss the night sky over the cemetery. Already he misses Rachel Rothstein and the boys, but there is nothing to be done about that. Soon he will be gone. But first he has to test something.

In the middle of his father's garage Miguel dumps the cow manure. Then he places the beetles a few feet away. At first they head toward the manure pile, but then he turns off the light so that the garage is almost dark but not so dark that he can't see their movement. Inside the darkened garage the beetles stagger. They cannot follow a straight line. He watches as they try to find their way toward the manure, then away, stumbling, uncertain of where they need to go. It is as if they are drunk.

Then he scoops them up again along with the manure. He goes into the driveway where he dumps the manure and the dung beetles beside it. In the twilight under the stars the beetles move forward and backward, carrying their spoils. Once more they move in a straight, orderly fashion. He watches them, and then he looks up. It is a bright, starry night. Cassiopeia is overhead, surrounded by her family, Andromeda, her daughter; Cepheus, her husband; and Perseus, who rescues Andromeda and marries her. At the horizon is the Big Dipper. And Polaris is due north. Again he looks at the beetles. Now he thinks he knows what they are doing. Like the ancient mariners they are navigating by the stars.

+

In the morning instead of running away Miguel goes to school. He shows up early before first period because he knows Mr. Garcia will be in his office. Miguel doesn't even bother knocking. He just bursts in. Mr. Garcia is standing at his desk, sorting through papers, getting ready for class. He looks up as if he's been expecting him. "So, Miguel, what's going on?"

"Dung beetles," Miguel says.

Mr. Garcia looks at him askance. "Dung beetles?"

"I think they navigate by celestial navigation. We know that other animals like birds and seals do, but it's never been applied to insects. If my theory is correct, then it's instinctual. And I think I can prove it. Here." Miguel thrusts some papers onto Mr. Garcia's desk. "I've filled out the forms for the scholarship."

Mr. Garcia shakes his head. "I don't know. This isn't what I had in mind."

"It's about explorers," Miguel says. "It's about history. I think I can prove that celestial navigation is in our DNA."

And Mr. Garcia sits down.

CHAPTER THIRTY-ONE

✳

APRICOTS—1599

ofia Pera de Torres knows that this morning, won't be like any
other. She is a woman who sees things even though she's not
sure that this is so. It's what Federico refers to as "her mystery."
Once she saw a log roll out of the fire, careening toward her youngest,
Enrique, who was playing with a puppy on the carpet in front of the
hearth. Except she saw it in her dreams the night before and when the
next morning she found Enrique on the floor near the fire, playing with
the puppy, she swooped down, scooping him up just as the log rolled to
the place where he'd been. The puppy managed to leap away.

That is how Federico sees his wife at times. Or rather how he teases
her. As if she has an animal's sense of what is to come. The way horses
bang in the barn and birds fly madly before a storm. And that morning
as he ran his fingers along the smooth lines of her back, Sofia knew that
it was not going to be a day like any other.

As she sips her cup of hot chocolate, she longs for what she left
behind. Perhaps it is her daily chocolate and the smell of stewing lamb
that makes her recall her parents' home in Mexico City. Though she
brought the recipe for the stew with her, Sofia has never been able to
replicate it. They tried adjusting the spices, rendering the sauce. They've
added more tomatoes or less. They've carved the fat off the meat or left
the fat on. But it never matches the sweet and savory dish her mother
made when Sofia was a girl. She wishes she could taste what she tasted
so long ago the same way she wants to smell her mother's garden or her

father's pipe. Instead she smells something fetid. Perhaps a mouse has died in the walls. She walks around sniffing. Sofia has an acute sense of smell. She can smell the venison that the natives are roasting in Santo Domingo and she can smell when something isn't right.

"Does it feel like a storm?" Sofia asks Bernadine as she rubs her hands against her arms.

"No, m'hija, I do not feel a storm in my bones."

"But do you feel something? Something strange in the wind?"

Bernadine shakes her head. The old woman is adjusting the stew. It is Friday and she is preparing the special meal that the family eats together on that evening. A chicken roasted over the flames, fried potatoes, fresh beans from the garden, and the lamb and garbanzo stew. It would not be Friday night without the stew. The candlesticks are polished and the table set. On Saturday Federico does not work in the fields. It is the one day that they are together. Sometimes they go into Santa Fe where Sofia shops for cloth to make new dresses and curtains or blue-corn flour to make flatbread, though on Friday they eat the rich buttery bread that Bernadine makes with eggs and braids into a golden loaf. Another recipe from Sofia's mother, but this one tastes the way she remembers it.

She helps Bernadine prepare the lamb. It is Federico's favorite dish, and though it is summer, he still expects it, and, despite the fact that she can never get it quite right, she makes it for him. It is one of the recipes that Federico also remembers from the old country. She smiles when she thinks of her husband with the sores she no longer sees and his fondness of cumin, turmeric, and ginger.

+

She did not love Federico when she first met him. It was a slow love that grew over time. It wasn't only the sores that he tried to conceal with his long, frilly cuffs and high-neck collars. Or the ones on his face that he covered with tinctures that made his skin glow like gold. It was his way of not really looking at her, his quiet voice that at times barely rose above a whisper, or the way his legs folded into themselves like a girl's when he was seated. Had he not been the son of the revered and wealthy Dr. Eduardo de Torres of Girona, Sofia was certain that her father would never have invited him into their home.

Sofia was still in love with her cousin Alejandro when Federico came to her father's house. She hadn't stopped thinking about him even though it had been years since he was taken to the Flat House. She had been a young woman and was hoping that the day had come when she would marry him. Instead she was present at his burning. Her father had explained that they had no choice. If they did not attend, they would come under suspicion as well. And so she had buried her eyes and determined that she would never look upon another man for as long as she lived.

Yet, the first time she laid eyes on Federico it was as if her heart had stopped. When he looked at her with those blue eyes, she thought Alejandro had risen from the dead. Though Alejandro had been dark-skinned and Federico was fair, it was as if he was her lover's pale double. "How is this possible?" Sofia wondered.

Her family didn't seem to see the resemblance. Her mother, who had adored Alejandro, saw only this man's effeminate side, with his silk handkerchiefs and lavender cologne, and her father only knew that he was the son of the distinguished Dr. Eduardo de Torres. But Bernadine noticed, and she crossed herself, fearing that it was a ghost come to take her away. Sofia almost shut the door in his face. The similarity with her dead lover was too much for her to bear. Besides Alejandro believed himself to be descended from a long line of Sephardic Jews and this new suitor made no such claim. He had been a Christian for as long as he could recall. But she didn't turn him away.

Federico was not like her other suitors—men who arrived unannounced, ate mutton with their hands, and thought nothing of putting their feet on the petit-point chairs her mother had brought from Spain. Sofia's feral dogs that growled at other men curled up and went to sleep at Federico's feet or followed him around, sniffing at his pockets where he hid pieces of cheese. He offered to help the servants carry heavy trays and to everyone's horror rinsed his teacup himself.

When the roses, whose cuttings her mother had also brought from

Spain, grew mottled, their leaves speckled with black mold and their buds drying up before they bloomed, Federico slashed them to the ground, washed the remains in saturated lime juice, and moved them to where the soil was sandy and the sun relentless, where they were watered within an inch of their lives until they brought forth a profusion of blooms that filled all the vases of the hacienda and perfumed every room with their redolent scent.

He did the same with the tomatoes. He searched the markets for varieties, and those he couldn't find in Mexico he had shipped from Spain. Whole plants arrived that grew in the sunny front garden, and Bernadine always had a pot going on the stove with thick sauces of plum tomatoes or prepared salads of ripe red ones. She roasted yellow tomatoes that she harvested in straw baskets and made broths of sweet cherry tomatoes and cream that she served at luncheons. In this way he won over the cook, the mother, and finally Sofia.

She came to look beyond his feminine manners and his skin as mottled as the plants he rescued and found a strength that surprised her and a gentleness that drew her in. He did not court her as the other suitors had. He did not come with a boisterous laugh and thirst for her father's wines. He sipped slowly and waited. He never asked anything of her until she was ready to give, and then made it seem to her as if this was what she had wanted all along. And when at last he announced his intentions, she asked matter-of-factly, "What took you so long?"

And he replied, "I was waiting for you." It was he who tamed her. He understood her wildness and, instead of trying to break it like other men, he had waited for her to come to him. This was not the same love she had known as a girl, but it was love all the same and one that had only grown with the years.

Their wedding was a simple affair. No more than one hundred guests in her father's garden where they drank his wine and ate the chickens Bernadine had been plucking for days. Musicians played on the harpsichords that had been brought over from France, and bouquets of irises were everywhere. Just before the ceremony her father took Federico into his study, offered him a cigar and a glass of port, and said, "You were aware, I assume, that you are marrying a Jew."

And Federico nodded. "I have my suspicions that I may be New Christian myself, though I cannot prove it. My mother always claimed we were Old Christians but I've had my doubts."

Sofia's father asked no more; he had also wondered. He knew of the Torres family and had heard the rumors of an ancestor who sailed with Columbus, a converso who died in the Bahamas. It would not be so surprising, would it? The great Coronado's wife was also a converso. And didn't Renaldo Pera once glimpse his future son-in-law as they urinated side-by-side into a stream on a family picnic in the Sierra? It was not lost on him that the young man who was hung like a horse had also had his foreskin removed. Renaldo had barely been able to contain his smile; it pleased him to think that his daughter was in the end marrying one of the tribe.

It was only after the marriage that Federico announced his intentions. He told the family that they would be moving north until he found a place where he felt safe growing garbanzo beans. Now her father could expand his mercantile empire throughout New Spain into the profitable area of commodities—grains and beans. But her mother wept until she learned that her friend, Maria of Lisbon, who had once dined with the king of Portugal, was imprisoned along with her daughter at the hands of the Inquisition where they would languish and die.

And of course she recalled the fiery deaths of her sister, Leonora; her niece, Magdalena; and nephew, Alejandro. It was only then that she agreed to release her daughter and let them move as far north as they pleased but within the viceroyalty of New Spain, and that they would take Bernadine with them with the understanding that for three months every winter her daughter and grandchildren would return to Mexico City to visit, and this was what they did for as long as Sofia's parents were alive.

A cloud passes over the sun or so it seems to Sofia. Is it the thought of her parents for whom she always longed despite her years in a contented marriage and the birth of her sons? But whatever darkness has fallen over her does not seem to be coming from such a distant place. "I think we will have a storm," she says to Bernadine who is setting the table, but Bernadine is too deaf to hear. Sofia smiles. The old cook has been her dearest friend. She has been with Sofia almost her entire life. She cannot bear to think of the day when she is gone. But of course Sofia herself has grown older. Indeed she can't bear to think of the day when anything might change. She has been blessed with a happy life. Perhaps not the one she imagined, but still it has been good.

+

Sofia bends forward to taste the stew. Putting the wooden spoon to her lips and blowing on it to cool, she glances outside. Right beyond the kitchen window, there it is. The flowering tree, ripe with its fruit. She laughs to herself. "Apricots," she says out loud. That is the sweetness that has been missing from the stew all these years. The ingredient her mother had forgotten when she sent her daughter the recipe. Why did it come to her now? It has been before her eyes all along.

That is when she hears the cries and shouting, the calling of her name. But she does not race into the fields. She does not move from where she stands. If it were possible, she would remain in this spot forever. If she could stop time at that moment, when she is tasting the broth and gazing at the fruit of the apricot tree, Sofia would stay here forever. But that is not possible. Because across in the fields soldiers are beating her husband with their truncheons until he falls to the ground, screaming for mercy.

Now Sofia grabs her shawl and races outside, her dogs nipping at her feet. They are barking and racing toward their master until a soldier slices one of her dogs in two with his sword. The others skulk away. Shrieking, Sofia rushes to her husband. "What are you doing?" she shouts at the soldier. Another soldier smashes her husband in the jaw. Blood spurts from his mouth. The soldiers have come with the bailiff and their priest. "Father," Sofia cries, "why are you arresting him?" Federico, his head bloodied, is being shackled.

"The order comes from the office of the Holy See in Mexico City," her priest says, turning away. "You are accused of practicing the dead Law of Moses."

"We are Christians," Sofia calls out. "We are good Christians."

"Sofia," her husband calls in a garbled voice, "do not anger them."

As Sofia rushes to help her husband, one of the soldiers spins her around, wrenching her arms. Pulling her hands behind her back, he puts shackles on her as well. Bernadine comes running out. She reaches Federico and grabs hold of the soldier who is dragging him away. "No," she is shouting, "not him." The soldier strikes her across the jaw and Sofia winces at the sound of bone cracking.

✳

CHAPTER THIRTY-TWO

A LETTER TO THE UNIVERSE—1992

Rachel Rothstein is driving north. She cruises along the four-lane highway of lowriders and pickups. Red clay cliffs line the road. She passes Camel Rock, a holy site of the Tesuque Pueblo. The boys were amused the one time they saw it. It looks just like a camel. In the months she's lived in New Mexico she's only driven north twice. Once was with Nathan when they'd first arrived and they'd driven the kids to see the dances at one of the pueblos. She loved the beat of the drums, the moccasins stirring up the dust. And she'd driven north that spring when she'd posted the flyers to find a babysitter and Miguel had phoned. And now he has vanished into thin air.

The road is wide and open. Buttes of red clay line the highway that has been carved through the middle of them. She's left the boys at a friend's house for the afternoon, saying she is going to take a drawing class. Nathan will pick them up on his way home from the hospital. There is no rush except she wants to find Miguel. She tries to remember where she posted all those flyers, the towns she stopped in. Tesuque, Española, Chimayó, it began with an E; that's all she remembers. Española. That must be the place. She is worried about Miguel. He probably blames himself. She passes a sign that reads ten miles to Española. The drive seems longer than she remembers. The distances seem farther. She doesn't recall driving this far when she put up those flyers. But she must have.

Rachel feels as if she could just keep driving. Nathan has barely said a word to her in weeks. Even now that Davie is better, he still won't talk to her. A week ago she confessed to him that she'd known almost nothing about the Hispanic boy who cared for their sons. That she'd wanted someone who wasn't like other nannies. Those girls from Germany and France who take care of kids but really want to learn English. She didn't want her boys to grow up and wear suits and ties and do what everyone else did. They should be exposed to real life, she told him. Nathan listened and said nothing. His anger festered. She believes that it's possible he will never forgive her. And then her marriage will really be over and she'll be divorced at thirty-two with two little boys and basically her life will be done. And perhaps it occurs to her that it already is.

+

At moments as she drives or makes dinner or waits for Nathan to come home, bad thoughts flicker through her mind. At times she thinks she could kill herself. But not really. It isn't something she'd really do. Long ago she ruled that out. When Rachel was a teenager, she wanted to be dead. She thought of many ways of doing this—messy ones, clean ones, but mostly what she wanted was painless. She did research in the library. Breathing helium with a plastic bag over your head was said to be the most painless and effective. There was a bluff behind the high school. Her junior year she would go to the bluff and sit at its edge.

Years ago this was where she believed she'd kill herself.

One hundred feet down the rocky bluff was a highway. She wondered why high-school students weren't flinging themselves off this all the time. There were so many reasons to do so. A failed exam, a broken heart, not making the varsity team. And yet no one had done so—perhaps until now. Rachel had had her own reason for wanting to die. She hated her life.

It was hard for her to be specific about what she hated. It was more an accumulation of small details that added up to a miserable childhood. Nothing she could put her finger on exactly, except that she wanted out of it and the bluff seemed, after long days of contemplation, the ideal place. It would be messy and it probably wouldn't be painless, but it would be effective and she didn't need to buy things—like poison or a gun—for which she might need her parents' permission. She would just jump and it would be over.

Many times in the night, as she drifted off, she pictured it. The moment when she could no longer feel the earth beneath her, when she was in mid-flight. Flying even. The bird's-eye view of the world. The weightlessness until gravity took over. She couldn't think of it past that point. She just hoped she would land on her back, not on her face. For some reason the thought of smashing her nose bothered her more than the shattering of her skull. She imagined that the nose would hurt before the bones shot like arrows into her brain. But she tried not to think of such things. She tried to think about her great moment of flight, an eagle catching the wind, and not everything that would follow.

She had picked a day in August. The summer camp where she was an arts counselor would be over as would her course in touch typing. She didn't want to miss work or school. She had always been an excellent, if somewhat methodical, student. It was a Tuesday, the third Tuesday in August, to be specific. Her mother had her mah-jongg game that day. Her father would be at work. Her sister heading back to school. And the cleaning woman didn't come on Tuesdays so she would have the house to herself. It was just a couple of weeks before students had to be back. Many of her friends would be away, touring Europe as part of an exchange program or on family vacations.

She made herself lunch. A chicken sandwich with mustard and mayo on whole wheat bread. She took a peach and an oatmeal cookie. She took a small bottle of Coca-Cola from the fridge. She would go to the bluff, have her lunch, perhaps write something in her journal or a letter to somebody. Her parents? She wasn't sure. Maybe a general letter to the universe. She put it all in the small pink satchel that she carried to school. Then she walked out the door. It was a hot day, muggy, and she could hear the cicadas chirping, so filled with life, their song rising and falling, then disappearing altogether.

None of the neighbors were out. It was the dog days of summer— that was what her mother called them. It was when she thought of dog days that she had a sense that she was being followed. Someone was definitely behind her. She turned and looked and there she saw him.

Just a few feet back. Bubbles was following her. Somehow he'd gotten out. "Bubbles," she said, "go home."

She clapped her hands. Bubbles stopped and stared. He was a black-and-white spaniel and they'd gotten him when she was a baby. Now he was old and probably deaf. She should take him home. But she was going to kill herself, and the last thing she wanted to do was go home. So she continued walking. She crossed Stanton Road. It was about noon. She turned to see if Bubbles was following her. When she didn't see him anymore, she kept going across the parking lot. Mr. Walkins, the head of maintenance, was on a mowing tractor, preparing the playing fields. He gave her a wave, but she just walked on. She cut across the parking lot along the edge of the playing fields. The smell of cut grass filled the air. From the end of the playing fields she entered the woods where it was cool and the smell was more loamy and fetid. She kept walking through the trees until she came to the path that led up the bluff. She scrambled up, sometimes crawling, until she reached the rocky outcrop.

She stood for a moment at the edge. Far below was the highway. A glacier had carved this passage through solid rock. Standing at the edge made her dizzy so she stepped back. She got that odd sensation one felt in the groin when standing at an edge. Almost like an orgasm of which thus far she'd had only a few, but enough to know how that feeling rippled through your body. Sitting on the ground she took out her picnic. On the brown paper bag she put down her sandwich, the peach, and the cookie. The peach had gotten a little mushy in her bag. The Coke was warm.

She ate slowly, thinking about death. Or rather thinking about why she didn't want to live. The sandwich was good and she ate it slowly. Then the cookie and finally the peach. She didn't drink the Coke. It tasted funny when it was warm. She thought of taking out her journal and writing something down, but instead she lay back. She looked up at the clouds rolling by, the different shapes. A bear, a snake, a flower. She laughed to herself. It was a game she used to play as a child. Naming the different types of clouds. She knew their scientific names but couldn't recall them just now. She just watched, the breeze blowing through the trees, the clouds sailing overhead. And she fell asleep.

When she woke, it was much later in the day. Perhaps even four o'clock. She decided that she would not kill herself that day. She didn't know why, but it wasn't the right moment. And she wasn't sure that jumping off the bluff was the way to go anyway. It wasn't how she'd really envisioned her death. She pictured something more elegant and romantic, not that messy splat like a bug on a windshield. Years later she learned that women tended to commit suicide with drugs, not with guns or by jumping. Women didn't like to leave a mess for someone else to clean up.

Rachel decided to go home and find another way. She climbed down the bluff, leaving behind the cool of the woods. As she reached the playing fields, she saw that the grass was all cut and that Mr. Walkins was puttering around in his garage. There was no longer the sound of the mower nor the scent of diesel. Only the smell of cut grass. Cutting across the playing fields to the parking lot, Rachel came to the exit where she'd traverse Stanton Road onto her own street, Willow.

She looked both ways. Out of the corner of her eye she saw something by the side of the road. She crossed the street and there in the drainage ditch was a body, black and white, something she couldn't quite recognize, something she could barely make out, but when she stooped down she saw. Bubbles must have followed her. He didn't go home. She hadn't heard anything. Not his yelp or cry when he was struck. She hoped it happened very fast. She wondered if the person who did this bothered to stop. If they looked at his tags and called her home.

Rachel had never seen anything dead before. Not like this. A fish maybe. But not something she had loved, walked, fed. Not something that had always been at her side. She had done this. It was her fault. She should have taken him home. But he was old, wasn't he? And he couldn't hear. He probably didn't hear her tell him to go home. He probably didn't hear the car.

She slipped her arms into the ditch and lifted him out. He didn't weigh more than twenty pounds but she was stunned at how heavy he was. Blood dripped from his mouth and nose, even his ears. Cradling him in her arms, Rachel carried Bubbles home. As she walked, she kept shifting her weight. His body was still warm and bulky and limp. She was surprised at what a dead body felt like. He had been alive moments ago and now Bubbles was dead. As she carried him, Rachel knew she would not kill herself. She did not want her body to become this warm, heavy, bulky thing.

Later her mother complained when Rachel padded Bubbles's home-made coffin with a silk pillowcase. But still she didn't want to kill herself and she doesn't want to die. Not now. Not yet. She'll figure a way to move on as she always has. She has her boys and she has her life, flawed though it is.

+

She's driving down the main drag of Española. It's part of the same four-lane highway. The map says it's called Riverside Drive, but as far as she can tell there's no river. It's a town of diners, auto mechanics, bodegas. She passes a taqueria called El Girasol with a big picture of a sunflower painted on the front. There are hair salons and thrift stores. Lowriders cruise along, some with elaborate designs painted on their hoods and sides. She has no recollection of stopping here. But perhaps she did. Perhaps she put up a few flyers in the stores and gas stations that line the main drag.

She pulls off the highway and stops at a convenience store. She walks into the store. Hispanic boys hang out in front, smoking ciga-rettes. They pause, checking her out. The shelves are almost empty and the clerk stands behind a thick plate of bulletproof glass. Rachel has no memory of posting a flyer here. She stops at a gas station farther up the road, where apparently you can also file for divorce. Rachel would have remembered that one. She drives up and down Riverside Drive but nothing about Española is familiar to her at all.

✳

CHAPTER THIRTY-THREE

THE EXPERIMENT—1992

O n his way home from school, Miguel heads to his father's
trailer. In the backseat is the large empty aquarium that he
purchased at a flea market, and he doesn't want to break it.
He also has a shovel, a decal kit of the night sky, a trash bag of manure,
and two dozen dung beetles in a margarine tub. As he drives past the
7-Eleven he slows down. He thinks he sees a Jeep Cherokee. Nobody
up here drives a car like that. In fact the only person he knows who
drives one is Rachel Rothstein. But what would she be doing in Española? Looking for a new babysitter? Or looking for him? He's tempted
to stop. He could walk into the convenience store by accident, run into
her. That would make it easier, wouldn't it? Instead he steps on the gas
and the aquarium rattles.

His heart is pounding as he pulls up to his father's house. He wonders if his mind isn't playing tricks on him. Why would she come looking for him? To talk him into turning himself in? Miguel breathes a
deep sigh. He's relieved to find that his father isn't home. Miguel has
work to do. He parks in the drive and carries the aquarium into the
garage, putting it in the middle of the floor. With the shovel he begins
to dig up dry patches of dirt, which he dumps into the aquarium. When
he has enough, he takes a hose and waters it down. Then he goes to his
trunk.

He takes out a large plastic bag filled with manure and brings it into
the garage. He digs out a shovel full and tosses it into the aquarium.
Then he gets the margarine tub that contains the dozens of dung bee-

tles he has captured over the last few days. These are his testers. He dumps some of them into the aquarium. Then he gets a ladder. On the ceiling of his father's garage he sticks on the stars. He puts up the constellations—Cassiopeia, Orion, the Big Dipper. He attaches the North Star. The moon. Then he closes the door of the garage, shining a small flashlight onto the ceiling with just enough light to illumine the stars. He observes the beetles, moving forward and backward in a straight line. In a notebook he makes a rough sketch of their trajectories.

Last week Mr. Garcia told Miguel that the ancient Egyptians worshipped dung beetles. They called them scarabs. The Egyptians observed how the beetle rolled its dung on the ground and it reminded them of how their great god, Ra, who is often portrayed with the head of a beetle, rolled the sun out every day, rolling it back at dusk. The beetles seemed to possess an orbit of their own. The Egyptians considered them sacred, infused with the power of the gods. They signaled rebirth.

Miguel pauses. What if the Egyptians had made the same discovery as he? Only nobody knew about it until now. Then he opens the garage door so that the light gets in. The stars are obliterated, and, without a vision of the sky, his dung beetles are utterly lost.

※

CHAPTER THIRTY-FOUR

THE CHARGES—1600

When the charges are read, Sofia almost laughs. If laughter weren't one of the accusations against her, she would. Instead she stands solemnly before her hooded judges and listens. The accusations are read with tedious precision. No accusers are named but there are specific dates, anonymous sources, testimonials. There are one hundred and thirty-two counts of heresy against her. She is accused of drinking hot chocolate on Good Friday, of bathing and changing her clothes on Friday, of changing her linens on Fridays, of trimming her nails, of not eating pork, of laughing when reading a book, of reading books in different languages, of lighting candles on Fridays, of not lighting a fire (but allowing the servants to do it for her) on Saturdays. She is accused of not going to mass often enough, of not dipping her hand in holy water each time she enters the cathedral. She and her husband slept late on Christmas three years ago.

The reading goes on for hours. She stands, listening to the man in his dark hood. Beside him a scribe keeps meticulous notes of every word, every sigh and exclamation with his stylus. Her bones ache. She wants to sit down, but she must remain standing. She is shivering and wants to rub her arms, but her hands are shackled. She listens to the sound of the pen on the paper. The bailiff, her jailer, and soldiers surround her, as if she could somehow escape from this dank prison. The four-month journey by donkey and cart to arrive in Mexico City has taken its toll. She is certain that the stiffness in her limbs will never leave her. She longs for a hot bath and to have warm oils massaged into her skin. She would give anything for a cup of hot chocolate. Her mind wants to drift but she forces herself to stay focused. She must convince these men of her innocence. Has she done many of these things? Yes. But does this mean that she is not a good Christian and has not always been a good Christian? No. Since the time of her family's conversion when she was very small, she has led a good Christian life.

She wonders about the lives of her inquisitors. Do they caress their children? Pet their dogs? What do they talk about with their wives at the end of the day? That they found someone guilty of bathing? Of preferring lamb to pork? How they sent someone to the flames for not confessing? How dull they must be in bed. These unimaginative lovers. Or perhaps they require unspeakable practices in order to feel pleasure at all. Do they inflict these tortures on those they love? Again she feels as if she could laugh. Or faint. The room smells of piss and sweat. Misery lives in these cold stone walls.

It occurs to her that perhaps she is losing her mind. She does not know how long she has been here. How long it has taken them to accumulate their evidence and prepare these charges against her. Weeks. Months. She spent two months in the jail in Santa Fe before they brought her here. It was chilly when they left Santa Fe and it is still chilly here. She wonders if she will live to see spring. If she will make it through the summer.

She has been told that she will be presented before the inquisitors three times. Once when the accusations are read, which is happening now. Once when she may defend herself. And once when she is read their decision. And she knows that the time between these can take up to a year. It is part of their strategy to wear their victims down. Boredom is also a form of torture. She did not realize it until now.

Her mind drifts. She wishes she could lie down and sleep, then wake and it will all be over. Finally the most ludicrous charge of all is read. She is accused of making a love potion by mixing chocolate and menstrual blood and serving it to one of the young Indian servants so that he would come to her bed. She snaps awake. She cannot refrain from an outburst. Grabbing at her head of graying hair, she shouts, "And where would I get menstrual blood?" Some of the soldiers can't help themselves and chuckle until the inquisitor bangs his gavel. He glares at her from beneath his hood. For the first time she sees his small, beady eyes. Then he puts down his papers and she knows he is done.

If these were wild dogs, she could tame them. She would feed them scraps and they'd grow docile at her feet. But these men aren't any kind of animal she's ever known. They are capable of doing anything to make her confess. They will torment her flesh and her mind. She saw what they did to Alejandro when she was a young woman. She trembles at the thought of what they have done to Federico. He was brought to the Flat House before her, and though she has tried to bribe her jailer with the few coins she was able to keep, she hasn't learned anything of his fate.

But it is Alejandro who comes rushing back to her like a flood. It is his hands, his lips. His love for her. Her first love, her young love. It is as if thirty years never happened. But now she is in the Flat House where he was once taken. She feels his presence. She imagines him in these walls. She knows what he suffered. It is as if she is losing her lover all over again. She has not thought of him in this way in a long time, but now she does. Is it possible that she has loved two men for all these years? A dead one and a living one? A memory and a husband? Why does she think of such things now? They should accuse her of this. It is perhaps her only sin.

"Do you have anything to say for yourself?" the judge asks.

"Where is my husband?"

"That is no longer your concern."

The finality in his voice sends a shudder through her, but she will not weep. She will not give these criminals the satisfaction of seeing her tears. "It is very much my concern."

"It would make it easier on all of us, but especially on you, if you would sign your confession now."

She glances around the room, then back at her inquisitor. "I would like a bigger cell." They stare at her as if she truly is mad. They cannot believe her audacity. No one, and certainly no woman, has ever addressed the tribunal in this way. "My cell is too cold and dank. I am unwell."

"Is that all?"

"I would like to keep the list of the charges against me. I wish to study them." There is a mumbling among the judges. "You know that I am capable of reading because it is one of the charges against me," she says with a wry smile.

Her accuser hands her the thick document. "You may review these if you wish." Then he orders her back to her cell.

✦

In her cell Sofia sits at the edge of her cot, shivering. Though she wraps her shawl around her shoulders—the only shred of warmth she has— she is still cold. More than anything she wishes she had a cup of hot chocolate. That dark, sweetened brew that she loved to sip daily and that has become, it appears, part of her undoing. It seems impossible to believe that you could be sent to prison for your laughter, your love of reading and chocolate. Except it is true.

She would bribe her jailer if she didn't think that it would become another accusation against her. Instead she calls him to her cell. He is not a bad man. He is never cruel to her and seems almost apologetic when he sees her suffering. But he will not break the rules. "I would like a candle," she tells him.

He makes a face and leaves her in the dark. But at daybreak he returns with a candle. It will burn for eight hours and the next day he will bring her another. Sofia places the candle on her small desk and proceeds to study the list of her crimes. She turns the dense pages slowly. There in the solitude of her tiny cell she does laugh. Who has spent so much time observing her every move, keeping a record of everything she did and did not do to prove her secret faith? She reads until the candle burns down and then she sits again in the dark. She sinks onto her straw pallet. She supposes she has been guilty of all these sins and more, but who could know this about her? A shiver runs down her spine. There is, of course, someone, but Sofia cannot begin to contemplate it.

In the morning when a thin light trickles in beneath her door, she begins to read again. When she is served her tepid tea and bread and her new candle is lit, Sofia turns to her jailer. "I would like paper and a pen."

The jailer is stunned by this request. "And why is this?"

"I wish to defend myself."

Shaking his head, her jailer leaves, but later that day paper, ink, and pen are brought to Sofia's cell. Again she sits at her small desk and, as the candle burns, begins to write. She writes slowly, day and night, as long as she has light. It is the job she must do. She answers the charges against her—one at a time. She ponders them, writing long and detailed responses. She reads in other languages because she was taught by an Italian tutor. She enjoys chocolate because her uncle was an exporter of cacao. She lights candles because it is her family's ritual to light candles, just as is taking a siesta or sipping a glass of port. She prefers beef and lamb to pork. She has not menstruated in years.

When she is finished, she gives the pages over to her jailer and asks if she may see the judges again. But weeks go by, and then months. She has time to think. Too much time. Every night in the darkness she feels as if she has solved a worrisome puzzle, but when daylight comes she is sure she is wrong. Finally the darkness wins, and one morning before her stale bread and tepid tea are served, Sofia knows.

Bernadine had been with her since she was a girl. They were raised almost as sisters. It was Bernadine who first braided her hair. Bernadine who held her as she sobbed upon learning that Alejandro was accused. Who stayed with her in her room after he was burned at the stake. It was Bernadine who accompanied her on her wedding night, who moved with her into the hills of New Mexico, who knew all the family recipes, who had helped birth her three children.

But it was Bernadine who had rubbed the salve into Federico's sores. It was Bernadine who kept the list of Federico's favorite dishes from home. Bernadine who drew his special salt baths and sprinkled them with rose water. Bernadine was not reaching for her, the woman she'd raised as a girl, but for Federico as she raced outside. It was Federico she wanted to save and for whom she'd sobbed. She'd never intended for him to be taken. Only Sofia. It is possible that she will never see Bernadine again. But if she does, she will tear her apart with her bare hands.

Finally her permission to appear before the judges again is granted. In the tribunal she reads her responses. She reads them as methodically and slowly as they read theirs—only her responses are longer than the accusations against her. She explains that she washes her hair not only on Fridays but whenever it pleases her because it takes her hair two days to dry. Once she did not go to mass on Good Friday because she had suffered a miscarriage. She explains that she does not drink chocolate because she is practicing witchcraft, as some women have been accused, but because as a child her nurse prepared it for her every day and it became her habit.

Her responses take three days to read out loud. When she is done, the judges say that she will have their answer, but they do not say when. And again weeks, then months go by. She languishes in her cell. They give her a Bible and she reads it over and over, not only because she is a believer but because seeing words on a page keeps her from going mad. She thinks she will die of the cold, and then in summer of the heat. She loses track of time.

At last on a hot summer day when she feels that she can barely breathe, her jailer informs her that her request has been granted. Without any further explanation she is moved to a larger cell. It even has a small window near the ceiling where, if she stands on a stool she has been given, she can breathe fresh air and see the sky. "Why am I being moved?" she asks her jailer when at last her belongings are arranged in the larger cell.

"Because you asked to be," is all he says. More weeks go by until at last she is called before them. She has decided she doesn't care what their verdict is as long as she doesn't have to wait any longer. If they plan to burn her, she hopes they do it soon.

Once more she is brought into the room where she has stood two other times. She expects that she will have to stand again for hours or even days, but the verdict takes only a moment. Her inquisitor does not look up when he tells her that she is found neither innocent nor guilty. "All charges against you have been dismissed," he says in the same flat tone in which he has told her everything.

She is stunned. All this time for nothing. "And my husband?"

"The charges against him have been dropped as well."

Sofia cannot help but smile. At last their ordeal is coming to an end. "When may I see him?"

"Unfortunately," her inquisitor says, "that will not be possible." He informs her that he died in prison. He has been buried. Sofia will not give these men the pleasure of seeing her grieve. She will not cry in front of them. She never has before. "Then give me his bones."

After almost two years in the Inquisition prison in Mexico City, Sofia Pera de Torres, accompanied by two servants, five aging donkeys, and a cart, walks through the gates of the Flat House and begins the journey home. In a wooden box she carries her husband's remains. It is fall when they set out. Sofia wishes she could wait until spring, but she senses that if she doesn't leave Mexico City now she never will. As they cross the plains of Mexico, the wind pummels them. In the mountains they almost die of the cold. They sleep on the hard ground and build fires when they can. One of her servants dies of starvation. When she thinks the trip could not be worse, the roads turn to mud. The wheels of the cart sink into the ground, and three donkeys die of exhaustion. Sofia is certain that she will never see her children again, but in the spring when the ground thaws and a grave can be dug, she arrives back in Entrada.

Her sons, who are tending the fields of garbanzo beans, cannot believe the strange entourage that wends its way up the trail toward the old hacienda. At first they stand motionless in the fields. Then Enrique, her youngest, falls to his knees, sobbing. José helps his mother off her donkey. She points to the box on the cart. "Be careful with that," she instructs them. "These are your father's bones."

His is the first death. She tells her sons to find a place high on one of the hills on the property. It should have long vistas and be close to the stars. There should be trees that can bring eternal shade. She does not want her husband plagued by the heat of the sun. They find a spot half a mile from the house on a hill where a young oak tree grows and there they begin the Torres family cemetery.

In time they will all be buried here. In his safe Federico has left instructions. He has requested that he be buried as a Jew. Sofia is stunned by his request, but he has written in a language Sofia can neither read nor understand what is to appear on his tombstone. She finds a man in the village who can carve the letters and make the Jewish star. They bury him on the hill that his sons have chosen.

Bernadine had, of course, disappeared shortly after Sofia and Federico were taken away. Sofia will live on for many more years and will be almost one hundred when she dies, but she will never recover from her sense of betrayal. During her widowhood she intends to tell her children that they are Jews, until the governor of Santa Fe, Francisco Gomez, is accused of having a tail. He is also required to have his foreskin examined by a panel of experts. The results will prove inconclusive though it is noted in the public records that he has no tail. Although he will be acquitted, Francisco Gomez Roybal will live the rest of his life as an outcast.

Sofia does not want her children to worry about having tails. It will only be a burden to them. Every time there is a family gathering she thinks she will tell them what they surely suspect, but she doesn't. What is the rush? Is there any reason why they must know now? And then Sofia begins to forget. At first she forgets that she was born and raised in Mexico City. She even seems to forget her life in New Mexico. On her deathbed she gazes into the eyes of her grandson, Diego, with a look of recognition on her face, and says, "Alejandro, is that you?"

Then she closes her eyes, leaving her children and grandchildren to wonder who Alejandro was and why their mother should see his face as she departed from this world. They bathe her body, trim her hair and nails, wrap her in white linen, in keeping with a tradition whose meaning they no longer recall, and bury her beside her husband beneath the oak tree at the top of the hill.

As usual Nathan is late. And Rachel has no sense of when he might be coming home. It is almost eight o'clock. The boys have had their dinner. Davie is watching cartoons but Jeremy has homework to do. A geography lesson. He is sitting at the dining-room table, studying a map of New Mexico. She checks on the boys and then starts to clean up. She slams cabinets closed, bangs pots and pans into the sink. As she does the dishes, Rachel is trying to decide when she will leave her husband. The question for her is no longer if. The only question remaining in her mind is whether she will move back to New York to be near her family—the family she did everything she could to get away from.

But leaving Nathan, Rachel has decided, won't be that difficult. It is as if they aren't really married anyway. They barely inhabit the same space. Since they moved to New Mexico, they've only been to a single powwow and their one camping trip was a disaster. In fact they've barely done any of the things she imagined they'd spend their weekends doing. And during the week they never have dinner together. How many meals has she made and then put in Tupperware, only to be tossed out a few days later?

She has been a single parent for a long time—and not a very good one, she fears. She will do better. She will find a way. "Okay, kiddies," Rachel says, "let's take our baths, then you can watch some TV." But Jeremy still hasn't finished his homework. He shows her the map of New Mexico.

"I have to pick out a city to write about," he tells her. Rachel sighs. All she wants to do is lie down, collapse. Outside the wind blows and she senses that winter is near. She will be more isolated than she already is. She tries to envision the winter with Nathan gone. And without Miguel. No one to arrive in the afternoon to watch the boys. No one to show them how telescopes work or tell them about the stars. Jeremy spreads the map out on the coffee table and kneels beside his mother. He's pointing to cities far to the south of Santa Fe. "Mom," he pokes her in the leg, "look."

She is tired and the map seems to swirl in front of her. She can hardly tell north from south. "It's upside down," Rachel says. She turns the map around. "Maybe we can pick a city nearby," she tells him. "One you can visit and learn even more about."

Jeremy nods. He thinks this is a good idea. He has become such a docile child since his brother's accident. At first she thought it was just his guilt but in fact he is a kinder person than he was before. "Look, here's Tesuque." With her finger Rachel traces the cities and towns going north. This map is fairly detailed and easy to read. She moves her finger toward Taos until she comes to Española.

Then as if her index finger has become a divining rod, she veers east on a narrow strip toward Chimayó until she comes to a tiny speck—a dot on the map that begins with an E. Entrada. She peers more closely until she sees it clearly. That is the name of the town Miguel comes from. Isn't that what he said? A warmth rushes through her. She will go there. She will try to find him again. If only to tell him that Davie is fine, that he did all the right things. And then perhaps he'll come back and teach Davie how not to be afraid.

+

The road between Española and Entrada is marked with roadside memorials. Every half mile, around every blind bend, every curve, she comes to another. Some seem new with fresh flowers, the cross standing tall. The names clearly marked. Others are more faded and neglected. She reads some of the names as she drives by: Martinez, Gonzalez, Chavez, Roybal. Pascual Roybal. This one seems the newest, almost fresh. Or perhaps just well-tended. The plastic flowers aren't tattered. The name on the cross is still clear.

Rachel slows down. Perhaps she should start heading back. It is later than she intended. She's not sure she wants to be on this road at night, and it is almost dark. In another twenty minutes or so it will be. It is almost winter and she can see the snow on the distant mountains. A light flurry falls, but it soon turns to rain. The pavement will be slick on her way home. Ancient willows and cottonwoods line this two-lane road taking her north. It is not like the highway from Santa Fe to Española.

She follows the signs until she comes to the town, if you can call it a town. She drives down its one main street and then sees the lights for the general store and something seems to awaken in her. She pulls up in front of the sign that reads Roybal's General Store. She thinks of the roadside memorial. Pascual Roybal—the same as the name on a painted board hanging above the porch. Standing on the porch it seems familiar. She steps inside.

The wooden shelves are lined in canned goods—carrots, peas, Spam. There is a shelf of bread and another of cereal. An old refrigerator is against the wall and on it are signs for the prices of milk, butter, and eggs. A handwritten sign says "Sodas, 50¢. 5¢ back on return." At the counter she almost knocks over the rack of beef jerky. An old man leans on the long wooden counter. Behind him are rows of cigarettes and small bottles of whiskey, tequila, and rum.

Off to the side is an old corkboard and on it are notices. Sofa for sale, $20 plus delivery. Puppies for adoption. Guns, cars, appliances—all for sale. Rooms to rent. Jobs needed. Jobs available. Rachel nods. She's been here before. She pushes some of the old notices aside and then she sees it, buried beneath others. Her old flyer with the smiley face. Only one tab has been taken. She looks at the old man at the cash register. "Hi there," she says with her brightest smile. It is an eye-catching smile, Rachel knows, and people can hardly say no to her when she beams at them in that way. "How're you doing today?"

The man stares at her skeptically. "About as good as any other day. What can I do for you?" She can tell he isn't accustomed to having a white woman come into his store.

"I'm looking for Miguel."

"Miguel who?" The old man puffs on a cigarette. "There's a lot of Miguels around here."

Rachel nods. She has a feeling he knows perfectly well whom she means, but she decides to play along. "Teenager. He's very tall." She raises her hand far above her head. "He's a stargazer."

"Miguel Torres." The old man nods, straightening himself up. And Rachel notices that this man is very tall as well. "Well, you can try his mother's trailer. But you'll probably find him up the hill. At the old cemetery under that oak tree. That's where he usually goes." The old man purses his lips, shaking his head as if he were understanding something for the first time—that he isn't the only person who is looking out for Miguel.

He walks to the front of his store and points to a winding trail that leads up a steep hill. In the distance Rachel can make out the silhouette of a tree. "That's the old cemetery. If he's anywhere nearby, he's probably there. Do you have a flashlight?" Rachel shakes her head. "You should have a flashlight."

Rachel doesn't carry a flashlight in her car. Or a first aid kit. Or bottled water either. She hasn't developed her survival skills in this part of the world. She knows how to watch her purse on a crowded subway, but she hasn't awakened her instincts here. Perhaps it is time to do so. She buys a flashlight, a small first aid kit, a water bottle, and two energy bars. So that she can survive. In case she gets stuck in the middle of nowhere.

She stands on the porch. Outside it is a clear night and stars fill the sky. The canopy is so huge that it frightens her to look up. She keeps her eyes to the ground. Besides, she could trip on roots or stones. As she walks, she feels the chill of fall in the air. That coolness in the breeze as winter sneaks in. Leaving her car parked in front of the store, Rachel begins the climb. Flashlight in hand, she hikes up the path. She turns the flashlight on. It isn't very strong. Just bright enough so that she can see the dirt path in front of her, riddled with the roots of old cottonwoods.

Halfway up the hill she pauses and turns it off. A shiver runs through her as she stands in the perfect darkness. This is why Miguel comes here. And it is frightening. Standing there, Rachel Rothstein begins to shake. She is utterly alone. She is nothing in all of this blackness. An irrelevant speck among billions of specks. The dust she sweeps away. Why would anything in her life matter? It is as if she'd been tossed into the middle of the ocean on a pitch-black night. She would die of fear before she drowned. Not the fear of sharks but the fear of being nothing at all.

Overhead the Milky Way stretches its huge canvas. She can barely bring herself to look at it. She's never seen so many stars. It rounds over her head like an enormous dome. A shooting star illumines the sky. She wants to turn around and head back. None of this matters. None of it will make a dust mote of difference, a hill of beans, a grain of sand. That is how tiny her concerns about her little life are. Still she feels she owes this to the boy. She turns on the flashlight and resumes her climb.

The hill turns steeper, surprisingly so. She almost has to scramble on all fours. Her feet slip on a rock and she stumbles and falls, bumping her knee, then rights herself. Pain shoots through her. She keeps climbing. At the crest of the hill she can make out the giant oak that the man told her about. She steps closer, and hears a rustling. Miguel is standing near the tree with his homemade telescope aimed at the stars. In a moment he'll notice her flashlight and it will annoy him. She flicks it off again, but he's already seen her. "Who's there?" he asks sharply.

"Miguel, it's me. Rachel." She hesitates. "Mrs. Rothstein."

There's silence, but she can see his eyes glistening at her.

"What are you doing here?" He turns back to his telescope.

"I've been looking for you for a while." She takes a step closer. The ground is rocky underfoot and she teeters.

"Why?" he whispers.

Rachel thinks for a moment. There's a long answer and a short one. She decides on the short version. "I wanted to see if you were all right."

Miguel breathes a deep sigh. "I'm so sorry . . ." His voice cracks. "It was all my fault."

Turning her flashlight back on, Rachel shines it straight ahead and takes another step toward his shadow, which is all she can see. "I'm sorry too." She walks in the direction of the sound of his voice. "I want to tell you that Davie is fine. Physically, that is. You did all the right things. That's what the doctor said."

"I never should have taken them for a hike."

"Maybe not, but it's all right." A cold wind blows, and Rachel steadies herself against a stone. "The snake didn't use much venom."

Miguel looks down, nodding. "It was an old snake."

In the dark she can barely make out his face. "I'm sure the kids felt cooped up. You took them for a walk. There was nothing wrong with that."

"I blame myself."

In the darkness he hears her voice. "I never blamed you. And everything is all right."

"Jeremy's a bully," Miguel says.

Rachel nods. "I know. But he's been better since the snakebite. He looks out for Davie now."

Miguel is quiet, but she is close enough that she can make out his smile. "I'm glad."

"But Davie isn't doing so well. He's afraid of everything." Rachel takes a step toward him. "So is this where you come? When you want to be alone?"

"It's where I come when I want to look at the stars."

She moves closer. "May I look too? I'd like to see what you see." She stands beside him. "I want to understand what brings you here."

In the cemetery he can barely see Mrs. Rothstein, but he feels her presence. She seems to float behind him like a ghost and yet he wants to reach out and touch her. He wonders if his hand will slip through her body or if he will really touch it. He realizes how much and for how long he has wanted to do just that. Perhaps since the first time he saw her. He wanted to feel her skin. Her smell is fresh like mint and almonds. He imagines that she uses soothing creams on her skin. That she gets her nails done and has all the calluses scraped away on the bottoms of her feet. He envisions her polished toes and her strong but elegant hands. He wants to hold them in his. But not in the way a man and woman touch. It is different. She brings him comfort. That is what he feels with her. Comfort.

Behind him he hears the sound of stones rolling and Mrs. Rothstein lets out a shout. Turning, he sees that she is stumbling, almost flying his way, and he reaches out his arms to catch her. Her flashlight falls, striking the crumbling stones. It shines weirdly on the stone like when you shine a flashlight under your chin to make a scary face. And though he manages to grab her arm, he hears the crunch as her knee strikes a slab. She lets out a sharp cry. "Mrs. Rothstein." Miguel holds her delicately in his arms. He will carry her down the hill if he has to. "Are you all right?"

She isn't sure. Moaning, she clasps her knee. It's the same place she banged just moments ago. Perhaps she has broken her patella. She's in extraordinary pain, but all she can think about is his arms and how strong this boy is. Rachel wonders if one day, years from now, when she is an old woman, one of her boys will catch her like this. Miguel holds her firmly, helps her up, and leads her to a rock where she can sit.

He bends down to pick up her flashlight. Miguel never uses a flashlight. He has good night vision. Like a raccoon. But now as he bends to pick it up, it shines on one of the fallen stones. Rachel stares. As Miguel begins to move on, Rachel stops him with her hand. "Wait. Can I see that?" With a groan she stoops down. As Miguel holds the flashlight steady, Rachel runs her fingers across the stone. "What is this place?" she asks.

"It's just the old cemetery. No one's been buried here since anyone can remember."

"Who is buried here?"

Again Miguel shrugs. "I don't know. My relatives, I guess. We've lived in this valley for hundreds of years. Why?"

She runs her fingers across the letters carved into the stone. "Because this is Hebrew," Rachel Rothstein says.

+

From his place at the counter of his store Vincent Roybal feels something change. Something in his universe has shifted. It has been a while, he realizes, since he's heard his dead son's voice. Pascual, Vincent mutters to himself. They named him for Easter because it is the time when everything rises from the dead. Perhaps at last that boy has found his rest.

Vincent grabs a cigarette and goes out into the night. He stands staring at the sky, his gaze moving up the hill. There under the oak tree all he can make out is a single beacon of light, but it is more than that. He knows in his bones that his story, the one he has been trying to tell for so long, has almost come to an end. And nothing will ever be the same.

+

In his mother's garage Roberto is working on Miguel's El Camino. He'd promised it to Miguel for his birthday but he's more than a month late. Now it'll be his Christmas present. He's already rebuilt the engine and chromed it. It's one of the best internal combustion engines anyone's ever seen. He still needs to realign the brakes and fix a leak in the exhaust pipe. Once that's all done he can finish the bodywork. He'll ask Miguel what he wants for his paint job, but Roberto is thinking big blue sky, the moon and stars. Maybe a telescope on the hood with the zodiac around it. Roberto is so pleased with himself that he thought of this. He's going to start drawing it tonight.

It's late, but he doesn't care. He likes to work on cars in the evenings. It keeps him away from the things he needs to stay away from. He jacks up the car in his driveway, gives it a shove. It is in place, the wheels are locked. She'll hold. With his wrench in hand, he slides under on the creeper. He checks the axle and the exhaust. But he still can't see where the leak is. He slides more deeply under the car. He'll get it into shape. Really into shape. Miguel has been asking for four-wheel drive. He'll make this a beauty for his son. And he'll paint it a shade of shiny blue because Miguel likes the sky so much. A comet shooting along the side. He wants to see him drive off in this car when he goes to college. He wants to see his son get into this car and drive away. Roberto is smiling. He has been sober for twenty-five days. He is going to show Miguel and MG that he can be responsible. After all, she hasn't divorced him yet, has she? Perhaps she's just biding her time. Perhaps this is how he'll find his way to get home to her. Under the car he finds a place where the pipe has rusted. He can stick his finger right through it. He'll have to replace that. He bangs on the pipe with his wrench, testing to see how weak the metal is. As he bangs on it, he hears the sound like a sigh. He listens, not sure what it is, but then he sees from the corner of his eye. The jack has slipped on the uneven ground. Not very far, but it is at an awkward angle. Carefully Roberto starts to ease the creeper out from under the car. But before he can, before he can do anything, the jack slips from its hold on the lip of the car. And the car falls on Roberto's chest.

He takes a deep breath as if this will keep his ribs from crushing. As if when he lets out that breath, he can lift the car off his chest. He presses his hands against the chassis. He just needs a little space to slip out from beneath the car. But he can't exhale and he can't breathe in. All he feels is the weight of the car pressing down. His ribs aren't strong enough to hold up a car. They are breaking, caving into his chest, piercing his lungs. With all the strength he can muster in his arms, he pushes against the bottom of the car. The car he wants his son to drive away in. As he pushes, he sees flames. He sees MG's face, lying beside him, her hair resting against his cheek. He watches her breasts rising and falling.

He sees a child, not Miguel, slipping out of her, being born, hears his first newborn cry. And he sees a creature coming out of the woods, cresting the hill. Perhaps a big yellow dog. It stares at him with its yellow eyes. Its coat is glossy as if it has just been bathed. He has never gone on his vision quest, but now it comes to him. Those yellow eyes, the shiny fur. Something wild that has eluded him for so long. He sees it there as the light of day is rising on the ridge. It is not afraid of him. Not at all. It is waiting for him, beckoning, there at the edge of the forest. It disappears among the trees from where it has come, and with whatever strength he can muster, Roberto follows the creature into the woods.

+

It's just after nine when Rachel gets back and Nathan still isn't home. In the living room the sitter is watching old episodes of *Star Trek* and Rachel pays her and tells her that she can go home. As the girl drives off, the house is so quiet, so still. It doesn't even occur to her to call Nathan. She already knows what she's going to say to him. It can wait.

She goes into the boys' rooms to check on them. Jeremy is spread out all over his bed, sleeping on his back like a cat, his mouth open. Gently she pulls the sheet up to his chin. He looks so peaceful in his sleep. Hardly the troubled boy he's been. She plants a kiss on his brow and then goes to check on Davie. When she gets into Davie's room, he is curled up into a ball, muttering to himself. Indistinguishable sounds that could be words. He looks pale and his forehead is damp. *My boys, my sweet, sweet boys.* As she kisses him, a tear slides from her eye and lands on his cheek. His pain is her pain. She wipes the tear with her finger and for an instant Davie latches on. "There, there," she whispers into his ear, and he lets go, drifting back into the place where sleep takes all children, troubled or otherwise.

It is difficult for Rachel to explain the fierceness with which she loves her children. How there is nothing she would not do to protect them. She would take a bullet for them. She would put herself between them and a wild beast. And now she has found Miguel again and he will help her boys be stronger. He will help Davie be braver and Jeremy softer. Rachel always believed that Miguel would.

Rachel goes into the living room and gently opens the sliding door that leads outside to her studio. It has been days since she's been out there but she wants to go now. It is one of those cold desert nights and she probably needs a sweater but she doesn't want to go back into the house. She wants to keep going. Overhead the sky is clear. It seems so odd that just hours ago she stood with Miguel under this very sky and read to him the words she could decipher from the headstones. And then as they were leaving he turned to her and said very matter-of-factly, "You know your husband is having an affair, don't you?"

And this had not surprised Rachel at all. "Yes," she replied, taking a deep breath. "I know."

She turns on the light. Her studio is a shambles. It is filled with random, unfinished things. All these hands and feet, extremities. She grabs a cardboard box and a trash bag. Into the trash bag she throws the objects she knows she will never complete, including the ones that shouldn't be finished. She picks out the ones that interest her, the ones that show some promise, and puts them into the cardboard box. Perhaps she will return to those. Perhaps she will not. She is done with body parts. No more heads or hands. She does not know yet what her new work will be, but she knows that it will be a work of the heart.

She is almost done tossing out what she doesn't want when she hears the car drive up. It is close to midnight. Rachel breathes a deep sigh. She doesn't look forward to her task, but nothing will change her mind. She flicks off the light in her studio and drags the bag of shattered limbs outside, ties the bag up, leaves it beside the trash, and walks toward the house. Nathan is already inside. He has found the house quiet, dark, except for the bathroom nightlight of cowboys and ponies and the tiny blue lights that illumine the hallways. She sees him from the patio as she walks to the house, but he does not see her. He has flicked on a light and is pouring himself two fingers of Scotch. It does not occur to him that Rachel is not in their bed.

When Rachel walks in, she startles him. "Oh my god," he presses his hand to his heart. "You scared me."

Rachel almost laughs. The cardiologist with the hand to his heart. Then she says without any hesitation, "Her name is Dawn and she's a nurse. She was taking care of Jeremy when Davie was bitten by the snake."

Nathan stands still, the glass trembling in his hand, the ice tinkling. "Rachel—"

"Everything that happens between us now will be for the boys. We won't fight. There will be no scenes. We will make it as easy for them as we can. We will decide together what's best for them. To stay here. To go back to New York. I'll need child support, of course, and probably ten years of alimony until the kids are older and I can get a profession going for myself. My mother can help out with college. I won't be asking you for more than what we really need so don't worry about that."

Nathan sits down in an armchair with a sigh. "You know I've tried."

"No, actually you haven't, but I understand. I'm not that easy to live with. I'm scattered. I can be erratic. But I am a good person and I do not hurt people."

Nathan is staring into his glass. He takes a sip, then puts it down. Then he picks the glass up again and takes another sip. "Look, I'm not in love with her. I can stop this. We can get help."

Rachel feels as if she has gone for a long swim in a cold lake. She is as fresh and clearheaded as she's been in years. "There's nothing more to say. Let's do this amicably."

As she turns to leave and go to bed, because for the first time in months she will sleep well, he calls out, "How did you know it was her?"

Rachel turns to him one last time. "Because she knew my name."

CHAPTER THIRTY-SIX

DENTISTRY IN THE DMZ—1956

P rivate First Class Rafael Torres sits in the dental chair, reading the final pages of *David Copperfield*. Though the room smells of disinfectant and the light is harsh enough for surgery, Rafael is engrossed. He has just finished a tattered copy of *From Here to Eternity* but found it reminded him too much of his present life. He prefers all the trials and tribulations of poor David. From time to time he pauses to read the essays of Emerson, which he recently found in the mess hall lending library. He had never known the pleasures of reading before, but now he cannot stop.

It is early and bitter cold outside. They have no appointments booked until eleven and the dentist, Art Rubin, hasn't arrived. A harsh wind blows through the Quonset hut, but Rafael has the heater pointed directly at him. He will stay warm as long as the generator doesn't give out. It is his job to get in early to warm the hut, get drinking water, put it in the #10 grapefruit juice cans and keep it from freezing. He washes the instruments and prepares the amalgams of mercury and silver for fillings or the mixes of zinc oxide and eugenol, which smell like clove and supposedly alleviate pain inside a tooth that has been drilled in half. Once his preparations are done, Rafael does whatever he wants until their first appointment, and usually that means he reads.

Rafael Torres has never had much of an opportunity to read until now. But then before the army he'd also known very little about teeth. In fact before arriving at the 38th parallel he had never been to a dentist or even a doctor, unless you counted the witch doctor at Santa

Domingo who cured him of a restricted bowel when he was five by making him drink a green potion whose taste has remained forever bitter in his mouth. He'd never had a vaccination that he knew of or his tonsils out. It wasn't that his parents didn't believe in doctors. It was that they didn't exist within thirty miles of the hills of New Mexico where Rafael was born on a plot of land that his father farmed. There was, however, a school where he learned the fine art of auto repair and the rudiments of reading.

He was sixteen when he dropped out of school. For a couple of years he fiddled with cars in a mechanic's shop. Then he was drafted. After ten weeks of basic training at Fort Leonard, he was sent to Fort Sam Houston for medical training. At first he thought it was a clerical error. His skills, such as they were, beyond auto repair, were in the farming and distribution of beans. He might make a good logistical officer. The closest he'd ever come to medical experience was birthing a goat. At Sam Houston he watched films about the various medical opportunities available to recruits. After hours of viewing, Rafael determined that the only guys who weren't crawling in the mud and dragging bodies away from the front lines were the dental assistants, and he was the first in his unit to volunteer for the post. Though later he would regale his children and his grandson with stories of combat, Rafael Torres spent his entire tour of duty in a Quonset hut.

For twelve weeks he studied the tooth and its structure. He learned about enamel and nerves. Then he was flown up to Seattle and was shipped off on a military vessel with twenty-five hundred other men who slept in bunks that were stacked five deep. Traversing the Juan de Fuca Strait they hit a major storm and everyone on board got sick. Rafael quickly understood the advantage of the upper berth. After three days at sea, he convinced the naval officers that he was a medic and they allowed him to sleep in the infirmary where he had a warm bed and no seasick soldiers who rained vomit down on him.

Arriving in In'chon, Rafael stared at the men carrying back-breaking loads and oxen pulling carts of wood and stone. As they disembarked, twenty-five hundred other soldiers heading home shouted, "If the gooks don't get you, the stink will." Days later Private First Class Rafael

Torres found himself in a cargo plane with the Seventh Infantry, heading up to the 38th parallel where he would live in the mountains that were not so different from his native New Mexico and dedicate himself to assisting a dentist in the polishing, filling, and extraction of teeth.

In his nineteen years he had rarely left Entrada de Luna except to go to Albuquerque for supplies or Santa Fe for drop-offs for his father at local grocery stores. He'd never met anyone who wasn't Hispanic or Anglo or Indian. It wasn't until he landed in the DMZ that he'd spoken to a black man, let alone a Jew. Rafael had no idea how or why he ended up in the DMZ. It was a couple of years after the shooting ended, but soldiers were still stationed here. He assumed he'd work on some army base back home, but instead he found himself in Asia, assisting a Jewish dentist. It wasn't unpleasant work though it was odd to see stalwart soldiers, who at a moment's notice could be asked to risk their lives, sit trembling in the dental chair. How their eyes bulged as the drill made its way into their mouth. Many pleaded for more pain-killers or gas. After they left, he and Art Rubin always had a good laugh.

Rafael leans way back in the dental chair. So far this morning no one has come in asking for emergency dental work. He has read a chapter or two about David Copperfield and now is plunging into self-reliance. Rafael enjoys Emerson's theories, but he prefers made-up stories. He has even read a novel by Jane Austen that someone has left behind. Some of the boys in the barracks call him a sissy, but Rafael doesn't care. He enjoys a good story. There are days he sits for hours with the light shining above him, just reading. Art Rubin doesn't seem to mind. He is busy writing letters home to a girl named Esther whom he plans to marry when his service is done.

Rafael is dozing when Art arrives. Opening his eyes, he finds Art arranging his instruments.

"Sorry, were you asleep?" Art is a short, stocky man with a broad face. He has dark skin and dark, kind eyes. Rafael hopes that his girl will wait for him. Rafael shakes his head. "I don't know. I don't think so."

"You were mumbling," Art says. They are an odd couple, everyone says, but they get along and to his surprise Rafael finds that he enjoys dentistry. He likes watching as Art cleans teeth, then pokes around.

The little pockets of decay fascinate him. The way the gums turn red and soft if you don't floss.

Their first patient of the morning is a KATTUSA, as they referred to the Koreans attached to the U.S. Army. This KATTUSA, named Peter (for all the KATTUSA are named Peter, Paul, or John for the purposes of the U.S. Army), shares Rafael's tent along with six GIs and another KATTUSA named John. Peter speaks no English, though Rafael has a sense that he understands more than he lets on. Peter has a toothache, and he doesn't look very good. Rafael motions for him to sit in the chair where Art examines the tooth. Art pokes around, and then shows Rafael. The tooth has a deep cavity that they have to fill.

The generator that operates the drill is slow and irregular, but Rafael gets it going as Art prepares the shot. As soon as Peter sees the needle, he begins to shake, then faints. Rafael is used to this. He's tried to tell Art not to show them the needle but just tell them to close their eyes and insert it, but Art insists on holding it up for them to see and asking if they have any allergies to Novocain or are frightened by needles, at which point at least once a week someone faints.

Afterward as Rafael cleans up, Art turns to him.

"I'm going out for sandwiches. We don't have another patient until two. Can I get you one?" Rafael sits up. "Yeah, sure. Not baloney, okay?"

"Sure, no baloney."

Rafael is finishing "Self-Reliance" when Art comes back with a couple of sandwiches, two apples, and a bottle of soda from the mess. He hands the sandwich to Rafael who looks at it askance. "What is this?" Rafael asks.

"I think it's ham and cheese or salami. Why?"

"I don't eat ham," Rafael says.

"I thought it's baloney you won't eat."

Rafael pushes the sandwich away. "I don't eat pork."

Art looks at him oddly. "But aren't you Mexican or something?"

Rafael shrugs. "I'm Hispanic from New Mexico, but we don't eat pork." Rafael opens his sandwich and stares. Soon his look turns to revulsion. "I can't eat it."

GATEWAY TO THE MOON

Art looks at his own sandwich. "What do you mean? Why can't you eat it?"

Rafael never can answer this question very well. How can he explain the place where he comes from? All the strange customs that people hold on to there? On the gravestones Rafael can trace his ancestry back hundreds of years. How many Americans can do that? How many can claim that their family has traversed the oceans with Coronado, that they had seen the actual halls of Montezuma, walked on the streets paved with gold. And yet they will not eat pork. He knows no one who does—at least he didn't until he came to Korea. Eating a pig is like eating the dirt itself. It is eating the worst possible filth. He stares at the ham sandwich that his friend has brought him and puts his book down. "I can't eat this," he says again.

Art is surprised. "Well, here. Take mine. It's turkey and cheese."

Again Rafael makes a face. "I don't eat dairy with meat."

"What's your deal?" Art looks at his assistant. "And I suppose you light candles on Friday night?"

"My mother does."

Stunned, Art shakes his head. "Are you a Jew?"

"Of course not." Rafael is offended by the question. "I'm a Catholic—born and raised," he says with the slight Spanish accent that he's never gotten rid of.

"So why do you do these things?" Art takes the cheese out and gives the turkey sandwich to Rafael, then sits down across from him. "Who are you?"

Rafael shakes his head of thick dark hair. "I'm nobody," he says. "I'm just me."

At night he writes letters to Rosa back in Entrada. He tells her about the weird dentist he works for and how he's developed a love of reading. They plan to marry when he returns. Rafael wants a family, children. He wonders what it would be like to go back to school, perhaps even study medicine. But that won't happen because Rosa will get pregnant and Rafael will open an auto-repair shop. She sends him packages. Warm sweaters she knits herself and tomato and beet preserves that arrive in cracked jars he has to pick the glass out of so he can eat them. In summer she sent him caps and suntan lotion for when the mountains at the 38th parallel are sweltering.

Sometimes she sneaks a bottle of whiskey into his package. She wraps it carefully in shirts. He hides the bottle under his bunk, sipping from it at night, trying to make it last. She thinks she is doing him a favor, but she isn't. He starts to resent the packages that don't have a bottle hidden inside. Soon it will be the only thing he looks for.

+

In the spring when the weather grows warmer, the soldiers begin building a stage. They don't know for whom or what. They are just told to build a platform. They are promised that it is for something special. All the men, except for Rafael, are glad for the distraction. It gives them something to do. Normally they just go on their patrols, waiting to see if anyone breaks the cease-fire. But for Rafael it interrupts his reading. He has just begun Tolstoy's *The Death of Ivan Ilyich.* On the other hand, it does keep him busy. It gives them all something to do.

When the platform is finally built they are told to expect visitors soon, and then a few days later they are ordered to bring chairs and set them up in front of the stage. While they wait, beers are served. Good cold Korean beer. The men consume it by the six-pack. In the end beer will be Rafael's drug of choice. He will drink it until years later when he drives his car into a canyon on the road to Taos. After what seems like an endless wait, as the day grows darker, some music is played from a Victrola and the most beautiful woman any of them has ever seen appears. She has flowing rich brown hair and a lithe thin body, tiny waist. It is as if she were a spirit more than an actual woman.

For an hour Rita Moreno sings and dances while the men shout. Rafael sits next to Art as they drink beer after beer, ignoring the fact that they both have to take a leak because neither wants to miss a minute of the show. They want to watch every moment. Rafael knows she will be famous. A few years later, when she gets the part of Anita in *West Side Story,* he'll tell anyone who'll listen that he knew she'd make it big. How could this Puerto Rican girl, the daughter of a seamstress and a farmer, be singing and dancing on the stage in the DMZ? As she finishes her show with "Bésame Mucho," sending kisses into the crowd, Rafael knows that anything is possible.

Afterward Rita agrees to take a picture with each man. All the soldiers line up. When Rafael's turn comes, he slips his arm around her slender waist and she seems to fold her body into his. He is holding an angel. Nothing will ever feel this good to him again. Nothing will ever satisfy him quite the way this moment does. He could spend the rest of his life carrying her in the crook of his elbow.

And then she has to leave. She waves goodbye, blowing kisses. It is late and all the men grow silent and moody. Most return to their bunks, but Rafael and Art go into the dentist's hut and drink a few more beers. Art sits in the dental chair and Rafael on the stool from which Art does his work.

"That was something, wasn't it?" Art says, leaning back.

"It sure was." Rafael nods as he feels Rita slipping away. Suddenly Rafael thinks he's going to explode. In a drunken stupor he lurches outside. He'll never make it to the urinals. In the light of the moon he pisses like a horse against a tree. Art is beside him, pissing a steady stream of his own. Suddenly Rafael can feel Art's eyes staring down at his penis. This has happened once before, but this time Rafael feels he has to say something. Or else punch this guy in the jaw.

"Excuse me," Rafael says.

"I don't mean to be staring," Art says, "but . . ."

Rafael feels his muscles contract. His nerves tingle. What does this guy want, looking at him in that way?

"But you're circumcised."

Rafael glares at Art.

"I'm not that way it's just that, well, it is unusual . . ."

Rafael zips up, not bothering to shake himself dry. He turns his back on his friend. "Not where I come from it isn't." Now suddenly sober, Rafael staggers back to his barracks and passes out on his bunk without even taking off his clothes.

After this Rafael will try to get a transfer out of the dental unit, but he fails. He will spend the rest of his deployment avoiding Art Rubin's eyes. He will never speak about this to anyone. But when the photo of him with Rita Moreno arrives he will guard it like a promise he must keep. Years later his daughter, Elena, will carry this portrait of her father with her when she leaves Entrada. It will remind her of another Spanish dancer who went to find her future in New York.

CHAPTER THIRTY-SEVEN

✳

VISION QUEST—1992

Elena knows the road north. She drove it a hundred times as a girl. She'd come back from performances or classes or competitions or auditions in Albuquerque. Sometimes driving herself. Sometimes her father driving her. Elena loved it when her father drove. It was the only time she recalls him being sober. She doesn't want to remember, but what choice does she have? She is driving home for her brother's funeral. No matter how angry she is, how her life has been changed, he was her brother.

When Elena got the call, she was just coming back from teaching a class. She had poured her first glass of wine. She was surprised to hear MG's voice leaving a message on the answering machine. Elena doesn't think that MG has ever called her before. Not in all these years. Elena wasn't going to answer it, but she panicked. What if something has happened to Miguel? Normally she would never think that, but something has been happening inside of her. Like pack ice breaking up. Feelings she didn't know she had are seeping through. When did it begin? When she walked into the planetarium or when she sent him the telescope? Or was it before that, in Morocco in the souk where she tasted her grandmother's stew?

What if he was in trouble? What if he got a DUI the way Roberto always did and she had to bail him out? Or worse. What if there'd been an accident? Elena was never the kind of person to ask herself what if, but now suddenly she was. She picked up in the middle of MG's message. "MG," Elena said, "I'm here."

"There's been an accident," MG told her, stifling a sob.

Elena's hand went to her lips. No, she pleaded, please don't let him be dead. Not before she can tell him the truth.

"It's Roberto," MG said.

She assumed he was drunk. And driving at night on those roads that cut through the hills between Entrada and Española. The road so lined with crosses that they call it the Via Dolorosa. But then MG explained. He'd stopped drinking weeks ago. He was crushed beneath the car he was working on for Miguel.

Elena hadn't wanted to come. It was her brother, it's true, but that's not why she has flown halfway across the country.

It's for Miguel. That's really why she's coming home, isn't it? To be there for him. Something she's never been able to do or wanted to do before. She has no idea what she'll tell him or even if she will. How do you tell a boy that his father is his uncle and his aunt is his mother? How will he make sense of any of that? And of course there is his schooling. His college. Because all the money she has saved is going to him. At some point he will have to know.

A light snow is falling. A thin layer covers the highway. The wind is strong as it blows across the plain. This highway has always been a wind tunnel. Now she drives quickly, her foot on the pedal, almost seventy-five, and then eighty miles an hour. She isn't aware of how fast she is driving.

From out of the corner of her eye she sees something coming across the snowy embankment. Where the traffic is heading south. It looks like a big yellow dog. It comes up on the ridge and hesitates. Then it steps into the road. Traffic speeds behind her and ahead of her. It is a four-lane highway and she is in the passing lane and she knows she can't stop. She can barely slow down. Elena looks at the traffic around her. As the creature walks into the road, perhaps five hundred yards ahead of her, she knows it is going to be killed. She is doing at least eighty. She takes her foot off the gas, trying to slow down. She begins to brake, but there are lines of fast-moving cars behind her. Elena still has her New Mexico driving instincts. She puts on her hazards and slows as much as she can, but she is on a crash course with that dog. Except now Elena sees that it isn't a dog. It is a coyote. A golden coyote.

The coyote makes it through the first lane of traffic, and then the second. Horns honk. There is a screech of brakes, but the creature doesn't stop. And just as she is about to strike it, the animal darts in front of her, leaping across her lane until it is on the median strip. And then, as she speeds by, it leaps through the next two lanes until it is safely on the opposite side of the road. It moves so swiftly that Elena wonders if she hasn't driven right through it. Or if it was even there at all.

+

As she pulls up in front of the trailer, it is difficult for Elena to imagine that she grew up here. It seems smaller as if it has shrunk over the years. How was it possible that four people once lived in this narrow, cramped space? The garage door is open, and the truck that crushed her brother is still in the driveway. She makes a mental note to have it towed away. But the garage gives her pause. Elena takes a deep breath. No one is left. Her father, drunk one night, drove himself into a canyon. Her mother dead five years ago of a weak heart, and now Roberto. Only she is left. And Miguel.

Elena gets out of the car, grabs her bag, and heads into the house. She climbs the three steps, the second one shaky, and kicks the door open as she always has. The door still sticks. You'd think Roberto would have fixed it by now. Inside is a mess. Dirty dishes, soiled towels. The bed is unmade and the sheets are filthy. On the floor are the T-shirts and trousers and underwear her brother hadn't gotten around to washing. She looks under the sink where she finds bleach, Comet, dish soap, detergent. Supplies she is certain her mother bought years ago and her brother has never used.

She begins in the kitchen. She washes all the dishes, scrubs the sink and countertops with bleach. Then she gathers the sheets and towels, her brother's T-shirts and underwear. She goes into the garage that is filled with her brother's airbrush paraphernalia. On the concrete floor in the middle of the room sits an aquarium that appears to be empty. Elena walks around the aquarium to the old washer and dryer her mother bought with the money Elena sent her when she was a ballerina. Her mother called her, crying, to tell her that she could now wash her clothes at home.

She throws in a load of whites. She lets the cycle begin, then adds more bleach. While the load is washing, she goes into the bathroom. The toilet has a rim of black mold and so does the sink. She cannot bring herself to even look at the shower. Elena finds a scrub brush and goes to work. The shower, the sink, the toilet. She scrubs and scrubs until the porcelain shines. Then she tosses the brush away. The whites are done and she puts them into the dryer, then she does a load of colors, including all the curtains.

She sweeps and vacuums, moving furniture aside, revealing the dust that has accumulated under the sofa and bed. She cleans the stove. She takes everything out of the fridge and tosses it into the trash. She washes the fridge and leaves the door open so it can air out. Then she gets in the car and drives down to Roybal's store.

She is glad that Esmeralda Roybal is at the cash register because she doesn't seem to recognize Elena. Perhaps she thinks she is just passing through, which she is. Elena picks up some juice, bread, diet Coke, beer, cigarettes, a few cans of tuna fish, cheese, pays and heads back. Except for the pungent odor of bleach, the trailer smells fresh and clean, and Elena puts the groceries away. Then she sits down at her mother's kitchen table and looks around. This is where she grew up. This is where she would have grown old. And she puts her head down on the newly cleaned table and weeps for the first time in years.

+

For weeks after her rape she couldn't stop crying. At times it seemed as if she would never stop. She cried until the corners of her eyes turned red and her body ached from endless sobs. But she won't tell her mother despite Rosa's pleas. "Tell me what happened to you," her mother begged. "Tell me who hurt you and I'll kill them." But Elena wouldn't tell. And in some ways she couldn't. She barely remembered that night or who they were or what really happened to her. All she remembered were hands and fingers and a searing pain. What little she did recall she'd never tell. She let her secret grow and fester inside of her. *My own brother. He let them take me. He laughed and drank his beer.*

But then suddenly the crying stopped and Elena grew tired. It was impossible to explain how tired she was. She dragged herself out of bed, to the bathroom where for days blood trickled into the bowl. She'd stayed home from school, but then when she returned, when she sat at her desk, listening to a teacher droning on and on, her eyes closed and she slept. The minute she lay down at night she was asleep until her mother shook her awake in the morning. It was as if every muscle, every cell in her body was tired. She'd wake to go to the bathroom, drink a soda, then go back to sleep. If no one woke her, she could sleep twelve, fourteen hours. Once Rosa put a mirror under her nose to make certain she was still alive. It was as if her whole existence was sleep and with the sleep came a kind of euphoria.

She was actually happy. The darkness lifted and this tired warmth gushed through her bones. Even exhausted, she was happier than she could remember being in a long time. Even in her dreams she was content. It was around this time that she noticed the tenderness in her breasts. An ache that surprised her but that would leave, she knew, as soon as her period came. Except it didn't come. Instead her breasts swelled. Her body thickened. And, just looking at her daughter, Rosa knew. "You are going to have a child." "No," Elena cried stubbornly, "I'm not." But of course it was true.

"Whose is it?" Rosa asked, though she was fairly certain she knew. It could be any of those boys. This baby's father was Entrada de la Luna, the town no one could ever leave. The town had created this child as much as any boy.

"I will get rid of it," Elena said.

But her mother, a good Catholic, would not allow it. "You will not murder my grandchild," Rosa said, "I will raise the baby."

A week later Elena moved to Albuquerque to live with her aunt. For the rest of her pregnancy her aunt home-schooled her so Elena could keep up her grades. And during that time, as her body grew and her breasts ached and this alien occupied her body, her heart turned to stone. It would never change. And then during a summer storm the child came. He was early by six weeks because Elena wanted to get rid of him. He knew she did not want him inside her body.

Elena lay in her bed that night, listening to the rain, as her body was shattered with pain. She refused to call out. It was better if the child inside of her died, and she would do what she could to make it so. She gripped the sides of the bed and bit into her pillow. She paced her room, then stared outside, watching the hard rain coming down on the asphalt, rivulets of mud and water, coursing down the side of her aunt's muddy yard. She squatted, clenching her sides, but she would not cry out.

She was silent even as the rain came harder and outside there was forked lightning as if the sky would rip in half, the way she was certain she would. She felt the child, pressing against her insides, splitting her in two, until a baby boy slipped onto the braided carpet, alive and wailing, covered in blood and his own sac. His dark eyes were open and fixed on her as if he already knew that she would never cradle or comfort him and that he would have to memorize her face before she was gone.

It was only then that Elena screamed and her aunt rushed in. Her aunt had not raised five children for nothing. With scissors she cut the cord. She made Elena hold the baby as she bathed it, but Elena would not nurse and she would not hold it any longer. She handed the baby to her aunt and, as soon as she was able, walked out the door. Six weeks later, which was the time when Miguel was due to be born, Elena was in New York, dancing with the American Ballet Theater. Miguel had stayed in the hospital where his aunt had taken him. It was at the time when Elena was to deliver that Roberto's wife, MG, hemorrhaged and gave birth to a stillborn child. In the hospital MG was told that she could have no more children.

For Rosa the decision was easy. She told her son, "You will raise your nephew as if he is your own." Because in some ways he really was.

+

In the morning, Elena gets up, goes into the bathroom and takes a shower. She washes her hair, her body. She dries herself off with the towels she laundered. Then she takes out the black dress she brought and a pair of black heels. She slips the dress on, zipping it up the back. She puts on the heels. Then she gets into the car and goes to bury her brother.

CHAPTER THIRTY-EIGHT

✳

THE PILGRIMAGE—1992

Hundreds of crucifixes line the fences at El Santuario de Chimayó. They have been carried by pilgrims—some for hundreds of miles—to reach this holy place where the earth itself is said to cure you. Some people crawl on their knees to get here. Rachel Rothstein walks past the crosses, leading her boys. "Come on," she says. "We're already late." The boys shuffle along. They are dressed in identical white shirts and black trousers with black ties. The only difference is that Jeremy is wearing sneakers and Davie is in leather boots. He has been wearing the boots since the snake bit him.

Singing comes from inside the sanctuary. A guitar strums out hymns in Spanish. Rachel takes each boy by the hand as they enter a room where thousands of crutches and braces hang from the ceiling. The boys look stunned. Rachel explains to them in a whisper, "People come here to get cured. They come on crutches and then they walk away." Then they enter the sanctuary. It is a simple dome-shaped room of adobe walls and it is about half full. In the center of the room before the altar is the coffin of Roberto Torres.

Miguel sits in the front row and Rachel goes up to him. "I'm sorry for your loss." She gives him a hug. At first the boys stand back. Then Davie grabs Miguel by the knees. Miguel squats down and whispers into his ear, "You won, big man. You fought the dragon and you won." He hugs Jeremy as well. Standing up with tears in his eyes, Miguel turns to Rachel. "Thank you for coming. I want you to meet my mother."

Rachel turns to face the woman sitting on the bench who looks just like Miguel. She is tall and thin with a long face and dark skin. "This is my aunt Elena," Miguel says, awkwardly directing her away. "Here is my mother." And he points to the woman sitting beside him. Rachel, who is confused at first, shakes MG's hand.

"I'm sorry for your loss," Rachel says to MG. But during the ceremony it is the lithe former ballerina whom Rachel keeps staring at.

After the service, Rachel, clutching her boys, goes up to the woman introduced as his aunt. "Excuse me," Rachel says, "but who are you?"

Elena looks at Rachel. "I don't live here anymore," she says with a sigh, "but Roberto was my brother."

Rachel nods, looking into Elena's eyes. "Yes, I can see the resemblance. I'm sorry."

Elena stares back at this bold, dark woman. "And you are?"

"I'm Miguel's employer." Rachel is proud to say it this way. "He's a very smart boy." She places her hands firmly on the shoulders of her children. "We've been lucky to have him."

+

Back at his mother's trailer metal tubs filled with cold cheese sit on the kitchen table. There are loaves of bread, mustard, catsup. As the guests serve themselves, Miguel holds back. He sits in a corner on a folding chair, a plastic cup of Coke in his hand. While everyone mills about in the narrow space, grabbing beers from the fridge, making sandwiches, chatting among themselves, Miguel is silent. He can't get over the way his father died. He can't stop thinking about it. At night sometimes he wakes up, unable to breathe. He envisions the weight of the car crushing his father's chest. The car he was fixing up for Miguel. Dying there alone on the cold garage floor. And no jack stands. How many times did Miguel have to tell him to use jack stands?

Across the room Elena is carrying platters of meat, pickles, bags of chips. She puts a chicken casserole someone brought on the table. Deviled eggs. Carrot sticks. Tamales. She moves like a dancer. Her head high, her feet out-turned. He watches as she crosses the room, those long, lanky legs, her straight dancer's spine. She sits down at the table, folding her legs beneath her. When she laughs, her mouth opens wide, revealing her shiny white teeth. As he watches her, Miguel feels that his life has been a puzzle and the pieces are coming together.

Just the way he wakes up from his dreams, Miguel feels as if he can't breathe. He has to get out of here. As he starts to leave, some of his school friends arrive. There's Pablo Martinez with his brother and their girlfriends. They're laughing, drinking Cokes. They come up to Miguel and pat his arm. They tell him that they are sorry. Mr. Garcia has come in as well. He's wearing a suit and a plain blue tie. Miguel is disappointed. He wishes he were wearing a reindeer tie. He doesn't want to see any of them. All he wants is to be alone. As soon as he can, he slips outside. He walks under the cottonwood tree and smokes a cigarette.

He needs to get away. He gets in his car. At first he drives around, heading toward Española, but then he turns around and drives to his father's trailer. He hasn't been back to the trailer since his father was found crushed beneath the truck by a customer who wanted an eagle airbrushed on his car. As he drives, tears stream down his face. His father died because his son wanted a four-wheel drive vehicle. And now his aunt is here, and observing her for the first time he realizes what he has suspected for some time.

He pulls onto his father's street. The El Camino his father was working on is parked off to the side. A sob catches in his throat. The tow truck that lifted it off his father left it there. They should have just towed it away. He tries to imagine what his father was thinking as the El Camino came down upon him. You stupid old man. Why didn't you use the jack stands like I told you? Miguel's eyes well up. What was his father thinking? The doctor told them he died quickly. But how quickly would you die if a car were crushing your ribs? Not quickly enough.

MG had watched Miguel leave. She saw him drive off, laying rubber as he swung onto the road toward Española. She knows her son. She has loved him since he was weeks old and put in her arms. She has taken Elena aside. "It's time," MG tells Elena. "It's time that Miguel knows the truth."

But Elena hesitates. "Why?"

"Because we all need to know where we've come from," MG replies.

"He's already left," Elena says and MG nods.

"Yes, but I can tell you where to find him."

+

Miguel stands in his father's driveway. Taking a deep breath, he walks into the garage. He hasn't been here since the accident and he wonders if his beetles are still alive. It seems absurd to think of beetles when his father has just died, but there they are, in their aquarium, staggering aimlessly. He closes the garage door and shines his flashlight on the ceiling, illuminating the night sky. His beetles right themselves. They begin their foraging again.

These are his tests. Soon he will show them to Mr. Garcia. Miguel will enter his dung beetles into the national science competition and prove that they navigate using the stars. He will receive an honorable mention. The following year he will receive a National Science Foundation scholarship to the college of his choice for an experiment in astrobiology and the possibility of water molecules on Mars. Both times Mr. Garcia will give him a high five. Later when Mr. Garcia becomes an inspirational speaker, he will include Miguel as one of his success stories. To his surprise, Miguel will attend one of his speeches and will get up and say that he would not be who he is if it weren't for his teacher. This will bring tears to everyone's eyes. Miguel will go on to study astronomy at the Massachusetts Institute of Technology on a full scholarship and eventually he will work for NASA. He will be among the scientists to enable the rover, Curiosity, to land on Mars. By then he will be a professor at the University of New Mexico. His wife and children will live in an adobe house on the outskirts of Albuquerque. He will tell people about his history. He will never hide from them the fact that he believes he is a Jew. Just before his first child is born, he will send his DNA to a lab in Atlanta and it will confirm his Iberian Jewish roots.

As he opens the garage door to let in the light, someone is standing there. For a moment he wonders if his father hasn't come home from wherever he's gone. Then he sees his Aunt Elena. "What are you doing here?"

"I'm staying here," she says. And then she adds. "This is my home." Elena steps inside the cool garage and looks down at the tank filled with manure and dung beetles. "What is this?"

"It's my experiment." And then he adds. "I don't want to talk to you. I know what you did."

"And what is that?" Elena asks.

"You had me and you left me, right?"

And Elena nods. "Yes, that is right. I did."

"But my dad was my real dad, wasn't he?"

Elena gazes at him perplexed. It takes her a moment to absorb what he is saying, and then she raises her hands into the air. "Oh no. He wasn't your father. I don't really know who your father was though I have an idea." Elena leans against the wall of the garage. "Could we go inside and sit down? I have something to tell you."

In the kitchen of Roberto's trailer Elena pours a Coke for Miguel. "This is very difficult to say to you." And she tells him about that night, about the drunken rape, and her need to get away from Entrada forever. "I'm sorry. I couldn't come back."

"So my real dad . . . he could be any one of them?"

Elena nods, then looks over Miguel's long lanky legs. "But I think I know who he was. He was very tall like you. In fact I liked him until that night. He died a year after you were born on this very road. And if I am right you have grandparents who are living in Entrada."

And suddenly Miguel feels sad for the two fathers he has lost, but also strangely happy for the mother he has found. MG will always be the mother who raised him, but as he looks into Elena's eyes, he finds his own. It is in her face that he sees his round dark eyes, his angular nose and wry smile. He sees his thin, lanky body and long legs. They do not have to speak of this and perhaps they never will. He understands that she had not known how to love him and others had, but now his three-body problem is solved, the mysteries of his own universe that have for so long eluded him are answered. He knows why his family settled in Entrada and why his own mother left him and why the parents who raised him loved him just as he understands how the moon is held in its place by Earth and the sun and how it is that we orbit among the galaxies and stars.

Miguel turns to his aunt, who is now also his mother. "And there's something I think you should know." And he proceeds to tell her who they are and where they came from. And why for the past four hundred years they have chosen to live on this dry, hard land. Elena sits, absorbing this information. As Elena listens to Miguel, it occurs to her that the recipe for the lamb with apricots and garbanzos that her grandmother made must have traveled the same distance that her family had. The recipe she tasted in Tangiers must have left Spain along with the Jews.

"I'm leaving tomorrow," she says. "I have a lot to take care of before I do."

Miguel nods. "Would you meet me this evening at Roybal's? I want to show you something."

"All right," Elena says, "I'll be there. What time?"

Miguel thinks for a moment. "Six would be fine."

Elena spends the rest of the day tying up loose ends and pondering what Miguel has told her. The people of Entrada are descended from Spanish Jews who fled the Inquisition. They settled here four hundred years ago and after generations they forgot that they were Jews. But they did not forget their rituals. It is more than she can fathom so instead she pays bills that her brother owed. She has been more or less put in charge of his estate, such as it is, and she focuses her attention on this.

At six sharp she drives to Roybal's General Store. Vincent Roybal is at the cash register and he gives Elena a nod. Elena decides that after Miguel shows her whatever he wants to show her, she will introduce Vincent to his grandson.

Miguel is waiting for her on the porch and he has something folded under his arm. He has a flashlight and slowly they begin their climb. Miguel shines a flashlight on the ground so that Elena won't trip over any stones or roots. He doesn't want her to hurt her ankle again.

"Where are we going?" Elena asks, and Miguel points to the top of the hill.

"The old cemetery," he says. Elena's eyes widen. "Don't worry." Miguel laughs. "It's just where I like to go." It's a cold night and the wind is blowing. "Are you warm enough?" Miguel asks.

Elena puts the hood up on her sweatshirt. "I'm fine. I'm glad to be here."

They cross the road to the dirt path and begin their climb. Elena struggles a bit. Her ankle is wobbly on uneven terrain, and Miguel takes her arm. Finally they reach the top of the hill and the cemetery. Miguel shines a light for her on the tombstones as he explains how these are the people who came here before them and what is written is in Hebrew. Then he sets up the telescope he's carrying. Not the one he made but the one she sent him. He used it only once, the day he received it, so he practiced during the day how to set it up and focus. Now he opens the tripod and adjusts the lens. He motions for her to join him. As they stand among the crumbling stones of their ancestors, Miguel teaches his mother how to follow the stars.

ACKNOWLEDGMENTS

This book has been an incredible journey for me, both in time and space. It's a story I began thinking about more than twenty-five years ago when we lived in Santa Fe and had a babysitter who believed he was a crypto-Jew. I don't remember his name, but I remember his face and the myriad of questions he asked about Jews and Jewish rituals. He was convinced that this was his family's narrative. For years this boy's story was the germ of an idea. Then, a few years ago, when my incredible agent, Ellen Levine, told me to write a novel that was "about something," she gave me pause. I recalled the story of this boy and the crypto-Jews of New Mexico. I dug up those journals and found notes for the material that has taken shape in this book.

I am indebted to Ellen as always for her commitment and wisdom. And to my indefatigable editor, Nan Talese, who loved this book as soon as she read it. Her enthusiasm has meant the world to me. For years now I have been so fortunate to have Ellen and Nan to work with, and I am honored and proud to dedicate this book to them. For all their support and attention, I want to thank Dan Meyer, Carolyn Williams, and Martha Wydysh. I also want to thank my various readers—Caroline Leavitt, who read the first draft and gave me so much encouragement; Barbara Grossman; Marc Kaufman for his insightful edits; and, of course, my husband, Larry O'Connor.

The phenomena of the crypto-Jews has been debated and it has its detractors. However I came to accept the research and academic work of Stanley M. Hordes, who wrote *To the End of the Earth: A History of the*

Crypto-Jews of New Mexico. It was a valuable source for me. Richard Zimler's *The Last Kabbalist of Lisbon* gave me a very good sense of Lisbon circa 1506. For the history of food and spices, Gary Paul Nabhan's *Cumin, Camels, and Caravans* was indispensable and inspiring. Martin A. Cohen's *The Martyre: Luis de Carvajal, a Secret Jew in Sixteenth-Century Mexico* helped me grasp the darkness of the Inquisition in Mexico. And Laurence Bergreen's *Columbus: The Four Voyages* and Kirstin Downey's *Isabella: The Warrior Queen* were excellent books of history, as were the journals from Columbus's first two voyages.

This novel has also been a journey for me through many parts of the world. I am grateful to the Bibliothèque Nationale in Paris for allowing me to spend an afternoon viewing Columbus's original portolan map. The Map Room and librarians at the New York Public Library were very helpful with early maps of New Mexico, the United States, and the expeditions of the conquistadors. I want to thank Rebeca Cordero, the historian I met when I stumbled upon the tiny Centro de Interpretación Judería de Sevilla in Seville. She spent a day with me and told me endless stories about the role of Spain, and specifically Seville, in the Inquisition. Meeting Rebeca was a gift. I am grateful to my friend Sonia Serrano Pujalras for encouraging me to come to Lisbon and for giving me a place in which I could stay and work, to Allison Markin Powell who put me in touch with Lisbon Explorer tours, and to Paolo Scheffer who became my guide through Jewish Lisbon and its mind-crushing Inquisition history that left me in tears in a café. This book would not be what it is if Paolo hadn't been my guide.

In New Mexico I spent time at the New Mexico History Museum where through an odd twist of fate two exhibits were going on side by side: one on the crypto-Jews of New Mexico and the other on the history of lowriders. And I am grateful to Jesse Hamilton who first told me about the crypto-Jewish exhibit, to my cousin Ethel Zimberoff, and to Andrew Sandoval-Strausz in Albuquerque who gave me safe haven on a very stormy night. The late Ron Chavez, whose diner we stopped at, took us to see his ancestral home where his people had lived for hundreds of years. And I want to thank my cousin Mike Bell, who shared with me his experiences during the Korean War and who has always regaled me with his wonderful stories.

I could not have done this travel without the Ellen Schloss Flamm and Family Endowed Fund for Faculty Research at Sarah Lawrence College that enabled me to do research in Spain, Portugal, and New Mexico. I am appreciative to the college and its advisory committee for their support. I also want to thank my research assistants, Nicole Saldarriaga and Dana Gillespie, who have helped make so many things possible. I am lucky to have them in my life.

I want to thank Marcia James and the Kimberly Hotel in Manhattan for providing an incredible work space and a week of silence as I was completing this book. And the dear Margani family in Puglia who let us use their farmhouse two years in a row and enabled me to turn an old cow barn and a Ping-Pong table into a studio where I accomplished so much. I also was honored to have a residency at the Writer's Room at the Betsy Hotel in Miami Beach and am appreciative of the quiet hours it gave me during the final stages of this work.

And finally, thank you to my family. There are no words to express how grateful I am for all the love and support Kate and Chris provide. I cannot imagine any of it without you. And my husband, Larry, whose literary acumen, compassion, and patience have enabled this work to come to fruition. Without whom none of this would be.

A NOTE ABOUT THE AUTHOR

MARY MORRIS is the author of numerous works of fiction, including the novels *The Jazz Palace, A Mother's Love,* and *House Arrest,* and of nonfiction, including the travel memoir classic *Nothing to Declare: Memoirs of a Woman Traveling Alone.* She is a recipient of the Rome Prize in literature and the 2016 Anisfield-Wolf Award for Fiction. Morris was raised in Chicago and lives in Brooklyn, New York. For more information, go to www.marymorris.net.

A NOTE ON THE TYPE

The text of this book was set in Requiem, a typeface designed by Jonathan Hoefler (born 1970) and released in the late 1990s by the Hoefler Type Foundry. It was derived from a set of inscriptional capitals appearing in Ludovico Vicentino degli Arrighi's 1523 writing manual, *Il Modo di Temperare le Penne.* A master scribe, Arrighi is remembered as an exemplar of the chancery italic, a style revived in Requiem Italic.